# Books by Judy Blume

## YOUNG ADULT AND MIDDLE GRADE

*Are You There God? It's Me, Margaret.*

*Blubber*

*Deenie*

*Forever . . .*

*Here's to You, Rachel Robinson*

*Iggie's House*

*Just as Long as We're Together*

*Letters to Judy: What Kids Wish They Could Tell You*

*Places I Never Meant to Be: Original Stories by Censored Writers*
(edited by Judy Blume)

*Starring Sally J. Freedman as Herself*

*Then Again, Maybe I Won't*

*Tiger Eyes*

## THE FUDGE BOOKS

*Tales of a Fourth Grade Nothing*

*Otherwise Known as Sheila the Great*

*Superfudge*

*Fudge-a-mania*

*Double Fudge*

## PICTURE BOOKS AND STORYBOOKS

*The Pain and the Great One*

*The One in the Middle Is the Green Kangaroo*

*Freckle Juice*

The Pain and the Great One series

*Soupy Saturdays*

*Cool Zone*

*Going, Going, Gone!*

*Friend or Fiend?*

it's not the end
of the world

# JUDY BLUME

it's not

THE END
OF THE
WORLD
March 2nd

𝓐
atheneum

A Richard Jackson Book
Atheneum Books for Young Readers
New York London Toronto Sydney New Delhi

ATHENEUM BOOKS FOR YOUNG READERS

An imprint of Simon & Schuster Children's Publishing Division

1230 Avenue of the Americas, New York, New York 10020

ATHENEUM BOOKS FOR YOUNG READERS is a registered trademark of Simon & Schuster, Inc.

Atheneum logo is a trademark of Simon & Schuster, Inc.

For information about special discounts for bulk purchases, please contact Simon & Schuster Special Sales at 1-866-506-1949 or business@simonandschuster.com.

The Simon & Schuster Speakers Bureau can bring authors to your live event. For more information or to book an event, contact the Simon & Schuster Speakers Bureau at 1-866-248-3049 or visit our website at www.simonspeakers.com.

Also available in an Atheneum Books for Young Readers paperback edition

Book design by Tom Daly

The text for this book is set in New Century Schoolbook LT Std.

Manufactured in the United States of America

0314 FFG

This Atheneum Books for Young Readers hardcover edition April 2014

2  4  6  8  10  9  7  5  3  1

Library of Congress Cataloging-in-Publication Data

Blume, Judy.

It's not the end of the world / Judy Blume.—First edition.

pages cm

"A Richard Jackson Book."

Originally published by Bradbury Press in 1972.

Summary: When her parents divorce, a sixth grader struggles to understand that sometimes people are unable to live together.

ISBN 978-1-4814-1435-7 (hardcover)

ISBN 978-1-4814-1116-5 (digest paperback)

[1. Divorce—Fiction.] I. Title. II. Title: It is not the end of the world.

PZ7.B6265It 2014

[Fic]—dc23      2013035876

*For John,*
*who married a monkey-face-maker*

# it's not the end
# of the world

1

I don't think I'll ever get married. Why should I? All it does is make you miserable. Just look at Mrs. Singer. Last year she was Miss Pace and everybody loved her. I said I'd absolutely die if I didn't get her for sixth grade. But I did—and what happened? She got married over the summer and now she's a witch!

Then there are my parents. They're always fighting. My father was late for dinner tonight and when he got home we were already at the table. Daddy said hello to me and Jeff. Then he turned to Mom. "Couldn't you have waited?" he asked her. "You knew I was coming home for dinner."

"Why didn't you call to say you'd be late?" Mom asked.

"It's only twenty after six. I got hung up in traffic."

"How was I supposed to know that?" Mom asked.

"Never mind!" My father sat down and helped himself to a slice of meat loaf and some spanish rice. He took a few mouthfuls before he said, "This rice is cold."

"It was hot at six o'clock," Mom told him.

Me and Jeff kept on eating without saying a word. You could feel what was going on between my parents. I wasn't hungry any more.

Then Daddy asked, "Where's Amy?"

"In the den," Mom said.

"Did she eat?"

Mom didn't answer.

"I said did she eat her supper?"

"Of course she did," Mom snapped. "What do you think I do—starve her when you're not around?"

My father pushed his plate away and called, "Amy . . . Amy . . ."

But my father said, "I'll have to scrape off the icing."

Mom looked right at Daddy and told him, "Don't do me any favors!" Then she picked up that beautiful cake, held it high over her head and dropped it. It smashed at my father's feet. The plate broke into a million pieces and the chips flew all around. It was one of our ordinary kitchen plates. I'll bet if it was an antique, my mother never would have dropped it like that.

Later, when nobody was looking, I snitched a piece of cake off the floor. Even though it had fallen apart it was still delicious.

But that was last week. Tonight Mom didn't throw anything but the sponge. As she ran out of the kitchen my father cursed, crumpled up his napkin and got up from the table. Jeff pushed his chair away too, but my father hollered, "You stay right where you are and finish your dinner!" He grabbed his coat and went out the back door. In a minute I heard the garage door open and the car start.

"You really picked a great time to dump

your milk," Jeff told Amy. He is fourteen and sometimes very moody.

"I didn't do it on purpose," Amy said. "You know it was an accident."

"Well, I hope you're happy," he told her. "Because the whole rotten night's ruined for all of us now!" He cursed like my father and Amy started to cry.

"I'm going to my room," she told us. "Nobody loves me any more!"

Jeff was the next one to walk out of the kitchen, leaving me there alone. I knew where he was going. To his private hideaway. It's on the third floor and it used to be the spare room. The ceiling is low on one side and the windows are small and up high. I don't see why anybody would want to sleep in there if he didn't have to.

Jeff spent a lot of time decorating it. There's a big sign on the door that says *Jeff's Hideaway / All Who Enter Do So at Their Own Risk*. Then there's a purple light hanging from the ceiling and a million posters all over the walls. It's very messy too. In the fall we had to have the exterminator because of Jeff. He took so many cookies and crackers and cans of soda up there we got bugs. My father was really sore! Jeff doesn't throw his garbage under the bed any more. And he's not supposed to drink soda anyway. It's bad for his zits. My mother calls them pimples and says he's lucky that he's only got one or two.

His zits don't stop the girls from calling though. They call all the time. My father has threatened to limit Jeff's phone conversations to two minutes. Jeff doesn't care. There's only one girl he wants to talk to anyway. That's Mary Louise Rumberger. She's in his homeroom. I've only seen her once. She has very nice hair and she smells like Noxzema.

I know what Jeff does up in his room. He lifts weights. Isn't that the dumbest thing! He wants to be on the wrestling team next year. My mother's worried sick because she's afraid he'll get hurt. I wonder if maybe Mary Louise Rumberger likes big muscles?

# 2

The house was very quiet. I was still sitting at the dinner table, making little designs on my plate with the spanish rice. I thought about clearing away the dishes and even stacking them in the dishwasher. But why should I? I didn't start the fight. It wasn't my fault dinner was ruined. I wondered if my mother had something special planned for dessert. I wasn't about to ask her though. She was probably locked up in her bathroom.

I went to the pantry and took down a box of chocolate-chip cookies. On my way upstairs I scooped up Mew, who was sitting on her favorite chair in the living room.

She is supposed to be the family cat but she loves me best. Probably because she knows I love *her* more than anything in the world. From far away it looks as if Mew's coat is dark gray, but when you get up close you can see that she's really striped—black, gray, a tiny bit of white and even some red here and there. She is also very fat. She wears a collar with bells around her neck. This helps do two things: One is, it warns the birds, which Mew loves to chase. And two is, it keeps her from sneaking up on you. She's very good at sneaking around. Sometimes she hides under our beds and when we walk by she jumps out. That's just her way of playing. Neither my mother or my father is crazy about Mew and her games.

When I got to my room I closed the door with my foot and put Mew down on my bed. I flopped next to her and she stretched out. She likes me to scratch her belly. I ate my cookies and let Mew lick up the crumbs. She has never put out her claws at me. And she doesn't rip up the furniture like other cats do. It's a good thing too, because if she did we wouldn't be able to keep her.

Some people might think Mew is a dumb name for a cat. But when she came to our door two years ago she was just a tiny kitten. She called *mew mew mew* and I gave her a dish of milk. She's been ours ever since. At first we all tried to think up clever names for her. But while we were thinking we got used to calling her Mew. So finally we gave up and agreed that would be her name forever.

She curled up and went to sleep as I sat down at my desk. My desk is very special. It used to be a part of somebody's dining-room set. Mom bought it for five dollars and refinished it herself. She's very good at that. Now it's bright yellow and has small gold handles on every drawer. My friends think it's neat.

I opened my middle drawer and took out my Day Book. My father gets one in the mail every December and he gives it to me. It has a plain black cover with gold letters that say *Global Insurance Company*. Inside there's a half page for every day in the year. It's not really a diary because it has no lock. It's more of an appointment book, but I don't keep a record of my appointments. If I have to go to the dentist or something like that my mother marks it on her calendar. I'm not interested in writing down that stuff.

I do keep a bunch of rubber bands wrapped around my Day Book just in case anyone happens to be snooping in my desk. They are arranged in a special way that only I understand. I took off all six of them and opened to Thursday, February 25. At the top of the page I wrote: *Fight—E.N.'s fault.*

E.N. are my mother's initials. They stand for Ellie Newman. Her real name is Eleanor but nobody ever calls her that. My real name is Karen and nobody ever calls me anything else. It's hard to make a nickname out of Karen.

I try to be very fair about my parents' fights. Tonight was definitely my mother's fault. She should have been nicer to Daddy when he came home. She knows he likes to relax with a drink before dinner. And she shouldn't have hollered when Amy spilled her milk. That can happen to anyone.

The time Mom dropped the cake on the floor was my father's fault. He started that one by saying he hates mocha icing. So that night I wrote: *Fight—B.N.'s fault.* My father's name is Bill—well, really William, but that's beside the point.

I put my pencil in my mouth and chewed on it for a while. When I was in first grade we had a contest to see who had the fewest teeth marks on his pencils at the end of the year. I lost. Biting on a pencil helps me think better.

I flipped back through the pages of my Day Book. I always give each day a mark, like on a report card. Practically every day this month has gotten a C.

My last A+ day was December 14. That was a really perfect one. First of all, Gary Owens, who is a boy in my class, chose me as his partner in a spelling bee. I hope it wasn't just because I am a good speller. And second of all, Mrs. Singer acted practically human. She didn't yell once. But the best thing about that day was the snow. We usually don't get that much snow so early in the season. It started in the morning and didn't stop until dinnertime. As soon as we finished eating, my father and Jeff went outside to shovel the walk. Me and Amy were dying to go out too. Finally Mom said, "Okay . . . if you bundle up good and promise to come inside when you get cold."

I helped Amy get ready. She has trouble with her boots. I tied up her hood and found her a pair of mittens. Then we went out together.

When Jeff saw us he called, "How about a snowball fight? Me and Amy against Karen and Dad."

"Okay," we called.

Daddy and I hurried around to the side of our house and I made the snowballs for him to throw. Jeff and Amy hid behind the big tree and pretty soon the snow was flying. I think Daddy and I won but it didn't matter because it was such fun. When we got tired of throwing snowballs Amy and me lay down in the snow and made angels. I was moving my arms back and forth to make really good wings. Then I looked up at the sky. There were a million stars. I wanted everything to stay just the way it was—still and beautiful.

When we got up we were both soaked and I was sure Mom would yell at us. But we ran inside and she just laughed and told us we looked like snowmen. After we got into our pajamas Mom made us hot chocolate with little balls of whipped cream on top. As I drank it I thought, I have never felt so good. Absolutely never!

Later I went up to my room and marked my Day Book A+. I didn't have to chew on my pencil to think it over. December 14 was perfect in every way.

But things have been going downhill since then. I'll bet my father will sleep in the den tonight. He's been doing that more and more. He tells us it's because my mother sits up in bed half the night watching the late show. But my mother says she can't get to sleep because Daddy snores so loud.

I marked Thursday, February 25 C-. Then I put the rubber bands back on my Day Book and went into the bathroom to brush my teeth. Maybe tomorrow will be an A+ day. I hope so.

# 3

Debbie Bartell has been my best friend since kindergarten. She lives two blocks away. We've only been separated twice in school—in second grade and fifth. This year we're both blessed with Mrs. Singer. Debbie has a younger brother the same age as Amy, so we really have a lot in common.

The trouble with Debbie is, she takes a million lessons. I only take piano, on Thursdays. But Debbie is busy five days a week plus Saturday mornings. I know her whole schedule. On Monday she's got piano. On Tuesday it's ballet. On Wednesday, Girl Scouts—on Thursday, ice-skating—on Friday, allergy shots—and art every Saturday morning.

It's all her mother's idea. Mrs. Bartell wants her to try out everything. Thank goodness we're in Girl Scouts together or I'd never see Debbie after school. I happen to know that Debbie wishes she had more free time to fool around and do nothing, but she doesn't want to hurt her mother's feelings. Now Mrs. Bartell has found out the indoor tennis club is giving lessons to kids every Sunday afternoon. Guess what Debbie got for Christmas? A tennis racket!

When I met her at the bus stop this morning Debbie said, "I don't need my allergy shots today."

"How come?" I asked. "It's Friday."

"My doctor's on vacation. If I start to wheeze my mother's supposed to call some other doctor."

"Great!" I said. "What do you want to do after school?"

"I guess I'll come over to your house. Do you think Jeff will be home?"

"No. He's never home on Fridays. You know that. He goes to the Y to swim."

"Oh," Debbie said. "I forgot. Well then . . . we might as well go to the library and get the books for our project."

Am I wrong to feel that lately Debbie is more interested in my brother than in me? Jeff can't stand her anyway. He calls her Fat-and-Ugly right to her face. She acts like that's some kind of compliment. Maybe because she knows she's not fat *or* ugly. The truth is, she's pretty. I think Gary Owens likes her. He's always tugging at her hair. I wish he'd do that to me!

Our bus came along then and we piled in. Debbie and I always sit in the same seats—the last row on the left. We've been sitting there since I can remember. It's a twenty-minute ride to school, counting the three other stops. This morning Debbie did her math homework on the way.

I do pretty good in school. I am also supposed to be mature, well adjusted and eager to learn. I saw this written on my permanent record card one day in the fall. Sometimes I don't feel mature, well adjusted and eager to learn. In fact, I think my fifth-grade teacher may have mixed me up with somebody else when she wrote that.

As soon as we got to school Mrs. Singer collected our milk money. I didn't know I'd forgotten mine until then. We eat lunch right in our classrooms because there isn't any cafeteria. If you don't bring your milk money on Friday you don't get any milk the following week. Sometimes, if you forget, your teacher will pay for you and you can pay her back on Monday. Mrs. Singer doesn't do that. She says it is our responsibility to remember and if we don't, we have to suffer the consequences.

If Mrs. Singer hadn't gotten married I'm sure she would still be nice. Last year whenever I went into her room with a message she was always smiling. But this year, on the very first day of school, she screamed at me in front of the whole class—just because I didn't hear her say we should open our math books. Is that a reason to scream at a person, even if I wasn't paying attention? I was just excited because it was the first day of school. Couldn't Mrs. Singer see that?

This is the first time I have ever forgotten my milk money. Now I will have to bring something from home to drink next week. Warm juice . . . ugh! I could already tell that this was not going to be an A + day.

# 4

My father didn't come home for dinner tonight. But that's not unusual. The store is open until nine on Fridays. It's called Newman's Modern Furniture and it's out on the highway. Nothing in our house comes from the store though. That's because my mother loves old stuff. She is an antique nut. Little china babies sleep on every table in our living room. We even have an old potbellied stove, which Mom painted blue. It stands in our front hall and holds fake geraniums.

When Amy asked, "Where's Daddy?" my mother said, "Working late."

On Saturday mornings my father leaves

very early, same as during the week, but the rest of us sleep late. He doesn't need an alarm clock to wake him. He gets up automatically. My mother is just the opposite.

It wasn't until Saturday night at about six that I began to wonder what was going on. My parents go out every single Saturday night, rain or shine, all year long. Sometimes they argue before they go—about what they're going to do or who they're going to see—but still they go out together. The only time they stay home is if one of us is really sick.

"What time is Mrs. Hedley coming tonight?" I asked, stuffing my second cupcake into my mouth.

"Don't talk with food in your mouth," Amy said.

"Oh, shut up," I told her. "What time, Mom?"

Mrs. Hedley has been baby-sitting since I was born. Jeff is getting pretty mad about having her come every week. He thinks he's old enough to stay alone. But my mother says if we stop using Mrs. Hedley some other family will grab her.

So Jeff complains but Mrs. Hedley still comes. She smells like gingersnaps. I used to like her a lot when I was little. Now I am not too crazy for her. For one thing, I am sick of holding my arms out with her knitting wool stretched across them. She spends Saturday nights making wool balls that must last her the rest of the week.

My mother sat at her kitchen desk reading the newspaper while the three of us had our supper. "Mrs. Hedley's not coming," she said.

"She's not?"

"No." Mom kept the newspaper in front of her face.

"How come?" I asked.

"We're not going out tonight."

"You're not?"

"That's right."

"How come?"

"We're just not, Karen."

"Goody," Amy said. "Then we can all watch TV together."

My mother put the paper down and got up

to clear away the dishes. "You can watch whatever you want. I just don't feel like any TV tonight."

"Are you sick?" I asked.

"No."

"Then what?"

"It's just that . . . well . . ." Mom stopped talking and looked at us. Then she shook her head and reached for a tissue. "I'll be upstairs," she practically whispered.

Amy finished her milk and followed my mother. Jeff took an apple out of the refrigerator, polished it on his shirt and went upstairs too.

I put the dishes in the dishwasher, then marched up to Jeff's room. I knocked. I'm not allowed in without his permission.

"What?" he called.

I had to shout because his record player was on full blast. "It's me."

"What?"

"I want to come in."

"Just a minute," he yelled. He switched off the music and opened the door.

"I'm scared," I told him.

"Of what?"

"I don't know. I think something's wrong between Daddy and Mom."

"Well, it took you long enough to figure that out."

"I mean *really* wrong, Jeff."

"Yeah . . . so do I."

"Do you know anything for sure?" I asked.

"I know Dad didn't come home to sleep last night," Jeff said.

"He didn't?"

"Nope. And I don't think he's coming back either."

"How can you say that?"

"I can tell by the way Mom's acting. Didn't you hear her at supper? She could hardly get the words out."

"But that doesn't mean Daddy isn't coming back."

Jeff shrugged and walked over to his record player. He turned it on and opened a book. He was through talking to me. "I don't believe you!" I told him. "You don't know anything!"

Jeff didn't answer. He didn't even look up.

I went to my room and took out my Day Book. I marked Saturday, February 27 *D-*. I wish something would happen to make my mother and father happy again. On TV everything always turns out all right. Once I saw a show where the parents were separated. Then their little boy was kidnapped and they got together to help the FBI find him. And naturally, when they did, the kid was fine. The mother and father were so glad to see him they decided to make up and everyone lived happily ever after. It was a very nice show.

I'm sure if one of us got kidnapped my mother and father would forget about their fights and everything would work out fine. I think it would be best if Amy was the one, since she's the youngest. And everybody says she's Daddy's favorite. But who'd want to kidnap her? She's such a funny-looking kid, with big rabbit teeth and snarly hair. She is supposed to have inherited her rabbit teeth from Aunt Ruth. My mother says she'll look a lot better after she has had braces. Jeff is the good-looking one. He has a dimple in his chin and his eyes are very blue. Aunt Ruth says it's a shame to waste that face on a boy!

I am in between Amy and Jeff in looks. If I had to describe myself I would say Karen Newman is ordinary looking. I plan to do something about that in a few years. I might wear purple eye-shadow.

My father is always home on Sundays. But I checked the garage early this morning and his car wasn't there. At first I thought, maybe he's been in an accident and he's in the hospital. Maybe he's even dead! Just thinking about it made me feel sick. But he couldn't be dead. My mother would have told us. You can't keep something like that a secret.

So I went into the kitchen and mixed the pancake batter. I do that every Sunday morning. I love to crack the egg into the blender, then watch the tornado inside. Even the time I dropped the eggshell in by mistake Daddy said the pancakes were good. A little crunchy maybe, but very tasty.

We eat Sunday breakfast at ten, but at quarter after there was only me and Jeff and Amy in the kitchen. Maybe the car is at the gas station for a check-up, I thought. And Daddy is upstairs with Mom. He took a taxi home late last night and I didn't hear him come in because I was sound asleep. So naturally he and Mom are staying in bed a little later this morning. They probably were up half the night talking things over. Daddy will have his arm around Mom's shoulder when they come down for breakfast and he'll tell us we're all going into New York for the day.

"Where's Mommy?" Amy asked then.

"Still asleep," I said.

"Where's Daddy?"

"Stop asking so many questions!" I shouted.

"The one who asks the most questions learns the most," Amy said.

"Well, today you can just learn to keep your big mouth shut!" I told her. Why did she have to interrupt just when I was planning a perfect A+ day?

I could tell Amy was going to cry. She doesn't come right out and do it like other kids. She thinks about it for a while. You can see her face scrunch up before the tears start rolling.

Jeff dug into the Sunday papers and came up with the funnies. I threw a few drops of water on the griddle to make sure it was hot enough. When they sizzle it's ready for cooking. "Why don't you put out the syrup, Amy?" I said. "Your pancakes will be ready in a minute."

"You're mad," Amy said, sniffling.

"No I'm not."

"You yelled at me."

"I didn't mean to. Honest."

"Well . . . okay then. I'll put out the syrup." She walked over to the pantry. "Karen . . ."

"What?"

"Do you know why the boy put his father in the refrigerator?"

"Yes."

"Jeff . . . do you?"

"Yeah," Jeff mumbled.

"Because he wanted cold pop! Get it?" Amy asked "*Cold pop*, like soda."

"That's a good riddle," I said.

"But you already heard it . . . right?"

"Right." I poured the batter onto the grill. I shaped it like a Mickey Mouse head. Amy loves it when I make her fancy pancakes. I shouldn't have hollered at her. After all, what does she know?

As soon as I gave Amy and Jeff their pancakes my mother came into the kitchen. "Good morning," she said. Her eyes were red and swollen.

"Look what Karen made me," Amy said, holding up her Mickey Mouse pancake.

Mom said, "That's beautiful. Be sure to finish it."

Amy cut off one Mickey Mouse ear, dipped it into the syrup and ate it. "Where's Daddy?" she asked.

Jeff looked up from his funnies. I think he was just pretending to read them anyway because he didn't laugh once.

"Daddy's busy," Mom said.

"Doing what?" I asked.

"He's got some things to take care of. Look,

you kids finish your breakfast while I go up and get dressed. Aunt Ruth will be over soon."

She was gone before I had a chance to ask exactly what things Daddy was so busy doing.

I am so afraid Jeff is right!

# 5

Aunt Ruth is my mother's older sister. She is also my mother's only living relative besides us, unless you count Mark, my cousin. But we never see him any more. He lives in Atlanta. My mother is ten years younger than Aunt Ruth and if you ask me Aunt Ruth enjoys acting like her mother. She is married to Uncle Dan, who is six feet five inches tall. When I was little he would hold me up to touch the ceiling and I thought that was really exciting. Aunt Ruth and Uncle Dan live in Maplewood. It takes about ten minutes to get from their house to ours. I wondered why Aunt Ruth was coming over on a Sunday morning. She never does.

I was in the bathroom rinsing out my toothbrush when Amy barged in. "You're supposed to knock," I told her.

"Karen . . ."

"What?"

"Do you know where Daddy is?"

"You heard Mom," I said. "He's busy doing something."

"I think I know what," Amy said.

"You do?"

"Yes. I think he's out getting us a puppy and it's supposed to be a big surprise."

"Where'd you get that idea?"

"In my head."

"Oh, Amy . . . I don't think that's it at all." I felt sorry for her then.

Amy sat down on the toilet.

I went into my room and made the bed. When I finished I sat at my desk and opened my Day Book to Sunday, February 28. I wrote: *Something is going on. I wish I knew what.*

I put the rubber bands back and took out my English homework. I nearly jumped right out of my chair when Aunt Ruth stuck her head in and called, "Good morning. . . ."

She has her own key to our house, so she doesn't have to ring the bell or knock. I never even heard her come in. She can be as sneaky as Mew. She should wear bells around her neck.

"You scared me!" I said.

"I'm sorry," Aunt Ruth told me. "Where are Jeff and Amy?"

"Jeff's up in his room and Amy's probably in the den watching TV." You can't pull Amy away from those dumb Sunday-morning shows. She likes the one where the kids throw pies at each other.

"Where's your mother?" Aunt Ruth asked.

"Getting dressed, I think."

"Well, suppose you tell Jeff and Amy to get ready and I'll tell your mother I'm here."

"Get ready for what?"

"Didn't your mother tell you?"

"Tell me what?"

"Uncle Dan and I are taking you out to lunch."

"But we just had breakfast."

"We're going for a ride in the country, Karen. By the time we get there it will be lunchtime. So get your coat and tell Jeff and Amy to hurry and get ready."

"Okay," I said. We never go out to lunch on Sunday. Sometimes we go out for dinner, but *never* lunch. We don't even eat lunch on Sunday. And Aunt Ruth knows it!

"Aunt Ruth . . ." I called as she was leaving my room.

"Yes?"

"Is Mom coming too?"

"Of course."

"And Daddy?"

"No. He's not coming."

"Where is he, anyway?"

"He's got some business to take care of," Aunt Ruth said.

Business? What kind of business would my father do on a Sunday morning? Unless he's selling the store! I'll bet that's it. Didn't he just tell us that sales are way down? So he's going to sell now and get some other kind of job. Jeff is wrong! Mom was upset because this means we'll be very poor. She might have to hock all her antiques. I'll get a job after school, to help out. Maybe I can deliver newspapers.

I ran downstairs and found Amy in the den. She was wearing her underwear. The rest of her clothes were spread out on the floor. I told her to hurry up and get dressed.

Then I went into the laundry room to check Mew's litter box. It was clean and I was glad. I rinsed her bowl and gave her fresh water. I filled her dish up with dried food. I didn't know how long we'd be gone and I wanted to make sure she wouldn't get hungry. She prefers canned cat food but I'm not allowed to leave that in her dish all day.

When I open a can of food for Mew I have to hold my nose. It really stinks. So does her litter box sometimes. But I have discovered that if you love someone the way I love Mew, you learn to overlook the disgusting things. And when I hold her close and she purrs at me it's all worth it.

When we were settled in the car Aunt Ruth drove down to her house to pick up Uncle Dan.

Then they switched places so Uncle Dan could drive. We rode all the way to Basking Ridge with Jeff, Amy and me in the back of the car. And when Uncle Dan drives he moves the front seat as far back as it goes because of his long legs. Which means whoever is sitting in the back gets squashed.

Aunt Ruth and Uncle Dan talked the whole time. About the weather and what a nice day it was and how it was just perfect for a drive and how all the snow melted since last week and that there is only one month to go until spring. When Aunt Ruth said that, she put her arm around my mother and added, "Everything will look brighter in the spring, Ellie."

Jeff leaned close and whispered, "You see . . . what did I tell you?"

"It's not what you think," I whispered back. I couldn't tell him in front of everyone that what Aunt Ruth meant was that then the store will be sold and Daddy will have a new job.

By the time we got to the restaurant Amy was carsick and she threw up in the parking lot. We are used to that. She does it every time we go for a long ride. She is so experienced she never even messes herself up. And she can eat like a tiger afterward. She never gets sick on the way home—only going. I wonder why?

The restaurant was called the Red Bull Inn and it had bare wooden floors and paper place mats that looked like lace on each table. I studied the menu. Our waitress recommended the curried shrimp. Jeff, Amy and I ordered hamburgers and french fries. My mother said she'd have an omelet and Aunt Ruth and Uncle Dan said they would try the curried shrimp. The waitress seemed really glad to hear that, as if she had been cooking all day and now at last somebody was going to eat her stuff.

When we were almost through, Mom said, "I have something to tell you." She wasn't looking at Aunt Ruth or Uncle Dan. She was looking at me and Jeff and Amy. "I wanted to tell you before, but I just couldn't. It isn't easy for me to say this and it won't be easy for you to understand . . ."

I dropped my fork then. It made a clink-
ing sound when it hit the floor. I bent down
to get it.

Uncle Dan said, "Let it go, Karen. The waitress can bring you another one."

"Go ahead . . . tell us what you were going
to say, Mother," Jeff said.

Mom took a deep breath and said, "Daddy
and I are separating."

"I knew it!" Jeff said, looking at me.

I felt tears come to my eyes. I told myself,
don't start crying now Karen, you jerk. *Not
now.* I sniffled and took a long swallow of
Coke. I guess I knew it all the time. I was just
fooling myself—playing games like Amy.

"What's separating?" Amy asked.

"It means your father isn't going to live at
home any more," Aunt Ruth explained.

"But he has to!" Amy said. "He's our father."

"Shush . . ." Aunt Ruth told her. "Everyone
can hear."

"I don't care," Amy shouted, looking around
the restaurant. But there were only a few
other customers.

Uncle Dan reached for Amy's hand. "Sometimes, when a mother and father have problems, they live apart for a while to think things over."

"Is he coming back?" Jeff asked. "Or are you getting a divorce?"

"We don't know yet," Mom told him.

"A divorce!" I said, when I hadn't planned to say anything. "You wouldn't! You wouldn't get a divorce!" Then I started crying for real and I jumped up from the table and ran through the restaurant. I heard Aunt Ruth call, "Karen . . . Karen . . . come back here." But I kept going. I didn't want to hear any more. I went out the front door and stood against the sign that said Red Bull Inn, letting the tears roll down my face.

Soon Aunt Ruth came with my coat. "Karen," she said, "put this on. You'll freeze to death."

"Go away," I told her.

Aunt Ruth wrapped the coat around my shoulders. "Karen . . . don't be like that. This is even harder on your mother than it is on you. She's very upset . . . if she sees you like this it's going to make her feel even worse."

You don't argue with Aunt Ruth. She has a habit of not listening to anything she doesn't want to hear. So I put on my coat and Aunt Ruth said, "Now, that's better."

We walked through the parking lot to the car. Aunt Ruth kept her arm around me. "Nothing is settled yet," she said. "Your father is home packing his things now. That's why we all went out to lunch. To give him a chance to move."

"But doesn't he want to see us? Doesn't he care? How can he move out of his own house?"

"Karen . . . there are some things that are very hard for children to understand."

That's what people say when they can't explain something to you. I don't believe it. I can understand anything they can understand. I got into the car but I didn't say anything else. I looked out the side window.

"You have to be the one to help your mother," Aunt Ruth said. "She needs you . . . more than ever."

I shook my head and pressed my forehead

against the window. Why did Jeff have to be right? Why couldn't it have been something else? If only we could go back a few days and start again maybe things would work out differently.

My mother came out of the restaurant with Amy and Jeff. Mom was carrying an ice-cream cone. "Here, Karen," she said. "I know you like dessert best."

I tried to smile at Mom because I couldn't say thank you. I knew if I said anything I'd start crying. I didn't want the cone, even though it was coffee, my favorite flavor. But I took it from Mom and licked it anyway.

"Dan will be right out," Mom told Aunt Ruth. "He's paying the check."

"Shove over, Karen," Jeff said.

"No, I like it here," I told him. "Get in on the other side."

"I said shove over!" Jeff repeated.

When I didn't, he climbed across me and stepped on my foot. I kicked him as hard as I could. He gave me an elbow in the ribs and my ice cream landed in my lap.

41

## 6

What will happen to me if they get divorced? Who will I live with? Where will I go to school? Will my friends laugh? I want a mother and a father and I want them to live together—right here—in this house! I don't care if they fight. I would rather have them fight than be divorced. I'm scared . . . I'm so scared. I wish somebody would talk to me and tell me it's going to be all right. I miss Daddy already. I hate them both! I wish I was dead.

On Monday morning I didn't get up. My mother came into my room to see what was wrong. "I'm sick," I told her. "I can't go to school."

Mom sat down on my bed. "I know how you feel about me and Daddy . . ."

"It's not that," I said. "I wasn't even thinking about you. It's my head and my stomach. I might throw up."

Mom put her hand on my forehead. "You don't feel warm."

"A person can be very sick without a fever," I said.

"You're right," she told me. "I better call Dr. Winters."

"Don't bother," I said. "I just want to sleep."

"Well . . . okay. But if you get any worse I'll have to call him."

"If I can just sleep I'll feel better."

"All right."

I heard Jeff and Amy getting ready for school. How can they go? How can they face their friends? I heard my mother calling, "Amy . . . Amy . . . hurry up or you'll miss the bus." Some things never change, I thought.

I stayed in bed all day. My mother made me tea and toast but I wouldn't eat it. Later she tried soup but I wouldn't eat that either. She said if I didn't take something she'd have to call the doctor. So I drank some juice.

Debbie stopped by after school, on the way to her piano lesson. She came upstairs and stood in the doorway of my room.

"Hi," she said. "What's wrong?"

"Everything," I told her. She looked pretty. Her cheeks were all pink from the cold. I wanted to tell her about my mother and father. I wanted to tell her so bad it made my head hurt for real. But I couldn't. Saying it would make it come true.

Debbie sat down on my other bed. "Your mother said it's not catching so it's all right for me to be in your room."

"My mother told you it's not catching?" I asked.

"Yes."

"Well, I'd like to know how she can say that."

"I don't know," Debbie said, "but she did. You look like you've been crying."

"So? Maybe I have been. Don't you ever cry when you're sick?"

"No," Debbie said.

"Well, this is an unusual sickness. It makes you cry!"

"Why are you mad at me?" Debbie asked.

"I'm not," I said. "I just don't feel like talking. Can't you see . . . I'm sick!"

"Want me to make monkey faces for you?"

"No—not today." Debbie can make very good monkey faces. She can look like a chimpanzee or a gorilla. Usually I crack up when she does them. But I didn't feel like laughing today.

"Will you be back in school tomorrow?" Debbie asked.

"No. I'll be out a long, long time. I may never get better."

"Oh, come on, Karen! You want me to bring you your books?"

"I've got my English book home."

"How about math?"

"No . . . I don't want it."

"Should I tell Mrs. Singer what's wrong with you?"

"No. Don't tell her anything!"

Debbie looked at the floor. I turned away from her and faced the wall. After a minute she said, "Is Jeff home yet?"

"How should I know? I'm in bed. Can't you see that?"

"I was just wondering . . . that's all."

"He doesn't like you anyway, so why don't you just leave him alone."

"Did he say that?" Debbie asked.

"He doesn't have to. Anyone with eyes can see it. And who did you come here to see anyway . . . me or him?" I was making Debbie feel bad and I was glad. Sometimes I am a mean and rotten person.

Debbie jumped up. "I came to see *you* and you know it! Whatever's wrong with you I hope it goes away soon because it's making you impossible!" Debbie walked to the door. "I'm going."

"So go!" I told her.

"I am."

Lying to Debbie did not make me feel any better. It made me feel worse.

Later Mom came into my room and told me

to put on my robe and come downstairs for dinner.

"I don't want anything to eat," I said.

"Karen, if you don't get up and come down you can't go to school tomorrow."

"So?"

"If you don't go to school tomorrow, you won't be able to have dinner with Daddy."

I sat up. "He's coming back?"

"No. He's taking you and Jeff and Amy out to eat. He wants to talk to you."

"Who says I want to talk to him?" I asked.

"Karen . . . don't be like that! Daddy is a wonderful person. He loves you."

"If he's so wonderful why are you separated?"

"Because we can't get along," Mom said.

"You could try!" I told her, feeling a lump in my throat.

"We have tried. Now I don't want to talk about it any more."

I put on my robe and went down for dinner. I wonder if anyone will ever talk about it!

# 7

Debbie was really surprised to see me at the bus stop the next morning. "I thought you were very sick," she said.

"I was. But I got better."

"So fast?" she asked.

"Yes. It was one of those twenty-four-hour bugs."

"Oh."

"Hey, look, Debbie . . . I'm really sorry I acted that way yesterday. It was just that my head was killing me and all. . . ."

"Forget it," Debbie said.

"Did I miss much in school?" I asked.

"No. Same old thing. Mrs. Singer changed

our desks around. I'm next to Gary Owens and Eileen."

"Where am I?"

"I'm not sure. But I think you're next to the wall on one side."

"That figures," I said. "One more way for Mrs. Singer to get me."

"I really don't think she's out to get you," Debbie said.

"Ha-ha."

"I mean it, Karen. You know I can't stand her either, but I don't think she treats you any worse than the rest of us."

"Well, I do."

When we got to school I handed Mrs. Singer my note from home. It said: *Please excuse Karen's absence on Monday. She wasn't feeling well.*

Mrs. Singer said, "I'm glad you're feeling better, Karen."

I looked at her. Did she know something? Did my mother call the school and tell them about Daddy moving out? Why else would Mrs. Singer act nice all of a sudden? She never says anything when you've been absent. One time Debbie was sick for a couple of weeks and when she came back to school Mrs. Singer didn't even smile. So why should she be glad I'm feeling better? If she knows the truth about my parents I will absolutely die.

My father called for us at five that night. He didn't come inside. He just tooted his horn. Amy ran out of the house first. "Daddy . . . Daddy . . . Daddy . . ." she yelled. Jeff and I followed. We got into the car and said, "Hi."

We went to Howard Johnson's on the highway. We sat in a booth in the back room and my father ordered a Martini. You have to sit in that section if you're going to have a drink. It was pretty quiet in the dining room. Maybe because it was so early or maybe because it was Tuesday night. Monday and Wednesday are the Big Fish Fry and Big Chicken Fry nights, where you can eat all you want for $1.98.

I can't remember ever eating out with just Daddy and not Mom too. I think we all felt funny. I know I did. There I was with my own father and it was like I hadn't seen him for ages instead of just a few days. He looked the same. I didn't expect him not to. But I thought there'd be something different about him now. I don't know what. But something that would let people know he didn't live at home any more.

After we ordered, Daddy said, "I miss you all very much."

Me and Jeff mumbled that we missed him too.

Then Amy asked, "Do you miss Mommy?"

My father looked sad and said, "No, I don't."

"Are you getting a divorce?" Jeff asked.

"Yes," my father answered.

"I thought you were just thinking about it," I said. "I thought it wasn't definite yet."

"We're definitely getting a divorce," he said. "It's the only way."

"Do you love somebody else?" Jeff asked. "Or does Mom?"

I never even thought about that! I couldn't picture my father with another woman or my

51

mother with another man. That was disgusting! How could Jeff even think of such a thing? I took a sip of water and waited for my father to answer.

"No . . . no . . ." he said. "It's nothing like that. There's nobody else involved. Your mother and I just don't get along. We can't go on living together. It's making a mess of our lives."

"Suppose we don't want you to get a divorce?" I said.

"I'm sorry, Karen, but this is between your mother and me."

"I want to live with you, Daddy!" Amy said.

"Don't be a jerk," Jeff told Amy. "The kids always live with the mother."

"Is that true?" I asked.

"Yes, usually," Daddy said. "Unless there's some reason why the mother shouldn't have the children."

"What about us?" I asked. "Where will we live?"

"With your mother."

"But where?"

"Right now you'll stay in the house."

"But for how long?" I asked.

"Karen . . . you're asking me questions I can't answer," Daddy said. "We haven't worked out any of the details yet. I'm seeing my lawyer tomorrow. You don't get divorced overnight."

"How long does it take?" Jeff asked.

"That depends. I guess about six months. Maybe more."

"Daddy . . ." Amy said, "please come home."

My father held Amy to him. Then he took off his glasses and started to clean them with his napkin. I think he had tears in his eyes. I didn't feel like eating anything.

After dinner Daddy took us into the motel to see his room. It has two beds and a TV. The bathroom is very small. "Are you going to live here forever?" I asked.

"No. Just until I find an apartment."

"Will we still see you?" I said.

"Of course you will. I'm your father and I'll always love you. Divorce has nothing to do with that."

After a few minutes Jeff said, "Well . . . I've got to get home. I have lots of homework to do." His voice broke on every word.

Nobody said much on the drive back to our house. When we got there Amy asked Daddy to come in and carry her up to bed like he always does. But Daddy said, "No, I'm not coming in."

*Tuesday, March 2*
*Divorce . . . it's the end of the world.*

# 8

In the middle of the night Amy shook me. I sat straight up in bed. "What's the matter?" I asked.

"I'm afraid to go to sleep," she said.

"Why?"

"I'm afraid if I do you'll all be gone in the morning, just like Daddy."

"That's silly," I told her.

She threw her arms around me. She was shaking. I held her tight. "Can I sleep in here with you?" she asked.

"I guess so," I said. But I really didn't want her to. I wanted to be alone. How could I cry with Amy in my other bed?

As soon as I tucked her in she fell asleep. But I tossed and turned for a long time. I wish I could talk to somebody about my parents. If only Debbie knew—I think I would feel better. I've got to figure out a way to tell her what's happening. She'll be able to cheer me up. Besides making monkey faces, Debbie has a very good sense of humor. I guess that's why everybody likes her. She doesn't even mind laughing at herself. I'm really lucky to have her for a best friend, even though I don't always show it. I am sure just having her know the truth will help.

On Wednesday afternoons Debbie and I walk to Girl Scouts together. Our troop meets at Willow Grove Church. That's just a few blocks from school. Then either Debbie's mother or mine picks us up. I used to love my Girl Scout uniform. But I am thinking of quitting after this year. So is Debbie. We are both sick of selling cookies and calendars to the same people year after year. If we had a good leader it would be different. But ours is a bore. If I was ever going to be a Girl Scout leader I would think up interesting activities for my group to do. And if they made a lot of noise I wouldn't yell that they give me a headache.

I planned to tell Debbie about my parents while we were walking to our meeting. But by three o'clock I was so mad at Mrs. Singer I couldn't think of anything else! Because this afternoon she called me up to her desk to discuss this month's book report. It was due last Monday. I scribbled mine out Sunday night before I went to sleep. I never even read the book. I just copied some stuff off the inside flap of the jacket. I've never done that before, but some kids in my class do it all the time.

Mrs. Singer said, "Did you enjoy the book you read this month, Karen?"

I said, "It was all right."

"Your book report wasn't nearly as good as usual."

"I was very busy," I told her. "I had to do it in a hurry."

"What did you think about the ending?"

"It was all right."

"Were you surprised by it?"

"A little," I said. I could tell that Mrs. Singer knew I hadn't read the book. Just as the bell rang she handed me my book report. I got a D—my first bad mark in school.

I could feel my face turn red as I walked to the back of the room to get my coat. Debbie waited for me at her desk. I picked up my books and marched out into the hall. Debbie called, "Good-by, Mrs. Singer," as she followed me.

Mrs. Singer called back, "Good-by, girls."

I didn't answer her.

When we were out of the building Debbie asked, "What's wrong?"

"Nothing!"

"What'd Mrs. Singer want to see you for?"

"Don't mention that witch's name! I hate her!"

"What'd she do?"

"Gave me a D on my book report!"

"She did?"

"Yes. There's something about me that

Mrs. Singer can't stand. This proves it!"

"She hardly ever gives out D's for book reports," Debbie said, "unless she thinks you didn't read the book."

I glared at Debbie, then I pulled my scarf up around my face. The wind was howling and it was really cold. We hurried along not saying anything for a while.

We only had one more block to go when Debbie said, "I heard about your parents . . . and I'm sorry."

"Heard what?" I asked, biting my lip.

"You know."

"Know what?"

"Oh, come on, Karen. That your parents are getting a divorce."

Well, there it was. Out in the open. But not the way I'd planned it. I was the one who was going to tell Debbie. And *she* was the one who was going to make me feel better. "Who told you?" I asked.

"Your aunt met my mother in Food Town and she told her."

"Oh," I said. I always knew Aunt Ruth had

a big mouth. It must have to do with her rabbit teeth. She's just like Amy.

"How come you didn't tell me?" Debbie asked when we got to the church.

"It wasn't definite." We went inside and jumped around a little to get warm. Then we hung up our coats.

"What's it like?" Debbie asked.

"What do you mean?"

"What's it feel like?"

How could she ask such a dumb question! "How do you think it feels?" I said, running for the bathroom.

"Hey, Karen . . . wait up!" Debbie caught me before I got inside. "I'm sorry. I didn't know it would be so bad."

"Well, it is."

"Are they going to have a fight over you and Jeff and Amy?"

"What kind of fight?"

"You know . . . about who gets the kids."

"No. We stay with our mother."

"Doesn't your father want you?"

"I don't know. He said we'll live with our

mother." Now I was getting all mixed up. Why did she ask if Daddy wanted us? Did Aunt Ruth know something else? Did she tell Mrs. Bartell something that Debbie knows? Oh . . . I hate everybody! I must have been crazy to think Debbie could cheer me up.

# 9

I have only one grandparent and that's Daddy's father. We call him Garfa because Jeff couldn't say "Grandpa" when he was a baby. When you are twelve you feel pretty stupid calling somebody Garfa, especially in public. So whenever I talk about him in school or to my friends I say "my grandfather." Only Debbie knows he is Garfa.

Garfa started Newman's furniture store when he was young, in the olden days. Daddy took it over thirteen years ago when Grandma died and Garfa retired. I never knew my grandmother but everybody says I look like her. I've seen some pictures though and I don't think there is any resemblance between us at all. But you can't argue about something like that with your family. Once they make up their minds that you look like somebody special, that's it.

Garfa lives in Las Vegas. The dry climate is supposed to be good for his health. But I have heard that he likes gambling. This is not something that the family talks about much. Last year Garfa got married again. His new wife's name is Mattie and she is sixty-five years old. Imagine getting married when you are sixty-five!

Garfa and Mattie visited us over the summer. The only thing wrong with Mattie is she doesn't like cats. She more than doesn't like them—she is terrified of them. So Debbie kept Mew at her house for two whole weeks.

I just found out that Garfa is going to pay us a visit this weekend, but Mattie is staying home in Las Vegas. Daddy called to tell him about the divorce, which is why he is coming.

On Saturday, Garfa came into our house alone. Daddy just dropped him off. The first thing

Garfa said after he kissed us and gave us the once-over was, "Well, Ellie, there hasn't ever been a divorce in our family. Not even way back. When the Newmans get married they get married for keeps. Or until one of them dies."

My mother didn't say anything. She just shook her head. I didn't think Garfa should discuss the divorce in front of Amy. But of course he didn't know she was so afraid at night.

"Listen, Ellie . . . everybody has problems," Garfa said. "Even me and Mattie have problems. But we're willing to work them out. That's what you have to do. Work out your problems with Bill."

"We can't," my mother said.

"Dammit, Ellie! Don't give me that! Of course you can. That's why I came. I want you and Bill to get away for a little while. All you need is a vacation. And it's on me."

"Oh, Garfa . . ." Mom said. "Thank you for trying but it's just no use. A vacation isn't going to solve anything. Don't you see . . ." Mom ran upstairs.

Later, after Daddy picked up Garfa, my mother drove downtown to get a box of Kentucky Fried Chicken for supper. Daddy can't stand that stuff. Well, now he'll never have to eat it.

I set the table while Mom cut up the salad. I didn't put out our regular paper napkins. I went into the den and came back with some of the cocktail napkins that say *Ellie and Bill*. I folded them up and put one at each place.

My mother called Jeff and Amy for supper. She didn't see the napkins until we were all seated. Then she looked at me and said, "I don't think this is very funny, Karen."

"I wasn't trying to be funny," I said.

"Then why did you use these?"

"Because there isn't going to be any more Ellie and Bill and I thought we might as well use them up now."

Mom collected the napkins and mashed them into a ball. She got up from the table and threw them away. "Where's the rest of the box?" she asked me.

"In the den, by the bar."

"Okay . . . after dinner get it and put it in the garbage."

"Boy, are you stupid!" Jeff whispered to me.

My mother didn't eat any chicken. I don't think she's been eating anything lately. She is getting very skinny. If she is so miserable without Daddy and he is so miserable away from us then why are they getting divorced? I don't understand.

On Sunday night Daddy took us out to dinner. We went to The Towers Steak House, which is my all-time favorite restaurant. I have never eaten out as much as in the week my parents have been separated.

During dinner Garfa tried to persuade Daddy to take a vacation with Mom. But it didn't work. Daddy said that was out of the question.

I could see how disappointed Garfa was at not being able to get my parents back together, so when we were alone for a minute I said, "Don't worry, Garfa." I thought of telling him about that TV show where the little boy got kidnapped. But I didn't. Because those things never happen in real life, do they?

"I can't help it, Karen," Garfa said. "I was so sure I'd be able to straighten everything out."

"Do you think I should try too?" I asked.

Garfa smiled at me. "It can't hurt."

Before he flew home to Las Vegas, Garfa told me to keep him posted on whatever was going on. "You're the most dependable person in this family, Karen. You're just like your Grandmother Newman. And you know something? You look more like her every time I see you."

"Oh, Garfa!" was all I could think to say.

# 10

Petey Mansfield seems to have moved into our house. He is Jeff's new best friend. They're always locked up inside Jeff's hideaway.

I don't know if Petey Mansfield is normal or not. He doesn't talk at all. Sometimes if you ask him a question he'll grunt at you, but otherwise, forget it. How does he manage in school? I wonder. His brother Brian is in my class. He never shuts up. Mrs. Singer is always yelling at him. Maybe that's why Petey doesn't talk. Maybe he doesn't ever get a chance.

Eileen Fenster, who is a girl in my class, says Brian Mansfield likes me. She knows because she spends every afternoon calling up boys. She asks them questions such as "Who do you like in our class?" or "What do you think of Debbie?" or something like that.

Debbie and I went over to Eileen's a few times. She knows all the boys' phone numbers by heart. The last time I was there she called up Gary Owens and I listened on the upstairs phone. She said, "Hi Gary. This is Eileen. Listen, Gary . . . what do you think of Karen?"

And Gary said, "Karen who?"

Imagine him saying that! How many Karens does he know anyway?

So Eileen said, "Karen Newman."

And Gary said, "Oh, her."

"Well?" Eileen said.

And then Gary hung up! Why did he go and do that? I'm never going to Eileen's house again.

Aunt Ruth came over tonight. She was full of advice for my mother because tomorrow is Mom's first meeting with Mr. Hague, her lawyer.

We were sitting around the kitchen table.

Aunt Ruth and Mom were drinking coffee and I was eating a banana. I only like bananas when they are pure yellow, without a spot of brown. That's why I hardly ever eat them.

Aunt Ruth said, "What are you going to wear tomorrow?"

And Mom said, "I don't know. What difference does it make?"

Aunt Ruth said, "You want to make a good impression, don't you? And remember, Ellie, you've got to tell him everything, no matter how hard it is for you."

"I know," my mother said. "Dan told me the same thing."

"I wish you'd try to eat a little more, Ellie. You don't look well."

"Oh, Ruth . . ." Mom said.

"I don't want to interfere, Ellie . . . I just wish you'd take better care of yourself."

Aunt Ruth is right. Suppose my mother gets sick? Then who'll take care of us?

Nobody said anything for a minute. Then Aunt Ruth asked Mom, "Do you remember Henry Farnum?"

"I think so," Mom said. "Is he the accountant?"

"That's the one," Aunt Ruth said. "From West Orange. Dan and I ran into him the other day. You know his wife died last year . . ."

"No, I didn't know that," Mom said.

"Yes . . . he's been very lonely. He's got a beautiful house and nobody in it. His children are both away at college."

"He ought to move to an apartment," Mom said.

I got up and threw my banana skin away.

"I'd like you to meet him, Ellie."

"Oh, please, Ruth . . . don't start in on that."

I sat back down at the table. Start in on what?

"Look, Ellie . . . that's the wrong attitude to take. Here I know a really nice man. He's lonely. So what's wrong with going out to dinner with him? I'm not saying you've got to marry him."

"Ruth, please! I'm not even divorced yet. I don't want to think about getting married again."

JUDY BLUME

"Okay. Fine. But a year from now when Henry Farnum is married to somebody else, don't come crying to me. And don't tell me you think Bill is sitting home alone every night!"

"Ruth . . . not in front of Karen . . . please."

Aunt Ruth looked at me. Does she know something? Why doesn't she just stay home and mind her own business! I hope my mother never goes out with Mr. Henry Farnum or any other man!

On Friday there was no school because of some special teachers' meeting. Debbie and I decided to go ice-skating. There is a pond in the middle of town, next to the library. When the blue circle is up it means the pond is frozen and safe to skate on.

Debbie's mother called for me and drove us downtown. I felt funny because Mrs. Bartell knows about my parents. I was scared that she would ask me something and I wouldn't know what to tell her. But she didn't mention one word about the divorce. She talked about keeping warm instead. And how she wanted

Debbie to wear a few pairs of underpants instead of just one. "That's the best way to get a kidney infection," Mrs. Bartell said, "sitting on that cold ice and getting a chill."

"I promise I won't sit on the ice," Debbie said.

I think Mrs. Bartell spends a lot of time worrying about diseases. She dropped us off right in front of the library and we walked down the path to the pond. There was already a bunch of kids there. I saw Eileen Fenster right away. She waved.

I love to ice-skate. I learned by myself when I was nine. That year I got my first shoe skates for Christmas. Debbie is always joking about her ice-skating lessons. She says it took her one whole year just to learn to stand up on the ice.

We were already wearing our skates, so all we had to do was to take the covers off the blades and skate away. I don't think Debbie was on the pond for two minutes before she fell down. I pulled her up. She started to laugh. "Three years of lessons and I still

73

stink!" she said. Then I started to laugh too. Eileen Fenster skated over to see what was so funny and pretty soon we were all standing there laughing. I had forgotten how good it feels to laugh. From now on I am going to concentrate on laughing at least once a day—even more if I can arrange it.

After an hour I could see why Mrs. Bartell wanted Debbie to wear lots of underpants. She wound up sitting on the ice more than she was standing on it! I skated out to the middle of the pond to practice my figure eights. When I turned around to look for Debbie I saw her standing on the grass talking to Eileen. I waved and called, "Hey, Debbie . . ." but she didn't notice. What were they talking about that was so important? Were they telling secrets? Was Eileen saying something bad about me? I skated across to them and said, "What's up?"

As soon as they saw me they stopped talking. Eileen said, "Oh, nothing. Me and Debbie were just saying it's fun to have a day off from school."

I knew that wasn't the truth. I could tell from their faces.

After Eileen went home I asked Debbie, "What were you talking about before?"

"Nothing," Debbie said. "Just forget it."

"I'll bet it was about me."

"Okay . . . so it was."

"About me and Gary Owens . . . right?"

"No. About your parents, if you want to hear the truth."

"My parents?"

"Yes. Eileen just found out they're getting divorced."

"Oh." I took my Chapstick out of my pocket and rubbed some along my bottom lip.

"You can't keep it a secret," Debbie said. "Sooner or later everyone is going to know."

"I never said it was a secret."

"Well, anyway . . . that's what we were talking about."

"What did Eileen say?"

"Oh, she was just asking me if your mother has a lot of money, that's all."

"Money? What's money got to do with it?"

75

"I don't know exactly. But Eileen heard her mother say that she hopes your mother has a good lawyer and plenty of money."

"I think Mrs. Fenster should mind her own business," I said.

"Well, so do I! Come on, now . . . just forget about it." Debbie made her chimpanzee face. I tried to laugh.

But I spent the rest of the day thinking about what Eileen had said. My mother has no money that I know of, unless Aunt Ruth and Uncle Dan are going to give her some. It's scary to think about my mother with no money to feed us or buy our clothes or anything. Maybe we will eat at Aunt Ruth's every night. And instead of giving all our outgrown clothes to some poor family someone will give their old clothes to us. I've got to talk to somebody about this. Maybe Jeff can explain things to me.

## ||

Trying to get to talk to Jeff is like banging your head against the wall. You just don't get anywhere. I've been tagging along after him for three days now but he says he's very busy and I should get lost. I think Petey Mansfield is a bad influence on him. I would tell that to my mother but suppose she says, "Why are you so anxious to have a private talk with Jeff?" What can I possibly answer without giving everything away?

I have come up with some information, though. From now on my father will be taking us out to dinner every Wednesday night and we will spend Sunday afternoons with him. This is part of something called a separation agreement. Daddy's lawyer's name is Mr. Levinson and he specializes in divorces just like Mr. Hague. Their offices are even in the same building in Newark. I wonder if maybe my mother and father will run into each other there.

Divorce is a very complicated thing. I always thought if you wanted one you just got it. But now I know that sometimes you need special reasons and each state has different rules. Uncle Dan explained this to me the other night. When I got into bed I thought of a million questions I should have asked him, like suppose I am sick on a Wednesday and can't go out to eat. Does that mean I don't get to see Daddy at all? I have *got* to talk to Jeff. If it takes me a week I am going to corner him. I will station myself outside the bathroom door when he is inside and I will not move until he comes out. There will be no way he can ignore me.

It didn't take me a week. On the second night, I sat down cross-legged right in front of the locked bathroom door. I listened as Jeff brushed his teeth and took a shower. When he opened the door he was really surprised to find me there waiting. He had a towel wrapped around himself and his hair was all wet.

"What are you doing?" he asked me.

"Waiting to talk to you."

"I'm busy," he said.

"I can wait." I wanted to say, "Please talk to me—I need somebody so bad." I felt tears come to my eyes. I think Jeff noticed.

He said, "Okay . . . go up and wait for me in the hideaway. I'll be right there. And here"— he handed me a tissue—"blow your nose."

I took it and ran up the stairs. I opened the door to his hideaway and sat down on his bed to wait. There was a picture of Mary Louise Rumberger tacked up on his bulletin board. She was wearing a bathing suit. She's pretty hefty.

When Jeff came up he was wearing a bathrobe and his hair was still wet but he had combed it. "What's wrong?" he asked.

"Does Mom have any money?" I said.

"What do you mean?"

"I mean does she have any money of her own . . . that's not Daddy's."

"I don't know," Jeff said. "I never thought about it. Why?"

"Because if she doesn't, what do you think is going to happen to us?"

"I think they make some kind of deal when they get divorced. Dad pays a certain amount of money to Mom every month. Something like that."

"Are you sure?" I asked.

"He's not going to let us starve, if that's what you're worried about."

"You're sure about that?"

"Yes, I'm sure. But if you don't believe me why don't you ask him yourself?"

"That's a very good idea. I think I'll do that. And another thing," I said.

"Go on . . ."

"Well, suppose I get sick and can't go to see him at all?"

"How am I supposed to know about that? You're thinking too much about the divorce."

"Do you mean you never think about it?"

"Well, sure I do. But we'll probably see more of Dad now than we did before."

"I don't care," I said. "It's not the same as having a father living at home where he belongs!" I started to cry again.

"You just better get used to it, Karen," Jeff said in a funny voice. "Because there's nothing you can do about it!"

That's what he thinks! I'm going to get them back together. I told Garfa I'd try, didn't I?

# 12

*Friday, March 26*
*My life is going from bad to worse!*

I found out today that Gary Owens is moving to Houston. His father has been transferred there. I wonder if he will start to like me before he moves? Probably not.

I forgot my milk money again. Mrs. Singer wants to know what's wrong with me. I told her nothing. Debbie said her parents bumped into my father at the Chinese restaurant. He was all alone, so the Bartells invited him to join them. Debbie said her mother told her not to tell me this—but my father is very lonely and unhappy. Why did she have to go and tell me?

If one more bad thing happens I just don't know what I am going to do!

My mother went to see Mr. Hague today for the second time. And when she came home she had a new haircut, a new dress and a smile on her face. So right away I thought, she's in love. Because I've been thinking a lot about that lately. Jeff says he is positive that Daddy and Mom are not too old for that stuff. I wonder!

Mom was in her room changing into a sweater and a pair of pants. I sat on her bed. "What's Mr. Hague like?"

"Who?" she asked, from inside her sweater.

This time I waited until her head was all the way through. "Mr. Hague," I said. "What's he like?"

"Oh . . . he's very nice. He's going to take care of everything." She fluffed out her hair.

"Do you want to marry him?"

"Marry who?"

"Mr. Hague."

"For heaven's sake, Karen! I've only seen

him twice. And he's already married, with five kids."

"How do you know that?"

"I saw a picture of his family on his desk."

"Oh. Then you're not in love?"

"No, I'm not. And what's all this *love* business anyway?"

"I don't know," I said. "You seem so happy today."

"Well, I am. It's a relief to know that soon everything will be settled."

"Mom . . ."

"Yes?"

"Will you tell me *exactly* why you're getting divorced?"

"Oh, Karen! We've been through this before."

"But there has to be a reason."

"There isn't any reason."

"How can there not be a reason? Is it a secret? Is that it? Something I shouldn't know about?"

"No . . . no . . ."

"Well then . . . what?"

"I mean there isn't just one reason. It's not that simple. There are so many reasons. It's just better this way. That's all."

"Does it have anything to do with your antiques?"

"Of course not. Whatever gave you that idea?"

"Oh, I don't know. Because the store sells modern furniture and you like old things."

Mom laughed a little. "Daddy likes antiques too. It just happens that his business is selling modern furniture."

"Well . . . does it have to do with the way you cook, then?"

"Oh, Karen!"

"Daddy's always saying you should try more recipes."

"But people don't get divorced over those things. You're all mixed up, aren't you?"

"I don't know," I said. "I guess I am."

Mom sat down next to me and took my hand. "I wish it was easier for you to understand. Daddy and I just don't enjoy being together. We don't love each other any more.

We love you and Amy and Jeff just the same, but not each other."

I took my hand away and fiddled with my chain belt.

"You're going to be a lot happier living in a house without constant fighting," Mom said.

I didn't say anything.

"You are, Karen. You'll see."

I nodded. If she was so sure, how come I didn't know it?

"Now let's go down to the kitchen and get dinner ready," Mom said.

We went downstairs together. Mew was on her favorite chair, bathing. She spends more time licking herself clean every day than I spend in the bathtub in a week.

# 13

On Sunday my father called for us at noon. Mom never comes to the door when she knows Daddy is outside. I don't know how I am going to get them back together when they never even see each other.

We went to visit Daddy's new apartment. He moved this week. The place is called Country Village and it has the kind of streets running through it where you can get lost pretty easy because everything looks the same. There are two swimming pools. One for Country Village East and one for Country Village West. My father's apartment is in West. Each section has four apartments.

Daddy's is in building 12, upstairs on the right. It's all fixed up like a magazine picture. Everything is brown-and-white and very modern. The kind of stuff that Newman's Furniture Store sells.

"Well . . . what do you think?" Daddy asked.

"It's terrific!" Jeff said. "It's a real man's pad. I'd like to live here myself."

That reminded me of what Debbie said. That Jeff might not want to be the only male in our house.

"Well, son," Daddy said, "you can stay here any time you want. That sofa opens up and I've got two rollaway beds in the storage room." He looked at me and Amy.

"I'll bet you're glad you're in the furniture business, right, Daddy?" I asked. "I mean, suppose you had to go out and *buy* all this stuff!"

"I don't exactly get it free, Karen . . . but I do save a lot," Daddy said.

"Well, that's good," I told him.

After we saw the apartment there wasn't much to do. Amy sat down on the floor in front of the TV and Jeff looked through my father's magazines. I went into the kitchen for something to drink. Daddy followed me.

"How's your mother?" he asked.

"She's fine and you should see her, Daddy . . . she looks great. She got a new haircut and—"

Daddy didn't let me finish. He said, "What kind of soda do you want?"

"I don't care," I said. He opened a Coke.

"Daddy, are you still going to pay for us?" I asked.

"Pay for what?"

"Oh, you know . . . our clothes and food and stuff like that."

"Of course I am, Karen. The lawyers will arrange for your support, and alimony for your mother."

"What's alimony?"

"An amount of money I'll be paying your mother every month."

So Jeff really knew what he was talking about.

"Anyway," Daddy said, "who's been putting all these ideas about money into your head?"

"Nobody," I said. "I was just wondering."

"You're sure no one told you to ask me?"

"Of course I'm sure." Who did Daddy think would tell me that?

"Because there isn't anything for you to worry about. I want to make sure you understand that."

"Suppose I get sick on a Wednesday or a Sunday and I can't come out with you. Does that mean I won't see you that day?"

"If you're sick I'll come to see you."

"You'll come up to my room?"

"Of course."

"But what if Mom is home."

"Listen, Karen . . . your mother and I aren't going to go out of our way to see each other. But if there's an emergency we won't let our personal feelings interfere. Now promise me you aren't going to worry about anything."

"I'll try not to," I said. But I was already thinking about getting sick next Wednesday so Daddy will have to come home. And once he's there he'll stay for dinner. Especially if I have a fever. How can I get myself a good fever? I wonder.

"There's a girl about your age in the apartment downstairs," Daddy told me. "I thought you might like to meet her."

"Oh . . . I don't know," I said.

"Her parents are divorced and she lives with her mother. They've been very nice to me since I moved in. I told her you'd be visiting today and she said you should come down. Her name is Val Lewis."

"Well . . ." I said.

"It might be nice for you to have a friend here."

"Okay . . . I guess . . . if you think I should . . ."

"It's apartment 12-B, on the left. Do you want me to come with you?"

"No. Did you say her name is Val?"

"Yes. Val Lewis."

"What's she like?"

"Oh . . . a little taller than you maybe and . . ."

"Not Val," I said. "Her mother!"

"Oh. She's a very attractive woman."

"Better looking than Mom?" I asked.

"In a different way. Why?" Daddy said.

"Just wondering," I told him.

I went downstairs and stood outside apartment 12-B. I wasn't sure if I wanted to meet this girl or not. Finally I rang the bell.

Val answered. "Oh, hi," she said. "I'll bet you're Karen."

"Yes . . . my father told me to come down."

"Come on in," Val said.

Daddy was right. She is taller than me. But not much. She has very long black hair and bangs that cover her eyebrows. Her eyes remind me of Mew's. They are the same color green.

"Excuse the mess," Val said when I walked into the living room. "I read the whole *New York Times* every Sunday. From cover to cover. I don't skip an inch!"

"That must take all day," I said.

"It does. And part of the night too. Let's go into my room."

I followed Val down the hall. "My father's only got one bedroom," I said.

"I know," Val told me. "All the apartments on the right have one bedroom and the ones on the left have two." When we got to Val's room she spread her arms. "It's small, but it's all mine," she said, pulling up her bed-spread. "I never make the bed on Sunday," she explained.

"That's okay," I said. The bed was up against the wall. There was a pink bulletin board that said *Valerie* on it hanging over the bed. She had a big desk with lots of drawers, plus a rug on the floor shaped like a foot, with toes and everything.

Val pulled her desk chair next to the bed and told me to sit down. "My mother's asleep," she said. "I know she'd like to meet you but she was out very late last night."

"With my father?" I asked.

"Your father?" Val laughed. "What gave you that idea?"

"I don't know. I just thought that's what you meant."

"My mother only goes out with one man. Seymour Chandler. Do you know him?"

"No."

"He's very rich. My mother wants to marry

him. Actually, my mother wants to marry anybody who's very rich."

"Oh," I said. I hope my mother won't be like that.

"She and my father have been divorced almost three years. My father lives in San Francisco."

"Have you been there to visit him?" I asked.

"No . . . I haven't seem him since the divorce. He's a runaround and he drinks too much and his checks are late every month. Once my mother's lawyer had him picked up for non-support."

"My father isn't anything like that," I said.

"Sometimes the children are the last to know," Val told me.

"How did you find out about yours?" I asked.

"Oh . . . my mother spent the whole first year after the divorce telling me what a bum my father is."

"My mother keeps saying my father is a great person," I said.

Val laughed and said, "Uh-oh! Watch out for that."

"Why? What do you mean?"

"Because she's not being honest with you, that's what."

"How do you know?" I asked.

"It says so—right here." Val reached under her bed and came up with a book. She opened it and read, "'If your mother never says bad things about your father it's because she thinks that it's better for you not to know about your father's faults. She may think that you can only love a person who is perfect.'" Val closed the book. "You see?" she said.

"What kind of book is that?" I asked.

"It's called *The Boys and Girls Book About Divorce* and it's just for kids like us. A doctor wrote it. I'm his greatest fan. I used to write to him once a week when I first got his book. He even answered me."

"Did your mother buy it for you?" I asked.

"No. I read about it in *The New York Times* and saved my allowance until I had enough. It's very expensive. It costs $7.95."

"For just one book?"

"Yes, but it's worth it. You ought to ask your

father to get it for you. Wait a minute and I'll write down all the information." Val got up and went to her desk. She wrote on a piece of notebook paper, then folded it and gave it to me. I put it in my pocket.

Val put the divorce book back under her bed and came up with another. "Do you know the facts of life?" she asked.

"Yes," I said.

"Oh. If you didn't I was going to say I'd be glad to tell you. I have a book about that too. See . . ." She showed me the book. It was a lot like the one I read at Debbie's.

"What grade are you in?" Val asked.

"Sixth," I said.

"I'm in seventh. I was twelve in September."

"I'm twelve too," I said. "We're just a few months apart."

"In age maybe," Val said. "But being in seventh grade makes a big difference. For instance, I wouldn't dream of liking a boy in my class."

"How come?" I asked, thinking about Gary Owens.

"Seventh-grade boys are babies. I like eighth- or ninth-grade boys."

"My brother's in ninth grade," I told her.

"Oh . . . I didn't know you have a brother."

"Yes, and a little sister too."

"Then you're the middle child?"

"Yes."

"Uh-oh! That's bad," Val said. "Middle children have all kinds of problems."

"Says who?" I asked.

"Everybody knows that. You're not the oldest and you're not the youngest. So you wind up with problems. The divorce will be harder on you than on them. But cheer up! I'm an *only* child. I have lots of problems too."

"Val . . . how do you know so much?" I asked.

"I told you," she said, "I read the entire *New York Times* every Sunday!"

# 14

Compared to Val, Debbie doesn't know anything. I don't think she's ever read *The New York Times*. And what does she know about divorce or alimony or support? Not much, that's for sure. It's funny how things can change all of a sudden. Now I have more in common with Val than with Debbie. Oh, we're still best friends but we don't see that much of each other outside school. Especially since Mrs. Bartell has decided Debbie needs dramatic lessons. She's going to get them every Saturday afternoon.

Now that Gary Owens has moved to Houston, Mrs. Singer's let me move my desk away from the wall and next to Debbie's. She said if there is any talking or giggling between us she will separate us again. It's too bad that Gary moved away without ever knowing that I've spent four whole months thinking about him. If I ever feel that way about a boy again I won't waste time. I'll let him know right off. At least I think I will.

We are studying about the Vikings this month. They were pretty interesting guys, but very mean. When they went into battle they acted absolutely crazy. They killed everybody, including the women and children. But they were smart too. For instance, they built great ships. We are going to make Viking dioramas. That sounds like fun, for a change.

This afternoon I tried to find out if Petey Mansfield talks. I waited until he and Jeff locked themselves up inside the hideaway. Then I crept up the stairs very quietly and stood outside Jeff's room, holding a glass to the wall. I pressed my ear against the bottom of the glass. Eileen told me this is the best way to try to hear something you're not supposed to.

It works too! First I heard them laughing. But then they switched on the record player and that was the end of it. All I got was an earful of music. If you ask me, Petey Mansfield can talk when he feels like it.

Debbie says if only I liked Petey we could have a double wedding. Meaning her and Jeff and me and Petey. I told her, "Ha-ha! I wouldn't marry Petey Mansfield if he was the last boy on earth." And anyway, I'm not getting married.

My mother is eating again. She goes around the house singing now. I still wonder if she's in love. I would like to get a look at this Mr. Hague because my mother has gone to his office a few more times, and once when I answered the phone it was *him.* Last week Val told me that women getting divorces always fall for their lawyers.

Tonight at dinner Mom gave us some big news. "I'm going back to school," she said.

Amy practically spit out her lima beans. "To school?"

"Yes," Mom said. "That way I'll be able to get a better job."

"A job?" Jeff and I said together.

"Yes."

"You're really getting a job?" Jeff asked.

"I hope so," Mom told him.

"Doing what?" I asked. "Refinishing furniture?"

"No," Mom said. "That's what I'd like to do but I have to be more practical right now."

What kind of job will she get? What can she do? Maybe she'll be a cashier in the supermarket. Or maybe she'll be a cocktail waitress. That's what divorced women on TV always turn out to be—cocktail waitresses. Imagine my mother dressed in a skimpy costume! Suppose Debbie comes over while she's getting into her waitress clothes. Debbie will say, "Why is your mother dressed up like a Bunny?" And I won't tell her the truth. I'll say, "She's going to a costume party." Then Debbie will say, "Oh. She looks cute." But I'll know that she looks terrible.

"I don't know what kind of job I'm going to get," Mom said. "That's why I'm going back to school. To take a course in typing and shorthand. I've signed up for an evening class at Seton Hall too. In English literature. The semester's half over, but I can still learn a lot."

"English literature!" Jeff said. "Why?"

"Because I only had one year of college before I got married. I had you when I was just twenty," she told Jeff. She finished eating her salad. Then she said, "I think I might like to get my degree. I never really had a chance to find out what I might be able to do."

"Well, don't let me stop you!" Jeff said. "I can always go and live with Dad."

My mother's face turned very red. "Did he tell you that?"

"He said any time I want to I can stay there." Jeff stood up. "At least he's not sorry he had us!" He clomped out of the kitchen and slammed the front door.

Mom pushed her chair away from the table. "Jeff is wrong," she told me and Amy. "You know I'm glad to have you."

Maybe you are and maybe you're not. Who can tell any more?

*Tuesday, April 6*
*Can Jeff really move out of our house?*
*That would be awful! Even though I can't*
*stand him sometimes, I would still miss*
*him a lot. I like just knowing he's around.*

But the next morning Jeff was back and Mom
was furious. She threw our breakfast at us.
"Where were you last night?" she asked him.

"That's my business," Jeff said.

"Just who do you think you're talking to?"
Mom asked. "From now on you're not to run out
at night without telling me first. And I want
you home by nine thirty during the week."

"Says who?" Jeff asked.

"Me!" Mom hollered.

"Since when are you the boss?"

"Jeff . . . stop it!" Mom said. "What's gotten
into you?"

By the time Jeff left for school my mother
was on the verge of tears. But when she saw
that he had forgotten his lunch she ran after
him calling, "Jeff . . . Jeff . . . you forgot your
lunch."

He yelled back, "Eat it yourself!"

*Wednesday, April 7*
*I hate Jeff today. He's making everything*
*worse, just when it was getting better.*

# 15

I have been trying to get sick. I don't wear a sweater when I should, and two days ago I walked in the rain without my boots and my feet got soaked. But so far nothing has happened. Debbie once told me about a girl in her cabin at camp who liked to stay overnight in the infirmary. She used to rub the end of the thermometer until it went up to 102°. Then she'd stick it in her mouth and the nurse would think she was really sick.

This morning I tried doing that but it never went above 94°—and I rubbed it for ten whole minutes. So I held the tip of the thermometer next to the light bulb in my desk lamp and it went up to 105°. I figured I'd put it in my mouth and walk downstairs like that. Then my mother would take it out and wouldn't she be surprised when she saw what a high fever I had!

The only trouble was I didn't know the thermometer would be so hot. As soon as I put it into my mouth I burned my tongue something awful! I spit the thermometer out. It fell on the floor but it didn't break.

I will have to think up a better way to get my mother and father back together. I can't waste my time trying to get sick. That could take forever.

I had my piano lesson right before dinner tonight. Mrs. Lennard told me to cut my nails shorter. She says she can hear a *click-click* sound when I play. And that from now on Mew can't sit on top of the piano when I take my lesson. I told her my cat is very musical and that she always sits on top of the piano when I practice. Actually, Mew is almost human, but I didn't say so.

Mrs. Lennard looked at me kind of funny. I'll bet she wishes she was still teaching Jeff and not just me. It's no secret that he's the one with the talent. But this year he quit piano. I don't think I play so bad. It's just that my fingers don't always do what I want them to.

Before Mrs. Lennard left she told me to practice the same songs for next week. She said I wasn't ready for anything new. I felt like asking her how she would play if her parents were getting divorced.

As soon as we sat down to dinner Amy said, "Wendy, my friend in school, has a Talking Jessie Doll. She brought it in for Show and Tell. I want one too. The kind with the hair that grows."

"Maybe for your birthday," my mother said.

"My birthday's not until the end of June," Amy told her.

"Well, that's not so far away," Mom said.

"Oh, please, Mommy! I can't wait until my birthday!"

"I'm sorry, Amy. But you'll have to."

"Why?" Amy asked.

"You know Mom doesn't have a lot of money to throw around," I told Amy. "Stop being so selfish."

"I'll bet you Daddy would get it for me."

"That's enough, Amy!" Mom shouted.

"*I hate you.*" Amy screamed. "You made Daddy go away just so you could be mean to me!"

My mother reached across the table and smacked Amy. Then she sent her to her room.

"I thought you said there wouldn't be any more fighting once you and Daddy were apart," I said.

Jeff laughed and got up from the table.

"Try to understand," Mom told us. "Won't you please try to understand?" She put her head down right on her plate and started to cry. She got gravy in her hair.

*Thursday, April 15*
*Sometimes I feel sorry for my mother and other times I hate her. And besides all that, I didn't laugh once today!*

# 16

Gary Owens wrote our class a letter. Mrs. Singer found it in her mailbox in the office. It said:

Dear Mrs. Singer and Class 6-108,
    Texas is neat. It's warm enough to play baseball even in the winter. We got a dog. His name is Alexander, like the Great. We call him Al for short. Most of the kids here are okay except for a few. They call me the new kid. Here's my address in case anybody feels like writing.

Gary Owens
16 Sanders Road
Houston, Texas

Mrs. Singer said we should all write to Gary and that would be our English lesson for the day. I wrote:

Dear Gary,
  It must be nice to be where it's warm. We made Viking dioramas. Did you learn about the Vikings yet? Your dog Al sounds very nice. I still have my cat Mew, but I like dogs too. By now you're probably not the new kid any more. Well, that's all the news from here.
                              Your friend,
                              Karen Newman
                  (I hope you remember me!)

Mrs. Singer made me copy my letter over because I didn't make paragraphs. There are a lot of things I would have told Gary, if only he had liked me before he moved away.

# 17

My mother got a job! She's going to be the receptionist at the Global Insurance Company in East Orange. She'll probably get to bring home a million Day Books next year. She says this is just a stepping stone—something to get her going until she decides what kind of work she wants to do permanently.

Aunt Ruth and Uncle Dan came over tonight. My mother was in the basement working on an old trunk she picked up at some sale. She's refinishing it and lining the inside with flowered material. It's going to be for Amy's toys, she says. So Aunt Ruth and

Uncle Dan went downstairs to see her. So did I. I wanted to hear what my mother had to say because I am almost positive Aunt Ruth doesn't want her to go to work.

"The children need you at home, Ellie," Aunt Ruth said.

"They're in school all day," Mom told her. "They won't even know I'm gone. I'm only working from nine to three and Karen will watch Amy until I get home."

"Except Wednesdays," I reminded her. "Don't forget I have Girl Scouts on Wednesdays."

"Amy can play at Roger's for half an hour on Wednesdays. I'll be home by three thirty."

"Suppose one of them gets sick?" Aunt Ruth asked. "Then what?"

"Mrs. Hedley can come. I'll make some kind of arrangement with her. Besides, they don't get sick that often."

Isn't that the truth? And I've been trying so hard.

"Ellie . . ." Uncle Dan said. "I wish you'd think this over for a while. Are you sure you can handle the responsibility of running a house and keeping a job?"

"Not to mention the children," Aunt Ruth added.

"I think I can manage," Mom said. "At any rate, I'm going to give it a try."

"What will people at work call you, Mom?" I asked. "Will you be Mrs. Newman or Miss Robinson, like before you were married?"

"I think I'll call myself Miss Newman. I'm used to being Ellie Newman. After all, that's who I've been for fifteen years." Mom opened another can of shellac and started painting the trunk.

After Aunt Ruth and Uncle Dan went home I asked Mom, "How come you didn't give in to Aunt Ruth this time?"

And Mom said, "I don't always give in to Aunt Ruth."

"Yes you do."

"That isn't so, Karen."

"Well, I think it is. Every time you go shopping Aunt Ruth tells you what to buy. And when Amy had all those sore throats

113

Aunt Ruth made you go to her doctor."

"You're wrong," Mom said. "I may have listened to Aunt Ruth a lot of times but I don't always do what she thinks is right. And from now on I'm going to be much more careful to make up my own mind about everything."

"Mom . . ."

"Yes?"

"What do you really want to do?"

"I don't know yet. But I'm going to try to find out."

My mother is grown up. So how come she can't decide what she wants? Does she want to go to work or does she want to go to college? "I sure hope you find out soon," I told her.

"It has nothing to do with you, Karen. It isn't going to change your life one way or another."

"That's what you say!"

"Look . . . some day you and Jeff and Amy will grow up and leave home. Then what will I have?"

"You see!" I raised my voice. "That proves

it! All you care about is yourself! You never think about me."

"That's not so and you know it!" Mom said.

"Oh, yes, it is so! You never ask me what I think or what I feel or what I want. . . . I wish I was never born!"

I ran upstairs, picked up Mew and took her to my room. I closed my door and put a chair up against it.

Pretty soon my mother knocked on the door and called me. I knew she would. "Karen . . . this is silly. Let me in. I want to talk to you."

"Go away," I told her.

I'll bet anything that Mom will change her mind about her job just like she did about Daddy.

A few days after my mother started her job I had a dental appointment. Mom said from now on she will schedule our appointments later in the day, but just this once Aunt Ruth would pick me up at school and drive me to Dr. Harrison's.

I am the only one in my family who has never had a cavity. I don't know if this is because I am a better tooth-brusher or because I was born that way. Whatever the reason, I'm glad.

Dr. Harrison sings while he looks at your teeth. He has a terrible voice. He makes up his own words too. Usually they don't make much sense but they always rhyme. When he cleans my teeth I laugh. I can't stand that tickle on my gums. And when I laugh he tells me not to, because I open my mouth too wide.

Today he said that my teeth are in good shape and that I don't have to come back for another six months. But he gave me a fluoride treatment and I almost threw up. I hate fluoride treatments!

When I was through I told the nurse my mother would call to make my next appointment. Aunt Ruth put away her needlepoint and asked me if I would like to stop for a snack on the way home. I said, "Sure."

We went to Grunings on the hill. They have the world's most delicious ice cream. Aunt

Ruth ordered a hot-fudge sundae with whipped cream and nuts. I guess she's off her diet this week. I ordered two scoops of coffee ice cream. I don't like sundaes. All that goo gets in the way and it makes you very thirsty.

When we were served and I took my first bite of ice cream I remembered that my teeth are very sensitive to cold and hot after a cleaning. The ice cream nearly killed me. I had to mash it all up and then lick it off the spoon so it wouldn't hurt my teeth.

"How are things going at home?" Aunt Ruth asked.

"Okay, I guess. Next week is Mom's and Dad's anniversary."

"That's right," Aunt Ruth said. "I forgot all about it."

"Are you sending a card?"

"No . . . when a couple is getting a divorce they don't want to be reminded of wedding anniversaries."

I don't agree with that but I didn't tell Aunt Ruth. I think if we remind Mom and Dad about their anniversary they will feel very bad about getting a divorce. They will remember how happy they were when they first met and all that. Then they will see how silly it is of them not to get along. "They'll be married sixteen years," I told Aunt Ruth.

"That's right. I remember it very well because Mark had the chicken pox and the wedding was at our house and your grandfather never had chicken pox so the doctor gave him a shot. But two weeks later he got it anyway."

"Garfa had chicken pox?"

"All over him." Aunt Ruth laughed a little. "You know . . . I haven't thought about that in a long time. Sixteen years ago . . . Mark was just a little boy and now he's all grown up."

"How long have you and Uncle Dan been married?" I asked.

"Twenty-six years."

"That's really a long time!"

"Yes, it is."

"Do you ever fight?"

"Sometimes."

"But then you make up?"

"Either that or we forget about it."

That's like me and my mother. We have just forgotten about the fight we had the other night. Neither one of us has mentioned it. Why couldn't she and Daddy have done that? "You know something? I don't remember my parents fighting when I was little."

"I suppose they got along better then," Aunt Ruth said. "It's only in the last six or seven years that things have been bad."

"That long?" I couldn't believe it! How could two people not get along for so many years?

That night I was sitting in the den with Mew on my lap. Her fur shed all over my sweater. I got up to get her brush, then settled on the couch again. She doesn't always like me to brush her. Sometimes she gets mad and tries to bite the brush. Tonight she purred and let me do whatever I wanted.

Mom and Amy were watching TV. Jeff never sits with us any more, except at mealtime. Amy was snuggled up close to Mom, which is really unusual for her. She always used to do that with Daddy. When I am cuddling Mew I never feel bad that my mother or father is paying attention to someone else.

As I brushed Mew's fur I started to think about what Aunt Ruth had said—that my parents haven't gotten along for six or seven years. And that's when it hit me! If the trouble between Daddy and Mom started that long ago, maybe it had something to do with Amy. That would have been around the time she was born. Maybe they didn't plan to have her. Maybe they only wanted two kids—me and Jeff. But then when Amy was born, Daddy liked her best. Mom was angry that he picked a favorite and she got back at Daddy by making Jeff *her* favorite. So really, if Amy hadn't been born they'd still be very happy.

I wonder if Amy knows about that? Probably not. She is too young to figure out such a thing. If you ask me Val has it all wrong. I might be the middle child, but it looks like I am the only one who is normal. Amy and Jeff have the problems. Poor Amy! No wonder she can't sleep at night. I am lucky to be no one's favorite.

# 18

On Friday night Mrs. Hedley came and Mom went rushing off to her class at Seton Hall. When Mrs. Hedley opened her knitting bag and pulled out a pile of yarn I left the room. Amy could help her make wool balls tonight! I had more important things to do.

I went up to the hideaway. The door was open. Jeff was lying on his bed with his eyes closed. Only his purple light was on. The whole room glowed.

"Hey Jeff . . ." I said.

"Yeah?"

"Did you remember that Monday is Mom's and Dad's anniversary?"

"So?"

"Don't you think we should do something?"

"Are you kidding?"

"No . . . I think it would be very nice to have a little party or something."

Jeff opened his eyes and sat up. "They're getting divorced, Karen."

"So?"

"So you don't go around giving parties for people who're getting divorced."

"Don't you even want to sign my card?"

"You bought a card?" Jeff asked.

"Two," I said, holding them up.

I bought them yesterday. One for Mom and one for Daddy. They are both the same. There's a picture of two bluebirds and it says *TO A SWELL COUPLE.* I'm going to mail them tomorrow morning because I want to make sure they are delivered on the twenty-sixth, and that's Monday. I'm sure when they remember that it is their sixteenth anniversary they will call their lawyers and cancel the divorce.

"Well," I said to Jeff, "you want to sign them or not?"

"You're nuts!" Jeff said. "You can't send them

anniversary cards like there's nothing wrong."

"Says who?"

"You just can't."

"Well, I'm going to. Amy's signing them and so am I and I think you should too."

"That's the dumbest thing I ever heard."

"This is your last chance to sign," I told him.

"Forget it!"

"Okay, I will." I turned and walked out of his room. Let him lie there forever—with his stupid purple light bulb!

When Amy came up to bed I showed her the cards. She liked them a lot. I told her she could sign them and she chose a different color crayon for every letter in her name. And she didn't just sign *Amy*—she signed *Amy Denise Newman.*


On Saturday morning Mom said I could ask Debbie to sleep over if I wanted because she was going out to dinner with Aunt Ruth and Uncle Dan. "I don't think we need Mrs. Hedley any more," Mom said. "Jeff is old enough to be in charge."

"I thought you said if we give up Mrs. Hedley some other family will grab her."

"They probably will," Mom said. "But it's foolish to pay her when we can manage by ourselves."

Did Mr. Hague tell Mom to watch her money? Or doesn't Daddy send enough for a baby sitter?

Debbie came over in time for supper, which we made ourselves. We had hot dogs, potato chips and chocolate pudding for dessert. The only part of the night that wasn't fun was telling Amy that she couldn't sleep in my other bed. She cried and carried on but before Mom left she explained that Amy has her own room and that's where she has to sleep from now on. I don't think Amy ever told Mom that she is afraid we'll be gone in the morning. Maybe I should be the one to tell my mother. I don't know—Amy might not like it if I did. That is supposed to be our secret.

Mom got all dressed up and I couldn't help wondering if just Aunt Ruth and Uncle Dan were taking her to dinner or if maybe Henry

Farnum was going along too. And I didn't want to ask her about it in front of Debbie anyway. Mom looked very nice and she smelled delicious. I think she was wearing the perfume Daddy gave to her last Christmas.

At ten o'clock Amy fell asleep in the den and Debbie and I carried her up to bed. We decided to leave her overhead light on all night. That way she might not get so scared if she woke up suddenly.

At quarter to eleven the phone rang. Debbie and I were in my room. I thought it might be Mom, checking to see how everything was. So I went into my mother's room and picked up the phone, but Jeff beat me to it on the kitchen extension. And it wasn't my mother either. It was Mary Louise Rumberger! I put one hand over the mouthpiece and called to Debbie, "It's Mary Louise . . ."

Debbie came running. We shared the phone and listened. Imagine Mary Louise calling my brother at quarter to eleven at night! And they barely even talked. They just laughed very softly at each other.

\* \* \*

I could hardly wait for Monday night. I hoped Daddy would call as soon as he saw his mail. Then he and Mom would talk about the day they got married sixteen years ago and they'd laugh about Garfa catching chicken pox!

Mom opened her mail as soon as she got home from work. I stood there watching her. After she read my card she did the craziest thing! She started to cry and she took me in her arms. She said, "Oh, Karen . . ." over and over again.

Later Daddy called. Only he didn't call to talk to Mom like I was hoping. He called to talk to me. He said, "Thanks, Karen . . . but from now on you have to remember we don't celebrate our anniversary any more. Try not to think of April 26 as a special day."

*Monday, April 26*

*How can I not think about this day? It is special and it will always be special even if I am the only one who knows it!*

# 19

Jeff has a broken toe. He has to wear a sneaker with a big hole cut in it. His toe is bandaged and he pulls an athletic sock over that foot to keep the rest of his toes warm. He broke it himself. He dropped a weight on his foot. Dr. Winters says he is lucky he didn't do more damage. He uses a cane to walk around. I wonder what Mary Louise Rumberger thinks of broken toes? She probably feels very sorry for him. She calls him every single night now.

Jeff doesn't talk to any of us. Not to me or Amy or my mother. He is getting just like Petey Mansfield. They can turn themselves off like radios. I am starting to really hate him!

Val invited me to sleep over Saturday night. I asked my mother if I could go. She said, "I don't even know her, Karen. How can I let you sleep there overnight?"

"Please, Mom! She's very nice. So is her mother." That was funny because I really don't know Mrs. Lewis. I've seen her twice. She says hello, but that's about it. She is the best-looking mother I have ever seen. "Daddy lives right upstairs," I told Mom.

"You'll have to call him and see what he thinks," Mom said.

"Now?"

"Yes, now."

I picked up the phone and dialed. "Hello Daddy? This is Karen. . . . I'm fine. . . . They're okay too. Daddy, Val wants me to sleep over Saturday night. . . . Yes, I'm dying to but Mom won't let me unless you say I can. Well, because she doesn't know Val or Mrs. Lewis. . . . Okay, I'll tell her you're going to be home. Thanks a lot, Daddy. I'll see you Saturday. Bye."

After that my mother said I could go.

The next night my father called to invite Jeff and Amy to stay over at his apartment Saturday night. Amy said she couldn't wait, but Jeff told Daddy he already made other plans. I'll bet they have something to do with Mary Louise.

On Saturday, before I left for Val's, I made my mother promise to take good care of Mew and to feed her *canned* food in the morning. I think Mom would give Mew food from a box if she could get away with it.

I picked Mew up and kissed her good-by. I am not allowed to kiss her. It has something to do with the possibility of her carrying germs. So I take her into the bathroom with me, lock the door and kiss her as much as I want to.

Later, when Daddy called for us, me and Amy were waiting by the front door. As soon as we were in the car Amy said, "Jeff doesn't like me any more."

My father said, "Oh?"

"And he doesn't like Karen either. He doesn't like anybody. He's so mean! He's almost as mean as Mommy. She won't get me a Talking Jessie Doll. The kind with the hair that grows."

"Your mother's not mean, Amy," Daddy said.

"How do you know? You don't live at home."

"Because I know your mother and if she doesn't think you should have a Talking Jessie Doll right now she must have a good reason."

"She's always leaving us alone," Amy said. "That's mean, isn't it?"

"I can't believe she leaves you alone," Daddy said.

"She doesn't," I told him. "We don't use Mrs. Hedley any more, that's all. Jeff is in charge when Mom goes out."

"That sounds reasonable to me," Daddy said.

Amy sulked the rest of the way to Daddy's apartment.

# 20

I rang Val's bell. She let me in. I got there in time to meet her mother's boyfriend, Seymour Chandler. He doesn't really look anything like a boyfriend. He looks more like a grandfather to me. His hair is silver and he's kind of fat. But Mrs. Lewis looked beautiful. I wouldn't want to have a mother that good looking. I'd spend all my time worrying about how I was going to turn out compared to her. Not that Val is ugly. She's okay. But she doesn't look like her mother.

Val introduced me to Mr. Chandler. She said, "Seymour, this is my friend Karen. Her father lives upstairs. He's getting a divorce." Then Val told me, "Seymour's divorced too."

"That's right," Seymour said. "I am. Twice, as a matter of fact." Then he laughed.

Twice! I never even thought about getting divorced more than once. That must *really* be awful!

"Well, girls . . . Seymour and I are leaving now. You have a nice time," Mrs. Lewis told us. She leaned close to Val and kissed her good night. I noticed that her lips didn't touch Val's face. It was an air-kiss. "Go to sleep by eleven, Valerie."

"I will, mother," Val said. She closed the door behind them and fastened the three extra locks on it.

It must feel funny to see your own mother go out on dates.

"Well . . ." Val said. "What do you want to do?"

"I don't know. I usually watch TV on Saturday nights."

"TV ruins your mind," Val said. "Let's wash our hair."

"Mine's not dirty," I said. "I just washed it Monday night."

"Oh, come on, Karen. It'll be fun. Then we

can soak in my mother's bubble bath. I always do that on Saturdays. Tell you what . . . I'll wash your hair first, then you can do mine."

We went into the bathroom, where Val attached a rubber hose to the sink. "It's like a beauty parlor. You'll enjoy it," she said.

"Well . . . okay."

Val fixed up a chair for me and spread a towel under my neck so it wouldn't hurt from leaning back so far. Then she went to work. I have never had such a good shampoo in my life. When I do it myself I don't get out all the soap, because my hair is so thick. But Val got it squeaky clean. She even gave me a cream rinse so I wouldn't get tangles. When that was done she wrapped my head in a big green towel.

Then it was my turn to do Val. I didn't do as good a job on her. I tried, but her hair is awfully long. She had to give me advice. She said, "Rinse behind my ears now. That's it. Watch it, Karen . . . the water's running down my face. Okay . . . now the cream rinse. Take two capfuls and rub it in all over. Good . . . rub some more in if that's not enough. Okay . . .

now give me another rinse. Careful . . . it's going down my back."

Val wrapped her head in a towel like mine, then she ran the tub. She poured in three-quarters of a bottle of bubble bath. While the tub was filling we rubbed each other's heads until they were damp. Val gave me a couple of barrettes to pin up my hair so it wouldn't get all wet when I took my bath.

She let the water run almost to the top of the tub and by then the bubbles were so thick you couldn't see through them.

I don't feel funny getting undressed in front of Debbie, because I have known her forever. But I did feel strange in front of Val. She could tell too. She said, "If you want I won't look until you're in the tub. You can hide under all the bubbles." Then she turned around and I took off my clothes, dropped them in a heap on the floor and stepped into the tub. When I did, some of the water ran over the side.

Then Val got undressed and I didn't look, even though she didn't care if I did. More suds overflowed when she got into the tub, but Val didn't pay any attention to that. She said, "When I grow up I'm going to be a nudist. People would get along better if they didn't wear any clothes. Then they couldn't pretend to be what they're not."

"But you'd get cold in the winter," I told her.

"Possibly. Maybe I'll move to a warmer climate."

That reminded me of Gary Owens. I wonder if there are nudists in Houston?

We soaked in the tub for half an hour. Neither one of us used soap or a washcloth. I guess if you sit in bubble bath all that time you're bound to get clean.

When we finally came out of the tub Val put on her mother's terry robe, which was about four inches too long. It dragged all over the wet bathroom floor. I got into my pajamas. We both smelled very nice. Then we brushed out each other's hair.

When that was done Val sat down on the closed toilet seat and rubbed some kind of oil all over her legs. "I have to shave my legs now," she said.

I don't know anybody who shaves her legs yet. Debbie says she will when she's fourteen or when her legs get hairy, whichever comes first.

Val ran a silver razor over her legs. *Zip zip zip.* She reminded me of my father, shaving his face. I used to love to watch him. He'd always put a dab of shaving cream on my nose when I was little. "Don't you ever cut yourself?" I asked Val.

"Oh, sure. But nothing serious. I've had lots of practice. I've been shaving since September."

"Did your mother show you how?"

"Nope. I learned myself. Want me to do yours?"

"No," I said. "My mother would kill me. She says the earlier you shave the more you have to keep shaving. And anyway, the hair on my legs is very light. See . . ." I held a leg up for Val to look at.

"You're lucky," she said, inspecting it. "I'm a very hairy person."

I noticed that when we were in the tub but I didn't tell Val.

When she was done shaving I helped her

clean up the bathroom. She took big handfuls of the suds that were left in the tub and threw them into the toilet. They made a sizzling sound. And even after she flushed three times there were still suds floating around. "I think I used a little too much bubble bath tonight," Val said. By then it was almost ten o'clock.

We went into Val's room. She has a trundle bed. It looks like just one bed, but underneath there's another one. It was already pulled out for me. I asked Val where she got the rug that's shaped like a foot and she said she saw an ad for it in *The New York Times* and cut it out to show her mother. Then she got it for her birthday.

"I put my new sheets on your bed," Val said. "Do you like them?"

They were pink-and-orange striped. "They're really nice," I said.

"I thought you'd approve." Val snuggled down under her covers.

I'll bet it's lonely for her to spend every Saturday night all by herself. And Mrs. Lewis goes out during the week too. No wonder Val hopes Seymour will marry her mother. Then she won't be alone so much.

"Val . . ." I said.

"Yes?"

"I still don't understand why you don't see your father. Couldn't you take a trip to San Francisco?"

"No. I told you before . . . he doesn't care anything about me."

"How can you say that?" I asked.

"Because it's true."

"Did your mother tell you?"

"No. That's one thing she won't admit. She says he's just busy."

"Then you don't know if he really wants to see you or not."

"Oh, I know all right. I'll show you," Val said, reaching under her bed. She came up with her divorce book. She opened it and said, "Listen to this. 'Fathers who live close by but do not visit—'"

I interrupted. "But your father doesn't live close by. He lives in San Francisco."

"Wait a minute," Val said. "I'm not done

reading." She started again. "'Fathers who live close by but do not visit and fathers who live far away and hardly ever call or write either do not love their children at all, or they love them very little.'" She closed the book, with her finger marking her place, and looked at me.

"It really says that?"

"It does."

"Do you believe it?"

"Of course I do. It's true. Why should I kid myself?" She opened the book again. "It says right here, 'There is something very wrong with an unloving parent. He deserves pity as well as anger.' I've gotten along without him for three years. I'll get along without him forever! He was never very interested in me anyway."

"What does your mother say . . . besides the bad things?"

"That he married her because she was pretty and he wanted to show her off, like a new coat or something. He never really loved her, she says."

"I think my parents loved each other when

they got married. Their wedding pictures look so happy. But my mother says they were too young."

"How old was she?" Val asked.

"Nineteen."

"You should never get married that young," Val said.

"I'm never getting married at all!" I told her.

"I am," she said.

That surprised me. "You are?"

"Yes. When I'm twenty-seven and I'm a successful scientist."

"You're going to be a scientist?" I asked. "I thought you were going to be a nudist."

"One thing has nothing to do with the other. I'll be both."

"What kind are you going to be? Scientist, I mean."

"I'm not sure. But I'm going to discover something important. I'll be very famous and my father will want everyone to know that I'm his daughter. I'll be very cool about the whole thing. I'll admit that we're related but I won't say anything else."

"If you get married . . . will you ever get divorced?"

"No. Never!"

"Me neither," I said. "You know something? I think if my father could see my mother now he'd move back in."

"Forget it. It'll never work."

"How do you know?" I asked. "You never even saw my mother."

"I'm telling you, Karen. Just forget it."

"I don't see how you can be so sure," I said. "My father's very lonely."

"But that doesn't mean he and your mother are going to get back together."

"Well, I still don't see how it can hurt to try."

"Go ahead," Val said. "Try . . . you'll see . . . you'll be the one who gets hurt." She put out the light then. "Good night Karen," she said.

"Good night Val." I'll bet she doesn't want my parents to get back together. Just because her father moved to San Francisco and never sees her. But I'm still sure it will work.

# 21

When Daddy drove us home on Sunday afternoon he asked me to run into the house and get Jeff. "I have something to tell all three of you," he said.

Jeff was playing the piano. I heard the music before I opened the front door. He's been spending a lot of time practicing lately. He writes his own songs. Most of them are in a minor key and sound sad. His newest one is called "Mary Louise . . . Please." Those are the only words. Please what? I wonder. But I wouldn't dream of asking him.

I went inside and said, "Hey Jeff . . . Daddy's out in the car. He wants to talk to you."

Jeff banged the piano with both hands before he got up and stomped out of the house. I followed him. We both got into the back seat of the car. Amy was up front with Daddy.

My father turned around to face me and Jeff. "I'm leaving for Las Vegas a week from tomorrow," he said. "I'm staying with Garfa for about six weeks and while I'm there I'll get the divorce."

"You're getting a Nevada divorce?" Jeff asked.

"Yes," Daddy told him.

"But why?" I said. "Why can't you just get it right here in New Jersey?"

"Because that would take a long time," Daddy said. "At least a year."

"So?" I asked.

"Well, your mother and I want to get things settled now. This isn't easy for either one of us."

What's the big hurry? I wondered. Why can't they wait? Why does Daddy have to go away for such a long time? Unless . . . unless there's some other woman that he wants to marry! Thinking about that makes me sick. But it is possible. One night last week I called

Daddy and there wasn't any answer. Maybe
he was out with her then, making plans! Or
could Mom be the one who wants the divorce
right away? Suppose she wants to marry
Henry Farnum! No, that can't be. We'd have
met him by now. It's got to be Daddy! I wonder
who the woman is? I hate her already. I will
never speak to her. Not as long as I live!

That night I helped my mother do the dinner dishes. When we were almost through I
said, "Is Daddy getting married?"

Mom turned off the water and looked at
me. "Where did you ever get that idea?"

"Well, is he?"

"No," Mom said.

"Are you positive?"

"Yes. The divorce has nothing to do with
anyone else. You know that, Karen."

"How can you be sure Daddy didn't meet
somebody last week and now he wants to
marry her?"

"I'm sure. That's all. Besides, he'd have told
me."

"Why should he tell you?"

"Just because. I know him. And he'd certainly tell you and Jeff and Amy. He wouldn't just run off and get married."

"Then why is he in such a hurry to get the divorce?"

"Oh . . ." Mom said. "So that's it!"

"Well?"

"He's going now because he can get away from the store now. In a few months he might not be able to."

I thought that over. And I had to admit it makes sense. Maybe things aren't as bad as I thought.

Later I called Val. I said, "If a person goes to Nevada for a divorce can he change his mind about it at the last second and tell the judge to forget the whole thing?"

"Who's going to Nevada?" Val asked.

"Nobody special. But just suppose somebody did. Do you think the judge would understand and cancel the divorce?"

"I don't think anybody changes his mind at the last second."

"But it's possible, isn't it?"

"Karen . . ." Val said.

"What?"

"I know your father's going to Las Vegas to get the divorce."

"You do?"

"Yes. He told my mother the other day. We're going to take in his mail and newspapers while he's gone."

"Oh." No wonder Val tried to discourage me last night. She knew about Daddy all along.

"So why don't you just forget about him changing his mind?" Val said.

"Listen . . . when he gets out there and sees how much he misses all of us I'll bet you anything he *will* change his mind!"

"Don't count on it."

"I've got to go now," I said. "I've got a ton of homework."

I hung up the phone and went to my room. Mew was asleep on my bed. I lay down next to her and rubbed my face against her fur. "I must do something, Mew," I told her. "I must do something right away to stop the divorce! There's only one week left."

# 22

I've got to get my mother and father into the same room. My new idea is this: I will ask Mrs. Singer if I can bring my Viking diorama home now, instead of at the end of the month. It's in the showcase in the hall, near our classroom. We have a whole Viking display. Everyone stops to look at it. Since my diorama is very fragile, Daddy will have to come into the house to see it. I wouldn't dare bring it out to the car or to his apartment. That's what I'll say anyway. He'll be very proud of me. I made a Viking ship with twelve small Vikings sitting in it. There are pink and purple mountains in the background and I used blue sparkle for the water. Even Mrs. Singer said I did an excellent job. I'm glad she noticed.

Once Daddy comes home and sees Mom, everything will work out fine. I just know it. First they'll look at each other then they'll touch hands. Finally Daddy will kiss her and they'll never fight again. Daddy will call Garfa to cancel his trip to Las Vegas and I will write to tell him how I got them back together. Garfa will write back that he knew I'd be able to do it all along. And won't Val be surprised! I'll never tell my parents I planned the whole thing. Let them think it was all an accident.

On Monday morning I went up to Mrs. Singer's desk and said, "I'd like to bring my Viking diorama home this week."

"But Karen," Mrs. Singer said, "it's in the showcase."

"I know," I told her. "But I have to take it home. So maybe we could put something else in the showcase."

"Like what?" Mrs. Singer asked.

"Oh, I don't know. A picture or a book. Anything."

"I'd rather that you wait until the end of the month when we change the showcase."

"I can't, Mrs. Singer," I said, raising my voice. "I need it now!"

"What for?"

"For . . . for . . ." But I couldn't tell Mrs. Singer why I needed it, even though I felt like yelling, "To keep my parents from getting divorced."

Instead, I turned around and walked to my desk. As soon as I sat down Debbie leaned over and whispered, "What's wrong?"

I made a face and shook my head toward Mrs. Singer. Then my nose started to run and I knew I was going to cry. So I ran out of the room. I stood in the hall with my forehead pressed against the showcase window. My Viking diorama was in the corner, with a little sign under it that said *Made by Karen Newman.*

Debbie came out into the hallway. "Are you okay?" she asked.

"I guess."

"Mrs. Singer said I should take you to the nurse's office."

"I don't need any nurse," I told her. We walked back to our classroom together.

I got through the rest of the day without doing any work. I made some plans though. If I could find the key to the showcase I could open it and take my diorama. That's not stealing. After all, it does belong to me! Mrs. Singer keeps the key to the showcase somewhere in her desk. I'm sure of that.

At two thirty I excused myself to go to the girls' room. I wanted to get a good look at the showcase lock. Maybe I could pick it open with a bobby pin. But when I looked in the window I saw a big book with a Viking on the cover in the corner where my diorama used to be. I ran back into the classroom and told Mrs. Singer, "It's gone! My diorama is gone. Somebody stole it!"

Everybody in the room started to talk at once, but I didn't care. Mrs. Singer shouted, "Calm down! No talking at all!" Then she reached into her bottom desk drawer and pulled out my diorama. "Nothing's happened to it, Karen. I took it out of the showcase myself. If it's that important to you, take it home."

I didn't say anything. I couldn't. I just nodded and took the diorama to my desk. I guess even witches have good days!

*Monday, May 3*
*I am counting the seconds until Sunday when Daddy calls for us and I get him inside to see my diorama.*

# 23

My mother, Jeff, Amy and me are getting to be regulars at Howard Johnson's on the highway. We go there every Friday night because of Mom's English literature course.

The Howard Johnson's hostess knows us by now. She tries to give us the same booth every week. My mother likes it because it's not near the kitchen and it's away from the front door.

Jeff has to sit on the aisle so he can stick out his foot. Next week the bandage is coming off his toe. If you ask me he likes his cane. It gets him a lot of attention.

Amy and I always order the same supper—

hamburgers and french fries. We drink Ho-Jo Cola too. I think that's really Coke, even though the waitress won't admit it. Tonight Jeff ordered fried shrimp.

"You never eat fried shrimp," my mother said.

"So I'll try it and maybe I'll like it," he told her.

"I don't think this is the place to try something like that."

"I feel like fried shrimp!" Jeff said. "So I ordered it. So now forget about it!"

"Okay," Mom said. "It's just that you'll have to eat them whether you like them or not."

"I said I'll eat them, didn't I?"

"I just want you to be sure."

"Daddy always takes us out for steak," Amy said.

"Daddy can afford to," Mom told her.

This is the first time my mother has ever said anything like that. She looked at Jeff. "Would you go wash up, please. Your hands are filthy."

"I washed at home," Jeff said.

"I'm asking you to go to the men's room and wash again."

Jeff stood up, grabbed his cane and left the table. When he came back our main course was served. He sat down, picked up one shrimp and nibbled at it. "Will you quit looking at me," he said to me and Amy.

I didn't look at anything but my hamburger for the rest of the meal.

When my mother finished her dinner she said, "Well, Jeff . . . how are they?"

"Not great," he said. "I didn't know they'd be all breaded like this."

"I told you," Mom said.

"Oh, lay off, will you!"

"Jeffrey . . ." Mom began.

But Jeff stood up then.

"Sit down," Mom told him.

"No."

"I said sit down!"

"No. I said *no*. Are you deaf or something?"

A lot of people were looking at us and my mother was embarrassed. So was I. I hoped we wouldn't see anybody we knew.

Jeff took his cane off the coat hook and walked to the front of the restaurant.

"Where's he going?" Amy asked.

"Out to the car," Mom said.

"How do you know?" Amy asked.

"Where else would he go?" Mom said.

"You want me to go see?" I asked.

"No," Mom said. "We'll have our dessert and when we're through we'll go to the car. Jeff's not going to spoil our dinner."

We all had ice cream. When we finished my mother gave me the check and the money to pay the cashier while she took Amy to the ladies' room.

But when we went outside to the car Jeff wasn't there.

"Karen . . . check inside the restaurant again. He must be in there somewhere. Look in the men's room too."

"Me?" I said. "Me . . . go into the men's room?"

"Just knock on the door and ask if anybody saw Jeff."

"Okay," I said. I went back inside. I checked

155

the counter. He wasn't there. I walked all through the restaurant, pretending I had left something in our booth. I didn't see Jeff anywhere. So I stood in front of the men's room. I didn't knock like my mother told me to do. I couldn't. Suppose somebody came to the door and when they opened it I saw inside? No, I didn't want to look inside the men's room. Even though I've always wondered what it's like in there. Tonight wasn't the right time to find out.

"You want something?" a man asked me.

"No," I said.

"Then, excuse me, please. I'm trying to get in here."

"Oh," I said, jumping away from the door. "Would you do me a favor?"

"Sure," he said. "What is it?"

"Would you see if my brother's in there?"

"What's he look like?"

"He's fourteen and he's got a broken toe."

"All right. Just a minute," the man said.

He went inside. I turned my back to the door. He came out right away. "Nobody's in here," he told me.

"Well, thank you anyway," I said.

I went back outside and told my mother that Jeff wasn't anyplace in Howard Johnson's, including the men's room. "Maybe he went home," I said.

"No. You can't walk from here," my mother told me. "There's no way."

"Well, then, where is he?" I said.

"I don't know," Mom answered. "Now stop asking me questions and give me a minute to think."

"The one who asks the most questions learns the most," Amy said.

"Oh, shut up," I whispered.

"Why don't you?"

After a minute my mother said, "We'll drive home now. Then I'll decide what to do. I can't think here."

When we got home Mom waited until nine o'clock before she did anything. Then she called Aunt Ruth and Uncle Dan. They came right over. Uncle Dan said the first thing to do was to call the police. But my mother didn't want to. So Uncle Dan said, "Okay . . . but that's what I'd do if he was my son."

Mom said, "Let's try the hospitals first."

So Uncle Dan sat down by the phone in the kitchen and called all the local hospitals. Jeff wasn't in any of them. I guess my mother thought Jeff got run over or something. Otherwise I don't know why she wanted Uncle Dan to call the hospitals.

Aunt Ruth said we should try his friends. So my mother asked me to make a list of all the kids Jeff might go to see. I couldn't decide whose name to put first—Petey Mansfield or Mary Louise Rumberger. I decided that Jeff, being in such a bad mood, would pick Petey. I handed Uncle Dan a list of twelve names. He called every one but none of them had seen Jeff.

"He could be at Bill's," Uncle Dan said.

"No. How would he have gotten there?" my mother asked.

"Maybe he hitched," I said.

"He knows I don't like him to hitch rides," Mom said.

Maybe he knows it, I thought, but he

hitches all the time. I've seen him do it. All the big kids hitch after school.

"And Bill wouldn't have been at the apartment anyway," Mom said. "It's Friday night. The store's open late."

"How about the store?" Aunt Ruth said. "Maybe he went to see Bill there."

"Want me to call?" I asked.

"No," Mom said. "I don't want Bill to find out about Jeff." She checked her watch. "Anyway, Bill must be home by now. The store closes at nine."

"He's going to have to know, Ellie. He is the boy's father," Uncle Dan said.

"Would you call him, Dan? I just can't," Mom told him.

So Uncle Dan called my father and when he hung up he said that Daddy was on his way over.

# 24

When my father got to our house I was hoping he would take Mom in his arms and kiss her and tell her not to worry, because everything was going to be all right. Instead he said, "Did you call the police yet?"

And Mom said, "Oh, Bill . . . do we have to? Why get Jeff mixed up with the police?"

"I suppose you have a better idea?" Daddy asked.

"No," Mom said. "I haven't any ideas at all."

"I'm not surprised," Daddy said.

Mom looked around. I think she wanted to throw something at Daddy. But there were too many people in the room. I saw Aunt Ruth raise her eyebrows at Uncle Dan.

My father walked into the kitchen and
picked up the phone. He called the police. He
told them his son was missing and gave them
his name and our address. When he hung up
he said, "They'll be right over."

We've never had a policeman in our house.
The only time I've ever been close to one is on
the street. Sergeant Tice got to our house in
ten minutes. He was chewing gum and he had
a pad and pencil with him, just like on TV.
Aunt Ruth showed him into the living room,
where we all sat down. He started asking questions right away.

"Name of the missing boy, please."

"Jeffrey Peter Newman," Daddy said. "We
call him Jeff."

Sergeant Tice snapped his gum and wrote
that down. "Age?" he asked next.

"Fourteen," my mother said. "He'll be fifteen in August."

Mew walked into the living room then. I
called, "Psst . . . psst . . ." and she came to me.
She jumped up on my lap, made herself into
a fur ball and started purring.

"Do you have a recent snapshot of him?" Sergeant Tice asked.

"I don't know," my mother said. "I think we might have one from last summer. Karen . . . would you see if you can find one?"

"I don't know where any pictures are," I told her.

Sergeant Tice said, "Never mind. Let's get a good description of the boy now. Later, if you can come up with a picture, fine."

"Well, he's about five foot seven," Daddy said. "And he weighs about one-thirty-five."

"Hair?" Sergeant Tice asked.

"Brown," Mom said. "Down to his collar in back and just over his ears in front."

"What's he wearing?"

"Jeans, a gray sweatshirt and a navy jacket," Mom said.

"Eyes?"

"They're blue," I said.

"Complexion?"

"Fair," Daddy said. "And he's got a dimple in his chin."

"And some zits on his face," Amy added.

"They're pimples if you don't already know."

My mother looked over at Amy then, as if remembering for the first time that she was in the room. "Go up to bed now, Amy. It's after ten!"

"No," Amy said.

"Ruth . . . would you take her up and get her into bed?" Mom said.

"No!" Amy yelled. "I want to stay . . . I want to stay and listen."

Aunt Ruth tried to pick up Amy but Amy kicked so hard Aunt Ruth couldn't get hold of her.

"Daddy . . ." Amy cried. "Don't let her take me away. Daddy . . . help!"

That sister of mine can really be impossible. And if you ask me she was doing it on purpose! But Daddy went to her and held her in his arms and stroked her hair and said, "It's all right, baby. Everything's going to be all right."

She really acts like a spoiled brat when Daddy is around.

Sergeant Tice cleared his throat to get our

attention again. "Any idea where he might be headed?"

"None," Mom said. "We've tried his friends but nobody knows where he is."

"Any reason you can think of for him running off?"

"He got mad at Mommy!" Amy said. "Because he didn't like his fried shrimp!"

Sergeant Tice looked at my mother.

"We did have a few words," she told him. "He got angry and walked out of the restaurant. Howard Johnson's on the highway."

Sergeant Tice wrote that down. "Is he on drugs?"

Daddy said, "Of course not!"

"Are you certain?" Sergeant Tice asked.

"Damn right I'm certain," Daddy told him, but he was glaring at my mother.

Sergeant Tice closed his notebook and stood up. "Well . . . these kids usually head for New York. We'll see what we can do."

Mom stood up too. "That's all?" she asked. "You'll see? What are we supposed to do in the meantime?"

"Just carry on," Sergeant Tice said. "Not much else you can do. He'll probably show up. Most of them do."

"He's walking with a cane," I said. "He's got a broken toe." I could just picture Jeff on his way to New York. He'd fall down every few miles and he'd be cold and hungry and nobody would help him. Maybe I'll never see him again.

"Well, he can't get very far like that," Sergeant Tice said. "I'll be in touch."

We all walked him to the front door. I saw him spit out his gum by our dogwood tree.

Aunt Ruth said she'd make some coffee and Uncle Dan excused himself to go to the bathroom. Daddy carried Amy upstairs and put her to bed. When he came back down he and Mom went into the living room.

Now that the police business is out of the way, they can have a chance to be alone, I thought. They'll see that they belong together. That we're a family. Any minute now Daddy will tell her he's sorry he left.

I stayed in the kitchen with Aunt Ruth and

Uncle Dan. I guess they wanted to hear what was going to happen as much as I did.

The first thing Daddy said was, "I want the truth and I want it now."

"I have nothing to say to you," Mom told him.

"You damn well better have something to say! Because I want to know why my son ran away!"

"Your son!" Mom shouted. "He's my son too . . . and don't you forget it!"

"When I left this house he was fine," Daddy said. "But you fixed that, didn't you?"

It's not going to work, I thought. They're just like they were before, only worse.

Mom yelled, "Did you ever stop to think maybe it was your fault Jeff ran off? You're not exactly a perfect father!"

"Shut up!" Daddy raised his voice too. "You want everybody to hear us?"

"I don't give a damn who hears! You make me sick!" Mom yelled.

"I'm warning you, Ellie . . ."

"Lay a hand on me and I'll have you locked up," Mom screamed.

Was he going to hit her?

"I wouldn't waste my time," Daddy shouted.

No, he wasn't going to hit her.

"That's the trouble with you," Mom hollered. "You think everything is a waste of time . . . me, the kids, the house, everything! The only thing you care about is the store! That goddamned store is your whole life!"

"I never heard you complain when the store got you a new car or this house or a vacation," Daddy yelled.

"Those aren't the only things in life."

"Come off it, Ellie."

"No, I won't! You never looked at me as a person. I have feelings . . . I have ideas . . . did you ever stop to think about that?"

Amy ran into the kitchen then. She was crying. Uncle Dan picked her up and held her to him.

"Now you listen to me," Daddy shouted.

"No!" Mom hollered. "I'm tired of listening to you."

"And I'm tired of the whole business. You don't know what you want. You never did.

And you never will! Because you never grew up! You're still Ruth's baby!"

Aunt Ruth pressed her lips together so tight they disappeared.

My mother shouted, "I should have listened to Ruth a long time ago. I should have listened the first time I brought you home. She saw you for what you are. Conceited, selfish—"

"One more word and I'm going to take the kids away from you!"

"Don't you dare threaten me!" Mom screamed.

"I mean it. So help me. I'll have you declared incompetent."

"You rotten bastard . . ."

There was an awful crash in the living room then and I ran in to see what happened. One of Mom's best china babies was on the floor, smashed, like the mocha-icing cake.

"That's how you settle all your problems, isn't it?" Daddy said with a terrible laugh. "Just like a two-year-old."

Mom started to cry. She bent down and tried to pick up the pieces of her antique. I

think it was the first time she ever broke anything she loved.

Then Daddy backed up and sat down on
the chair by the fireplace, right on top of Mew.
Mew howled and Daddy jumped. "Damn cat!"

I shouted, "You never liked her, did you?" I
could see that Daddy thought I was talking
about Mom, but really I meant Mew.

I don't know what they started yelling
about then but I couldn't stand it any more so
I put my hands over my ears and I started to
scream. And I screamed and I screamed and I
screamed, without stopping to take a breath. I
saw Aunt Ruth and Uncle Dan and Amy and
my mother and my father, just standing there
like idiots, watching me scream, but still I
didn't stop. I kept on screaming . . . until
Daddy slapped me across the face.

And then I cried.

# 25

When I opened my eyes it was morning. The first thing I saw was my Viking diorama sitting on top of the dresser. The sunlight coming through my window hit the blue sparkles and made them shine. I threw off my covers and jumped out of bed. I grabbed the diorama and flung it against the wall. It didn't break. Two of the Vikings fell out of their ship but the box was okay. So I stamped on it with both feet until there was nothing left but a broken shoebox and a lot of blue sparkle all over my rug. Then I kicked it as hard as I could, again and again. *Stupid, ugly Viking diorama! I hate you!*

I got back into bed and pulled the covers over my head. I was all set to cry, but the tears didn't come this time.

I must have been a crazy person to think that my silly diorama could work magic. Now I know the truth. My parents are not going to get back together. And there isn't one single thing I can do about it! My mother doesn't think Daddy is a wonderful person. She was feeding me a bunch of lies. Val was right. Not that Daddy thinks much of Mom either. Well, I'm through fooling myself.

I rolled over. I wonder where Jeff is. I think he would have liked the way I screamed last night. I'm sorry he missed it. I'll bet he wishes he had some of those fried shrimp with him, breaded or not. He must be hungry by now. I hope he's okay. I don't want anything bad to happen to him, even though I did hate him for a while. If he doesn't come home Daddy won't be able to go to Las Vegas on Monday. Hey, I'll bet that's why Jeff picked last night to run away! Maybe he knew what he was doing after all. Except for one thing.

He didn't hear them fighting so he doesn't know that they're hopeless. Poor Jeff! He ran away for nothing.

The phone rang, but I didn't jump up to answer it as usual. My mother came into my room. I closed my eyes and pretended to be asleep.

"Karen . . . are you awake?" Mom asked.

I didn't answer her.

She stood next to me and shook my shoulder a little. "Karen, your father wants to talk to you."

This is the first time she's ever called him my *father*. I still didn't answer.

"Karen . . . are you okay?"

I could tell by her voice she was getting upset because I wouldn't open my eyes. So I got out of bed on the side away from where Mom was standing and I said, "I'm up and I'm fine." I walked from my room, across the hall, to hers. I picked up the phone. "Hello."

"Karen, about last night . . ." Daddy began.

"I don't want to talk about it," I told him.

So Daddy said, "Well, I want you to know it

172

was just because we were so upset about Jeff."

"Sure," I said.

"And I don't want you to worry about your brother either. Because I've already hired a private detective and he'll certainly find him if the police can't."

"That's good," I said.

"Listen, Karen, the only reason I slapped you last night was because you were hysterical. And that's what you have to do when someone's hysterical."

"That's okay," I told him. I haven't ever been hysterical before. I wonder if I ever will be again?

"Are you still flying to Las Vegas on Monday?"

"I don't know yet," Daddy said. "It all depends on Jeff."

"If he doesn't come home you're not going?"

"I'm not going anywhere till I know Jeff's okay. My trip can wait a week or two," Daddy said. "If you need me for anything I'll be at the store all day."

"Okay. Bye." I hung up and went back to

my room. My mother was making my bed. She looked very tired. When she was done she sat on the edge of the bed and said, "Karen, about last night . . ."

I told her the same thing I told Daddy. "I don't want to talk about it."

But she said, "I think you should know that it was just because we were so worried about Jeff."

"Sure," I said. "I know."

"And we didn't really mean any of the things we said."

"How about Daddy taking us away from you? Can he do that?"

"No, of course not. That was just his way of hurting me. I told you, we didn't mean anything we said last night."

I didn't believe that. I think they really meant *all* the things they said to each other.

My mother blew her nose. When she was done she asked, "What happened to your Viking diorama?"

"It broke," I told her. "But don't worry about the mess. I'll clean it up."

"I wasn't even thinking about the mess. I just think it's a shame that it broke. It was beautiful." Mom stood up and checked her watch. "It's almost nine o'clock. I've got to run downtown to police headquarters. I found a picture of Jeff for Sergeant Tice."

"Which one did you find?"

"His school picture," Mom said, pulling it out of her pocket. She showed it to me.

"That's a nice one," I said.

Mom nodded. "Hurry and get dressed now, Karen. I want to go right away."

"Why can't I stay here and watch Amy?"

"Amy's not home. Aunt Ruth picked her up early this morning."

"Well, you go ahead and I'll stay here and clean up my room."

"I don't want to leave you alone," Mom said.

"But suppose Jeff calls and there's no answer. What will he think?"

"I never thought of that," Mom said. "You're right. You better stay here just in case. I won't be gone long."

As soon as my mother left the house I went

175

down to the kitchen. I was very thirsty. I felt like drinking a whole giant-sized can of pineapple juice. I gulped down two full glasses, then poured a third and walked into the living room. The smashed china baby was gone, but all the drawers in my mother's antique chest were halfway open and the floor was covered with photos. There were so many of them!

I put my glass on the coffee table, sat down on the floor and picked up a picture. It was of me when I was little. My two front teeth were missing. I was standing next to a huge fish and crying. I remember I was really scared. I thought the fish could bite me. I didn't know it was dead.

There was another picture that showed all of us at a picnic. I must have been about eight. That was the day Jeff's kite got caught in the tree and I fell into the brook.

I found our baby pictures. And one of Daddy and Mom at a costume party. My mother was wearing some dumb-looking Cleopatra wig. She and Daddy were laughing.

I grabbed up the photos and stuffed them

back into the drawer. Then I ran upstairs to my room and took my cat bank off the dresser. Jeff gave it to me for my last birthday. He said he knew I'd rather keep my money in a cat than in a pig. I pulled the stopper out of the bottom of the bank and dumped all the money onto my bed. There was $10.49. Good! The divorce book costs $7.95, Val said. So I have enough.

I got dressed, threw my diorama into the garbage and took out the vacuum. There was no other way to get rid of the blue sparkle all over my rug.

When my mother got back from police headquarters I was still vacuuming.

"You didn't have to do that," Mom said.

"I felt like it," I told her. "Did Sergeant Tice find out anything yet?"

"Not yet," Mom said. "But he will. Especially now that he has the picture. That should help a lot. Jeff might even be home this afternoon."

"Sure," I said.

"You know what I'm going to do?" Mom asked.

"No, what?"

"I'm going to give Jeff's room a good cleaning. The closets and everything."

Why would she do a silly thing like that?
Jeff likes his room messy. The messier the
better.

Mom took the vacuum. "I want his room to
look really nice when he comes home. You
want to help?" she asked me.

"I can't," I said. "I have to go over to the
shopping center. I need something for a school
project."

Mom acted like she hardly heard me. "Be
careful" was all she said.

The shopping center isn't that far from our
house. I rode my bike straight to the bookstore. I had the paper with Val's information
on it tucked away in my pocketbook. I asked
the saleslady for *The Boys and Girls Book
About Divorce* by Richard A. Gardner, M.D.,
published by Science House, Inc., illustrated
by Alfred Lowenheim, with a foreword by
Louise Bates Ames.

She seemed pretty impressed that I knew
so much about it. She smiled at me a lot. Then

she said, "I'm sorry, but we don't have that book in stock. We'll have to order it for you."

Imagine not having such an important book in stock! What is the matter with this bookstore? I asked her how long it would take to get it and she told me *maybe two weeks*. I said I didn't think I could wait that long and she smiled again and told me she'd put a rush on it and it might come through sooner. I had to pay in advance and write down my name, address and phone number. I don't know how I am going to last two whole weeks without that book!

# 26

Sunday, May 9

Dear Ganfa,

  How are you? I hope you're fine.
Yesterday <u>I ordered The Boys and Girls Book
About Divorce</u>. Did you ever hear of it?
It's a very famous book and I need it a
lot. I need it because Daddy and Mom are
definitely going to get divorced! I've tried
hard to get them back together. Honest!
But nothing works. I have discovered
something important about my mother and
father. When they are apart they're not
so bad, but together they are impossible!
  Anyway, I hope you understand and

won't be too disappointed, even if this is
the first divorce in the history of the
Newman family. Do you want to hear
something funny? When Daddy told us
he was flying to Las Vegas to get the
divorce I still didn't believe it would really
happen. Now I believe it! Another thing I
think you should know is this—I don't look
like Grandmother Newman at all. I just
pretended to agree with you. I don't look
like anyone but ME! I hope Mattie is fine
and that you are having fun.

Love,
Karen

Maybe I should have mentioned something
about Jeff in my letter but I think that would
upset Garfa even more. And I am hoping that
by the time my letter gets to Las Vegas Jeff
will be home.

I folded the letter, put it in its envelope and
licked it closed. I had to sneak an airmail
stamp out of my mother's desk. I didn't want
to ask for one because then I would have to

explain why I was writing to Garfa. After breakfast I walked down to the corner and dropped the letter in the mailbox.

My mother spent all of Sunday morning washing and ironing Jeff's shirts. If you ask me she was just keeping busy so she wouldn't have to think about all the awful things that might happen to him.

That afternoon Aunt Ruth and Uncle Dan brought Amy home. Then we all sat around in the living room, waiting for something to happen. But nothing did. Uncle Dan called my father a couple of times. Daddy didn't want to leave his apartment in case Jeff decided to go there. Mom called police headquarters once, but Sergeant Tice wasn't in and there weren't any messages for my mother. It was a very gloomy afternoon.

At three thirty the phone rang and I jumped up to answer it.

"Hello, this is Mary Louise Rumberger calling. Is Jeff home?"

At first I didn't answer her. I didn't know what to say.

"Hello . . ." she said again. "Is anyone there?"

"Yes," I told her. "I'm here."

"May I please speak to Jeff?"

"No . . . he's not in right now," I said. "Can I take a message?"

"Who is this?" she asked.

"It's Karen . . . his sister."

"Oh. Well, tell him I called and ask him to call me back."

"Okay . . . I'll tell him."

"What time do you think he'll be home?"

"I don't know," I said. "Maybe around five or five thirty." I don't know why I said that.

"Okay. Thank you," Mary Louise said.

"You're welcome." I hung up the phone and went back into the living room. "That was Mary Louse Rumberger," I said. "She wanted to talk to Jeff."

"I hope you didn't tell her anything," Mom said.

"I just told her he wasn't home right now."

"That was very good thinking, Karen," Aunt Ruth said.

"Is it a secret that Jeff is lost?" Amy asked.

"Kind of," Uncle Dan said. "Can you keep a family secret?"

"I guess so," Amy said.

An hour later Aunt Ruth ordered some pizzas for supper and I went outside to wait for the delivery truck. It was a good excuse to get away from everybody.

I sat down on our front steps. Mew ran out of the bushes and rubbed up against me. I picked her up. Her front paws smelled like mouse. Mew loves springtime. She sleeps a lot during the day and prowls around at night. The Great Gray Hunter, I call her. She brings a mouse or a mole to our door every morning. This doesn't make my mother happy. And to tell the truth, I don't like to be the one to get the shovel and scoop up Mew's catch. I love her a lot and I'm glad she's happy, but I wish she wouldn't bring home so many surprises.

In a little while I saw a girl walking up the street. When she got to our house she turned and came up the driveway. It was Mary Louise Rumberger. I knew it right away. And if I hadn't recognized her face I'd have known her by the Noxzema smell.

She said, "Hi. I'm Mary Louise."

I said, "I know. I'm Karen."

Then we just looked at each other until Mary Louise said, "I brought Jeff a book he wants to read."

"Oh, that's nice," I said. "You can leave it with me and I'll give it to him."

"I'd rather give it to him myself."

"Jeff isn't here right now," I said.

"Where is he?" Mary Louise asked.

I knew she'd say that sooner or later. "He's not home," I told her.

"I know," she said. "You already mentioned that."

This conversation might last forever, I thought. I'll keep telling her Jeff isn't here and she'll keep saying she knows.

"Well, where is he?" Mary Louise asked again.

"Who?"

185

"Jeff!"

"Oh, Jeff. He should be back soon."

"Do you know that somebody called my house Friday night looking for him?"

"Yes," I said. "That was my uncle."

"Why did he call my house? Didn't he know where Jeff was?"

"I guess he thought Jeff was with you. But really he was in New York visiting his friend from camp." There, that sounded pretty good.

"None of this makes any sense to me," Mary Louise said.

"It does, if you really think about it," I told her.

"I didn't know Jeff was going to visit his friend from camp."

"He doesn't tell you everything, does he?"

"I don't know," Mary Louise said. "I thought he would have mentioned something like that. He was supposed to meet me at the Y Saturday night."

"Oh, well probably he didn't mention it because it was a last-minute thing. He didn't plan to go. He just went."

"Why didn't you tell me that when I called?"

"I don't know," I said. "I guess I forgot."

"How long will Jeff be gone?" Mary Louise asked.

"Oh, he'll be back any day now."

"You mean you don't know *exactly* when?"

"Sure I do," I told her. "Any day. Soon. This week, I think!" I was getting in deeper and deeper.

Mary Louise shook her head. "I'm having a party Friday night. Jeff is supposed to be there. If he's not coming back I'm going to cancel my party. Why should I have a party without him?"

"I don't know," I said. I wished she would stop sniffling like that. I didn't want her to cry.

"You can tell him for me that if he doesn't come home by Friday I never want to see him again!" Mary Louise started down the front walk, holding her book tight against her.

"Hey, Mary Louise . . ." I called.

She turned around. "What?"

"I think he'll come back for your party."

187

"I hope you're right," she said as she walked away.

I hoped so too.

*Sunday, May 9*
*I am so afraid J.N. is dead!*

# 27

Mom didn't go to work on Monday and when I got home from school I found her sound asleep on the living-room couch. I called Aunt Ruth. "Did you hear anything about Jeff?" I asked.

"No, not a thing."

"Mom is sleeping. Should I just leave her alone?"

"Yes," Aunt Ruth said. "I finally got her to take one of the sleeping pills the doctor prescribed. You know she hasn't slept since Friday."

"I know it," I said. "I can take care of Amy when she comes home. So don't worry."

"Thanks, Karen. I'll be over with something for supper about five o'clock."

"Okay. Bye."

I got a blanket from upstairs and covered my mother. I'm worried about her. If anything happens to Mom what will become of me and Amy?

Where is that detective my father hired? And how about Sergeant Tice? What is he doing besides chewing his gum?

I've got to try to find Jeff myself.

On Tuesday I went to the Mansfields' after school. I had to start somewhere and Petey was number one on my list. Brian answered the door.

"Hey, Karen," Brian said. "What are you doing here?"

"I came to see Petey," I told him. "Is he home yet?"

"Yeah, he's upstairs. What do you want to see him for?"

"It's personal," I said.

"Oh, yeah?" He started to laugh. "How personal?"

"Look, Brian, just tell Petey I'm here, will you?"

Brian turned away from me and yelled up the stairs. "Hey, Petey . . . somebody's here to see you about something personal."

"Very funny," I told Brian.

"Yeah . . . I'm a riot . . . everybody knows that!"

I wonder if it's true that Brian likes me?

Petey came running down the stairs, but when he saw me he stopped.

"Could I see you alone?" I asked him. "Outside maybe?"

Brian made a noise then. It sounded like *woo-hoo*!

Petey nodded at me and we both walked outside. He even shut the front door in Brian's face so he wouldn't be able to hear anything.

"Listen, Petey," I said. "If you know anything about my brother you better tell me. Because my mother's really sick about him. I mean it . . . she's sick! And if he's dead . . . if Jeff is dead . . . I want to know it! And I want to know it now!" I put my hands on my hips and waited.

Petey did the craziest thing then. He started to laugh. And that got me mad! "I don't see anything funny," I said. "Maybe you think it's funny that my brother could be dead in some alley, but I don't!"

Petey just kept laughing.

"Do you understand me, Petey? Please tell me if you at least understand what I'm saying."

Petey stopped. "Jeff's not dead," he said in this deep voice that surprised me. So he can talk!

"How do you know he's not dead?" I asked.

"I just do, that's all."

"You tell me where he is, Petey Mansfield!"

"I don't know."

"Then you don't know if he's dead either, do you?"

"I'm telling you, Karen, he's not dead! Now that's all I'm going to say!"

"Well, if you know that then you know where he is and you can just tell him for me that if my mother has a heart attack or something, it's all his fault. You hear that, Petey? It's all his fault! You just tell him that for me. And if you're lying about Jeff being dead and anything happens to my mother then it's all *your* fault!"

"You're really something, Karen. You know that? You're really something!" Petey said.

I took a good look at him. Maybe he's not so bad. Maybe if he was the last boy on earth I would marry him. That is, if I was going to get married at all, which I am not.

I went home. I wanted to tell Mom not to worry, that Jeff wasn't dead. But I had no proof. So I didn't say anything.

Later that night, after Amy was in bed, I went into the kitchen to get an apple. While I was peeling it the phone rang. I answered. It was Jeff! He said, "Hello Karen." Just like that. When I've been worrying he might be dead! *Hello Karen.* Like there was nothing wrong at all. I hollered, "MOM . . ." and dropped the phone.

"What is it, Karen? What's wrong?" Mom asked.

"It's Jeff," I said. "On the phone."

"Oh, thank God!" Mom said. She picked up the phone. "Jeff, Jeff where are you? Are you all right? Oh, Jeff please come home . . . yes . . . yes, no questions. I don't care where you've been as long as you come home. Where are you now? Jeff . . . Jeff . . ."

My mother put the receiver back on the hook. "He hung up," she said. "I don't know where he is, but he's coming home."

"When Mom? Did he say?"

"I don't know. Tonight I think. Karen . . . you go up to bed now."

"Oh, Mom."

"Please, Karen! I don't want Jeff to have to face anyone but me tonight. You'll see him tomorrow . . . or whenever he's ready to see you. Okay?"

"Okay . . . if you say so."

As I went upstairs I heard Mom phone Aunt Ruth. "Jeff's okay," she told her. "He's coming home. . . . Oh, Ruth, I can't. . . . You call Bill for me."

I went to my room, took out my Day Book and wrote:

*Tuesday, May 11*
*J.N. is alive! I heard his voice. He is*
*coming home. M.L.R. doesn't have to worry.*
*He'll be able to go to her party.*

I didn't get into bed. I turned out my light and sat in front of the window. I waited and waited. Finally I saw Jeff come up the walk.

Maybe Petey did know where Jeff was. Maybe he told him to come home. I wouldn't be surprised if that's what happened. Or maybe Petey didn't know a thing. I suppose that's possible too. Jeff could have decided to come home all by himself. I'll probably never know the truth.

I sneaked out into the upstairs hall. With the lights turned off nobody could see me, but I could see down. My mother hugged Jeff for a long time. Then she held him away to get a good look at him. While she was looking he started to cry. Just like a little kid. Imagine Jeff acting like that! They sat down on the bottom step then and my mother held him tight. I always knew she loved him best.

# 28

"Jeff is back!" my mother told me and Amy at breakfast the next morning. "I'm taking the day off from work."

"Where is he?" Amy asked.

"In his room . . . asleep," Mom said.

"Where was he?" Amy asked.

"Wherever he was he's home now. And that's what counts. We aren't going to ask him any questions. I want you both to understand that completely."

"The one who asks the most questions—" Amy started to say.

But my mother didn't let her finish. "Never mind about that. No questions!"

"Okay," Amy said. "You don't have to yell."

"I'm not yelling," Mom told her.

Amy fiddled around with her waffles. We eat them every morning now. They're the frozen kind that you pop in the toaster. I think they're good. We never had them when Daddy lived here. Daddy doesn't trust frozen foods.

That afternoon when I got home from school, I went up to Jeff's hideaway. The door was closed but I heard Jeff grunting, so I knocked.

"Yeah . . ." He sounded out of breath.

"It's me, Karen."

"Oh."

"Can I come in?"

"Yeah . . . I guess so."

I opened the door. Jeff was on the floor doing push-ups.

"Hey . . . your toe is unbandaged!"

"Yeah . . . Mom took me over to Dr. Winters. It's fine now."

"That's good."

Jeff was counting. "Eighty-five, eighty-six,

eighty-seven . . ." When he got to ninety he stopped and lay flat on his stomach. He was breathing hard.

I sat down on his bed. "Mary Louise Rumberger was over on Sunday," I said.

"I know . . . I talked to her before."

"She wanted to make sure you were coming to her party."

"I know."

"Are you?"

"Sure."

"That's good. Jeff?"

"Yeah . . ."

"Did you have fun when you ran away?"

"I didn't run away," he said.

"Oh. Well, was it fun when you were gone?"

"No."

"I'm not supposed to ask any questions . . . I know that. But I just want to tell you one thing. If you went away because you wanted to stop the divorce, you better forget it. Daddy and Mom had an awful fight Friday night. They yelled and screamed and called each other a lot of names. They're just impossible together."

"I know that, Karen."

"Then you didn't run away to stop Daddy from flying to Las Vegas?"

"No," Jeff said.

"But I was sure you did."

"Well, I didn't."

"Oh."

"Dad was over to see me this morning."

"He was? Was Mom home?"

"Yeah."

"Well, what happened?"

"Nothing. She stayed upstairs the whole time."

"Is Daddy going to Las Vegas?"

"Yeah. Tomorrow."

"I guess I knew he would," I said. "Jeff . . ."

"Yeah?"

"I'm glad you came home."

Jeff turned over and looked up at the ceiling. "Don't ever run away, Karen. It stinks!"

"I won't. Not ever. I promise."

*Wednesday, May 12*
  *I will never run away. Running away*
*does not solve anything! Also, I will never*
*tell anyone I went to see Petey Mansfield*
*yesterday. If J.N. knows, let him tell me.*

I have started to mark my days again. I am back to C-. I just had an awful thought. Suppose there aren't any more A+ days once you get to be twelve? Wouldn't that be something! To spend the rest of your life looking for an A+ day and not finding it.

# 29

I got two postcards from Daddy. I wrote him back while Mrs. Singer was giving us her daily lecture on manners. She told us we haven't had a real sixth-grade day all year. Now isn't that too much? Here we are getting ready for junior high and she's telling us we don't act like sixth graders yet!

Debbie says if Mrs. Singer sprays hair stuff on herself once more this year she's going to report her to the principal. Imagine a teacher spraying herself in front of the class and then telling *us* we have no manners. I will be so glad to be rid of her!

This afternoon we had to fill out little green

cards for next year. One question was about parents. You had to check a box telling if they were deceased or divorced. I checked *divorced*. I might as well get used to admitting it.

Tonight I found out my mother is going to sell our house! How can she do such a thing? She says she *has* to put our house up for sale. It has something to do with the divorce. I can't believe it.

I asked Mom, "What about us? Where will we go?"

"I haven't made up my mind yet," Mom said, "but I'm thinking about Florida. We might as well move someplace warm as long as we're going to move."

"Florida! That's about a million miles away," I said. "I'll never see Debbie again. Or Val. And what about Daddy?"

"Oh, you could see him during school vacations. It would be fun. But nothing's definite yet. So don't start worrying."

"I'm not worrying. I just want to know what's going on."

"Right now the only thing I can tell you for sure is that we're selling the house."

"Daddy won't let us move to Florida," I said. "It's too far away."

"It's not *that* far," Mom said. "You'd be able to write and phone."

"That's not the same as seeing him!"

"Karen . . . I don't want to argue about this," Mom said. "I have a lot of thinking to do before I make up my mind."

"But we *are* going to move?" I asked.

"Yes . . . but I don't know where."

"When will you know?"

"By the end of next month I hope," Mom said.

"You mean we'll move over the summer?"

"Yes. I want everything to be set before school opens in the fall."

"You mean I might go to a different school?"

"You probably will," Mom said. "Even if we wind up in an apartment around here you'll all have to change schools."

"You mean we might take an apartment near Daddy?" I asked.

"Well, it's a possibility. Or we might take one in New York. I've always wanted to live in the city."

"But what about your job at Global?" I said.

"It's a temporary job, Karen. I'll get a better one if we move. Or I might go to school full time until I get my degree."

"But what about Aunt Ruth? How could you leave her?"

"That will be good for both of us," Mom said.

"But . . . but . . ." I couldn't think of anything else to say.

Later when I got into bed I remembered that Gary Owens said it's warm in Houston. So I went back downstairs. "Hey Mom . . . if we have to move, how about Houston?"

"Houston!" she said, like I was crazy or something. "Why would we want to move there? That's in Texas."

"I know it," I said. "Somebody from my class moved there. It never gets cold."

Mom said, "Look, Karen . . . if we move someplace warm it will be California or

Florida. But Texas is out of the question. And nothing is settled yet. I told you that before."

I hope my mother knows what she is doing this time. Suppose we move to Florida and then she decides she doesn't like it. Do we move back to New Jersey or do we try California or what? I have always lived right here on Woods End Road. I love our house. I don't want to move anywhere.

# 30

I got my divorce book!

Debbie is very interested in divorce. Now that I have my book it will be easy to teach her all about it. Even though Debbie says her mother and father are not going to get divorced it can't hurt her to know the facts. This way she will be prepared for anything!

I talked to Val this afternoon. She says maybe my mother will meet a man when we move. I guess it could happen. Suppose she gets married and her new husband doesn't like kids? Suppose he's mean or else very old? There are too many things for me to think about.

If I do move away Val promises to keep an eye on my father and let me know if anything important comes up. I think the idea of my leaving has her feeling pretty sad. She's not looking forward to summer at all.

"I'll be around for at least another month," I told her. "And maybe my mother will decide to stay near here after all. We might wind up living closer than we do now."

"Or we might not," Val said.

"Oh, well . . . even if we don't we can still write and phone and see each other over vacations."

"That's not the same," Val told me.

"I know it," I said. Poor Val. I wish there was a book to make you feel happy when you're not. I would get it for her.

I got a letter from Garfa:

Dear Karen,

I'm sorry that your mother and father are going through with their divorce. But I'm glad you're getting used to the idea. Mattie tells me not to be so upset. I'll try to accept the situation too. Don't blame yourself. You are still my most dependable Karen.

I'm going to buy the divorce book you wrote about. Maybe it will help me understand too. Your father is here and he's fine, but he misses you a lot.

Love,<br>
Garfa

## 31

Today the sixth graders were invited to spend a day at the junior high. Debbie and I went together. We toured the whole school and had our lunch in the cafeteria. There was plenty of room for us because all the ninth graders were over at the high school getting their tour. I guess Jeff feels pretty grown up now that he's almost done with junior high.

We met some of the teachers, and the principal made a short speech. He looks fairly young and sounds very nice. I wish I wasn't going to move away.

On the way home from junior high Debbie said, "I'll really miss you this summer, Karen.

I wish we weren't going away on vacation."

"I'll miss you too," I told her.

"You're my best friend."

"You're mine."

"Do you think you'll have moved by the time I get back?"

"I'm not sure. Nothing's definite yet. You know my mother."

"Well . . . I hope Jeff doesn't forget about me," Debbie said. "My mother always says, 'Absence makes the heart grow fonder.'"

"Mine says, 'Out of sight—out of mind.'"

"Oh, Karen!" We both laughed. Debbie knew I was just teasing.

When we got to my house I said, "Come on in . . . I want to show you my divorce book."

"I can't," Debbie said. "It's Tuesday—I've got ballet."

"That's right. How could I forget?"

"Karen . . . I've got something for you." Debbie reached into her skirt pocket and pulled out two pictures. "Here—" she said.

I looked at them. They were of Debbie making monkey faces.

"My father took them just for you."

I will never find another friend like Debbie.

Jeff came out of the house then. "Hi, Fat-and-Ugly . . . long time no see—" he said. I haven't seen Debbie smile like that in months.

We had Kentucky Fried Chicken for supper. We ate it right out of the box because Mom is taking us to the movies and we don't want to be late.

While we were eating Amy said, "Hey, Karen, why did the man put Band-Aids in his refrigerator?" She didn't wait for me to answer. She went right on. "Because it had cold cuts! Get it? Cold *cuts!*"

"I get it," I said. Then I laughed. Imagine Amy telling riddles again!

I had a B+ day today.

# Judy Blume talks about writing *It's Not the End of the World*

When I wrote *It's Not the End of the World* in the early seventies, I lived in suburban New Jersey with my husband and two children, who were both in elementary school. I could see their concern and fear each time a family in our neighborhood divorced. What do you say to your friends when you find out their parents are splitting up? If it could happen to them, could it happen to us?

At the time, my own marriage was in trouble, but I wasn't ready or able to admit it to myself, let alone anyone else. In the hope that it would get better, I dedicated this book to my husband. But a few years later, we, too, divorced. It was hard on all of us, more painful than I could have imagined, but somehow we muddled through, and it wasn't the end of any of our worlds, though on some days it might have felt like it.

Divorce laws have changed since I wrote this book. You don't have to go to Nevada or anyplace else to be divorced these days. And unlike Karen's mother in this book, many women have jobs outside the home, regardless of whether they're married or have children. Not that a new law or having two working parents makes divorce easy. It still hurts. It still causes the same fears and feelings Karen experiences in this story.

»«   The Revolt of the College Intellectual

# The Revolt of the College Intellectual

BY EVERETT LEE HUNT

*Dean Emeritus and Professor Emeritus, Swarthmore College*

HUMAN RELATIONS AIDS / 104 East 25th Street, New York 1 9 6 3

# Contents

# Preface

The exuberant explosions of old college days have traditionally been forgiven as somewhat enviable expressions of the
high spirits of exultant youth. Of course the boys and girls
were immature, but who expected college students to be mature? Now that young intellectuals are the dominant group
in many colleges, and they avow a lofty contempt for the rah-
rah activities of earlier years, are they less adolescent and
more mature, or do their immaturities merely manifest themselves in different ways? As intellectual individualists the students do not usually care for group explosions unless they are
for social causes such as the rights of minorities. But their
adolescence often manifests itself individually in a superior
condescension or in depressive inferiority complexes.

The more vocal of these adolescents often move toward
college journalism. A concerned reader of the undergraduate
publications of the Ivy League colleges, or of other institutions where intellectuals dominate, will note a deep discontent with life on and off the campus. Instead of the much-
criticized undergraduate complacency and passivity, he will
find an interesting combination of an idealistic passion for
reform and a vigorous adolescent rebellion. All these assertions of the independence of their own generation may be

quite necessary to adolescents in finding themselves and an indication that at last self-education is proceeding admirably. But the unhappiness and discontent are often as truly adolescent as the less intellectual gusto of another era, which still lives on in "undeveloped" colleges. These dissatisfactions are only made endurable by the sense of intellectual superiority manifested in perceiving their situation. Their complex attitude is evident in the remark of a Harvard senior to a neophyte: "Well, Harvard really is a terrible place to be, but where else would you go?"

The phenomena of late adolescence have only lately begun to receive careful study, and the college is now recognized as the best place for such observations, where the culture is the culture of adolescents, where adult responsibilities do not impose their discipline, where the trial-and-error period of self-discovery is recognized and encouraged. The adolescent rebellion of individuals is an anciently-observed and permanent phenomenon, but it is only in recent times that whole group cultures have become dominated by adolescent intellectuals.

In their earlier stages it was natural that studies of late adolescence should deal almost entirely with those disturbed personalities who appealed to departments of health for therapy. There was then a feeling that such studies, if made known to the public, would seem to reflect unfavorably on the college. In the Preface to his book, MENTAL HEALTH IN COLLEGE,[1] Dr. Clements Fry of Yale says:

This report analyzes mainly those factors of Yale life associated with histories of maladjustment and emotional disturbance, with the result that many constructive aspects of Yale life are taken for granted, or at least not stressed. . . . No society suits all its members. This report . . . is not specifically concerned with the possible reform of Yale society. . . . So long as personalities are changing and developing, they will find that aspects of their environment may disturb emotional equilibrium. Yale society is not peculiar in having such effects on its members; and we do not wish to be understood as criticizing the general organization of the College community because some members find it difficult to adapt themselves to its system.

To this disavowal of any intent on the part of the author to criticize Yale, its president, Charles Seymour, added the following in his Foreword to the book:

The problems dealt with by the psychiatrist are so widespread among students and so severe in individual cases that our institutions of higher learning cannot safely ignore them. . . . Yet it is only in recent years that the practice of mental hygiene has come to be recognized as an important aspect of the student health service of colleges and universities; and even today relatively few institutions are adequately equipped in this regard.

Dr. Fry's book draws upon a decade of experience with such problems, as encountered on one university campus. The cases which he describes and analyzes are by no means peculiar to this particular environment; they have been selected as typical situations that might be found anywhere throughout the academic world. The conclusions which Dr. Fry draws from his own experience are therefore pertinent to the needs of colleges generally. We may hope that the publication of this book will serve to promote essential and more effective service in behalf of the students of this country.

In 1949 Vassar received from the Old Dominion Foundation a gift of two million dollars given by Paul Mellon in memory of his wife, Mary Conover Mellon, Vassar '26, "with the possibilities of applying to the development of the individual during the educational process some of the insights and techniques provided by the new sciences of psychology and psychiatry." President Blanding immediately found it prudent to issue a public statement to the Vassar constituency that the mental health of the Vassar community was normal. The studies supported by this grant have developed and broadened, and have been published in part under the title PERSONALITY DEVELOPMENT DURING THE COLLEGE YEARS.[2] The studies are by no means confined to those who seek therapy, but representative students are regarded in a scientific manner. Although the conclusions have not yet been published, they have already stimulated similar studies by other investigators on a nation-wide basis.

In 1957, Dr. Dana L. Farnsworth, head of the Harvard University Health Services, published MENTAL HEALTH IN COLLEGE AND UNIVERSITY. A nontechnical book addressed to educators, it presented a broad view of the historical development of the concern for factors of mental health. It also included references to prejudice and indifference concerning the removal of emotional inhibitions to learning. According to Dr. Farnsworth:

Mental health is not something new to be added to an already overcrowded curriculum; neither is it a specialized technique, a specific doctrine, or a limiting factor. Instead, mental health represents a point of view which tends to encourage freedom with responsibility, flexibility, self-reliance, and a genuine concern for the common welfare. It is a vital aid to traditional education, enriching teacher and student alike.[3]

In 1958 Dr. Fry's successors in the Department of University Health at Yale dedicated to him a book entitled PSYCHOSOCIAL PROBLEMS OF COLLEGE MEN that was based on their work since his book of 1942. They too describe the salient features of the Yale culture that impinges on the student, but say:

The observations on Yale and its students have not been softened in any way. Yale is a university with its own characteristics, one of which is the capacity for critical self-evaluation.[4]

A somewhat more technical book published in 1961 by members of the Harvard Health Services, EMOTIONAL PROBLEMS OF THE STUDENT, asserts even more strongly that the problems of Harvard students are problems of students *over the country:*

. . . people wonder why a college like Harvard, supposedly occupied in educating the most promising young men in the country, should need the services of eight full-time psychiatrists. . . . Many people seem to feel that psychological experience with a Harvard population does not count. Somehow we cannot believe that. . . . Harvard men are human [and therefore] show forth action of the laws of human nature.[5]

All these studies and numerous others are devoted to the college of the present; they include little of the history of changing mores and cultures. The absence of a modern psychosocial point of view in the older histories makes impossible scientifically valid comparisons of then and now. Because of the complexity of the forces producing social change, it is difficult to say what factors are due to college policies, to the cultures from which students come, or to the reputation of the college, which attracts certain types of applicants. Nevertheless, regardless of the complexity of causes, there are in different epochs clearly marked and easily described differences in student attitudes, behavior, public expressions of ideals and purposes, and inner moods and morale. These are worth observing for their impact on social history and their effect on the atmosphere for adolescent development. There have been repeated requests for more accounts of the development of individual colleges, both for the better understanding of particular groups of students and their cultures, and—as studies accumulate—as a basis for wider generalizations.

This volume, then, is a case study of one small college, Swarthmore, that has repeatedly been rated at or near the top for intellectual distinction. This writer believes the college is worth commendation, and even imitation, for other than intellectual reasons, not the least of which is its spirit of eagerness, so perceptively described by David Boroff in his article "Eager Swarthmore," in *Harper's Magazine* for October 1961. It is the intellectual results, however, that have been easiest to measure and record and that have therefore received most public attention. It is obvious that adolescent intellectuals have played an influential part in molding the institution and that there are likely to be some unpredictable results in any educational changes that encourage student participation with freedom of expression.

To many critics of conformity, the intellectual revolution on this and other campuses has seemed to promise a new era for individual development and unhampered creativity, in addition to heightening hopes for social progress under the leadership of a new generation. Critics of a different temperament are likely to comment on the difficulty of establishing any sense of community among intellectuals and to predict even greater extremes of individualism from the adolescents. The change from conformity to individualism as the dominant pattern on the more intellectual campuses raises again the old questions about the relation of group loyalties to emotional stability and morale and about the place given to human relations as a source of maturity. But we are here concerned to set forth what has happened and leave the answers to the reader.

These observations of a retired dean offer pictures of student life in the eras of religious nurture, secular conformity, and intellectual individualism. A concerned reader may find elements in each of these startlingly different cultures that he would like to include in his own educational utopia.

For support in this study the author is indebted to the Grant Foundation, whose many appropriations to Swarthmore and other colleges and institutions have been designed to carry out Mr. W. T. Grant's philosophy that "the well-being of peoples depends in large part on the discovery and comprehension of human relations which contribute to the welfare of all."

Everett Lee Hunt

Swarthmore, Pennsylvania
June, 1963

# Introduction

Indignant protests of undergraduates against being treated as adolescents suggest that the term carries connotations even more offensive than the epithet "childish," and yet we recognize childhood as a normal period of life that poets praise and most of us love. Adolescence, properly understood, has the same possibilities, but the term "adolescent intellectual" seems to have doubly irritating associations. It describes a youth such as Aristophanes portrayed beating his father and then justifying his action with the new-fangled logic taught by Socrates; or it applies to such youth as Aristotle described as being "great lovers of the wit which is educated insolence."

And "intellectual," too, has its own equally irritating implications. Some critics and historians have attempted to attribute all our American anti-intellectualism to our primitive frontier traditions, in which practical versatility with physical vigor seemed more important than specialized knowledge. But the criticism of intellectuals goes back much farther than this and has been best expressed by intellectuals themselves. Aristotle asks, "Why is it that all those who have become eminent in philosophy or politics or the arts are clearly of an atrabilious temperament?" Lucian, Horace, Erasmus, and many others have satirized the unsociable and self-centered scholars. The

Florentine physician and humanist, Ficino, wrote a serious book to teach the scholar how to keep his melancholy happily tempered. He was all the more concerned because he believed:

If men of letters can avoid the melancholic diseases to which they are prone, they are the happiest of men. The melancholic mind enjoys the contemplation of the innermost secrets of nature and the highest truth of heaven.

Elizabethan dramatists satirized the type known as the malcontent—the man with the sense of neglected superiority, a man who has persuaded himself that he is melancholy because melancholy signifies astuteness or profundity of mind. He snarls at the world because it has not perceived his talents. He is too preoccupied with weighty matters to attend to his personal appearance; he is taciturn, unsociable, and morosely meditative. Richard Burton in his seventeenth-century ANATOMY OF MELANCHOLY has a chapter on the various effects of the scholar's "sedentary, solitary life, free from bodily exercise and those ordinary disports which other men use."

Such observations on intellectuals by intellectuals cannot be dismissed as coming from Philistine or bourgeois ignorance. They constitute a valid source for the vestiges of distrust of the intellectual, even after Adlai Stevenson's appeal to egg-heads of the world to unite and John Kennedy's elevation of Harvard intellectuals to positions of power.

And yet we should turn at least briefly from those who see the arrogance or the humility of adolescence heightened or deepened by becoming intellectual to a more sympathetic view. Shakespeare was under thirty when he wrote

Crabbed age and youth cannot live together. . . .
Age I do abhor thee, youth I do adore thee.

He still preferred to abhor or adore rather than to pass a cold judgment, but he later said many of the wisest things about the relation of the generations and retained an enviable sympathy for both.

Robert Louis Stevenson wrote:

For God's sake give me the young man who has brains enough to make a fool of himself. If we wish to scale Mt. Blanc, to go down in a diving dress, or up in a balloon, we must go about it when we are young. There is some meaning in the old theory about wild oats; and a man who has not had his green sickness and got done with it for good, is as little to be depended on as an unvaccinated infant.

Randolph Bourne's essays on YOUTH AND LIFE were written in his early years, and he did not live to attempt any revision. The book offers a creed that is quite generally accepted, often unconsciously, by the more active and confident young intellectuals:

It is the young people who have all the really valuable experience. It is they who have constantly to face new situations, to react constantly to new aspects of life. It is only the first collision with life that is worth anything. Youth therefore has no right to be humble. The ideals it forms will be the highest it will ever have, the insight the clearest, the ideas the most stimulating. It is only the young who are contemporaneous; they interpret what they see frankly and without prejudice; their vision is always the truest, and their interpretation always the justest.

These opinions of literary and philosophical figures are a long way from the tests and measurements and statistics of our social scientists. But we cannot afford to forget the insights of literature. Indeed, it has become quite impossible to do so. The growth of adolescence toward maturity, or the repudiation of contemporary maturity, forms a dominant theme of contemporary fiction. Critics tell us that no great literature has come out of the college scene, even though some fifty novels have been published about Harvard alone; the prospects grow dimmer as college life becomes more intellectual. The social scientists, however, are now beginning their research on late adolescence, and they are already asserting that educators cannot ignore their findings. Education, they say, has been concerned with everything but the students; the timeless wisdom of the humanities cannot provide guidance for our bursting colleges and universities, even where its voice can be heard.

When Woodrow Wilson made his oft-quoted remark that in our universities the side shows had swallowed up the main tent, he did not regard Princeton adolescents as intellectuals, and no one seemed to expect that the time would ever come when the main tent might swallow up the side shows. Wilson seemed to resign himself to his situation rather easily by reminding his students frequently that they would soon forget practically all they had learned in college anyway; what would remain, he hoped, was the character and personality developed in the pursuit of knowledge. He did not suggest that character and personality owed more to the side shows than to the main tent, but he might have quoted Macaulay as asserting that the greatest men had come out of Oxford when studies were at their lowest ebb or Cardinal Newman as saying that students were much more influenced by one another at Oxford than by all the dons, the lectures, and the examinations. This observation by the Cardinal has been accepted rather placidly for many years. But now, when it is repeated by the social scientists in the form of psychological studies on the relative ineffectiveness of the curriculum as compared with "peer culture," it induces something of a state of shock among educators.

When Frank Aydelotte, after residence in Oxford as a Rhodes Scholar early in this century, wrote THE OXFORD STAMP AND OTHER ESSAYS,[1] he was in entire agreement with Newman and quoted him with great approval. He liked the "peer culture" of Oxford. It was not to be described as a side show. It seemed in harmony with the best traditions of that seat of learning. And when he selected Swarthmore, a small, rural, Quaker college, as the best place to try to create an equivalent of the Oxford atmosphere in America, he was sure that the small college had the best means of mobilizing student interests around intellectual concerns. He hoped to intellectualize the "peer culture." And he did, with some surprising results. What has happened at Swarthmore since he became president in 1921 has been described by outside observers as "controlled metamorphosis." But to one who has lived through it in close association with student life, the phrase suggests nothing of the dramatic conflicts that often made the "control" seem a little doubtful.

The intellectual revolution at Swarthmore occurred two or three decades ahead of similar movements in many other colleges. A group of institutions has since become recognized as intellectually elite, and there has grown up what might be called a "new criticism" of higher education. This has been based in part upon the methods of the social sciences and has grown out of "scientific" observation of the most intellectual colleges and universities. It now seems evident that the "main tent" in the form of the graduate school is actually swallowing up the side shows of the older collegiate life, both in those colleges that are parts of universities and in the separate colleges that call themselves liberal but now seem to face domination by faculty departments intent on training their students primarily for graduate schools. The obvious neglect of undergraduate education at Harvard led to the much-publicized program of "general education," which, according to some contemporary studies at Harvard, has been quite unable to resist the pressures of the specialists in the graduate school. Yale College has put up the most determined resistance to Yale University, but it, too, is being subordinated. President Hutchins's reforms in the college of the University of Chicago were made necessary and possible by the indifference of the graduate school to the undergraduate college, but his over-intellectualized program for adolescents has had to be largely abandoned. The Princeton preceptors have not been able to maintain their position in the face of graduate school demands for publication and research.

There have been numerous attacks on graduate school influence on the colleges as overly analytical, cold, inhuman, destructive of values, fragmented, and overspecialized. Back in 1935 President Aydelotte collected letters from graduates of Swarthmore Honors seminars that tell of their impressions of the graduate schools. So acute were the disappointments of these students, even though they were making superior records, that President Aydelotte protested vigorously to the American Association of Universities. Some recent books indicate that the situation has worsened since the Aydelotte protest. But in reply to all this Bernard Berelson points out, in an exhaustive survey of graduate schools and opinions about them,[2] not only that the graduate schools are now the dominant influence in American higher education and that their methods are in harmony with scientific and technological research, but also that college presidents might as well save their breath instead of protesting, because they no longer have any real influence. They no longer represent the consumer's market for the products of the graduate schools. Their graduates now mostly enter industry and governmental agencies where present salaries and future prospects make teaching seem uninviting. In the process of bringing about such a situation the so-called liberal influences seem to have lost their appeal.

Along with the increasing tensions of competition and specialization among students has come an increasing recognition of nervous disorders and problems of mental health and personality development. In recent years the annual meetings of the American College Health Association have become increasingly psychiatric. The number of psychiatric consultants in college health departments has grown out of proportion to the increase in enrollments. Books on the mental health of college students show that emotional problems interfere seriously with the intellectual achievement of gifted students.

If the intellectual utopias envisioned by some educators have proved disappointing, the psychologists and sociologists point to their research on the personality development of college students during late adolescence as giving new authority in support of some humanistic values. Some of these investigators aver that they are the *new* new humanists. When the academic studies of the great works of literature and philosophy, they say, have grown so analytical and esoteric that they have little human significance, the scientific students of human problems reassert some ancient virtues and values, both individual and social, and even suggest means for putting them into practice.

If we are approaching a new era in education—and it surely is being forced upon us—there is some reason to speculate about which of the old values commended to adolescents should survive and which will no longer be accepted. To aid in this speculation we offer concrete observations of some dominant personalities and customs that molded the intellectual, emotional, and religious atmosphere of a small college from its beginnings. This may help to determine what values a college may see in its traditions, whether and when predominantly intellectual criteria become dehumanizing, whether the pioneer distrust of the intellectual was a form of primitivism to be outgrown as soon as possible, and whether there are some "nonintellective" values in an intellectual community that contribute to emotional stability and the development of personality. All this, perhaps, is one way of asking what future the small liberal arts college has in American education as it becomes statistically a smaller and smaller part of the whole picture.

Although the development of personality is still one of the major concerns of the liberal arts college, the dominant opinion seems to be that not much can be done about it directly. To quote Courtney Smith in his inaugural address as president of Swarthmore in the fall of 1953:

One tries to create the conditions in which personality can blossom and mature, conditions in which the latent creativity of the individual is encouraged, and yet learns the essential adjustments required by group living. Whether the mind will broaden and inform our senses of the possibilities of life depends upon a complex of factors, not the least of which is living in an integrated community, where there is a healthy respect and lively concern for values. It is not a dogmatic community that I have in mind. Indeed the Quaker tradition is in quite the opposite direction, holding that the experimental approach, under conscience, is the way to a knowledge of truth and right conduct. What we want, then, is a community that values values.

This utterance is quite consistent with what Edward Parrish said in taking office as the first president of Swarthmore in 1869, if stated in present-day terms, and it could be supported by quotations from all the Swarthmore presidents.

The method of this book is to give a concrete account of the values evolved by the Swarthmore College community and of some of the effects these values seem to have had upon the growth of personality. It is perhaps a "then-and-now" account of how it felt and how it feels to live in the Swarthmore community. The book is an attempt to describe the intellectual and emotional climate of the college, with enough selected pictures to give a sense of the past, and the changes that have led to the present climate. Very few of these changes are peculiar to Swarthmore, except that some of them occurred earlier and faster here. Very many colleges are traveling the same road, and their changes obviously reflect changes in American culture. It would be a hopelessly complicated task to try to describe all the cultural influences that produced the freshman who was nurtured upon Louisa May Alcott's LITTLE MEN and LITTLE WOMEN, or even Booth Tarkington's SEVENTEEN, and then to contrast him with the one who finds his adolescence reflected in J. D. Salinger's widely read CATCHER IN THE RYE.

The observations in this study spring from the author's teaching experiences at Swarthmore from 1925 to 1958 and from those as dean for twenty years. It is not possible, even if it were desirable, to eliminate all the nostalgic tendencies of the emeritus professor, nor to erase the continuing loyalty to the memories of his relatively primitive and unsophisticated but warm-hearted college community in the pioneer West. If this book should occasionally seem like our agrarian writers' attempt to re-establish the values of the old South, it has been written with an acceptance of the fact that much of our older culture here too has gone with the wind and with a major concern for what lies ahead in all our colleges.

A professor may lose himself in his subject, but a dean cannot escape the influence of campus personalities. A dean usually has a hand in selecting students for admission; he cooperates with his committee in following the hunches of an interviewer and judging character and personality as well as college board scores. He lives with his mistakes and successes. His worst mistakes often come back years later to tell him proudly of their subsequent achievements. He is inevitably concerned with advising, rewarding, disciplining, and, later, writing reams of letters describing students to professional schools and to future employers. The whole experience has created a great sense of indebtedness to the students for all the joys and all the sorrows they have brought to him.

In the early years of these experiences this dean was almost wholly ignorant of any psychological theories about personality. Cases never fell into types; each student was unique. But sooner or later he often had to attempt diagnoses, in which he frequently needed the help of the college physician and the consulting psychiatrist. He was forced into thinking of college mores and morale in the light of mental health. He wondered if some generalizations about emotional maturity might be acceptable to intellectual adolescents who were scornful of all moralizing.

To what extent some of the vanishing values of the older culture may be restored by the more specialized findings of the students of mental health is a matter of concerned debate. Much of this debate among scholars and educators has seemed to go on without adequate knowledge of what it feels like to be a student today. This writer may be too old to understand the students fully, but he has listened sympathetically and tried to quote understandingly from what students have said both in public and private. He hopes that these accounts of student life may lead to a greater appreciation of the many attempts to understand the development of personality in college today and may give this understanding a more important place in college life, both curricular and otherwise. It is well to treat intellectual adolescents *as if* they were adults, but it is important for them and for their elders to understand why they are not adults and why development proceeds at such different rates in different personalities, in different communities, and in different times.

»«  The Revolt of the College Intellectual

# 1

# Awakened colleges

In 1930, after a long experience with varied aspects of education at Harvard and a brief but disillusioning term of service as president of the University of Michigan, Clarence Cook Little published THE AWAKENING COLLEGE.[1] It was not a tactful book. Reviewers referred to Mr. Little as an irritated and impatient idealist who obviously lacked the realism so necessary for a successful administrator. He found so much wrong that he had to fight on all fronts at once. But if his prophetic zeal seemed to lead only to his resignation as president, the developments in American education since his day at Michigan have followed so markedly the lines he laid down that his call to an awakening deserves to be characterized as a remarkable instance of educational insight and foresight. Fundamentally, he said, our hope for an awakened college lies in a vastly increased interest in the character and personality of the individual student. Neither the admissions offices, nor the deans' offices, nor the teachers, he said, had faced the fact that the largest and certainly the most tragic cause of failure in college is emotional in nature. He therefore urged that steps be taken to control and simplify, wherever possible, the extent and nature of emotional and social problems in order to clear the way for action on the intellectual level. The college entrance requirements of the future, he wrote, were to include, among their most significant features, a measure of each student's emotional maturity and balance. Here Mr. Little anticipated some of the most important developments of college admissions, developments that still need much more study in many colleges and by many organizations that award scholarships on a national scale.

After his selection on an inadequate basis, the difficulties of the entering student, he said, were increased by the type of professional scholar selected to teach him. The prescribed training of college and university teachers tended to create, select, and reward overspecialized, cold, self-centered individuals who had too little interest in their students or the human values of their subjects. So far as possible these teachers (or worthier successors) should be brought to realize that the main function of the first two years of the college curriculum should be to arouse the students' intellectual curiosity and interest. Mr. Little's acquaintance with students, however, led him to believe that in this respect most introductory courses failed dismally. Certain contemporary studies seem to support Mr. Little's belief. The second half of the college period should seek to teach the student the joy of intense and constructive work for definite ends, leading in many cases, at least, to creative work. Here again, his disappointment has led to a growing national emphasis upon the importance of his aims.

Thus far Mr. Little has referred to educational reform as a struggle between those who had faith in youth and those who did not. But in dealing with some of the phenomena of adolescence, the elders, he felt, had left youth too much to themselves in a manner quite contrary to the methods of Nature. Nature always protects a developing new structure with a fixed and simple environment—an outer shell or chrysalis. But in college we wait until the students have reached the age of the most disrupting physiological and psychological changes and then we change their geographic environment; their social environment, which presents new and oftentimes false and unreal campus values; their emotional environment, which often allows and encourages unrestricted experimentation with subtle and powerful forces; and their mental environment. We then require them to clarify and correlate new facts and theories whose significance is not understood.

It is this situation that demands that we control and simplify emotional and social problems. But, he continues, we have neglected our duties in allowing fraternities to be breeders of a shallow group psychology, a false sense of values, and social distinction that is undemocratic and to hinder the development of a mature, independent, and individual point of view. We have allowed the use of automobiles and liquor in an uncontrolled and unbalanced manner that complicates the already difficult problem of orientation and adjustment, and we have allowed coeducation to lead to unbalancing problems of emotional adjustment at a period when students most need to form and establish habits of intellectual activity. We have not protected the active interest of students in athletics from the exploitation of selfish interests, and have permitted a situation in which normal and healthy instincts are exploited and allowed to prevent the growth of intellectual interests.

If Clarence Cook Little had been president of Swarthmore College in 1927, he would probably have resigned when he read I. M. Rubinow's "Revolt of a Middle-Aged Father" in *The Atlantic Monthly.*[2] In this article a distinguished intellectual set down his virulent observations about Swarthmore as he attempted to discover some signs of intellectual interest on the campus during repeated visits to his daughter. As one living and teaching on the campus at the time, I am not convinced that his description reveals the whole truth about the college. Nevertheless, it is graphic and forcible, and shows that he was a keen observer. The beautiful campus, he says, is obviously a place of vacation and not of vocation. Any ideal of education and culture, he maintains, is held by only an infinitesimal proportion of students; neither the college nor the students encourage the effort to seek an education or culture. In something of a quiet rage he set about questioning students regarding their habits of work and found that thirty hours a week for classes, laboratories, and study was considered ultralaborious. In despair and disgust he sent his daughter to a Midwestern state university in the hope that there she might be given some intellectual stimulus.

For two years following its publication I presented this article to classes of students. They were generally agreed that the thirty-hour work-week for Swarthmore students was much too high, except possibly for a few Honors students, who were regarded as queer creatures anyway. Ten years later, when I presented the article to other groups, the general opinion was that this was grossly unfair; that no one, not even a "Course" or "pass" student, could do his work in thirty hours a week; and that sixty hours was a more accurate average.

If this increase in hours of work had resulted merely from the "crack down" of a production manager, it would not have been especially significant. But it actually was a result of gradually changing student attitudes and motivations that may well be regarded as an awakening.

In recent years an increasing number of studies have attempted to assess the intellectual productivity of colleges, and in some of these the results of the changes at Swarthmore have been noted and published. One of these assessments was the Roster of Scientific and Specialized Personnel, which was compiled in Washington to make instantly available by push button the names and addresses of specialists in all fields whose services would aid in our world war struggles. The compilation of the roster naturally gave rise to questions about the origins of these men, the influences that had produced them, and what might be done to recognize and spread the influence of those colleges that had been markedly successful in the production of scientists of distinction. In 1952 R. H. Knapp and H. B. Goodrich, carrying out a research study authorized by the trustees of Wesleyan University, published their findings in a book entitled THE COLLEGIATE ORIGINS OF AMERICAN SCIENTISTS.[3] One chapter devoted to "Four Institutions of Broad Intellectual Emphasis" (Antioch, Oberlin, Reed, Swarthmore) comments on the intellectual quality of their student bodies on the basis of tests and the production of scientists and on the superior status of scholastic achievement leading to a disregard of conventional social and athletic activities and to a venturesome spirit and a lack of traditionalism that is termed "the spirit of vanguardism." To these writers Swarthmore seems to represent a "controlled metamorphosis." It has looked to the European scene (Oxford) for the inspiration of its reforms, as contrasted with Antioch, which turned to the American industrial scene. The authors did not discover at Swarthmore the degree of radicalism and individualism that seemed so obviously prevalent at Reed. Both the students and the college seemed comparatively wealthy, with an abundance of material resources and an excellent faculty functioning under favorable conditions. The writers seem impressed that almost in spite of these things there should be such an atmosphere of intellectual vigor so little affected by the distractions that beset the conventional college. The principal stimulus to all this they found to be the dynamic leadership of Frank Aydelotte (president from 1921 to 1939), and the acknowledged and growing success of the Honors system he had inaugurated.

A year later Professor Knapp, with a new collaborator, Professor Joseph J. Greenbaum, published THE YOUNGER AMERICAN SCHOLAR: HIS COLLEGIATE ORIGINS,[4] extending their interests to the origin of younger scholars in all fields who had graduated since 1946 and who seemed to be on the road to intellectual distinction. A purpose of the study was stated in an introductory section:

If we are to maintain and increase the intellectual strength of the country, we must have some way of recognizing those with high research and scholarship potential, so that we may support their growth and help to actualize their intellectual potential.

Only a few institutions, like individuals, they find, have scholarly creativity. They believe that there must be individuals of high talents among the unproductive institutions, but

so marked a degree of specialization in the production of younger scholars as we have found seems to approach a monopoly and to leave undeveloped and unproductive large segments of the American system of higher education.

Only a very few colleges of "general intellectuality" elevate the scholar and the intellectual to the position of "culture hero." An over-all index based upon the percentile production at such institutions of scholars in science, social science, and the humanities places Swarthmore at the head of the list.

The impulse to study such institutions in order to understand the forces that produce them was strengthened by the publication in 1957 of Philip Jacob's study, CHANGING VALUES IN COLLEGE.[5] Summarizing the results of many research studies, Professor Jacob concluded that American colleges have little effect on the values of their students and that their values on leaving college are not too commendable. The publication of this report created much discussion among educators who were unwilling to accept his conclusions, who questioned his methods, and who called for other studies of broader scope and sounder techniques. Professor Jacob's statement that he had studied only a few colleges and that there might well be some of "peculiar potential" that deserved commendation led to numerous suggestions that colleges should be classified and sufficient examples studied within each type to show what college attributes are related to what effects on what kinds of students.

But not only did colleges differ among themselves. Within the same colleges there are periods of creative and intellectually exciting activity that should be studied to determine what personalities, what social processes, what types of students, and what faculty-student relationships produced such results. Can any useful advice be found for institutions that would like to create or sustain high levels of intellectual achievement?

The effect of all this concern is to concentrate more attention on the student, his origins, his personality, his abilities, his progress, and his later career. Instead of merely aligning ourselves with the educational theories of Woodrow Wilson, Charles Eliot, John Dewey, Robert Hutchins, and the like, we want to know what actually happens to Joe Doakes and why.

The University of California Center for the Study of Higher Education has begun a study of a few of the colleges that are rated high on the index of intellectual productivity by Professor Knapp in THE YOUNGER AMERICAN SCHOLAR: HIS COLLEGIATE ORIGINS. Professor Knapp did not have the time or means to include the students and their backgrounds and abilities in his studies. He merely characterized briefly the colleges from which these superior students came. Now we are to learn why these students selected these colleges and what influence they had on the college, as well as what influence the college had on them. A whole generation of college students is to be studied, tested, and measured, with special attention to the changes from the freshman through the senior year. Qualified sociologists and psychologists are studying the social structure of the college and the personalities of the students. When these studies are published five or six years hence, we shall know more about Swarthmore, and about colleges in general, than we have ever known.

To become at all familiar with the batteries of tests, the statistical methods of validation, and the theories of personality is to make the layman fearful of hazarding any observations on the meaning of his experience. Nevertheless this volume is a layman's account of the college as he saw it in the Dean's Office at Swarthmore under three presidencies. It cannot have the validity of a scientific study, nor the scope of a history of the college. It is limited to an account of what interested him most: the attitudes and feelings of the students in their relations with the college and its institutions and with one another. Allowance must be made for the fact that this is inevitably a dean's-eye view. The Dean's Office is a focal point for those who are in difficulties—those who are dragged in and those who come for help. Since about nine-tenths of these difficulties are emotional in origin, a dean becomes something of an amateur psychiatrist in spite of himself and soon learns to seek the advice and support of those who are professionally trained to deal with the difficulties of arriving at emotional maturity. This bias is very likely to make his account of a college somewhat like the pictures of wedded life in current fiction. So few novelists attempt to make happy marriages interesting. Of the critics who have praised the colleges that produce a high percentage of professional scholars and have blamed those that do not, none thus far has seemed to consider the happiness of students a relevant consideration. Emotional costs are not counted. It is assumed that a college that produces scholars in quantity is a successful college and that no other questions need be asked, except how other colleges could do the same. It is probable that studies now in progress will reveal that an intellectual adolescent is an adolescent still. It is also probable that they will reveal the inadequacies of my personal observations. But in the meantime the account of one who has lived among students in an official capacity may suggest new problems for investigation, lead to new conclusions, and have some human interest in and of itself.

This is not a history of the college (that, too, by the well-known Quaker historian, Professor Frederick Tolles, is forthcoming). For the sake of appreciation by contrast, it is well, however, to give a short account of earlier Swarthmore days and the origins of its traditions, with special attention in each period to student feelings and attitudes. It is important also to note that only in more recent times has student self-expression been so completely uninhibited and so easily accessible.

We may take three periods: the early period, in which the religious purposes of the founders were dominant in keeping the college apart from the world; a middle period, which reflected the prevailing values and mores of the time and in which the college was in and of the world; and a third period, in which intellectual values gained dominance and which some critics have called the period of eggheads in the nest.

We wonder what kinds of personalities fare best in a rarefied intellectual atmosphere and what kinds suffer most. How do these personalities reveal themselves? What impressions do they make on each other? Are intellectuals predominantly introverts, nonconformists, less stable emotionally? Do they reinforce one another's propensities and create a sense of alienation from the world? Or is it here that the creative individual is unleashed and encouraged to discover his real self, and thus enabled to perform his greatest service for society? Instead of attempting to arrive at unsafe generalizations, I have tried to describe what has gone on and how various types of personalities have felt about being at Swarthmore.

In leaving Princeton to accept the presidency at Swarthmore, Courtney Smith seemed to sense both the possibilities and the problems of the small college of intellect. In his inaugural address he cited with pride the intellectual distinction of the college:

We have no intention of relinquishing our academic excellence. . . . But it is not enough for us to be a training ground for scholars. It is not enough to develop intellect, for intellect by itself is essentially amoral, capable of evil as well as good. We must develop the character which makes intellect constructive, and the personality which makes it effective. . . . A balanced community requires more than the valedictorian and salutatorian, and the academician must ponder the fact that Franklin Roosevelt's record at Harvard, and Adlai Stevenson's at Princeton and Dwight Eisenhower's at West Point, were scarcely, I am told, pace setting.

Mr. Smith quoted, with apparent approval, from an Englishman's protest against limiting admissions to Oxford College to those who won scholarships by competitive examinations: "Intellectuals, by themselves, make a bleak sort of society."

President Smith here echoes President Aydelotte's answer to the same question about the limitation of Swarthmore to Honors students. "No," said Mr. Aydelotte, "we need the humanizing presence of the Course students."

The writer's personal experience in living on the Swarthmore campus began four years after President Aydelotte had announced his aims and hopes for the college and while the surge of the new life was beginning. But he has had enough contacts with the older alumni to be conscious of their great affection for the college of the days of Presidents Magill and Swain, and it is enlightening to study the sturdy roots of the college before describing Swarthmore's flowering into national recognition.

The Quaker origins of the college differ enough from those of most church-related colleges in America to justify some attention to the rise of the Quaker tradition of a guarded education and to the values Friends hoped to preserve in this tradition of a peculiar people.

With President Swain's administration, beginning in 1902, while the Quaker tradition among the Board of Managers was strong and the president himself was a devoted Quaker, worldly ways kept creeping in. The students conformed to the ways of the other college campuses to an extent that makes it possible to describe this period as an age of conformity and high morale during which students were inspired by successful conformity in gaining recognition.

With President Aydelotte's appeal to break the academic lock-step, the era of individualism began and proceeded through many rebellions, academic and social, to make the nonconforming intellectual the dominant campus figure. All of this, of course, is closely related to the many social and ideological changes in American life and to patterns of education in the lower levels of schooling. The "controlled metamorphosis" produced by Aydelotte's policies, however, had the effect of selecting and developing enough nonconforming intellectuals to change the whole structure and atmosphere of campus life. In a recent study of Amherst entitled PIETY AND INTELLECT AT AMHERST COLLEGE [6] there is the implication that piety stifles intellect and that, with the development of intellect, piety fades away. But the Quaker tradition of nonconformity is such that the present young intellectuals, quite regardless of their religious affiliation or lack of it, are often closer to the Quaker spirit than the students in the age of conformity. But we must not drift too far into generalizations before we have described what happened.

# 2

# William Penn
# and guarded education
# at Swarthmore

William Penn's Holy Experiment in Pennsylvania was inspired
by what he felt to be a Divine Mandate: to create in the
wilderness an ideal Christian Commonwealth in which religious men of all faiths would be free to set a shining example
before all nations. He had been outraged by the tyrannical
persecutions that the combined church and state had inflicted
upon him and his Quakers; he was sickened by the wickedness of the courtly life of the nobility, with which his position
and rank made him familiar; and he was depressed by the
decline of rural life and the simple virtues.

The year before Penn became Lord Proprietor of Pennsylvania he was close to despair. "There is no hope in England,"
he wrote, "the deaf adder cannot be charmed." In a letter to
a friend in America he said: "There may be room there though
not here, for such a holy experiment. Mine eye is to a blessed
government and a virtuous, ingenious society."

Penn's inner consciousness was not the only evidence of
Divine guidance in the Holy Experiment. Penn had traveled
widely in Europe and had familiarized himself with European
governments. It seemed to him that governments could hardly
do worse, and he was haunted with the idea that he could do
much better.

A visit from George Fox, who had just returned from the American colonies, brought his rather vague ideas to a focus. Fox had been greatly impressed by the potentialities of the Indians and was deeply concerned for the Negro slaves. He wanted a sanctuary in the New World for persecuted white men everywhere, and not only for his Quakers. When in America he had looked into the possibilities of purchasing a tract of land from the Susquehanna Indians. His fervor brought to Penn's mind an inherited bad debt from the Crown. Charles Stuart owed Admiral Penn, William's father, 16,000 pounds. The wilds of America meant little to the English King, and the Quakers were a minor nuisance; if he could get rid of the debt and the Quakers at the same time, it would be a happy solution. And so William Penn, this seditious Quaker preacher, before he was forty, became in 1681 the feudal Lord of Pennsylvania.

But "the founder of an over-seas colony," writes Professor Tolles of Swarthmore,

needed something more than lofty ideals and religious dedication. Plenty of high-minded attempts at colonization in the new world had come to grief because their sponsors, impractical visionaries, expecting manna in the wilderness, had taken insufficient thought for the practical aspects of the venture, such as how to live through the first winter. . . . But Penn's religious faith, though spiritual, was not other-worldly. . . . Penn expected Pennsylvania not only to provide a haven for persecuted Friends, and an example of liberty and democracy to the world, but a comfortable living for himself and family, coming from the prosperity of the colony.[1]

For seventy-five years the Quakers remained in political control, exercising power under the terms of Penn's constitution. But the Assembly of the colonists rejected Penn's Frame of Government when it stood in the way of profits. They wished to sell rum to the Indians, exploited them in ways that led to hostilities, and encouraged illegitimacy among Negroes in order to increase the slave population more rapidly. All but a few faithful Quakers regarded Penn as a nuisance, and were glad to see him return to England. The Quakers could no longer administer the affairs of Pennsylvania to the satisfaction of the Crown and the adjoining territories and remain Quaker. In 1701 they were asked to allot money to purchase ammunition to fight the Delawares and to offer bounties for their scalps. It became clear to certain weighty Quakers that they could no longer hold office and retain any consistency. Partly upon the advice of London Quakers, they resigned, and after them many Quaker members refused to stand for re-election. Here, according to many historians, ended the Holy Experiment, and began those processes of government that in later years made Philadelphia known, not as the Holy Experiment, but as "Corrupt and Content."

One result of this withdrawal from political power was to strengthen the conviction of many Quakers that they should always be a minority group, too devoted to their spiritual and moral convictions to descend to the compromises and subterfuges of political administration. Among widespread Quaker communities this conviction led for long periods of time to what is often termed Quietism: a withdrawal from the world to maintain themselves as a peculiar people that emphasizes all those habits of dress and speech that separate them from the world and makes an orthodoxy out of picturesque but minor manners of community life—a community life such as was so effectively portrayed in Jessamyn West's FRIENDLY PERSUASION, although that is not all so quiet. But for the most part it is characterized by sweet, serene withdrawal to the simplicities of pastoral life.

William Penn, for all his love of rural life and his enjoyment of philosophical retirement, where he could pluck the Fruits of Solitude and write his most-quoted words, had earlier declared that a man's religion ought to enable him to live in the world rather than withdraw from it. But Quaker influence naturally suffered a great decline during the dominance of Quietism from the 1770's until almost a century later. This partly accounts for Friends' lack of concern for higher education. When other religious groups were founding colleges fired with missionary zeal for the production of religious leaders, the Quakers saw little connection between higher education and religious leadership. This view was in part inherited from earlier and more active days of Quakerism. George Fox, uneducated and only semiliterate, had reflected a marked contempt for seventeenth-century education. Having achieved an understanding of the ways of God without benefit of academic training, he doubted the value of the experience. The early Quakers were excluded from the English universities; in response they attacked the English clergy, asserting that "God teacheth his people himself" and that "We need not that any man should teach us save as the Holy Spirit teacheth us."

Sent away from Oxford for his activities in leading a small minority of individualists, William Penn characterized universities as "signal places of idleness, profaneness, and gross ignorance." In his old age he wrote: "We are at pains to make boys scholars, not men; to talk, rather than to know, which is true canting. It were happy if we studied nature more in natural things, and acted according to nature, whose rules are few, plain, and most reasonable."

In 1828 occurred the split between the Hicksites and the Orthodox, a split that would never have happened, President Sharpless of Haverford said, if there had been a few men in each group with a broad and liberal education. There then began to emerge some pressure for education above the level of those guarded schools that were to "preserve our youth from the contaminating influence of the world." Among the wealthier Friends, sons began to go to Harvard and Yale and even to Catholic colleges. These young men felt the need for a level of education that would fit them for their positions of inherited leadership. Others desired to rise above the humble circumstances of their parents. Finally there was the obvious need for educational and religious leadership within the Society of Friends.

These demands for education were felt first among the Orthodox Friends, and represented their higher standard of wealth and culture. Haverford School, which was soon to become Haverford College, was opened in 1833, with a stern, uncompromising, and disciplined approached to education. The superintendent and teachers were admonished by the managers to "instill" into the minds of the students "a love and esteem" for Quaker doctrines and testimonies—a charge that included dress, speech, and conduct most minutely circumscribed. "No periodical publications except *The Friend* are to be brought to the school for the use of students, nor any books except school books, which should be subject to the approval of the council."

Isaac Sharpless, one of the great presidents of Haverford, who served from 1887 to 1917, gained his early experience as assistant superintendent of the Preparatory School and College. He suffered acutely from the rules he had to administer— rules, he later wrote, imposed by men who had high moral standards and who intended to perpetuate them by forbidding whatever in their judgment would jeopardize them. His life, he said, was one of alternate pleasure and confusion. He wrote:

When we got into healthy human relations, talking sports or studies, there was much enjoyment in their honest earnestness. To meet them in their rather reckless disregard of rules for disregard's sake when they set fire to the leaves in the fall without caring for damage to trees or buildings, when at midnight they went through the operation of burying an unpopular author with heathen ceremonies, then it became an intolerable burden to keep pace with them, and after one year's trial I declined further service in the field. . . .

How easy it would have been as seen by future experiences, to have controlled with pleasure and profit this little group of worthy students, from good homes and no bad intentions. To have removed one-half or more of the little restrictions and depended on public sentiment and honor to maintain standards. . . . But it was two decades or more before the Alumni became influential enough to make themselves felt in Quaker Councils, and liberalize the restrictions and discipline insisted upon by the fearful Quakers. They applied school discipline to college material, but gradually the tradition passed on by Alumni to undergraduates made it seem possible to feel the pulse of change, and slowly all the elements of the college population became infused with a common loyalty to rational living.[2]

The Hicksite Quakers, having a larger proportion of farmers and rural tradesmen, were more influenced by the fear that education would lure their children away from the farm. Even so there was discontent with their low educational status. In 1865 Edward Parrish, later the first president of Swarthmore and a man ahead of his time in many respects, said in his EDUCATION IN THE SOCIETY OF FRIENDS (still greatly worth reading):

We find the Society now quietly resting in its traditions and forms, its members generally illustrating in private life the virtues which have grown out of its discipline and teaching, but almost devoid of the *anima* (spirit) which made their predecessors a great power on the earth.[3]

And Martha Tyson of Baltimore, one of the most ardent founders, answered the doctrine that only the Holy Spirit could teach by saying that before their children could be "taught of the Lord," they must learn to know His voice. She expanded the idea with a Biblical analogy:

We believe there are many precious Samuels among our people, who have their rest broken by a voice they would gladly obey, but who for the want of parental Eli's to teach them who it is that speaks, and what to answer, continue in a distressed and disturbed state, to their great spiritual loss.[4]

However high the hope of relieving the distressed and disturbed state of students, there was a great fear for the state of students brought up in the conventional pattern of education. Thomas Hallowell of Baltimore wrote that "Education as at present conducted is no security against disorder and wickedness"; and Edward Parrish, who was sent on tour to investigate schools and colleges, reported: "A common fault with popular seminaries is their aim at a superficial polish which will make their pupils shine in society, without being well grounded in sound learning."

The program of Swarthmore College, then, was to be a departure from the program and atmosphere of the colleges that were visited and disapproved. Swarthmore was to have an atmosphere of its own. First, it was to be coeducational, in accordance with a long-standing Quaker tradition of equality of the sexes. In this it differed from Haverford and the orthodox Quakers who were more sensitive to accepted practice. Secondly, its curriculum was to provide extensive practical acquaintance with the natural sciences. Here again there was a contrast with Haverford, which was more indebted to classical tradition and literary culture. Thirdly—and here there was agreement with the orthodox—the atmosphere was to be "guarded"; that is, it was to conform to Quaker standards of dress and conduct, and its population was to be primarily Friendly.

With these issues decided, the delay during the Civil War years provided time for agreement that the control should rest completely with the Quaker Board of Managers and that, for a while at least, a preparatory school should be a part of the scheme. But the issue that aroused the strongest feeling was the location of the college. Groups in New York and Philadelphia favored the city because it provided more convenient access to museums and libraries and made it possible to hire part-time teachers and lecturers more cheaply and easily. But the Baltimore Friends said that the Quaker tradition required a rural location. "The clear advice of the Quaker past was to avoid the tarnish of metropolitan influence, and to locate in an atmosphere of Nature and God." Baltimore Friends finally withdrew most of their interest because they were displeased by the selection of a site within easy striking distance of Philadelphia.

There was no doubt that the loyalty of the first two presidents, Parrish and Magill, was devoted to the idea of a guarded education for the protection of Quaker ideals, although President Parrish was enough ahead of his time to agree with Benjamin Hallowell and a small minority of Quakers that they should create a college whose instruction should equal the best in the land. He also had ideas about discipline that were much more liberal than those of most of his contemporaries. President Magill had had experience with preparatory schools. As head of the Boston Latin School he knew school discipline, and Swarthmore was still in large part a preparatory school. He also knew of the skepticism of rural Quakers about college life and the shocked fears of the public about coeducation. He therefore had published in pamphlet form for general circulation the One Hundred Rules of Swarthmore College. They have been so often quoted that I need not go into detail: girls could leave the campus only in groups of four, and accompanied by upperclass attendants; men wishing to leave the campus should leave their cards with the president; girls were to be in by dark; boys and girls were not to sit together on a bench; boys and girls were to walk on different sides of the asphaltum, and so forth.

So far as I can learn, the students were not consulted about these rules. They rested upon Calvinistic assumptions of youthful potential for evil. But as in the case of all church-related colleges over the country that started with the domination of more conservative members, youth was rebellious. The attempts to make students answer all questions regarding their movements, the condemnation of books bought by the literary societies, the dismissal of boys for playing football without faculty permission all resulted in student demand for greater liberty. Attempts to set the gymnasium on fire and to cut off the college water supply, in order to increase the length of the coming holiday, probably had their origin as much in rebellion against authority as in inherent sin. It all led the managers to appoint a committee to see if there were any relation between the student discipline and the decline in enrollment. For the first time the committee took into account the attitudes of the student body. President Magill, influenced greatly by Dean Bond, changed his attitude, and life for a time at least seemed happier for being less guarded.

There were, of course, many personalities on campus during those years who greatly influenced the students. Some of them have been characterized by President Magill in his SIXTY-FIVE YEARS IN THE LIFE OF A TEACHER.[5] Many others are also worthy of tributes from an historian. But one figure was so unique in her personal influence, and it is so impossible to see her like again, that I cannot omit her in any discussion of the influence of personality on adolescents. Emily Cooper Johnson has written a very eloquent and complete biography [6] of Elizabeth Powell Bond, and I draw upon this, together with reminiscences from older alumni, one of whom in his will so generously provided the Dean Bond rose garden that delights all who come to the campus.

Mrs. Bond's higher education consisted of a two-year normal course, taken in one year, and one year at a collegiate institute, where she was chiefly interested in botany. She later taught in the country school she had attended when she was little older than her pupils. Her early interests were greatly affected by her Quaker family associations with the abolitionists. She went to Boston to study physical culture, and while there formed close connections with the Alcotts and the Emersons in Concord. A little later a friend recommended her to the "Vassar Female College," where physical education was greatly emphasized because of the fear that the mental strain of higher education would be too much for the female mind. The rules governing student behavior were of much the same restrictive nature that President Magill and his Board of Managers had imposed upon Swarthmore. After four years of especially happy relations with the students of Vassar she resigned to become religious counselor to the Free Congregational Society in Northampton, Massachusetts, where she gave Sunday afternoon addresses on such subjects as "The Ministry of Nature." Here she met her husband, who left her a widow after ten years of happy married life. As a result of her reputation at Vassar she was invited and came to Swarthmore as matron, bringing her young son David. Her duties as matron concerned discipline and social relationships. She assigned places at table, gave permission for going out of bounds, received excuses for absences, had oversight of conduct—a set of duties that to some might well have seemed very trivial and tiresome. But as Emily Cooper Johnson said:

We now can see that she successfully worked at a problem in social psychology. She dealt with the mental habits and the points of view

»« *William Penn and guarded education*

of the student body; she wrought changes that made a new Swarth-more. . . . She developed a relation between faculty and students that made discipline not a book of statutes but a community enter-prise, a relation among the students themselves that grew into unusually successful coeducation, a relation between students and herself that was their mental and spiritual enrichment.[7]

This achievement was the more remarkable because it was scored amidst difficulties that would make it entirely impos-sible in this generation. The Quakers, almost abashed at their own boldness in sponsoring coeducation, kept up the pressure to enforce the strictest rules. Martha Tyson, a prime mover among the founders, had written President Magill:

I learned from a friend interested in the cause that the inter-course between the sexes was about constant—that they ate all their meals together—walked together on the campus—and a good deal more of promiscuous intercourse. On my daughter's return I made use of the first private opportunity that occurred to ask her if the report was not a fabrication. I heard that it was all true, an asser-tion that I was pained to hear.[8]

Mrs. Bond was able to allay such fears, to command respect for her standards, and yet to hold the affection of her wards. When she showed her faith in her students by allowing the seniors to spend a social hour in her parlor without a chaperon, one of them responded by saying later that the experiment was quite safe

for the pictures and the books and the open fire were Mrs. Bond almost as distinctly as if she had been present, and established an ideal of refinement which we could never lose.

Such a social hour was one of the more exciting times in a life that would have been unbearably monotonous for later generations. Athletics were undeveloped, there were no danc-ing and no music, there was no village. Students who wanted to see a train come in could not go too near the station. But perhaps the monotony was Mrs. Bond's opportunity. She introduced hymn singing and later extended it to songs of many lands. She read aloud to her students, with interpretive comments. She carried to them her interest in botany and led them to study the plants of the campus, with a special interest in roses. She would return from vacation trips to England with ivy plants from various cathedrals and would plant them by the walls of Parrish. Thus originated the traditional senior Ivy planting, accompanied by the Ivy oration. In all these activities Mrs. Bond stood entirely on her own personality. She had none of the prestige that came with the authority of academic learning; she never taught any courses at Swarthmore. Her title was changed in 1890 from matron to dean, which was a recognition of the position she had created for herself. She acted as hostess in entertaining most of the official guests of the college and made speeches representing the college in various parts of the country. She spoke frequently in Friends Meeting, and her talks have been collected in two small volumes called WORDS BY THE WAY.[9] They seem about as quaint and old-fashioned today as most of the speeches of the period. But it says as much for the student personalities of those days as it does about her own personality that they responded to her with such tributes of affection. All this implies an acceptance of common standards that is increasingly rare in the relations between the generations today.

## The early graduates

President Magill liked to say that the history of a college is largely a record of the actions of the men and women who have been educated there. Fifteen years after his retirement from the college, when he was eighty, he took pleasure in compiling an HISTORICAL CATALOGUE OF SWARTHMORE COLLEGE that gives in some detail brief biographies of those who graduated in the first twenty classes from 1873 to 1892. When we consider that there was no competition for admission in those years, that the student body for much of the time consisted largely of preparatory students, and that the college could not have met the requirements of any of the contemporary standardizing agencies, we may say to ourselves that we ought not to expect much of these graduates. But if we also reflect that going to college was not a matter of custom in those days, that students by their very presence probably manifested a genuine interest in getting what the college had to offer, we need not be surprised that President Magill could contemplate his Historical Catalogue with pride and satisfaction and could conclude his autobiography with this sentence:

It is my earnest conviction that no other college in the country has accomplished a greater work in its first half-century, in the general diffusion of education, mental, moral and spiritual, given to both sexes alike from the beginning, than Swarthmore College.

If we care to examine the basis of this feeling of pride by looking at his catalogue, we may feel that he was not unduly complacent. The number is small, an average of fifteen students to a class for the first twenty years. The statistics do not reveal so much as do Dr. Magill's comments and notations, showing a close personal acquaintance with his students. The "guarded education" did not keep them from entering actively and successfully into the life of the world, and the absence of any professional Quaker ministry was perhaps one factor that helps to explain why so little religious leadership seemed to emerge from the group. There were disappointingly few Samuels who spoke to the world about the voice of the Lord, but their deeds spoke for them.

If we look first at the women, who were under scrutiny to see what they would do with an education, we note that in the first graduating class was the first woman in America to receive the Ph.D. from an American graduate school. It remains only to add that she was the daughter of President and Mrs. Magill of Swarthmore.

Also in the first class of women a number continued their pioneering in education by studying medicine, mostly in women's medical colleges. Teaching had a strong appeal, and many of them taught in the Friends schools in the Philadelphia area. A number served with distinction as principals, as was also the case with the men who frequently returned to the Friends schools from which they came. But the number of students coming to Swarthmore from Friends schools in the rural areas between Philadelphia and Baltimore did not result in any large return to their native environment. Only eleven male graduates reported themselves as associated in any way with agriculture, and the women, although most of them married, were not content to report themselves merely as housewives (the almost universal custom of mothers of children entering Swarthmore today) but recorded many community activities, advanced study, and European travel.

The practical interests of the college curriculum and of the students who came to it were reflected in the thirty engineers who graduated and who attained high administrative and executive positions in railroading, bridge building, corporation management, and mining enterprises.

# 3

# Conformity to the ways of the world

The quiet rural college could not escape the contagion of current educational adventures. Vassar, Cornell, and Johns Hopkins, pioneers in educational revolt, all received dramatically large gifts and all were free from religious restrictions. A fundamental issue, at first obscure but which became increasingly clearer, was: Could the college run by and for a peculiar people remain guarded and rural, and still hope to be distinguished for intellectual excellence? Swarthmore's President De Garmo saw the issue, and attempted a program that called for "keeping the college fully abreast of the best colleges in the country in requirements, and also in quantity and quality of teaching force and equipment." This program was really an attempt to carry out the aims and ideals of the first president, Edward Parrish. But it seemed at the time so impossible of attainment that President De Garmo resigned to accept the chair of the art and science of education at Cornell. Swarthmore's Board of Managers then selected as president William Burdsall, a devoted Quaker who was the principal of Friends Central School. He made a gallant attempt to build up a Quaker constituency that might keep the college unique and independent of worldly standards, but resigned after four years.

Convinced that they could not return to the simplicity and piety of earlier years and that they must loosen the bonds of a conservative tradition, the Board next turned to Joseph Swain, the president of the University of Indiana. A tall, impressive, powerful figure, he had been a student leader in his undergraduate days at Indiana, especially active among the "barbs," was distinguished academically, and had served as professor of mathematics at Stanford. A Quaker by birthright, he was devoted to his Society. By training, academic connections, and personality he seemed capable of satisfying the ambition of the Board to make Swarthmore a great college. Swain said that when his Society of Friends called him to head their college, he could not find it in his heart to say "No." He also stipulated that the Board must agree to raise a substantial sum for endowment and must give him powers of real leadership, including the power of appointment and dismissal. The way in which he and the Board cooperated to achieve his aims is an important part of the history of the college.

Swain's inauguration as president was an occasion for addresses by presidents of leading universities and colleges and by alumni of distinction who emphasized in various ways the function of the small college in the development of personality.[1]

One alumnus, the Honorable John Kelvey Richards, Swarthmore '75, Solicitor General of the United States, said:

While Swarthmore is not my only Alma Mater, she is my *own* Alma Mater. The other and later one, fair though she is, seems but a step-mother to me; she helped train my mind, but she never touched my heart. The influences and ideals which mold one's character and shape one's career, I found here.

An almost equally well-known alumnus, Alexander Griswold Cummins, '89, agreed, saying:

We believe in this college, which provides for the highest development of the individual, and the molding of personal character by the closest possible contact of the student with the teacher; we believe that a college should create something more than mere bookishness, that its highest mission should be to equip men with useful knowledge of their fellows, not that they may outwit others, but may serve as brothers.

This moral idealism, characteristic of the alumni of the period, was supported by a new recognition of the importance of the college and its new president. President Thomas of Bryn Mawr declared:

We are met to celebrate not only your inauguration, but the transformation of Swarthmore from one of the smaller colleges to one of the few well-endowed colleges in the United States. For of the 496 colleges enumerated by the United States Commissioner of Education less than thirty-one possess income producing funds of one million. (When President Swain raised the endowment to three million dollars it seemed to give substance to his ideals.)

President Harper of the University of Chicago said:

Those of us who have gone from the East to the West and who know how greatly to be desired is the presence of every strong man in that vast country, look with great regret upon the transfer back again to the East of men who have made for themselves a name and a place in the West. The West mourns one of its strong leaders, but the West joins with you in congratulation upon this event.

The inaugural address of President Swain showed that he, as every college president must, looked to both the past and the future. He declared:

A college cannot in any high sense belong exclusively to a class or creed, or have geographical or other similar limitations. It cannot be confined to a generation or a time. It must be so conducted that while serving each generation in its turn, it will ever adapt itself to the new and larger wants of the rising one. . . .

Thus for the future, and now for the past:

From the time of Benjamin Hallowell and Martha Tyson, Swarthmore has never departed and does not propose to depart from the conception of a guarded education for the children of Friends and others who wish such influences as are approved by Friends to be thrown about the daily lives of young women who come here to study. But quoting Lucretia Mott, "we must never degenerate into a sectarian school."

And again to the future:

Swarthmore is not local, and for the future she must enrich her curriculum, multiply facilities for instruction in books, apparatus, teachers and buildings, and maintain the highest standards of character, personality, and scholarship in faculty.

With this evidence of new hopes for Swarthmore we may see the justification of the faith placed in President Swain by examining a few tributes to his character and personality at the close of his administration. A volume of about one hundred letters covering intimate associations from his boyhood to his retirement from the presidency of Swarthmore College was collected by Dean W. A. Alexander (another much-loved campus personality). Bound under the title OF WHAT SHOULD A MAN BE PROUD IF NOT OF HIS FRIENDS, it was presented to President Swain on June 30, 1921.[2] One letter is from Herbert Hoover, who thanked Swain for

the kindly and human assistance you extended to a boy in Portland, Oregon, now thirty years ago. Had it not been for your personal interest I should obviously have failed of entrance to Stanford University.

Another letter of thanks for the same kind of service is from Joseph Willits, Swarthmore '11, who wrote:

When I first entered your office I was strictly "to let." I have many times since thanked you for your wisdom. . . . The atmosphere of Swarthmore seems to insinuate into a man's psychology that there is some higher goal than the mere accumulation of wealth. When an institution does that it really educates.

Dean Henrietta Meteer quoted one of her students:

Perhaps thee remembers that one of thy boys said "When I am with him I feel so safe, as if his cloak were folded about me."

William Ridgway, '74, wrote:

Ever since that night when Billy Sweet and I took the college to task for "heathenism" and you came out and put your arms around me and thanked me, I have loved you.

The only other statement I shall quote from the many and varied expressions of loyalty and devotion is from the dedicatory statement in THE HALCYON for 1922, written by Dean Alexander and appended to the letters:

As a builder of material things he is great, but he is greater as a builder of men. He has unusual power in making people believe in themselves. There are men in all parts of the world who were inspired by him to do things which they thought they could not do. He has the unselfishness and sacrifice required of the give and take of friendship. His deep concern for the welfare of his students and friends, the encouragement, advice and inspiration which he gave to others is his greatest work. A Swarthmore man writing from the Middle West attests this in the following words: "I have met scores of people out here who were directly influenced by Dr. Swain, and who regarded him almost as a father."

Some may feel that there is an atmosphere of outmoded rhetorical sentimentality about both the inaugural oratory and the letters of personal tribute; but it is worth while to look further into the spaciousness of the old rhetoric in nurturing beliefs and building morale.

## Oratory and morale

Historians of American culture often refer to this period in our history as still in our age of innocence. They say that it is characterized by an optimistic faith in progress and a confidence in a morality based on external verities. All this, they say, we have now lost. Few speakers addressing this generation dare to base their appeals on the beliefs that were so long accepted by American orators and their audiences. But such unity of faith as can be found in any generation is the capital of our orators; if no unity is discoverable, then we go down to defeat at the hands of those who do have a faith. The object of an oration (and we hardly dare use the word any more) is not so much to "make people think" as it is to remind people of what they have already thought—and believed. Oratory is spacious because it seeks to discover the highest grounds of unity.[3] It is spacious in the same way that liberal education is liberal; the assertion has been made that a correlation can be shown between the decline of liberal education and the decline of oratory. But even if we are in a decline, that need not prevent us from trying to understand one of the sources of morale that we sometimes seek with difficulty to recapture. The speeches of President Swain were relatively simple and direct in style. Nevertheless, he was called on so often to speak both in the college and over the country, and his speeches were so frequently printed, that he acquired standing as an educational sage and prophet. The National Education Association passed resolutions commending his national influence. His achievements and recognitions were recounted with such pride in the editorial pages of the *Phoenix* that his receptions to students in his home were made to seem like pilgrimages to the great, where the warmth of greeting conveyed a sense of importance to everyone. His addresses in Collection, in Quaker Meeting, were not the utterances of a lonely Quaker mystic; they were the counsels of a figure who had won the recognition of the world of education and who honored Swarthmore by his presence.

Another figure who increased the unifying power of rhetoric and oratory was Paul M. Pearson, of the Public Speaking Department. Those of his pupils who won the contests in debate and oratory seemed assured of future leadership; anyone who cares to investigate the subsequent careers of these winners will see that the expectation was fulfilled. The graduation recitals of his majors in elocution were college events of great importance, and the critical analyses of their performances that were published in the *Phoenix* approach in technical expertness the critical analyses of performances of visiting musicians now published by music majors. But perhaps the Public Speaking Department exercised its greatest influence in publishing the talents of the college abroad through the Chautauqua. In 1912 Pearson went to his friends among faculty, Board members, and alumni to tell of his altruistic dream of community betterment by establishing Swarthmore Chautauquas throughout Pennsylvania and neighboring states. It was enormously successful, and spread from forty-one towns that year to 776 towns when Swain came to Swarthmore ten years later. It only collapsed with the coming of the media of mass communication. There are numerous accounts of the Chautauqua movement by social historians; we need only say here that the campus was suffused with the exhilaration of the summer triumphs in drama, debate, oratory, music, and elocution. Paul Pearson's widely given lecture on the "Joy of Living" and his recitals of James Whitcomb Riley were representative of the Chautauqua spirit. Again, the later careers of the students who participated in Chautauqua would be an interesting chapter in the development of personality in college.

Many ceremonial institutions in the college life of the period increased the unity of the college through eloquent expression of loyalty to its traditions. Founders Day in October brought Woodrow Wilson, state governors, a number of whom were Swarthmore alumni, and national figures whose presence seemed to bring distinction to the college. There is much quotable oratory from these occasions that had its effect in its day and that bears the stamp of its time. I select from one occasion two statements that called forth most perfectly the combination of alumni pride and loyalty, and the exhilaration that the undergraduates expressed in belonging to such an audience.

First, Congressman A. Mitchell Palmer, Swarthmore '91, introduced Woodrow Wilson as follows:

Mr. President and friends of Swarthmore: Swarthmore College, named for the home of George Fox, the founder of the Religious

Society of Friends, and standing within sight of Upland, where William Penn, the founder of our Commonwealth of Pennsylvania, first set foot upon his domains, very properly harks back to times far in advance of its own actual founding in the celebration of this day. While the work of establishing a seat of learning here came really two hundred years after these men had walked upon the earth, it was the desire to advance the teachings of the one and work out the ideals of the other which really actuated the Friends who founded this institution. It is the fondest hope and constant prayer of those who are today carrying on the work here that the men and women who, in the character-forming years of their lives, seek inspiration and learning within these halls, may, so far as within them lies, exert upon their fellows, their state and their country, influences akin to the teachings and ideals of George Fox and William Penn. It is more than the casual meeting upon the same day which marks the significance of the dual celebration in which the President of the United States has today participated.

Then President Wilson responded:

No one can stand in the presence of a gathering like this on a day suggesting the memories which this day suggests, without asking himself what a college is for. There have been times when I have suspected that certain undergraduates did not know. I remember that in days of discouragement as a teacher, I recall the sympathy of a friend of mine in the Yale faculty who said that after twenty years of teaching he had jumped to the conclusion that the human mind had infinite resources for resisting the introduction of knowledge, and yet, I have my serious doubts as to whether the main object of the college is the introduction of knowledge. It may be the transmission of knowledge through the human system but not much of it sticks. Its introduction is temporary for the discipline of the hour.

Most of what a man learns in college he assiduously forgets afterward—not because he purposes to forget it—but because the crowding events of the days that follow seem somehow to eliminate it. But what a man ought never to forget with regard to college is that it is a nursery of principles and of honor. I can't help thinking of William Penn as a sort of spiritual knight who went out upon his adventures to carry the torch that had been put in his hands so that other men might have the path illuminated for them which led to justice and to liberty; and I can't admit that a man establishes his right to call himself a college graduate by showing me his diploma. The only way he can prove it is by showing that his eyes are lifted to some horizon which other men less instructed than he have not been privileged to see. Unless he can carry freedom of spirit, he has not been bred where spirits are bred.

This man, Penn, representing a sweet enterprise of the quiet and powerful sect that called themselves "Friends" proved his right to the title by being a friend of mankind and he crossed the ocean not merely to establish estates in America, but to set up a free commonwealth in America and to show that he was of the lineage of those who had been bred in the best traditions of the human spirit. I would not be interested in celebrating the memory of William Penn if his conquest had been merely a material one. Sometimes we have been laughed at, by foreigners in particular, for boasting of the size of the American continent, the size of our own domain as a nation, and they have naturally suggested that we did not make it. But I claim that every race and every man is as big as the thing he takes possession of and that the size of America is in some sense a standard of the size and capacity of the American people; but the extent of the American conquest is not what gives America distinction in the annals of the world. It is the professed purpose of the Quaker, which was to see to it that every foot of that land should be the home of free, self-governed people who should have no government whatever which did not rest upon the consent of the governed. I would like to believe that this hemisphere is devoted to the same sacred purpose and that nowhere can any government endure which is stained by blood or supported by anything but the consent of the governed, and the spirit of Penn will not be stayed. You cannot settle him as to such mighty adventures. After their own day is gone, their spirits stalk the world, carrying inspiration everywhere they go and reminding men of the fine lineage of those who have fought for justice and the right.

It is no small matter, therefore, for a college to have as its patron saint a man who went upon such a quest, and what I would like to ask you young people today is, how many of you devoted yourselves to like adventures? How many of you will volunteer to carry these spiritual messages of liberties to the world? How many of you will forego anything except your allegiance to that which is just and that which is right? We die but once and we die without distinction, if we are not willing to die the death of sacrifice. Do you covet honor? You will never get it by serving yourself. Do you covet distinction? You will get it only as a servant of mankind. Do you forget then, as you walk these classic places, why you are here? You are here not merely to prepare to make a living—you are here in order to enable the world to live more aptly, with greater vision, with a finer spirit of hope and achievement. You are here to enrich the world and you impoverish yourself if you forget the end.

The *Phoenix* editorial entitled "A Great Celebration" by Paul Cuncannon, '15, later Professor of Government at the University of Michigan, expressed the response of the under-graduates:

Never should the heart of an undergraduate or an Alumnus have vibrated with as much genuine respect for its Alma Mater as did the hearts of Swarthmoreans on Saturday last. Not alone did the hearers absorb the references to Swarthmore, their eloquence only seemed to intensify the beauty of general thought in the speech rendered. The underclassmen may have a right to feel proud over Saturday's picturesque story. To them it was a revelation; to the gray-haired Alumnus, it was a realization. . . . Was it any wonder that the hearts were deeply touched as they literally sang "Staunch and gray, Thou stand'st before us, on the campus fair—Thy high spirit guarding o'er us, who Thy blessing share."[4]

This quotation from the Swarthmore Alma Mater as a fitting climax to such a deep feeling illustrates the changed responses that the passage of time has wrought. No under-graduate today can be induced to learn the words of Alma Mater or to sing it except under the compulsion of the commencement exercises. It is "kid stuff." And the speeches of that day that lent fervor to Alma Mater also reveal a marked difference. Even Woodrow Wilson, whose protest against the side shows swallowing up the main tent was so widely quoted, joined the educators of his day in expressing doubt about the ultimate significance of learning, except as, in the process of acquiring it, eternal principles that form character and per-

»« *Conformity to worldly ways*

sonality may be absorbed. And he had the courage to assert what he thought some of those principles were and to appeal to the emotions of his hearers for their support.

The enthusiastic response to appeals of visiting speakers was heightened by the general esteem for persuasive personalities in spreading the sway of "the conventional wisdom." The national honorary public speaking fraternity Delta Sigma Rho installed a chapter at Swarthmore in 1910; almost all of its members became distinguished and influential alumni. Its annual initiation ceremonies in 1915 were typical of its proceedings. It was a large public occasion graced by a nationally-known preacher and Chautauqua lecturer, Dr. N. Magee Watters, who spoke on "The Omnipotence of the Spoken Word." Citing compelling examples, he concluded: "Always the people who talk are the people who draw the world to themselves. Every great crisis in the world's history has lingered on the spoken word. Lovers, mothers, poets, prophets, teachers have always been the rulers of the world." The response of the *Phoenix* was equally enthusiastic about the substance and the art of the speech.

Another student institution for uniting feeling through appeals to an audience was the Ivy oration. Each year, in connection with the Class Day exercises of the graduating class, a senior was chosen to deliver an oration at the planting of the class Ivy. The exercises also included the placing of a stone in the walls of Parrish Hall that carried a class motto—first in Greek, later in Latin, and finally in English—until the whole idea of mottoes, proverbs, and "conventional wisdom" fell into disrepute while a belief arose that class spirit and Class Day exercises were idle sentimentalities that should be, and were, abolished. The Ivy orator spoke to an audience of students suffused with feeling about their approaching departure from a loved spot, and he usually spoke with affectionate loyalty of the ideals that should dominate their future. After reading many of these orations,[5] which in those days were often printed in full in the *Phoenix* and which presented interesting variations in student interpretations of college life and its influence, one cannot help regarding them as significant reflections of the times, moods, and personalities of their day.

Hugh Denworth, '16, later a banker, spoke about the significance of the ivy as a symbol from ancient legends down to contemporary literature, and perhaps best exemplified the literary tradition in these speeches. Columnist Drew Pearson, '19, appealed solemnly to the sense of duty toward the future, taking as texts the last recorded words of four Swarthmore boys who died in World War I. Detlev Bronk, '20, later president of Johns Hopkins and the Rockefeller Institute, gave the most affectionate and nostalgic pleas for loyalty to the college. James A. Michener, '29, the author, showed the earlier stages of the critical spirit on the campus:

For the Faculty only the student exists; for the student body, only the big-man-on-the-campus. So far the main failing of the college has been the impossibility of reconciling these two differing classes.

Clark Kerr, '32, later president of the University of California, showed still further the changing attitudes of Ivy orators and students:

In former days, class day exercises of wills, prophecies, histories and the like, served a need, aroused large interest, and were well done. During recent years, the need, the interest, and the successful presentation of the exercises have largely disappeared. Loyalty in past years has been largely expressed by attendance at athletic contests. Organized athletics, however, seems to be in a period of decline. The loyalty expressed through these channels will have to have some other outlet. Our student body is changing and their activities and interests are also in a period of transition toward intellectual pursuits. . . . I suggest that the college make an increasing effort to arouse Alumni interest in the intellectual activities of the college.

Class days and Ivy orations survived Mr. Kerr's pronouncement for ten years, when the war with its year-round schedules helped in the destruction of many leisurely commencement activities. But Class Day, with its orations, was never revived, and the few suggestions that they should be resumed met with a shudder from undergraduates. Clark Kerr was right in saying that the increasingly dominant young intellectuals would regard the friendly intimacy, the gay humor and oratorical interpretation of college years as sentimental and juvenile.

Along with any lament for the passing of the loyalties of old-fashioned rhetoric should go the recognition that today's college students listen to many more speeches than their predecessors. The number of student organizations whose chief activity is importing speakers is legion. These speakers have much more specialized knowledge, make fewer appeals to general principles, avoid moralizing, deal more in criticism than praise, and are more subjected to rigorous questioning. They aid in producing the highly controversial and critical atmosphere that now prevails. Every national cause has its speakers bureau with attention trained on the college campus, and the representatives of these causes often inspire protest marchers among the students.

A triumphant example of a surviving but changing tradition is the compulsory weekly assembly known as "Collection." It has survived generations of student attacks, and now has their hearty support. The students are active on the committee that suggests speakers and programs, and show a great versatility of ideas in selecting speakers who can appeal to the young intellectuals. Scientific research, literary figures, the performing arts, foreign visitors of significance, political and economic issues, philosophical and religious values—all are represented and given impressive attention if the students are convinced that they are not listening to platitudes. Any student who can convince the president that he sincerely objects to compulsory attendance may be excused if he will agree to stay away from all the scheduled collections. This group of excused students, once a club of twenty, has declined to three members at the present writing. Rhetoric in its higher sense does continue to excite adolescent intellectuals, even if it more often divides than unites them.

## High-jinks and hazing

Some of the same feelings of affectionate loyalty that supported the orators of the day also supported the ancient and primitive custom of hazing. It was in part a reflection of the belief that the rebellious adolescent should realize the necessity of conforming to the traditional institutions of the new society he was entering as he left his home and family. There was no question that the traditions of the campus were superior to any assertions of an individual. Submissiveness was enforced by such freshman customs as wearing a garnet cap with green button, tipping this cap to all seniors, no wearing of conspicuous socks or ties, and no placing of class numerals on college property, with variations from time to time. Added to these were the various forms of class struggles between the freshmen and sophomores, with elaborate rules for governing keg fights, poster fights, tugs of war, and the like. These events often dominated student feelings during early days of the school year with much more intensity than Orientation Week produces now. They aroused class loyalties and a sense of participation in school life. But while there was no doubt of the need to make the spirit of the place felt, by enforcing traditions upon newcomers, there were various reactions to the procedures, with their frequent excesses. One of the approving comments was an editorial in the *Phoenix* by the editor, John E. Orchard, '16, later a distinguished professor at Columbia and a member of the Swarthmore Board of Managers. Reviewing the chief factors for the high morale of the student body, he wrote with hearty approval of the class scrap:

To the incoming students these class scraps will be an educational factor of themselves. Since there are many student government regulations and college traditions to be learned which are not in the annual catalogue, if approached in the right spirit, they will be invaluable in getting the newcomers acquainted with their fellow classmen.

But in another year national excesses in student fights were creating serious difficulties, and in April 1916 a *Phoenix* editorial declared:

Since the fatality of the bull fight at the University of Pennsylvania, there has been much agitation in the college world against the continuance of the custom of underclass scraps. Williams, Purdue, and many other colleges have taken similar steps. At Swarthmore we have a contest just as dangerous in its rivalry as the bull fight of the University or the flag scrap of Penn State. Our annual Keg rush between the Freshmen and Sophomores cannot be defended as a safe outlet for class rivalry. . . . But by abolishing the Keg Rush, the need for it would not be removed. There must still be some form of contest between the two lower classes to develop healthy class rivalry and class spirit. . . . A college is inconceivable without some kind of class rivalry to produce spirit and loyalty.

The attacks on hazing also conceded that underclass discipline of some kind was a necessity. On April 18, 1916, the *Phoenix* said:

Three years ago the Men's Student Government Association attempted to reform hazing without abolishing it. General hazing was abandoned and in its place was substituted a form of discipline which was to accomplish all the good of hazing without any of the evils. In spite of all the arguments advanced in favor of the new system, it has proved to be an absolute failure. Hazing should neither be reformed nor modified. It should be abolished. . . . Underclass discipline is a necessity, but with a proper organization of it we believe that more respect will be shown by the Freshmen; that the college traditions will be observed and that many of the problems that are now so perplexing will disappear.

Even the strongest attack on hazing, written as a letter to the *Phoenix* two years earlier by Paul F. Gemmill, '17, now a distinguished economist, seems to admit a need to support traditions somehow:

The students who took part in a discussion of hazing at the recent meeting of the Men's Student Government, both the advocates and the opponents of this practice, were unanimous on one point—that the Freshmen must be taught to respect the upperclassmen and the traditions of Swarthmore College.

But those who were so warm in their defense of hazing of "the good old days," and even the students who supported the present system, seem to forget that true regard seldom comes to the man who demands it.

The mission of hazing is that of producing in the newcomer a love of the college and its traditions. Are we expected to take this suggestion seriously? Is it not, on the contrary, rather conceivable that the Freshman's affection for his Alma Mater would be turned to aversion if he should discover that she regards with indifference practices so repulsive that they would not be for a moment tolerated off the college campus?

Let the upperclassman determine, then, which brand of "respect" is the more desirable. If he is so petty as to crave cringing submission to his authority, then by all means let us have hazing, and plenty of it. But let him bear in mind that genuine esteem comes only as spontaneous recognition of true personal worth.

Despite vigorous attacks by eloquent intellectuals and individualists, hazing and class scraps continued for more than a decade as somehow satisfying the instincts of the dominant personalities on the campus. Arguments on this issue seem to have little effect on the type of personality that delights in physical domination; this type also seems to be able to accept such discipline with pleasure. Instead of feeling outraged at the insult to their personal dignity they seem to think with delight of the time to come when they will be top dog and to feel that the whole procedure is both healthy fun and a beneficial part of growing up. One of the best indictments of hazing that I have read was written by an Annapolis student as late as 1946. He wanted to enter Swarthmore, but not if such practices were condoned at the Quaker college. Consequently, he sent his manuscript to the dean to see what reception it would get. When he was satisfied that he would feel more at home at Swarthmore than at Annapolis, he resigned as a midshipman, published his attack in *The Atlantic*

*Monthly*,[6] entered Swarthmore, and graduated with a record of superior scholarship and student leadership. Ralph Lee Smith, '51, was the only student I have known who had an essay published in *The Atlantic* before entering Swarthmore, and I felt some pride in showing it to Swarthmore students and noting how enthusiastically they endorsed his position. The civilian colleges, he said, welcome the maturity of the post-war students, but the Naval Academy had no time for those who regarded its traditions as childish:

The plebe system is based upon the theory that it is permissible for one person to cause unnecessary discomfort to another person. It appeals to the narrow-minded, the unintelligent, and the very few actually sadistic members of the upper class. The men of intelligence and sympathy have no part in it. Ordinary college and fraternity initiation is nothing but tough and old-fashioned horseplay. It pretends to no lofty purposes or attainments. But in Annapolis it is carried out with the noblest pretensions and under the loftiest banners.

These generalizations are illustrated with some well-chosen examples from life at Annapolis; but when I showed the essay to a number of Naval officers, Annapolis graduates, they said, in effect: "Yes, he has his incidents and facts straight enough, but we loved it all and hope it never changes."

## Athletics

Differences in personality types are even more obvious in attitudes toward athletics. It would have been surprising to find such a physical specimen as President Swain wholly absorbed in his field of mathematics. Early in his administration he championed the cause of sports against the disapproval of some Quakers. A clipping from a Philadelphia daily preserved in the scrapbook of Howard Cooper Johnson, '96, very gaily captures the spirit of the conflict. Headed "Quaker Meeting An Arena for Sports," it reads:

Quaker Meeting at Fifteenth and Race Streets today was so engrossed in a discussion of school athletics, that the quaint house with its severely plain wooden benches rising in tiers might, with a slight exercise of the imagination, have been converted into a stadium. The question came up when the Committee having the management of George School submitted its annual report, which was read by Charles Francis Jenkins, Assistant Clerk of the session. Football, baseball, and the entire gamut of sports was run and their champions and opponents were as strenuous as ever a gridiron star was. Dr. Richard Darlington of West Chester Meeting insisted that a halt be called to a sport at Friends Institutions which, he said, had caused the deaths of over two hundred youths in the United States last year and had resulted in injuries more or less serious to nine hundred boys and young men. He said that football gave an impetus to the military spirit which was unfortunately too rampant in the country.

A venerable gray-bearded Friend from Abington rose and asserted that baseball as played at Abington, by young men in suits, was brutal. Friend Lukens Webster suggested that sawing of wood be substituted for sports as an outlet for surplus strenuosity. "There is just one objection that I desire to urge to Friend Webster's suggestion," interjected a Friend from a far corner. "My objection is that the Professors would be obliged to saw the wood." The sallie (*sic*) did not in the least disturb the gravity of the session. It was not until the giant form of President Swain of Swarthmore moved to the front of the Meeting House that the tide turned in the favor of school sports. He said, "Every boy and girl must have a playground. This committee could not, if it would, forbid participation in what is called 'Athletics.' My experience of twenty-five years with the young convinces me that they cannot do this. The athletic field is a necessity."

President Swain had found football in full vigor when he came to Swarthmore in 1902. That year Swarthmore had beaten New York University 11–0 and had held Penn to a score of 11–6. In 1905 Swarthmore beat Cornell 14–0, Lafayette 27–0, and Wesleyan 50–6. The Lafayette game was declared to be for the championship of the Middle States, and *The Philadelphia Ledger* published pictures of President Swain in the grandstand along with the Mayor of Philadelphia, Isaac Clothier, and Joseph Wharton. The *Ledger* said of the whole season:

Swarthmore has had a team this season which no small college has ever before surpassed. The players have been the pride of the College but have also been greatly admired by the entire East. The victory against Cornell was probably the greatest surprise of the season for Swarthmore as well as for Cornell.

At the football rally and celebration of the Wesleyan victory President Swain was the chief speaker, supported by alumni and faculty.

At this time there was a national agitation against the brutality of football, and college presidents met with President Roosevelt to see what could be done about it. President Sharpless of Haverford was quoted in Philadelphia papers as saying:

It would have been an easy matter for Haverford under the guise of scholarships to have bought up a ton or so of muscle and made a football team, but we realize that football and other sports are purely auxiliary to the college training, and we do not wish to lose the respect of Alumni, undergraduates, or our own respect by converting the institution into a football factory.

The *Illustrated Outdoor News* printed an article by Joseph Swain on reconstructing the game of football. Swain did not take too seriously the charges of brutality. He said football was rough but not necessarily brutal. He also approved of not permitting an undergraduate who came from another school to play on the college team the first year. But it is obvious that, in the main, President Swain was a supporter of football.

An unexpected test soon came about. Anna T. Jeans, a wealthy and philanthropic Quaker lady whose benefactions have enriched Philadelphia life and who felt that Swarthmore's overemphasis on football was taking it from its Quaker traditions, left an estate of coal lands, at first reported to be worth three million dollars, to the college on condition that it abolish intercollegiate football.[7] Soon the value of the lands had shrunk, according to newspaper reports, to one million dollars. When the committee of Quakers appointed by the Board to investigate presented their report, they estimated that the land was worth no more than forty thousand dollars and probably less than that. But President Swain, acting promptly on principle, had already written to leading college and university presidents, asking their advice on the acceptance of gifts with strings that bound the future of the college. President Benjamin Ide Wheeler of the University of California and many others wrote that by accepting such a gift the college would be governed by the dead hand of the past and that the gift should be refused. The Board confirmed the judgment of President Swain and his colleagues, and refused the gift. However, the following expression of opinion is recorded in the minutes:

The Board again affirms its belief and sympathy with many of the views as to intercollegiate athletics which have been expressed by Friends from time to time, especially in *The Intelligencer,* and it is believed that good may grow out of the otherwise fruitless discussion, and that a healthful and restraining influence may result not only at Swarthmore, but over a wide field. To this end we recommend that the President and the Faculty consider the widespread concern of the Friends on the subject, with which concern we sympathize.

In the process of reaching this decision, and in order to show that he had an open mind on the subject, President Swain did suspend football for the season of 1908. When it was resumed the following year, with a much poorer team, many Quakers felt that the guidance of the inner light had been abandoned in favor of worldly diplomacy. As one correspondent protested in *The Philadelphia Ledger:*

Would the Friends of George Fox's day have written to all the leading colleges for opinions to strengthen their position? Would they not rather have gone apart into their secret closet and closed the door and asked the Father's will about it all, and hearing, given it fearlessly to the world as the Father's will?

As the Friends turn more to the outer world, and they are doing it, they are losing that spiritual power which was given them freely in the early days of the Society.

For a couple of years after the hiatus of 1908 the Swarthmore football scores were substantially lower, but they soon started to climb again. In 1916 Swarthmore beat Penn and Columbia, but, *mirabile dictu*, was beaten by Haverford. In 1917, when Swarthmore scored 238 points to its opponents' 40, it beat Haverford 57–7, and Haverford severed relations with many charges of professionalism. But this did not seem to lessen the pride of Swarthmoreans in their victories. The *Phoenix* turned to impressive quotations from current articles, citing the number of governors, senators, judges, ambassadors, mayors, attorneys general, and industrialists who had played football. The student paper repeated quotations from many of these men to the effect that football had been the strongest influence in preparing them for public leadership. And there is a statement from William Rittman, Swarthmore '01, whose researches in chemistry contributed notably to the development of our weapons in World War I, saying that only his football training enabled him to concentrate for such long hours in the laboratory. Anyone who cares to look through the list of names of players on the football teams of President Swain's administration will be impressed by the private success and public influence of these men. He will not be content to characterize them as several tons of muscle bought by the college. He may not be certain to what extent football merely developed personal characteristics that were already present, but certainly the sport added to their dominance on the campus and increased the prestige of the "command presence."

But it was not only personal dominance that was exerted. The genial warmth of the physically inclined students was rewarded by food and fellowship at the homes of alumni who loved the athletes. Dr. Edward Martin, '78, a distinguished surgeon who was Commissioner of Health for Philadelphia and for whom the Martin Laboratory is named, for many years entertained the teams and their dates either at his farm home on the Crum or at Lamb's Tavern. The *Phoenix* writer obviously expects the whole school to glow with pleasure at his account of such an occasion:

The annual Martin's May Moon Meeting for the football men and their best girls was held at the home of Dr. and Mrs. Edward Martin. About thirty-five couples attended, and every individual who was fortunate enough to be included declared it to be absolutely the greatest event of the year. Starting with the ride over from Parish Hall to the beautiful home in Crum Valley, the good time ended only when the two big four-horse busses discharged their passengers at the head of the Asphaltum again, just as the chimes were striking twelve.

This personal warmth toward the students was displayed by many alumni, whose fondness for the college was stimulated most frequently by athletics. For years Morris Clothier, '90, seldom missed football practice, to say nothing of the games. He conceived the idea of putting the names of the graduates on plaques in the dining room; to insure the project's success, he paid the bill for the first forty-one tablets. The warmth of his feeling is shown in the conclusion of a letter he wrote to the *Phoenix:*

Now that the task is done and the tablets are in place, one feels anew the thrill of loyalty to the college as one views the names of those who after four years or more of life within the walls of Alma Mater, have passed from thence into the world of business and professional life with her stamp of approval upon their academic standing. Already many of the names engraved there in enduring brass are written large upon the scroll of fame. Swarthmore men and Swarthmore women are achieving distinction in all walks of life, and as the years roll on and each new group of graduates passes from college into active participation in the affairs of the world, it will be the delight of all Swarthmoreans to see upon the walls of our college buildings the names of many who shall add to the fair name and fame of our Alma Mater.

This hopeful sharing of future fame spread over into affectionate remembrance of the humble, and there were tablets to the memory of watchmen and servants, with a loving observation of their habits and peculiarities.

## Seeds of skepticism

The approach of World War I turned the attention of the undergraduates increasingly toward national and world affairs. The *Phoenix* devoted more space to these issues and to what Swarthmore students should do about them. In comparison with such questions some of the campus activities seemed trivial, and the term "goat-feathers" was increasingly applied to many pursuits that previously seemed all-important. These early criticisms did not immediately threaten the dominant institutions of the campus, but they did decrease their importance. The issues of the war, of course, overshadowed all others for a time. There was deep concern, both individually and institutionally, as to the course of action for Quakers. President Swain declared that he stood ready to help any student in following any course of action that his conscience dictated. After considerable hesitation and delay the Student Army Training Corps was placed upon the campus, but without guns. This acutely embarrassing situation endured for only a short time, and was terminated by the ending of the war. THE HALCYON for 1919 was a war memorial issue, and contains accounts that deserve to live.

Even before the end of the war, critical restlessness increased. In 1916 there were eloquent letters to the *Phoenix* from women who belonged to sororities but had developed grave doubts about them. And there were equally eloquent letters of reply by men who regarded fraternities and sororities as guardians of the most precious values of campus life. By 1919 President Swain had to ask for a truce in the fraternity debate for a year.

The criticism of Swarthmore football as involving athletic scholarships emerged into the open in letters to the *Phoenix*, and the charges seemed to be sustained by the evidence. The editorial columns renewed the criticisms that students were as seriously deluded by "goat-feathers" as the Kaiser's men were by uniforms and medals. The hope was expressed that

the veterans will come back with a pretty accurate idea of what braid and tinsel amount to in the world. They write back that when they return they will turn from the goat-feathered froth to the rougher road of work.

This they did, and there are many evidences that the college was ready to welcome the changes that were to come with President Aydelotte. But the vigorous fight put up by the alumni of the college of the Swain era against later changes at Swarthmore that seemed to threaten their values shows their loyalty—not wholly nostalgic—to the influences that most of them passionately believed had prepared them for the struggles and successes of their later years.

Perhaps the most discerning judgment as to the power and limitations of these campus institutions in molding personality was made by a distinguished alumnus who was inwardly an "intellectual," an individualist, and a nonconformist, but who drove himself to the peaks of success as measured by all the altitude markers of the campus in his day.

As an indication of Alan C. Valentine's place in the estimation of the students and faculty, I quote the words of an editorial by a contemporary, Richard Slocum, '22, an editor of the *Phoenix* and later managing editor of *The Philadelphia Bulletin*:

*Scholar, Athlete, Man*

In all the long list of Swarthmore graduates to whom honor is due, there is none we delight so much to honor as Alan C. Valentine, newly elected Rhodes Scholar from Pennsylvania. Others may have equalled him in ability and character, but none, it seems to us, have excelled. His record testifies to his ability as a scholar, an athlete, and a leader of men.

His citation as Ivy orator recalled that he was on the debating team as a freshman; played football for the next three years; served as class president, captain of Varsity debate team, editor of the *Phoenix,* and president of the Men's Student Government Committee; was elected to Phi Beta Kappa; and was a member of Book and Key, Kwink, and Delta Sigma Rho.

Now let us look at the picture as recollected by Alan Valentine years later in the chapter on his Swarthmore days entitled "In Pursuit of Praise" in his autobiography TRIAL BALANCE.[8] He writes about himself in the third person, usually referring to himself as "Angus":

He accepted the general opinion that the real measure of collegiate success was the length of the list of honors, from football to Phi Beta Kappa, after one's name in the college yearbook. The "all-round man" was the most popular while in college and the most likely to be offered a good job on graduation. Even as a freshman, Angus suspected that most all-round college heroes were not first rate in anything, but that suspicion did not deter him from wanting to be one. He liked to be different, but schooldays had finally convinced him of the advantages of keeping in line.

His real independence was soon tested, and on the issue that would trouble him always—his personal relations to organized society. Even before he set foot on the Swarthmore campus he met it in a seductive form. In spite of the fact that the college offered an intense social life of its own, that its smallness called for close internal social unity, and that it professed the simplicity and democracy of Quaker ideals, fraternities flourished there and three-quarters of the students belonged to them. . . . There were many good reasons for joining. Not to do so would disappoint a cousin who had been graduated from Swarthmore as president of his class and a leading member of Phi Kappa Psi. The boys he met there were the most attractive he had ever seen, and he was flattered as only a freshman can be flattered by the attentions of urbane and potent upperclassmen. The few men who declined fraternity membership were regarded resentfully by men of all fraternities as socially subversive. Most of the attractive girls were members of sororities that had informal "sister" affiliations with the men's fraternities, and did not "date" with nonfraternity men. The fraternities were powerful units in college elections, and Angus's ambitions for college honors were almost certain to be frustrated if he lacked fraternity backing.

Yet many of Angus's instincts opposed his joining. College fraternities seemed in principle undemocratic, and arguments to the contrary were unquestionably specious. The basic lure of membership was to belong to something exclusive, and because he had known the pains of being excluded he disliked the effect of the system on those who were being left out. . . .

Angus staggered everyone, including himself, by declining to join. Under heavy pressure he agreed to reconsider after a month, and the intervening period was a trying one. . . . The pressures were too much, and the attractions too, and before the month was up—a little ashamed of himself for giving in so quickly—Angus joined. The results were on the whole happy, and he discovered that once he had established himself as a figure of importance in college, he could be more independent in his friendships than he had thought the fraternity would allow, and in his Senior year, against the strong pleas of his fraternity, he roomed with a friend who, being a Jew, was a nonfraternity man.

Angus wanted success; college and society were teaching him what success was, and the practical ways of gaining it. . . . To agree with Lincoln Steffens, even to admire Norman Thomas, while a Sophomore in college, was a healthy sign of an open mind, and a warm heart, but one should recognize it as a stage through which one must pass, and restrain oneself from words and activities that might later be embarrassing. . . . The quest for personal standing should precede the quest for the welfare of society. All this was in the atmosphere one breathed, and Angus and his classmates, with only exceptional and minor groups, accepted it.

Quakerism seemed on the whole to provide the most reasonable basis on which he might ultimately build his personal religion. He liked its simplicity and its emphasis on "Faith through works." It appealed to him particularly because it let him alone. By making each man directly responsible to God it left it to the individual to decide when and how he would call upon Him. And best of all, if a man might follow his inner light, then he could believe as he pleased and still be a Quaker; no one could overrule him except God, and Angus felt that he had reached a mutually satisfactory arrangement with Him.

In social, political, and religious attitudes Swarthmore was not much different from other colleges of the time, but it did create habits of living more sensible lives than many of them. Its social sanity redeemed its overemphasis on social respectability. In rather different ways than its Faculty intended, the college prepared its students for the century they would live in, where one could be successful without ideas and happy without excellence if one accepted majority opinion and got on well with people of one's kind.

Such is the picture of conformity at Swarthmore painted by one who experienced similar feelings of inner emptiness in his conformities at Oxford, at Yale, as University of Rochester president, and as a figure in public life. Some thirty years later, in 1956, he concluded:

No man can find unity with others until he has learned to live in understanding and amity with himself. . . . When unity is carried to excessive conformity, or organized to excessive complexity, it is harmful; when diversity destroys social order or fosters rampant egos, it is harmful. Human history can be viewed as a constant struggle between unity and diversity, and civilization as society's effort to find the proper balance between them.

To Angus, conformity at Swarthmore brought every success, and at the time that was most important to his happiness. To many others conformity brought the pleasures of loyalty, enthusiasm, and satisfaction, unaccompanied by his inner skepticism. To those who would not or could not conform, it gave the feeling of being an outsider, and this, in some cases, was a stimulus to achieve satisfactions elsewhere. But the point that seems pretty clearly established is that, for better or worse, it was a period of conformity; and that, in general, it was a conformity cheerfully and happily accepted until a more critical intellectualism began to assert the values of individualism.

# 4

# Revolt of the intellectuals

When Joseph Swain's failing health brought about his retirement after twenty years as president, there was universal regret that such a wise, distinguished, and beloved leader was no longer to direct the conspicuous progress of the college. There were scattered expressions of dissatisfaction with the low level of intellectual life, expressed chiefly by the able scholars he had brought to the faculty. These faults had been laid at the door of the collegiate life of the times, lamented by so many critics of the American college, and there was hope that a new leader might advance the progress that Swain had made. All this made it natural to look to Swain for his choice of a successor. In view of his successful faculty appointments drawn from Indiana, it was not entirely strange that he should nominate as president a man who also had grown up in rural Indiana.

## President Aydelotte and the academic lock step

Frank Aydelotte distinguished himself, after his graduation from Swain's Alma Mater, the University of Indiana, as a football coach, a Rhodes Scholar, a teacher of English at Massachusetts Institute of Technology, and the author of distinctive essays on teaching, literature, and the values of an Oxford education. His own career aims were becoming more clear and definite to him. He would assault mediocrity in American life by breaking the academic lock step and giving a new freedom to the gifted and creative student. His most difficult choice at this stage was to decide whether the Swarthmore presidency would be a step toward the achievement of this purpose. As he said in a letter to President John Nason long afterward, he spent his time on his first visit to Swarthmore

in going from one member of the faculty to another, saying to each that it had been suggested to me that I should become President of Swarthmore, that I was not interested in becoming just another college president; but that if there was any chance of working out the Honors plan, I would be distinctly interested. It was the replies I got from these queries which decided me to accept and you know, of course, how gloriously the Swarthmore faculty vindicated my decision.

In setting down some results of the Aydelotte intellectual revolution at Swarthmore, it might be observed paradoxically that many of the personal characteristics that made for Aydelotte's success were not intellectual. He had none of those qualities of detachment, reserve, coldness, introversion, and alternating superiority and self-doubt so often attributed to intellectuals. He was warm, enthusiastic, self-confident, interested in others, bent on action, intensely competitive, and not given to philosophical dialectic. His most extensive bit of research, ELIZABETHAN ROGUES AND VAGABONDS,[1] was not a reflective book; it was done under the direction of Professor Walter Raleigh of Oxford, who made no secret of his dislike for academic life and academics and who would much rather have been an Elizabethan explorer than a Shakespearean scholar.

Although Frank Aydelotte was a spokesman for the intellectual life, he would not have understood or approved some of its later consequences in the intellectual revolts on the campus. He never would have condoned cynicism, skepticism, and pessimism on the ground that these were attitudes common to many intellectuals. He did not see any necessary connection between intellectuals and radicalism; he often said publicly that a college should be ahead of its time intellectually, but, in its attitudes and mores, it was just as well to be half a generation behind socially. He did not believe that there was necessarily any conflict between the established social institutions of the campus and the good life. He enthusiastically helped to raise money for new fraternity and sorority lodges, and supported senior honorary societies. His most revolutionary extracurricular step was to insist, as a condition of accepting the presidency, that there should be no athletic scholarships.[2] This did not seem to him to involve any necessary decrease in the intensity of the games or delight in watching the play, although he shared the British belief that the game should be played for the fun of it and that students generally might well be more interested in playing than in watching. He had little of the intellectual's superiority to nonintellectual interests, and when he often advocated intensity as the most essential quality of college life, he did not mean to restrict it to intellectual pursuits.

There were intellectual revolutions fomenting at Harvard and Yale about this time, but in general it may be said that it was about thirty-five years after Aydelotte first showed concern over the special stimulation of the intellectually gifted that this kind of concern became nation-wide and spread to all levels of the educational processes. It was not surprising, therefore, that Aydelotte, although originally supported by his faculty and increasing numbers of the students, faced widespread opposition among the alumni. It was not merely that football victories declined to a point where traditional competitors had to be abandoned, with consequent decline of campus morale, or that Honors students were regarded as a little group of English tea hounds, who did not count in the serious affairs of the campus even as they had not counted in the school life before college. There was a fear that qualities of character and leadership were endangered. The alumni were very proud of the prestige conferred upon the college by the political and business leadership of its graduates, but they were not yet conscious of the prestige created by the production of Ph.D.'s. They were in the habit of associating leadership with vigor on the athletic field, fraternity presidencies, Book and Key membership, and class loyalties and activities. The student body selected its leaders for the same qualities that brought recognition in the world of affairs. The feelings of the alumni were forcefully expressed by William Tomlinson, '17, when, as the newly elected president of the Alumni Club, he addressed the annual banquet of the Swarthmore Club in February 1935. President Aydelotte's program had been in operation for a dozen years, and many influential alumni urged Tomlinson to express their fears for the college. Writing from his office as vice president of Temple University to give permission to quote from a speech given twenty-five years earlier, Tomlinson said:

If I were to deliver the "Men Wanted" speech today it would be a vastly different declaration; but I still believe ardently in the potential of the whole man, and I have the feeling that today's Swarthmore recognizes that the human being must be endowed with resources beyond the purely intellectual if he is to be effective under the stresses and challenges of modern life.

However, he feels that he did speak in a manner that represented the feelings of those who elected him president of the alumni. Anyone acquainted with their feelings in those days will agree that he spoke with moderation. The entire speech is still symbolic of the times, as illustrated by these excerpts:

Over the years, Swarthmore has sent forth her sons into wide and diverse fields of the world's work. They have won honor and distinction in the professions, in public service, in education and in a host of other high callings. A study of the statistics, however, reveals that something over 70 per cent of Swarthmore men eventually find themselves pursuing careers directly associated with some form of business or industry. If my analysis is correct, after the first three or four years of adjustment, some 72 per cent of Swarthmore men finally select business or industry as their calling, while approximately 15 per cent enter educational fields. About

5 per cent study medicine and about the same number enter the Law. The remaining 3 per cent engage in Public Service and other callings.

Such is the apparent capacity of the varying branches of the world's work to absorb Swarthmore men. In my mind this distribution of our trained human resources is a wholesome and fortunate one because it indicates that the influence of Swarthmore is flowing through the channels of life's activities in almost representative proportions.

There are those who cry out dismally that we face diminishing opportunities in business and industry. That is the lament of the Defeatist. We have resumed our forward march and we see bearing aloft the encouraging signs, "Men Wanted."

Men Wanted: and what manner of men will be wanted? Whatever else they may possess as qualifications they must be men of mentality, courage, determination, understanding and vision. For these are the qualities of leadership—and leadership is the hope of our nation. . . .

The qualities of courage and determination may be developed in a variety of college activities; they are derived particularly from college athletics. I saw these qualities of courage and determination manifested in a way that thrilled me with pride last fall when the Swarthmore football team played Amherst. Those of us who watched that game instinctively felt that Amherst had the more powerful team. But a superior courage and determination—and the will to win—triumphed for Swarthmore. And my only regret is that this unconquerable spirit has not played a still greater part in the destiny of Swarthmore teams—and that it has not permeated more deeply the whole student body. . . .

There is abroad today in the ranks of the alumni the fear that men are being selected for Swarthmore on the basis of scholastic attainments without proper regard for the broader qualities of manhood. There is the fear that the purely academic functions of Swarthmore are crowding out those vital activities that have to do with the development of ruggedness, courage, determination and better human understanding.

As President of the Alumni Association of Swarthmore, I am all too conscious of these fears. And they are dangerous and unfortunate, not only because of their own implications, but because they seem to be driving a wedge between Swarthmore and a large part of her alumni body.

Here we have represented the dominant physical type and the dominant philosophy of the Swarthmore graduate of the Swain era: hardly Quaker, rather the noble Roman; ambitious, courageous, and energetic; interested in the achievement of political or economic power; resolving doubts by vigorous action; regarding competitors as forces to be opposed as resolutely as rival athletic teams, but loyal to the rules of the game and impatient of quibbles over them. These attitudes had been characteristic of those the alumni had shown during undergraduate years in relation to problems of school discipline. The college rules were often broken boisterously, but they were not attacked with philosophic arguments. They were rules of society and accepted as such, and offenders endured their punishment. Learning was not a matter of prime importance. They were assured of this over and over, even by such educators as Woodrow Wilson. They were told that they would soon forget their textbooks and examination questions, that what mattered was character and attitudes developed in the years of schooling. But what alumni heard about the college under the new program of President Aydelotte filled them with the feeling that what had been a preparation for Wall Street or political leadership was becoming an introduction to Greenwich Village or to permanent seclusion in the groves of academe.

What was it they heard about the college, and how did they hear it? The football scores, of course, spoke for themselves, as did the dropping of the old rivals and the decline of athletic morale. One of the more conspicuous changes was in the character of the college paper, the *Phoenix*. Although it had formerly conducted crusades for college improvement in various ways, its dominant tone had been one of loyalty and enthusiasm. It was widely read by alumni, partly for the excellent alumni notes provided by Caroline Lukens, '98, and partly because it was believed to be representative of the opinions of the student body as a whole. The alumni and faculty were represented on the board of control of the paper, and editorial policies were discussed in relation to their representative character. But early in President Aydelotte's administration this was overthrown as imposing limitations on the freedom of the press. The advisory board had vetoed the *Phoenix* staff's choice of an editor on the ground that his contributions to the paper had outraged both student and alumni opinion and that as editor he needed to recognize that he had something of a representative function. This was explicitly denied by the staff. The veto on this particular editor stood, but the board was abolished and student independence was effectively established. Occasional faculty advisers were appointed, but none of them cared to act as censors or to take initiative in bringing their opinions to bear. Freedom of opinion and its expression was unquestioned, and there were no sacred cows. Published letters and editorials on campus affairs became almost wholly critical. The curriculum and the Honors programs were vigorously attacked; news of campus social affairs made way for reports of the activities of the American Student Union, the Swarthmore Improvement Association, the East-West Society, the Young Progressives Association, the Liberal Club, and the Forum for Free Speech. There were full reports of Communist and alleged Communist speakers, who were usually questioned vigorously by many students; but even these joined in the general satisfaction that freedom of speech was not challenged. Existing campus institutions—sororities, fraternities, honorary societies such as Mortar Board and Book and Key—were attacked as undemocratic; rules of the college concerning liquor, cars, and limitations for men and women in each other's dormitory rooms were assailed; almost every disciplinary case produced letters and editorials raising philosophical objections to rules that were regarded as unjustifiable infringements on individual freedom. In occasional letters alumni objected to the generally negative attitudes, but their principal reaction was to drop subscriptions and to support the new alumni publication, which has since developed into a superior organ of communication that emphasizes the achievements of students, faculty, and alumni. These achievements do much to show that adolescent rebellion has its educational values and often leads to constructive careers.

## Demise of sororities

Among the various institutions attacked by Swarthmore intellectuals, the sororities were the first to go. Neither the fraternities nor sororities at Swarthmore ever had any residential functions, and it is usually assumed that they were therefore less influential and less divisive in a small college community. Three national sororities were established at Swarthmore from 1891 to 1893. Although they created strong loyalties and enthusiasm and gave a sense of national significance to this rural Quaker college, they had too few members to give the outsiders a feeling of not belonging. From 1912 to 1919 three more national sororities were formed and flourished; they raised the total membership to something like 85 per cent of the women students and established (along with the fraternities) the dominant tone of the campus social life. The small minority of dissatisfied students (including a number of members) suffered in silence. There was a feeble agitation in 1911, and the *Phoenix* staff of 1913 launched an attack for which it received little support. It is of interest to note that when Professor R. C. Brooks, in 1922, asked for confidential autobiographies in a course in "Political Motives," both men and women protested the effects of sororities on their lives, but were unwilling to have their names made known in the publicity that Professor Brooks gave to his results.

A seventh sorority was founded in 1928 and received its national charter in 1930. This occasioned a public discussion of the situation in which the seven sororities left the few outsiders conspicuous and ostracized. The fat was in the fire. A determined group, the most prominent of whom were sorority members, led the attack.

Scattered letters and comments about the women's fraternities began to appear in the *Phoenix* in 1928. Some of them

are editorial comments apropos of suggested changes in rushing rules and other matters of procedure. The first editorial to
take serious notice of the situation, entitled "The Fraternity
Question," was published in November 1931. (Throughout
the Swarthmore discussion the sororities are referred to as
"women's fraternities.") The editorial read in part as follows:

It is obvious that at the present time the Swarthmore women are
going through a period of social unrest. Part of this unsettled social
condition is due to the fraternity system, and it is the discussion
of this question that will be brought to a focus at the meeting of
fraternity and nonfraternity representatives tomorrow.

The real underlying question, stripped of all unessentials, is:
Is there a place for fraternities on the campus as small as Swarthmore and in a college in which the ideals are fundamentally opposed to any restriction on individual freedom? Basically the problem is for both men and women to solve. However, it must be
admitted that the social side of college life does play a more important part in a woman's undergraduate life than in that of a man.

The edtiorial went on to summarize all the suggestions that
had been made to date for improving the situation and then
concluded:

A real step towards social readjustment would be made if the
women of Swarthmore would grasp the idea that fundamentally
the fraternity system is at odds with a much broader conception of
college life, and that a small college can thrive more contentedly
without fraternities than with them. If the women seeking a more
mature perspective would realize that almost all the advantages of
the fraternity system could be obtained in other social groups, and
that most of the disadvantages of the present system could be
alleviated by a readjustment into simpler social principles, then a
real step would be achieved towards the solution of this problem.

In tracing through the utterances of the *Phoenix* on this
subject it becomes obvious that most of the writers are anti-
fraternity people. It is of course nearly always true that the
objectors to any system are more vocal and that all college

papers have increasingly become agents of reform. But if one attempts to cite the personality of any three or four radical or ultraradical reformers in such a movement as this, it will be seen that this is not really a wholly adequate explanation, because the agitation continued over too long a time and too many people participated in it. But some will speculate that an increasing proportion of the student body was composed of "nonaffiliative" types.

Before Christmas of 1931 the situation had crystallized to the point where President Aydelotte was asked to address a meeting of the fraternity and nonfraternity women and to comment specifically upon the various proposals that had been made to remedy the situation. As the administration's part in this whole affair has been so much discussed, it is worth quoting from his speech at some length:

In commenting on the progress of the discussions of the fraternity problem, I should like in the first place to emphasize the point that this discussion was not originated by me, or by the faculty of the college, but rather by student and graduate members of the fraternities. I emphasize this for the information of friends of the college outside who may find it difficult to believe.

As you all know there have been during the past few years two movements originated entirely by undergraduates for the abolition of fraternities. So far as I am aware no member of the faculty took any part whatever in either movement, as I certainly did not myself. Undergraduate social life ought to be a matter for undergraduates themselves to manage and I should like to emphasize the point that so far as the faculty is concerned, this is your problem and to you will be left the problem of solving it.

I wish to say very frankly that I approve strongly of the discussion, that I feel it is timely and needed, and that I admire very much the spirit in which the undergraduate girls of the college have attacked the problem.

I can readily understand the surprise which is felt by the public at large that we should have here a group of undergraduates who are too keen and too idealistic to accept the highly artificial working of the fraternity system as if it were one of the laws of nature.

I congratulate you on your realization of the difficulties of the fraternity plan as it works here at present and upon your determination to improve it.

When I spoke to you three weeks ago I expressed the wish that your discussions would not be too long drawn out. I begrudge the time which the leaders of the undergraduate body are compelled to give to these discussions. I know that most of you are leaders not merely in social affairs, but in your studies as well and that this fraternity discussion necessarily interferes a great deal with your academic work. Nevertheless I should like to say that I hope you will not hurry your decision. What you are trying to do is something new, undergraduate opinion is divided, and it is clearly the part of wisdom not to allow yourself to be hurried, but to take time for thorough discussion before acting.

What you are trying to do at Swarthmore is to create a more democratic and a more delightful social life. The task is an important one. It seems to me that in an educational institution, it ought to be a part of the training of character that you should learn to think that no distinction is really important which is not based upon merit. It is for this reason that I believe that you ought to contrive it so as to prevent fraternity membership from bulking too large in undergraduate life and from standing too near to the center of the stage.

When any new proposal is made the first thing thought of is objection to it, and I am told that a certain number of the fraternity women are so impressed with the objections and difficulties in the way of any kind of reform that they are coming to feel that perhaps the best solution is the total abolition of the fraternity. This may be the best course, but I myself am inclined to doubt its wisdom. It seems to me that there is a great deal about the fraternities which is good and that your task is to preserve that good and to eradicate the very real evils which now accompany it. My own predilections are always strongly in favor of reform rather than wholesale destruction. I want whatever solution is reached to be your own and I give you advice only for the sake of what you may find it to be worth, but I hope you will first explore every possible method of eradicating evils and of making the very real good which is inherent in the fraternity system available for everyone before you decide on its abolition.

61   »« *Revolt of the intellectuals*

I hope you will attack this problem in an experimental frame of mind. Any step you may take will not be irrevocable. If you try some solution which does not work, you or the next generation can try another. One of the fortunate things about our small size is that we can make experiments, can closely study their working, can alter them on short notice if necessity demands. If you approach the problem with the same experimental attitude that the faculty has already shown in problems of academic work, I shall be confident of your success.

In arriving at your decision you can have an opportunity not merely to make a great contribution to social life at Swarthmore, but also to do something for the American college fraternity as well. As you doubtless know, the fraternity system is under criticism from a large number of forward looking colleges and universities throughout the country. Many of the evils which you feel at Swarthmore are felt by students and members of the faculties of other institutions. If you can reach a solution of the fraternity problem which will make the fraternity system a force which will assist in the development here of a democratic and happy social life, and which will work for the intellectual ends for which the college exists, you may be sure that your experience will be watched and that the measures you take will be imitated insofar as they are successful. If the fraternity system is so inflexible that it cannot be changed, then it is as good as dead, but my contact with national officers of a great many fraternities leads me to think that they do not consider the fraternity system perfect and that they are eager for any suggestions or any experiments which will lead to its improvement. The opportunity to make that experiment is now in your hands and I hope that in working it out you will be bold, large minded, imaginative and wise. This may seem to you a good deal to expect of undergraduates, but I may as well confess to you frankly that this is what I expect of you.[3]

Following this speech, a series of meetings discussed various proposals for changing rushing rules and modifying fraternity life in numerous ways. The whole problem was dumped in the lap of a committee of fraternity members, alumni, and the dean of women. The committee approved a proposal that provided for a year's moratorium on initiating new members, a sharp curtailment of all fraternity activities, and a great expansion of all college dances and table parties under the direction of the Women's Student Government.

After a year of comparative quiet on the issue, the Women's Student Government set a date for voting on whether to continue with the experiment of the past year, to try other experiments, or to abolish fraternities. Before this meeting Dean Blanshard addressed the students and the *Phoenix* published a summary of student arguments, pro and con. Dean Blanshard had earlier (January 1932) reminded the women that the administration had no intention of abolishing fraternities, since they were not considered a serious detriment. If they were to be abolished, she had said, it must be on the initiative of the active chapters, and if the girls voted for abolition, President Aydelotte had asked that the administration be allowed to "play with" the fraternities for awhile, to see if anything could be made out of them. Dean Blanshard had also pointed out what she considered to be the advantages of fraternities. But in a later meeting, on February 26, she assumed an impartial role and summarized the advantages and disadvantages in a detached manner.

From the wealth of published undergraduate statements, frequently expressing hostility and bitterness on both sides, I have selected two that seem cogent and courteous. The first, signed by six members of the class of '35 and one from '34, favored fraternities: [4]

Fraternities fulfill a definite and helpful function in bringing about contacts between upper and underclass women. The seniors, having acquired their own interests during their first three years, have little incentive to form friendships with women in the freshman and sophomore classes. Fraternities make it imperative for these upper class women to make contacts leading to friendships. . . .

The same thing applies to the alumnae. It is almost beyond question, we think, that alumnae are more apt to return to college if they have fraternities to come back to. This is not, as has been implied by critics of the system, due to the fact that the fraternity tie is more binding on an alumna than her college spirit. It is simply that a fraternity provides a permanent place for the alumnae to go to on the campus—a house where the alumnae can count on a wel-

come and can meet college girls and become acquainted with them
and their problems. . . .

We feel that entirely too much emphasis has been laid on the social
side of fraternities. This is shown by the fact that a social program
has been offered as a substitute for them. In our opinion one of the
chief virtues of fraternities is that they stress standards other than
the standards of social popularity. In any coeducational college,
social success, popularity with men, "getting around" are all bound
to loom large. . . . A fraternity, in its insistence on a certain minimum standard of scholarship, and its demand that its members
conform to a high standard of social conduct, decreases this emphasis on social popularity at any cost. . . .

We come now to what is finally the most serious charge against
fraternities—that their exclusiveness causes needless unhappiness
to the girls who are left out. We sincerely regret that every girl in
college does not receive the benefits of fraternity membership, but
fraternities, to be effective, must select their members largely on
a basis of congeniality. . . .

Lack of social success, failure to achieve prominence in any chosen
line, psychological maladjustments to life in general and college in
particular—these things cause the real unhappiness in college, and
fraternities, though definitely not responsible for them, have become a convenient peg on which to hang the blame for the unhappiness they cause. There is no magic in a fraternity which
brings happiness and success to its members. A fraternity is simply
a group of girls working for their mutual good through an organization which stresses and maintains definite standards. And we
feel that the disappointment and temporary feeling of inferiority
which the nonfraternity girls must have is far outweighed by the
permanent gain which the fraternity girl receives.

The second statement, written by a fraternity member who
had cooperated with reform plans but who was now a determined leader of the abolition movement, read:

What are the values of fraternity life? Where can they be found
elsewhere?

(1) They give one the opportunity of working in a small group and
thus they are of definite value in learning how to cooperate. . . .

All these values can be found in any group organization, the *Phoenix*, the Manuscript, departmental clubs, athletics, etc.

(2) Fraternities aid a girl in gaining social grace. This is very true. It is achieved, however, through associations with upper class women. This association need not be limited to fraternity life, but can with planning be achieved in a college without fraternities.

(3) Fraternities get girls interested in extracurricular activities and those broaden them. This is true in a vicious sense. It so happens, however, that this year, the Freshmen women have gone into various activities in greater numbers than ever before.

(4) It is held that fraternities run the social life of the college in an excellent way. This is possibly true, but we have seen this year that it is possible for the student government to plan our social life in a very delightful manner.

The values which are claimed for fraternities are inherent in college group life rather than in fraternity group life.

There are certain faults in the fraternity system which will always exist. Namely, rushing, organized groups rejecting certain girls and causing great unhappiness, artificial social prestige, use of time and energy out of proportion with other functions of college life. Is it too much to ask that we abolish fraternities and do away with the faults and unhappiness when we can find the merits and happiness in other ways?

The final vote favored abolition. In both votes the majority of fraternity women had voted for abolition, but in the second vote the majority was increased. Since President Aydelotte had taken the property issue out of the contest by announcing that the college would purchase the lodges for all-college use in the event of abolition, there were no further complications except the burning resentment of the faithful alumnae who had just furnished the handsome, newly constructed lodges. The Board of Managers therefore supported President Aydelotte in his feeling that undergraduates should form their own institutions and ordered the fraternities discontinued at the end of the year.

As he stated in his annual report of 1934, President Aydelotte had advised the students in the first year of his administration that the social life of the college should not be exclusively dominated by the fraternities, and he proposed a couple of all-inclusive social functions each year. Student interests were becoming increasingly individualistic, however, and were being directed away from all-college activities; it was evident that such functions could not provide a satisfactory social life. The fraternity functions themselves, with their alumnae participants, were too large for many of the members, and dissatisfaction with this aspect of fraternity life explains many of the votes of members for abolition. It is a little pathetic to read the protests of alumnae on abolition because they now had no place in which to become acquainted with the undergraduates and then to read the statements of fraternity members that they were tired of having alumnae members dominate the chapter and would prefer to preserve their independence even if it meant relative isolation.

The gap between the generations seemed to be widening. Whether continuing alumnae associations with undergraduates could have helped to bridge the differences between the generations is an interesting subject for speculation. At any rate, the undergraduates have never shown interest in any revival of fraternity life. Since the abolition of fraternities they have expressed dissatisfaction with social life as sharply and frequently as ever, but have not called for all-college functions. Instead, they want cars to get away from the campus, freedom from restrictive hours for returning to the campus, and privacy to entertain visitors in their rooms.

In taking over the direction of social life the undergraduates showed full realization of the responsibilities of student government. As one of the student leaders wrote in the same issue of the *Phoenix* just before the final vote:

If women's fraternities are abolished for the purpose of increasing the sum total of the college's happiness, there is obviously a big job of social reconstruction awaiting the de-fraternized student body. That such reconstruction after our little civil war will be a large undertaking is unquestionably true but that it is feasible is evidenced by the fact that this year's infant social program is already proving himself a bouncing baby boy with plenty of room for growth. . . .

It is hard to emphasize sufficiently the potentialities of a program which can get into full swing only when the hair splitting fraternity fracas is dead and buried, when a greater college unity is made both feasible and necessary, and staunch retentionists have found that their group enthusiasm can be broadened to meet the demands of reconstruction.

Year after year the social committees of the student government have tackled their problems with loyalty, enthusiasm, and unflagging vigor. They have been as effective as could have reasonably been hoped, but unsatisfied longings creep into querulous print. It is pointed out that there are now practically no social relations between alumnae and undergraduates, that chaperones disappeared with the women's fraternities, that cliques devoted to contemporary musical composers, Bohemian dress, or social reforms are more narrowly exclusive than earlier organizations that prized a congenial sociability. Dress was much better, it is said, when the women's fraternities were dominant, and if they perhaps overdid it, many prefer that to contemporary slovenliness. But in spite of nostalgic laments, any realistic observer of the young intellectuals who dominate campus life today knows that the life of the women's fraternities has gone with the wind.

## The attacks upon fraternities

Although the men students were not asked to vote upon the abolition of the women's fraternities, there were so many similar issues that attacks upon the men's organizations inevitably followed. The Swarthmore Improvement Association led off with satirical, slashing assaults upon fraternities, honor societies, and campus big wheels.

Some alumni replied with letters to the *Phoenix* in which they contrasted student joy and pride in the old Swarthmore with the universal, self-centered discontent voiced in letters and editorials. They asked the ancient question, "What is the matter with the younger generation?" But the men's situation was not really so disturbing. In most years fewer than half the freshmen joined fraternities. This contrasted with well over three-fourths of the women who were members of sororities. The initiative in dating continued to rest with the men, in spite of occasional agitations to the contrary, and the growth of student government offered increased opportunities for student leadership entirely independent of the fraternities. Many of the nonfraternity men had no feeling of being outsiders and cherished no resentment against the fraternities. The activities of the Student Council increased until over sixty student committees were under its direction. Not every student was fortunate enough to serve immediately on the committee that interested him most, but practically all students with energy and ability found an outlet in some committee. This led to one crisis in fraternity life when there was a direct conflict of authority between the Student Council and the Interfraternity Council. The Student Council members, citing their constitution to the effect that they had supervisory powers over all student organizations, ordered the fraternities to postpone their rushing season until the sophomore year. This issue, important as it was, was promptly forgotten in the more exciting question of what right the Student Council had to tell the Interfraternity Council anything. Was not the Interfraternity Council a powerful organization years before the Student Council was heard of? A dramatic and sometimes belligerent debate in the peaceful atmosphere of the Friends Meeting House on a Sunday afternoon stirred the student body, but the conclusion was to retreat from the issue and effect a compromise. The Student Council decided that it was unwise to force the issue authoritatively, but it was evident thereafter that the Council was the dominant voice in student affairs. Many fraternity members told the Dean's Office that they were bored with a merely social role and tired of fraternity meetings devoted exclusively to planning dances; they suggested that the administration designate certain useful functions in student life as belonging properly to fraternities. This was a delicate matter since students saw no reason why such services as reading for the blind, serving the county family society, and clearing the college woods should be undemocratically limited to fraternity members. But it did indicate progress when the fraternities transformed their initiation practices from begging old size-13 shoes to soliciting for the Heart Association.

One fraternity function that at this time had a divisive effect was the nonintellectuals' banding together in solace and comfort for their inferiority feelings. The administration imposed no minimum grade level for membership on athletic teams or fraternities. The national fraternities have urged local chapters to maintain minimum grade levels, but the Swarthmore chapters have observed this only very occasionally. As a result, a few of the fraternities that were very active socially lost a majority of their initiates at the end of the freshman year. But while these boys were still on the campus they reassured one another that if activities of no greater importance demanded their attention, they were perfectly capable of equalling in their grades the grinds and "turks" who spent all their time studying.

With increasing competition for admission to college and graduate school, this state of affairs changed and fraternity membership was no longer accepted as an adequate solace for inferior academic achievement.

The change was perhaps less desirable in another direction. With the disappearance of sororities, social life for both sexes centered increasingly in the men's lodges. Requests for increasing the number of hours during which women could be entertained in the lodges and the students would be unchaperoned were gradually granted until women were freely present at fraternities whenever they could be out of their own rooms. A few men grumbled that no longer was there a place a man could go without a woman and that "fraternity" was now a misused term. These men could only seek refuge in barber shops. For a time numerous complaints reached the Dean's Office from shocked parents of girls shocked at behavior in fraternity lodges, but as high school behavior also became increasingly freed from old restraints, the parental worry seemed to diminish. There were, of course, questions of the violation of the campus liquor rule. Garbage cans were full of bottles, and rumors of antisocial behavior flew about. Occasionally, when charges were proved, fraternities admitted their guilt and were penalized by fines or by being closed temporarily to social activities. The fraternities never officially attacked the college rules. The alumni pledged the college administration their support in enforcing regulations and suggested that the real laxity was with the dean. On occasion they cited with serious approval a statement of the national chapters that used to be read more frequently in all the locals:

A Resolution of the Greek Letter Societies of America in Convention Assembled.

It is our earnest wish and desire to inculcate in our various chapters the principles of true womanhood and manhood; to promote the moral welfare of all our members; to stimulate and encourage scholarship; to prescribe obedience to all authority; to encourage loyalty to and active interest in the institutions where they may be located; to foster a democratic and friendly spirit between our members and all others, and to inspire among our members a true, loyal and lasting friendship.

The support given to qualities of obedience, loyalty, and morality by alumni and national chapters made it easier to deal with fraternities than with the more individualistic students who were inclined to flout obedience and loyalty as restricting personal freedom and to regard "morality" as "bourgeois mores."

Although there was vigorous controversy over fraternities at the beginning of the war period in 1942, the issue that actually brought the question to a student vote ten years later was racial discrimination. Negroes were not admitted to Swarthmore until after World War II, and the Jews had been too small a minority to be effectively vocal. But with the increasing enrollment of Jewish students, the battle against discrimination began in colleges all over the country.

The *Phoenix* summarized the development of the struggle against discrimination in the local chapters in the northern part of the country and pointed to the entrenched conservatism of national chapters as a valid reason for abolishing fraternities. But 57 per cent of the students voted in 1952 against abolition, and none of the agitations since then has come to a referendum vote.

Since all the Swarthmore fraternities have attacked national rulings favoring discrimination, the college administration has not felt it necessary to set a deadline for the achievement of freedom from national rules. It has contented itself with expressing the hope that all fraternities would have complete freedom of choice in selecting members. But the question continues to raise its head. Three fraternities have gone local; in another a substantial group of members has resigned in protest against the national chapter. In a statement published jointly with those who elected to remain in the fraternity they declared that their only disagreement was whether to wage the battle against discrimination from within or without.

In one sense the removal of discriminatory clauses makes the fraternity problem more difficult. If a man knows that he is excluded from a certain group because of his race or religion, he may resent this, but he does not usually feel that there is anything personal about it. To most people it is much less frustrating to be excluded for reasons of race or religion than because one is personally unpopular. A member of a minority group who happens to be very popular often hesitates to accept membership in what seems to be an exclusive student group lest he should be deserting his fellows; he often suffers from a violent tug of war between his conflicting loyalties and in many cases refuses to join the fraternity, preferring to remain loyal to his religious or racial group.

FRATERNITIES, BEARD GROWERS, AND
FOLK DANCERS

As we turn from racial issues to deep-rooted differences in temperament and personality, two incidents will illustrate how difficult it is to make sympathetic understanding prevail, even on an idyllic rural campus.

The first concerns tastes in beards. Shortly after the war, when feeling between veterans and nonveterans was as much a complication as fraternity membership, four athletic veterans belonging to the same fraternity took a nonathletic, nonfraternity beard grower to their fraternity house and told him to shave "or else." He shaved. This roused great indignation in some quarters and gratified amusement in others. Another nonathletic, nonfraternity individualist immediately announced that he would grow a mustache, and publicly and repeatedly dared any person or persons to interfere. Shortly before graduation day, the same four veterans visited this boy in his room at night and with clippers cut two perpendicular swaths in his hair. One of the liberal student organizations drafted a document that should frequently be taken from its obscurity in the faculty minutes in which they asserted the rights of every individual to grow his hair as he pleased and demanded that the faculty punish any persons who attempted to violate this right. The faculty was somewhat divided between the indignant and the amused. They first promptly voted to recommend "severe punishment" to the disciplinary committee, but on pressure for reconsideration voted "appropriate punishment." The disciplinary committee suspended the four boys for a semester, but later, when it was pointed out that this would cost the veterans their government financial aid under the G.I. Bill and would mean the termination of their college careers, the penalty was changed to allow the students to return to college in the fall without participating in athletics. In the fall the battle was renewed between those fraternity alumni who said that the administration had no sense of humor and the students who charged that it lacked courage to resist alumni pressure. All this naturally increased attacks upon fraternities. But with the increasing popularity of beards and the declining feeling among fraternity members that they can successfully interfere with nonconformists, this particular issue has faded away even though the temperamental differences remain.

The divisive effect of personality differences between the fraternal conformists and the "arty individualists" was further illustrated by the controversy over folk dancing. The annual spring folk festival had grown rapidly for several years. An outgrowth of the modern dance group, it had been conducted by the Women's Physical Education Department. Well-known folk singers were invited to come and give a concert as the climax of the two- or three-day festival. During the daytime there was informal folk singing by groups of students who gathered in various places on the campus; in the evening there was folk dancing in the field house. The festival was enormously successful. It was a sort of Dionysiac festival for the springtime; groups of folk singers came to it from points as distant as Chicago, Boston, and Chapel Hill. They often descended upon the college without warning or invitation. Some brought their bedding with them and slept on dormitory floors; others camped up and down the Crum Creek or on the campus. Far into the morning there was singing in various dormitory rooms.

It is a little hard to describe a folk singer or a folk-singing group without recording the prejudice of the observer. As the singers scattered over the village, many gave some onlookers the impression of being ill-kempt, nonconformist, either gay or surly people who regarded themselves as members of a somewhat oppressed minority and nostalgic seekers for a return to the primitive and who here at last had congregated in a grand occasion where they were actually in the majority. In the eyes of others they were creative artists who rise above the amenities of formal social life and greatly prefer an imaginative return to the simplicities of real folk-dancing days to all the artificialities of an Arthur Murray dance studio. It is a notable fact that very few persons who regularly frequent fraternity dances are folk dancers and that very few of them would be caught at a fraternity dance. If one wished a simple, rough test to divide the students into conformists and nonconformists, one might perhaps go about asking them as they come down the hill, "Are you a folk dancer?"

The students who descended upon the college in such large

numbers for this folk-dancing festival created a serious problem. It was hard to feed them, and impossible to find places for them to sleep or to approve of some of the places where they did sleep. As the word passed through the country that here was a glorious spring celebration for folk-dancing groups, it also seemed impossible to control the numbers arriving for the occasion. Some members of the college community found the invasion so disagreeable that they planned a vacation of several days to escape it all. Others found it the point of highest joy in the year. Administrative officers and members of the Women's Physical Education Department, which had borne the chief responsibility for the festival, talked with students about this, but there seemed to be no immediate way of checking the ever-increasing attendance. The administrative officials therefore decided to cancel the folk dance for one year in the hope that some groups might forget about it or might not consider themselves invited, or that in one way or another, as the result of a year of careful planning, some means of controlling the occasion might be hit upon.

When this decision was announced there was a tremendous outburst of student indignation. No such decision, they said, should be taken without consulting the entire student body. It was arbitrary, it was high-handed, it showed the desire of the administration to suppress the nonconformist groups in the college. It was unduly deferential to the village, which, after all, was composed mostly of successful Republicans who did not have the artistic taste to properly appreciate folk singing and folk dancing. Letters of denunciation appeared upon the bulletin board, committee meetings were held, and a gulf appeared between those students who felt greatly relieved that there was to be no folk festival and those who apparently dragged out a bleak existence in the time between these annual occasions. The following year, with the full blessing of the administration, it was planned to reinstitute the folk festival. Vigorous appeals had to be made to secure cooperation in timing and conducting it. There were as many folk-dancing enthusiasts as ever, but when the festival had not been forbidden, its organization and staging somehow seemed a matter of sheer labor. These divisions in taste run deep; one of the important functions of a small college is perhaps to enable people with such differences to learn to get along together, to appreciate one another, and to understand those natural differences in personality that lead some students to find so great a delight in successful conformity and others to pronounce the very word conformity with such bitter contempt. Surely folk dancing is spontaneous and gay; affords an adequate outlet for the creative instinct; is in itself beautiful and sociable; and gives an imaginative release from the confines of our daily conventions. And yet when it comes to standing up and being measured according to the vital principle "Are you or are you not a folk dancer?," the question is capable of dividing a whole community with intense bitterness.

There are still many who feel that the easy way out of this struggle is to abolish all conformist institutions on the campus, fraternities in particular, and who predict that this is part of the wave of the future. However, to abolish such institutions is to deny the fundamental right of voluntary association that is deeply imbedded in our government and in our whole social life. It is also to ignore the tremendous difference in the kinds of satisfaction that are sought by different personality types. Naturally gregarious boys who enjoy relaxing in the presence of others, have a certain love of polite ceremony, enjoy affection and approval, have a pleasant orientation to people, turn naturally to people when in trouble, and are equally glad to talk to them about their troubles—such boys find their best self-realization in the group activities offered by fraternities. To deprive them of this would be indeed a very serious loss.

Another type of boy, often of superior intellectual attainment, is characterized by a certain restraint and tightness in his relations with people. He is temperamentally secretive, restrains his emotions, and is self-conscious in the presence of others. He may be a fairly solitary sort of person most of the time, and in time of trouble he prefers to be alone. His presence does not make other people become expansive and take pleasure in him. Much of the world's distinguished work is performed by persons of such temperament. They are not likely to be happy at fraternity gatherings, and yet their feeling of being an outsider is increased by their knowledge of the very existence of fraternities. Some of these boys learn to relax, to enjoy the amenities and the trivialities of social life, and are undoubtedly better for it. There is probably no complete cure for this situation, and there may always be some sense of stress and strain between persons who are easily and happily sociable and those who are not.

The future of fraternities in a college of intellect will be determined by several somewhat unpredictable factors. One is the growth toward maturity of the fraternities themselves. In the past they have often been refuges for the immature and have been dominated by them. But there are many signs that this is changing. The abandonment by fraternities of the attempt to dominate campus affairs, the introduction of moderation and open-mindedness in the rushing of freshmen, and the declining number of rah-rah boys in the entering classes all eliminate many ancient and deserved criticisms. The declining number of rah-rah boys admitted speaks of changes not only in admissions procedure, but also in the life at secondary schools. In many schools it is no longer thought weird to be a "brain." High College Board scores are less and less a sign of abnormality. Admissions committees can and do look for students who will enrich community life without sacrificing intellectual achievement. As fraternities insist less and less upon rigid conformity, and individualists also feel less need to conform to their own eccentricities, the free associations of campus life may diminish the controversies over fraternities.

## The rise and fall of Book and Key

The college honor that was once the most-prized recognition of success on the Swarthmore campus was membership in the Senior Honorary Society Book and Key. All this was a cause of surprise to some campus visitors who would ask if a simple Quaker college conducted rituals in an Egyptian tomb. Swarthmore was spared much of the campus life that led

Abraham Flexner to protest to a Yale faculty committee that "the continued exaltation of the social, fraternal and athletic interests would make the American college an important agent in the demoralization of the well-to-do." Nevertheless, Yale campus life had an important influence in molding the aspirations of Swarthmore students who had understandable yearning for a more sophisticated society, especially since the Friars and the Sphinx flourished at Penn.

In President Swain's era campus life at Swarthmore became so organized as to make a senior honorary society the capstone of a prestige system that powerfully influenced the development of character and personality. The Swarthmore fraternities were extremely simple, nonresidential groups in rented off-campus quarters, but they were dominant forces in college politics. To be a nonfraternity man was to be one of a small group of left-overs in the social system. The class organizations were powerful forces for unity and conformity. The sophomores were entrusted with employing the inscrutable wisdom of tradition to take the vainglory out of freshmen. The numerous class activities formed a theater in which the naturally dominant could prove their worth in upholding the established loyalties of college life. In such a close-knit community, where dissenters were mostly silent and ignored, those who seemed most useful to the college as undergraduates and most likely to reflect glory upon the college as alumni had established such reputations by the end of the junior year.

In this situation it was not strange that Swarthmore students should wish to imitate the famous Yale senior societies of Skull and Bones and Scroll and Key, established respectively in 1832 and 1842, with a Greco-Egyptian tomb on High Street and an incongruous Moresque Temple on Wall Street. These societies reveled in the prestige of members who had become Yale presidents, governors, senators, industrialists, and endowers of the college in the course of careers dedicated to the service of "God, country, and Yale."

In 1902–04 the Swarthmore organization began to take form, and its members proceeded to select alumni as far back as 1875 whose careers represented the kinds of loyalty and achievement they hoped to stimulate. By 1910, with the vigorous moral and financial backing of Herbert Tily, '85, Morris Clothier, '90, Isaac Clothier, '96, and Howard Cooper Johnson, '96, they had established the Temple Trust with endowment funds, had built their mausoleum on Elm Avenue, had instituted Tap Night, and had their choices recorded annually in THE HALCYON as one of the securely established institutions of the campus. The number of students initiated each year was usually seven. Early on a May evening the juniors obeyed a summons to be on the campus. The senior bookies would run around, glancing here and there as freely as though those to be initiated had not already been selected, approaching and retreating from juniors who were attempting to conceal their anxiety, while the college as a whole looked on with feelings that ran the gamut from grave to gay. Every seven minutes a man was tapped and led away. A week later at seven minutes of seven the initiates were marched at seven-minute intervals to the tomb, where a bloody hand reached out to welcome them. The initiating ceremony, I have heard, contained very solemn charges of a lofty, ethical character, but all the neighborhood ever knew was that the gong sounded hourly all the night long.

In the spring on Thursday nights the Book and Key members would rise early from dinner and march in solemn silence to their weekly meeting. Their departure from the dining room was regarded as a traditional ceremony to be gazed upon with respect and awe. It was indeed a revolution in campus attitudes that later produced boos and laughter, and even resulted occasionally in barricaded dining room doors.

During Book and Key's active years, about 400 members were tapped. If anyone acquainted with Swarthmore alumni over these years were to study the careers of these men, he would be profoundly impressed with the sound judgments these little groups of seniors had made in selecting their successors. Their decisions, of course, were made according to the standards of the peer group. Anyone who has sat on a college admissions committee, and has for some years followed through on his choices, will recognize the advantages in the intimacy of those days. Any of today's foundations that can record equally distinguished successes from its investments in young scholars and researchers may be congratulated: it is difficult for awards for the solitary pursuit of knowledge to have the emotional effects of the plaudits of one's community for service to it. The Book and Key motto, *Acta, non verba,* was perhaps not chosen in order to recruit poets and novelists; but as a group the society's members are distinguished for loyalty, character, and achievement. Men of affairs and industrial and political leaders are the dominant personality types in the group, but there are also distinguished scientists, scholars, educational administrators, editors, journalists, physicians—men who in all walks have shown a high degree of intelligence and energy. Of course some mistaken selections were made, and it was not only the disappointed who were conscious of this. It could not be seriously maintained, however, that it would have been possible to select any group more representative of the values of the period.

The attacks upon the whole idea of such a publicly applauded elite go back a long way in the history of such societies as Yale, even long before community life became sufficiently complicated to make selection difficult and to a time when the rebellion could still be attributed to the normal amount of resentment that the unhonored felt in the presence of the honored. In the early eighties the tombs at Yale had been disfigured, and the society members had been denied class offices and violently waylaid. But even so the prestige of the societies was reputed to be so high that fathers hesitated to send their sons where so large a majority were doomed to public disappointment, and the societies were blamed for a serious decline in the Yale enrollment. In time the increasing diversity in campus life shifted the standards of selection away from their concentration on social and athletic achievements, and the rise in popularity of dramatic productions and student publications enabled students of literary and artistic attainments to reach a wider public than the traditional campus hero. The most conspicuous type of student writing was satirical. The rising stock of young intellectuals even in the midst of Yale conservatism brought about a shift of emphasis in the whole prestige system. There emerged a brilliant group of iconoclasts described by the eminent Yale historian, Professor G. W. Pierson, as loud in speech, brutal in analysis, and enthusiastically uninhibited in their attacks on the old tribal gods.[5] Their new organ, *The Harkness Hoot,* attacked the Gothic architecture of the new Harkness quadrangles, the "medieval" character of the curriculum, the exhibitionism of popular Yale faculty lecturers, fraternities, and, of course, senior societies, which were assaulted under such titles as "The Elks in Our Midst" and "Descent to the Tombs." Stephen Vincent Benet was quoted as saying on Tap Day, "I have seen that poor, dumb, pleading look as in pre-butchered steers—and I begged the juniors to stay in their rooms." But the frontal attack failed, even though it led to a general recognition that the senior societies no longer dominated campus values.

Some Yale men and other social critics have said that *The Harkness Hoot* was greatly influenced by H. L. Mencken and his *American Mercury.* Certainly there was a similarity in tone and temper, and the literary intelligentsia were delighted at the attention they received. Architectural magazines all over the country quoted the attacks on Collegiate Gothic. *The Nation* editorialized:

The thing that has put Yale University "on the map" during the present academic year is not the pronouncements of its president or governing boards regarding educational policy, nor the scholarly achievements of the faculty, but the pungent criticism of its methods and ideals by the undergraduate publications. . . . The indictment has importance far beyond the academic limits of Yale.[6]

Beginning with those days the tone of undergraduate journalism throughout the country has changed from one of predominantly loyal support, with occasional bursts of vigorous criticism, to one of slashing attack. Few football stars or fraternity presidents can now have the constituency in campus politics of the left-wing journalist.

If the Swarthmore of Joseph Swain's day was influenced so

much by the established institutions of the conservative Yale of Hadley's administration, it is not surprising that Aydelotte's aims for Swarthmore—so similar to those of President Angell, who arrived at Yale from the Middle West about the same time, with very similar ideas about the overdevelopment of athletics and the underdevelopment of intellect—should have produced similar changes. Angell's task at Yale was to make a national university out of an entrenched and conservative small college. He had to put the emphasis on intellect, whereas his predecessor, Hadley, had been most strongly concerned about personality and character. Aydelotte's aim at Swarthmore was not to create a university, but to influence the intellectual character of the college so that it might approach the quality of the Oxford colleges he loved so much. He cooperated enthusiastically with Book and Key, and foresaw no conflict between it and his aims. He did not seem to suspect that the conflict between the old and the new Swarthmore might be very similar to the conflict that arises when a university grows out of a college. This conflict has been so eloquently stated by Professor Pierson, a loyal son of the old Yale College and an influential member of the new university faculty, that I quote from his comment at some length:

The true college is not just a chance collection of teachers and students, but an organic society, with a way of life, a system of beliefs, and an *esprit de corps* all its own. One hall mark is intimacy. . . . A second essential is to realize that the college has functions that are social and spiritual as well as intellectual. "Truth is but dimly perceived by the intellect alone." Hence the college must use varied ways of "teaching young men, and letting them teach each other."

All this makes it clear why a college and a university are not the same thing, and why indeed they are almost irreconcilable. For in all fields of instruction—the spiritual, the social, and the intellectual—the aims of the university are distinct. Our colleges were religious foundations; spiritually they stood for the Christian belief; they taught the art of faith. By contrast American universities were created to advance learning; their truth was to be discovered, not revealed; their point of departure was clearly secular. Again the college educated the emotions, and especially the emotions of enthusiasm and loyalty; until the disillusioning 1920's Yale College was one of the most enthusiastic societies in the whole nation. By contrast the university teaches analysis, criticism, even skepticism; its emphasis is rational, not emotional. Where campus life gives rise to group loyalty and a community point of view, the graduate school puts the student on his own, and on the town.

Intellectually the contrast is no less sharp. The college may be defined as the school of the highest *general* learning, but the universities must cultivate the still higher special learning. The aim of one is broad understanding by means of a balanced curriculum; in the other it is mastery via specialization. Where the college undergraduate is an amateur, to be disciplined to good citizenship, and instructed in the inherited culture, the university student is a prospective professional, to be encouraged and guided to his self-education, so that he may even create something new.[7]

There are educators who will say that this is a nostalgic picture of the old college of Skull and Bones or Book and Key days; that analysis, criticism, skepticism, and cold rationality in the spirit of research are an indispensable part of the college approach, especially in the last two years. At any rate, these attitudes have filtered down from the graduate schools that train the teachers, and the college is inevitably transformed by them.

Even before President Aydelotte arrived in the "disillusioning 1920's" there were active signs of discontent with the intellectual limitations of the old college. The *Phoenix* repeatedly published editorials about the overorganized and futile character of many campus activities, and dubbed much of college life a vain pursuit of "goat feathers." A number of men who edited the *Phoenix* from 1915 to 1922 and were Ivy orators and Ivy medalists (and, incidentally, members of Book and Key), plead for more serious intellectual interests and more concern about national and world affairs. Their careers since then have reflected great credit on the college they criticized so constructively. And even more symptomatic than the serious and even solemn criticism is a new satirical gaiety in laughing at what had been taken so seriously. The college annual, THE HALCYON, inaugurated a section devoted to lampooning, in which the editors could "laugh at the college as it really was." This little parody on Robert Service is typical:

*Song of the Big Man*

I wanted each job and I sought it,
    I fought every step to the goal,
I wanted each honor and I bought it,
    And paid for it out of my soul,
I paid the price and I got it,
    But now that the race is near run
I find that the things I discarded
    Are the things I ought to have won.

The first attack on Book and Key that appeared in this section of THE HALCYON, in 1917, was as much in sorrow as in anger, but still in fun:

*Plaint of the Would-Be Bookie*

"What makes a Bookie?" How freshman, can I,
Who have never passed the sacred portal, hope
To tell thee what has wrung sad hearts for years?
Can I, who am profane, tell thee what I would,
But know not? Yet this much, alas, I know,
That I am not a leader in my class—
That I am not among the blessed seven
Who know the secrets of our Swarthmore heaven.

Today I know that, when I knew it not
They weighed me in the balance which by few
Is seen, and seen is ne'er described. They found
That I, with puny mind and body weak,
Could not be trusted with sacred things
All Bookies know—but knowing ne'er repeat.
Ah, Frosh, to that great end thy thought incline;
Beware the awful fate that now is mine.

I stand before thee here, a hopeless wreck,—
A failure,—bankrupt in the marks of life,
I stand alone—forgot—outside the pale
My classmates entered. I, alas, am left

To drain the stein of bitterness. In shame
I hang my head; by all my name is scorned.
I'm down and out: my vest is unadorned!

These plaints increased and became more angry than sor-
rowful. Almost suddenly students seemed to feel that Tap
Night was a cruel exhibition. Many juniors refused to come
out; as a result, Tap Night was changed to a procedure
whereby those elected were notified twenty-four hours in advance and were marched solemnly at the old seven-minute
intervals from the Parrish dining room to the Temple, where
the same bloody hand welcomed them. The ceremony retained a diminishing number of spectators for a few years, but
a number of factors contributed to its loss of hold on the
attention of the college. Public criticisms declared that Book
and Key performed no functions and had no interests outside
itself. This was hardly fair. One of the policies of Book and
Key was that it would take no public actions as an organization. College problems were discussed earnestly, and often
members were delegated to act quietly and unofficially to see
what should be done. There can never be any adequate recognition of the services thus rendered; the wisdom of this policy
was seen in what happened when the Dean's Office suggested
that Book and Key help officially with the orientation of freshmen. The work was undertaken enthusiastically and effi-
ciently. But by this time the Student Council had evolved an
elaborate system of committees for practically all student
functions and had demanded that it assume the responsibility
as the only democratic group. The same fate awaited several
other suggested functions. Whereas some said that Book and
Key was an honorary society and did not need to do anything,
that election to it was somewhat like receiving an honorary
degree, others argued that many of the traditional paths to the
coveted honor had vanished. The disappearance of class organizations, functions, and spirit, the shifting of many local
social interests to concern with larger matters off-campus, the
growing recognition of individual achievements unrelated to
the community, such as the increasing awards by foundations

for specialized pursuits and skills, the virtual disappearance of fraternities from campus politics, the diversity and sometimes even hostility among different campus groups all made any attempt to select and salute the "seven leaders" seem rather arbitrary and unreal. As a result more and more students declined the honor. The experiment of enlarging the number selected each year was tried, but it was not successful. Many men still refused to be considered, and those who would accept often seemed so diverse that no unity could result from their association. The last student proposal was to suggest that Book and Key should have the function of recognizing all the increasingly divergent groups in student life. This has not seemed feasible to those who cherish the traditions of the organization, and the students themselves seemed to have no serious interest in it. No satisfactory solution seems to be immediately on the horizon.

Are we then to abandon the purposes of those early organizers of honor societies and say that their aims are as outmoded as their methods? Shall we say that because secret rituals, oriental ceremonies, and social exclusiveness sometimes seemed dominant, we should abandon all attempts to recognize and reward effectiveness of character and personality that seem to emerge from the peer culture? Many faculty members wearily struggling with the problem of the awarding of ivy and oak-leaf medals have been heard to say that no qualifications but grades should be considered. Character and personality are not measurable; awards should be publicly made only for strictly measurable achievements.

This problem is now occupying the attention of contemporary educators armed with the latest sociological and psychological ideas. A recent book, RECOGNITION OF EXCELLENCE,[8] reports a long and careful survey of all the forms of recognition of excellence in America. The distinguished educators who contributed to it conclude that there are plenty of awards for distinction in the sciences, or for almost any specialized pursuit, and that what is needed is more recognition for that old, old character, "the whole man."

Thus we find that educators armed with all the instruments

of scientific measurement and prediction seem to revert to an old aim very similar to that cherished by Book and Key. Perhaps experts might offer advice on how such aims might be pursued in the changed college of today.

## The struggles for new freedoms

President Aydelotte's favorite phrase for his educational reforms was "breaking the academic lock step." He was not by temperament a breaker of other lock steps, and he did not expect his young intellectuals to apply their habits of breakage to the social mores around them. He agreed with Bernard Shaw that if one is to be an influential radical, his private life should meet with the approval of the conservatives. He often said that a college should move with the times; that it might well be in advance of the times intellectually, but at least a half a generation behind the times socially. This was sound administrative wisdom, and if he could have induced his adolescent intellectuals to have accepted it, he would have avoided many headaches. But he never succeeded in making social conservatives out of his intellectual radicals. The campus institutions that his students inherited and attacked as conformist and undemocratic were thoroughly in harmony with the nonacademic life of their times. Success in campus activities was a harbinger of success in later years. But this did not enable them to hold the respect of the young intellectuals. And when conformity to these institutions was so largely abandoned, the same habits of nonconformity spread to the social mores generally. When President Aydelotte and his administrative associates desired fraternity dances to be held in the Borough of Swarthmore in order to keep them within the bounds of propriety, fraternity and nonfraternity men alike joined in protest. I quote from the *Phoenix:*

The borrowed car argument, the accident argument, the applied argument concerning the moral well-being of youth in general, and the financial argument are familiar to all. The whole thing is based on the assumption that it is the duty of the college to guard the morals of its students.

Tomorrow evening President Aydelotte will address the fraternities on the proposal which they have rejected. It is evident that the words of the President of the college should carry a great deal of weight, regardless of their import. It is also possible that the import of the words themselves would also merit consideration. But we must, as college students, striving for a balanced mental outlook and freedom from prejudice, distinguish between the words and the speaker. Let us remember, with all due apologies to President Aydelotte, that we cannot afford to relinquish our views simply because one whom we admire opposes us.

This utterance is noteworthy chiefly because it contains traces of lingering respect for an administration that was opposing student desires. Such traces grew rarer in succeeding years.

The administration held to its ruling for a short time and then abandoned it. It is interesting to note in how many of the struggles for freedom the students have been victorious. As older faculty and alumni view such changes over the years, they are usually able to accept changes of the past rather philosophically, as representing inevitable progress. But as for continuing to grant new freedoms in the future, they usually say the limit has been reached and that the time for firmness has come.

DRESS

The next struggle has dogged the college for years and still arouses more intense feelings than any academic issue. On September 30, 1930, the *Phoenix* carried an announcement from Dean Alan Valentine reaffirming the rule requiring students to wear coats and ties for both lunch and dinner. There were strong editorials of protest, again recounting the history of the objections to informal student dress and the protests of the newly-constituted student government officials, and repeating their concern that the administrtaion should override student government in the matter.

The *Phoenix* carried an account of a student mass meeting

in which a resolution was passed condemning the administration for its action with regard to dress in the dining room. They quoted the Executive Committee of the Men's Student Government as saying that it was prepared to make student government an active and effective association, or to resign immediately. In an attempt to make effective the student vote condemning the administration, the student government summoned the president, the dean, and the chairman of the Board of Managers, Wilson Powell, who then lived in New York, to attend a mass meeting and hear the opinions of the students. This meeting, as I still remember it, was an excited gathering and showed again how difficult it is to impose a rule upon rebellious students. Mr. Powell was accustomed to speak with authority, and his bearing certainly commanded respect. In the heat of the argument, however, he told the men that appearances must be preserved, that he did not care what they wore below the table, but that above it their coats and ties must be visible. This raised vigorous objections from the floor, all to the point that the Quakers had always been more concerned with the inner man than with the outer appearance and that it was in no sense good Quaker doctrine to tell the boys to look well above the table and that the rest did not matter. Richard C. Bond, '31, now president of John Wanamaker's, was president of the Men's Student Government Association and called the meeting together. The opposing argument was presented by Robert Kintner, now president of the National Broadcasting Company; Carl Dellmuth, now vice president of a large banking corporation, suggested that in the future the administration ask the opinion of the men students before passing such a rule. The arguments of Dean Valentine, President Aydelotte, and Wilson Powell are all summarized in the news account in the *Phoenix*; it is obvious from the story that they made no impression at all on the students. As a result of this meeting, however, the coat rule was suspended for a trial period of two weeks. At the end of this time the administration was not satisfied with the appearance of the boys, and the rule was reinstated. On November 4 Dean Valentine issued the following statement:

Two weeks ago the men students of the college accepted a proposal that for a trial period of two weeks they be allowed to show that their own standard of dress in the dining room at lunch could meet the approval of the college. It was agreed that the administration would judge with open mind the standard set and then make a decision which would be accepted with good grace by the student body.

We have made every effort to perform our half of this agreement. A majority of students appeared to have done the same. Too large a minority, however, have taken advantage of the privilege, and hurt the cause of the student body by appearing not only in sweaters, which is contrary to the expressed wish of the administration, but also frequently without ties, which is below the standard which the men students as a body agreed should exist.

It is a regrettable fact that a responsible majority must frequently submit to rules made necessary by an irresponsible minority. This is the present case. The rule making coats necessary in the dining room at lunch and dinner must again become effective until further notice. Men entitled to wear Varsity sweaters may wear them at lunch on Friday.

Since the student government executive committee has not adopted our suggestion that it become responsible for this rule, the administration must take over its enforcement. We ask the cooperation of all undergraduates, confident that they will accept this solution as sportsmen and gentlemen.

The issue of the *Phoenix* containing Dean Valentine's statement has also a vigorous editorial in reply, the final paragraph of which read:

Men's student government has refused to aid in enforcing the coat rule or to take charge of order in the dining room. The *Phoenix* believes that it is right in taking this attitude. The administration has retained the coat rule to which the men students do not adhere. It would not be fair to ask student government to enforce this regulation in which they do not believe. We also think that they are right in their refusal to take charge of dining room order. The administration says that dress is a part of order, and refuses to allow student government to control the same. It would not be consistent for the men's executive committee to take charge of the order when the administration refuses to allow student control of dress which they declare is a part of order.

One response of the students to this rule was to appear in the dining room in great numbers with coats wrong side out and to insist that they were observing the letter of the rule. For a time a serious effort was made to exclude from the dining room those students who did not seem to meet the new requirements, but this practice was gradually abandoned. When I became acting dean upon Dean Valentine's departure, the practice I inherited was to ask the head waitress in the dining room to report to the Dean's Office cases of flagrantly bad dress and appearance and to call such boys to the office for expostulation and reproof. The reproofs were not very effective; they produced vigorous counter-arguments about the right of the individual to dress as he pleased. The laboratories were given as a reason for bad dress at lunch. The men reported that they were unable to dress after athletic practice in the evening. There was no disposition to accept, as there had been formerly, the dictum that the evening meal at least might have a certain element of formality about it. The student government attempted to secure greater formality in dress in the evening by requiring men and women to eat together. For a short time proctors were placed at the door. Women who did not have to participate in athletics in the field in the evening came much earlier and had to wait around for the men; they expressed great dissatisfaction with this arrangement. In fact, it elicited almost no support from the student body, and this attempt at regulation was also given up. What can we say now about more recent student dress?

The most vivid account of both the facts and the state of feeling in the situation is given in a statement in the "Reflections" column of the *Phoenix* written by Barbara Pearson Lange and published on November 16, 1949. Barbara had grown up on the campus as a faculty child. She was in college when Valentine first attempted to improve dress. Some time after graduation she had returned to the college as Director of Dramatics and had resumed the old family connections in the village. She had made a reputation as having a sympathetic understanding of students; twenty years after the issues were first joined she was probably the person best qualified to know and understand the many points of view about the matter of dress. Her article appeared immediately after a number of student articles had criticized both the curriculum and the faculty for stifling the creative spirit. Whether there is any connection between the feeling of oppression at required courses and the desire to express individuality by flouting current customs and manners in dress and appearance, it is interesting to note that as students demand freer intellectual creativeness, the alumni and citizens of the village find the students increasingly impossible. The ancient town-and-gown controversy seems eternal. But to return to Barbara:

Controversies rage in local so-called society and alumni gatherings about the Swarthmore student. The female version as seen by the village housewife, when encountered in the Acme, is not only carelessly dressed, but her entire appearance, from coiffure to sockless legs and feet shuffling in heelless loafers (how aptly we use the English language at times), seems designed to be unattractive. Our local ladies are not so shocked as bewildered, for they question whether their daughters, now in high school, will disintegrate into the sloppy coed.

The college male as seen in the druggie by alumni who cherish memories of their years of good fellowship and rowdy pranks, is a puny, bespectacled, over-confident, long-haired egotist, who knows the answers to be found in most books except the book of etiquette. Stories spread with no realization of their inconsistency. He spends all his time in the library, none on the athletic field. He studies abstract theories, learns nothing about life. He is a communist. He gets drunk every night, keeps whiskey under his Wharton bed, and has even been known to hide a coed there. "What," they cry, "is the matter with the authorities? Why do they let the college get in such an awful state?"

There are three stock answers to give the inquiring and bewildered soul who questions me: One, the obvious one that appearance is only skin-deep, etc. (I am so tired of it I can't repeat it here.) Two, the students they notice in the vil and on the campus are only a minority. They don't see the polite, healthy, well-groomed, well-informed individuals with keen minds and appalling fund of knowledge and a capacity for independent thinking. Three, the "times have changed" theme. As youngsters we never saw our parents drink, or heard them swear. This is a new generation, conditioned very differently. This is my defense in your behalf.

But I am weakening. Every day as I walk from Trotter to Parrish, and am pushed from the sidewalk by students changing classes, I find it more difficult to remember your virtues. After a few days of straightening chairs, sweeping cigarette butts and picking up all manner of debris in Commons my faith is badly shaken. I need to be recharged.

The faculty and administration are also frequently attacked. The faculty is labeled as "foreign," "communist," "ivory-tower intellectuals," "impractical idealists." The administration is "unable to enforce discipline," "incapable of choosing the well-rounded students," "hypocritical in statements to the faculty, the students, the alumni and the Board," and "employ(s) psychiatrists for the students, but until this year had no course in religion." The defense here is an obvious one. Put the critic's name on a list of people who periodically come to visit the college. This may be a headache to students and faculty. But the administration is smart enough to realize that it is the only way to combat criticisms which usually arise from misinformation and ignorance.

Naturally you don't care about the opinions of the village housewife, the memory-ridden male alum, the Board of Managers—or the faculty. No student body ever has, but the strange fact is that in four short years you will be, oh horrible thought! a memory-ridden alum and your viewpoint and perspective will change with amazing rapidity. You will become quite protective and very proud of the institution that now it pleases you to attack. And then in a few years you will look very critically and somewhat distastefully at the new generation of students, at the curriculum, the administration and the faculty, and mutter "it wasn't like that in the good old days."

This weekend will bring a horde of alumni to the campus. You and they will seem separated by generations—but a college generation is only four years. As these strangers swarm through your buildings, dance with awkward and ridiculous steps on your floor and perhaps eye you and your behavior with some disapproval, realize that their loyal support of your college has made possible many of the advantages you enjoy. Realize, as I must, when they confront me with their criticisms, that their considerable sacrifice and time and money gives them the right to question and be answered. You too will soon be demanding that right. In four short years present *Phoenix* editors will scrutinize the efforts of future editors and murmur, "It was certainly a much better paper when I was in college." It was ever so.

This eloquent expostulation had about the same effect as the more authoritative statements of the president of the college and the president of the Board. Ten years later the situation is somewhat the same, except that casual dress has spread so widely that, when reasonably clean, it is less shocking. One finds eminently respectable village housewives shopping in the kind of dress so well described by Barbara. Both parents and alumni have become so accustomed to the dress of the younger generation that they do not feel that what they see in the Swarthmore dining room necessarily represents depravity. In fact, a good many parents, and those who often show considerable style and distinction in their own dress, often comment very favorably upon the long, crowded, disorderly line of students waiting in the hall, dressed in the most miscellaneous fashion, apparently quite unconscious of the differences, and talking gaily. The parents often envy the success of such a gathering in bringing the students together and enabling them to know one another. Surely, they say, no one can be lonely here.

When I left the Dean's Office it was still the custom to exclude barefoot students from the dining room, and this in the spring was becoming something of an increasing problem. The natural love of casting off shoes and stockings and cavorting barefoot upon the green was spreading widely; it is indeed hard to look upon this custom with disfavor. Mildred, whose long service as head waitress in the dining room is beyond all praise and who commands general respect for her judgment and vigor, occasionally reports students to the Dean's Office.

From time to time there have been sporadic campaigns to add a little more formality to Saturday night and Sunday dinners, and the managers of the dining room have celebrated such occasions by providing table cloths. Alumni whose memories have grown fonder with the passing of the years often speak of the days when they sat in assigned places at a table for a year at a time and developed the greatest affection for all their table companions. The cafeteria service, the long wriggling line of students awaiting entrance, the hasty exits all make college dining seem a revolting spectacle. Many suggestions for restoring dignity, leisure, and some of the amenities of gracious living have been made; and yet the crowded, hasty informality of the dining room is probably one of the most successful social institutions in the college in producing unity.

What can be said for the possible future of any administrative attempts to improve dress in the dining room and on the campus generally? In the first place, dress even among the intellectuals does vary somewhat from time to time according to influences of contemporary fashions; jeans will be succeeded by Bermuda shorts, and the ponytail hair-dos are, after all, only transient. President Smith has made some excellent speeches in Collection about the state of college dress. Delivered with tact, wisdom, and humor, the speeches were as good as any that could be made upon such a subject. They were, I believe, influential for the better, and did at least let the student body know that the college did feel some concern in the matter. There is no doubt, however, that it stiffened the backs of many students with a vigorous resentment. The talk about making a little Princeton of Swarthmore very much resembled the campus talk about making an Oxford of Swarthmore in President Aydelotte's days. The temper of the times and of the student generation is so markedly against authority that any edicts about dress are almost sure to unite the student body in determined opposition; the best dressed will vote with the worst dressed to express disapproval of any attempts to impose conformity. The wave of the future, barring some unforeseen power in the realm of fashion, is probably with the current trend of the undergraduates. This circumstance, of course, is nation-wide. It is often said that Swarthmore ought to be above nationwide tendencies, but the Quakers must accept some responsibility, I think, for their general reputation for nonconformity. Perhaps one of the best ways to make Quakers of all the students on the campus would be to tell them that they must wear prescribed garments. The shades of George Fox would be invoked immediately. Attendance at a recent six-choir festival at Haverford, where the musical performance was of the higest standard of excellence and where the program was one that could not possibly have been performed by any of these college students fifteen or twenty years ago, brought to mind the sharp contrast between the artistic intelligence, energy, and initiative of these students and their utter nonconformity in dress. The number of beards observable in the men's choruses and the high degree of informal dress in the final rehearsal contrasted sharply with the idea of this festival as one of the great cultural achievements of a group of Eastern colleges. At the evening performances, which were followed by dances, the beards, of course, remained, but the dress showed a high degree of sophistication. One error sometimes made by critics of this generation is that the college needs to teach the students how to dress. This, I think, is not true. They are a very sophisticated group. Many of the worst dressers come from families of the greatest elegance, and when they wish to conform to a different set of surroundings, they do so instantly and easily. They feel that the college is their club, that it belongs to their generation, that they have the same right to dress casually that is enjoyed by members of the most-exclusive country clubs.

Some of the aberrations, of course, are somewhat neurotic in origin. There are the natural exhibitionists, who seem to feel that conspicuous defiance of custom is the only way to attract attention. There are girls who have not succeeded in getting dates and who apparently wish to show their defiant disregard of this situation by dressing in a way that makes them as conspicuously unattractive as possible. And there are always a few couples, noted for their constancy and their steady devotion to each other, whose dress will be about equally disreputable. One will see some of these couples in torn tennis shoes, patched jeans, dirty shirts, sometimes with beards and tousled hair, walking arm in arm along the walk or across the campus, their gaze fixed straight ahead as if they felt that they were the only two individuals in the world who understood each other and who had their eyes fixed upon some far-off Eden where they might dwell eternally as predestined soul-mates. All this is a part of adolescence and must be viewed with sympathetic understanding. It is necessary to remind ourselves, perhaps, that this same group of disreputably dressed students has vastly more social consciousness, more concern for the affairs of the world, greater artistic achievement, more intellectual interests, a more significant group of student acitivities than their predecessors, whose pictures in THE HALCYON now seem so quaint and formal.

When the students leave the campus they can and do adjust to other mores with ease. When I congratulated one of our notable beatniks on his appearance as he returned to the office a year after graduation, he replied, "In me, sir, you see the birth of a salesman."

But while one who lives in this outing-club atmosphere can accept it philosophically and remain fond of the youngsters who are finding themselves, the general public expresses more indignation over appearances than it would over academic deficiencies. The public has not yet realized that what we have here is a nation-wide declaration of adolescent independence, made more easily attainable by the prestige of being in college. Many students in city universities who live at home and commute to classes regard their nonconformist uniform as a badge of membership in a superior culture, and look with condescension on the conventional dress of the "wage slaves" who travel with them in train or bus or subway. Many of those who live on rural or semirural campuses feel as hesitant about donning conventional dress as they would about wearing formal evening clothes to a campfire supper in the woods.

Somehow this gap in manners and appearance needs to be bridged. Either the public will come to understand and tolerate adolescent dress as a transient symptom of a need for self-expression, or college administrations will be forced to adopt some highly unpopular rules, as they have already done in some places, and to answer the student protests with the observation that to treat them as adults just hasn't worked.

## THE RIGHT TO PRIVACY

Traditionally, college social life, like social life in general, has involved relations with other persons and groups; but the social life of our young intellectuals is increasingly becoming a private affair. Social life was once a matter of serving on large committes, decorating dance halls, hiring orchestras, appearing in formal dress, and enlarging one's circle of acquaintances with pleasant small talk. But this brings little pleasure to many intellectuals who dislike crowds of any sort, who prefer intellectual companionship in their own often somewhat specialized realm of interest, and to whom formality of all kinds is a mask of insincerity. They will attend lectures and concerts in great numbers if they are free from the vulgarities of mass communication, but there is no necessity for formality even here. Beyond this, the best social life is in very small groups of like-minded—with emphasis on the mind—and, best of all perhaps, groups of two. But here enters the question of the right to privacy. Aside from questions of conventionality, it is difficult for a college to provide private sitting rooms for all couples. But the solution, students say, is simple if prudery can be laid aside. A dormitory bedroom is a student's home. Why should he not be at home when and to whom he (or she) pleases? As a student wrote in the *Phoenix:*

When we are at home, all of us have members of the opposite sex visit us in our homes, and our rooms are the only homes we have while we are at college. The fact that they are bedrooms and have real beds with sheets and blankets on them, where people sleep, seems to constitute an immoral situation in the eye of the administration.

The issue of the *Phoenix* in which this appeared is illustrated with a photograph of a girl and a boy comfortably posed on a bed in a dormitory room, obviously concentrating on books.

Swarthmore was somewhat slow and conservative in granting such privileges, but the freedoms of other Eastern seaboard colleges were cited as proof of the inconsistency between our intellectual and our social freedom. Somewhat grudgingly the administration consented to open house in the women's dormitories on Sunday afternoons. At first there were house parties, with gay crowds going up and down the halls and entering rooms to which the doors were open. Gradually this privilege was extended to include the men's dormitories. Crowds lessened, doors were closed, and privacy seemed attained at last. But a scandalous episode made the administration insist upon open doors in open houses. This, the students felt, was an invasion of their right to privacy, and so they refused. The open houses were cancelled for a time. Then the Student Council and the Student Affairs Committee proposed a Friday night open house with open doors. The hall presidents in the women's dormitories and the proctors in the men's dormitories said that they had no intention of being policemen to see if doors were open. Here the matter rested for a time, but in 1957 it was raised again and presented to the president and Board of Managers. The managers said that this was properly a decision of the administrative officers of the college. Here the matter rests, with students visiting other colleges, publicizing their more liberal house rules, and asking why Swarthmore is so stodgy.

One group of students attacks limitations on privacy as a matter of undue suspicion about a perfectly normal and healthy desire to talk together, study together, and listen to records together. But another group, citing anthropological and sociological evidence, attacks restraints upon sexual freedom as outworn and unrealistic. A notable example of this position was an editorial entitled "Kinsey," which appeared in the *Phoenix* on January 16, 1948, shortly after the Kinsey report was published. The editorial raised such a tempest of controversy that part of it must be quoted in order to understand the states of mind on the issue at the time:

Our first response to reading the Kinsey report was to write a blasting editorial, quoting devastating statistics on the amount of sexual activity of the college male, and to call on the administration to face the realities of the situation by finding more adequate facilities on the campus for sexual expression by the student body.

Second thought, however, suggested that such an editorial might well be self-defeating. All the groups that are connected with the college policy—the administration, the faculty, the Board of Managers, the alumni, the parents of students, the community of Swarthmore and the student body—all these groups tend to enjoy the same basic sexual behavior. They all tend to fall in the highest educational category, the same occupational categories, and the some parental-occupational categories; and the categories reveal a distinct pattern of sexual behavior. The members of these categories tend to rationalize their sexual behavior in terms of morality, and historically have tended to institutionalize their behavior in terms of patterns in the political and social organization they control (notably in legal codes). Moreover, in control of the most important institutions, they have tried to enforce this pattern of sexual morality on other groups in the population. Swarthmore College is no exception to such social pressure.

The Kinsey report shows also that the amount of sexual activity on the part of the college male is far in excess of that recognized by the institution of college, the total sexual outlet for the typical single white male in the top educational category between the ages of 16 and 25 being approximately two orgasms a week.

With such a conflict of sexual practice and sexual mores, the evident conclusion is that one or the other should be revised; and this being the *Phoenix,* we would be expected to call for a revision of the institutional mores. The argument would go that we should examine the facts of sexual behavior in the college community openly and without prejudice, and change the institutional pattern in terms of the reality of the situation as revealed by the Kinsey report. . . . It is evident that the liberalization of administrative policy on sexual affairs can only be achieved *sub rosa,* without the publicity attendant upon open avowal.

President Nason resisted the pressure of indignant alumni and Board members to drop the author of the editorial from college. It was impossible to drop him as editor, since this was the last issue of his editorial term. The *Phoenix,* however, was forced to suspend publication until such time as the Student Council could offer assurance that it would accept greater responsibility for editorial policy. The suspension lasted three weeks. The *Harvard Crimson* led a national assault of college journalists upon the Swarthmore administration for violating academic freedom, a position taken privately by several college presidents. Only the *Daily Pennsylvanian* had a word in defense of the administration. It said they viewed the editorial as a discredit to college journalism and as calling for disciplinary action.

The editorial did warrant the fears of its author, now a reputable sociologist, that it might be self-defeating as far as administrative policy was concerned, but many students applauded it as expressing their individual beliefs.

There are still conservatives who fear that the constant liberalizing of dormitory visiting hours may be carrying out the *Phoenix* editor's advice to adjust the changing sexual standards *sub rosa.* Such an experienced and wise psychoanalyst as Carl Binger, writing on "Emotional Disturbances Among College Women," says that educators should look the facts in the face:

If they relax parietal rules sufficiently to permit girls to go to boys' rooms and remain there until late, then they should realize what the consequences are likely to be.[9]

Professor Binger writes as one concerned with mental health rather than as a moralist, but he says he is not devaluating ideal goals, however remote or difficult to achieve.

There are no restrictions upon behavior involving cars, liquor, sex, and dress that the young intellectuals will not rationalize away. And it is not only those who pride themselves on being radical who reason thus. They are more and more representative of the majority of their generation, the high-minded idealistic youth interested in social justice, in a better world, in self-sacrifice for causes. They cannot be dismissed as merely irresponsible pleasure hunters, and they are distrustful of all "moralizing." They earnestly desire to see the college assume leadership in placing the social standards of behavior at least half a generation in advance of current mores. They identify Victorian and present standards as equally outmoded, and believe that instead of being influenced by adolescent emotional desires, they are the ones who are truly rational. Their insistence upon their point of view may not mark a change in the behavior of adolescents so much as a change in the attitude of their parents, whose general permissiveness has encouraged the belief that anything the younger generation insists upon will be the pattern of the future. Surely there is much in our society, in college and out, to justify such adolescent convictions. At present the students appeal to the "behavioral sciences," to psychology, sociology, and anthropology, in support of a relativistic point of view in morals and ethics; they assert that the "conservatism" of the college is in part due to the absence of sociology and anthropology from the curriculum. They are not yet acquainted with some of the very significant trends in sociological and anthropological thinking, and it may take some years for them to learn that the "behavioral sciences" may reach some conclusions that are not so different from some ancient insights, after all.

## THE STUDENT BATTLE AGAINST DISCRIMINATION

In 1932 a Negro from a Philadelphia high school decided to apply to Swarthmore. He was a prominent athlete; had a good background in classics, his major interest; was president of Student Government and popular with his fellows; and, except for his color, was a logical candidate for an open scholarship. The admission of colored students had never been approved by the Board of Managers, and so the Admissions Committee referred the application to the Board. After a long discussion it decided by a large majority that Negro students could not yet be admitted to a coeducational college like

Swarthmore. Their admission would raise too many problems and create too many difficulties. There was general satisfaction at the happy solution presented by Dean Speight, just arrived from Dartmouth, when he got the boy accepted there with a large scholarship. A men's college seemed just the place for him. The question of admitting Negroes to Swarthmore did not become acute again until the year before John Nason's inauguration as president. In 1940 a Student Committee on Racial Relations was organized with the avowed purpose of bringing about the admission of Negro applicants. The students began with a program of recitals by Negro performers, and with exhibitions of Negro art, painting, and sculpture. They had a number of meetings with speakers furnished by the National Association for the Advancement of Colored People.

When President Nason came into office, the students sent him a memorandum requesting him to begin his administration with active attempts to secure the admission of Negroes. Remembering some remarks of President Aydelotte about the danger of trying to fight all battles on all fronts at once, President Nason replied that the question seriously interested him, that he hoped to do something about it later, but that he could not tackle it immediately. Then the war came, and all of his efforts were absorbed just in keeping the school going on the year round basis that the war demanded. After about three years, as the course of the war led to more and more arguments about the future of oppressed minorities in the world, President Nason thought the time had come to raise the question again. He therefore presented to the Board of Managers the memorandum presented to him by the students; to his great delight and to the delight of the students, the Board by a very substantial majority passed a resolution changing the admission policy to permit the admission of students regardless of race, color, or creed. There was no great rush of Negro applicants, either qualified or unqualified. Probably the cost of going to college at Swarthmore made it out of the question for most applicants, and there were no scholarships specifically for Negro students. Gradually, however, there were from three to five Negro applicants a year, of whom two or three would turn out to be sufficiently well qualified to be admitted. The Admissions Committee felt that it would not be doing a Negro student a favor to admit him if his general record showed that his chances of graduation were very small. On the other hand, they did perceive that they often needed to recognize superior motivation in a student who had lacked earlier opportunities but who, by reason of great ambition and industry, wished to make the attempt to come to such a college as Swarthmore. From time to time the Student Race Relations Committee has written letters to schools in the South and sometimes to schools in other sections of the country that had a large proportion of Negro students, urging them to apply to Swarthmore.

Representatives of the National Association for the Advancement of Colored People have talked to Negroes in southern schools about the advantages of coming north, and the Association has been able to raise a considerable amount of money to offer scholarships for this purpose. Some Swarthmore graduates have worked in this capacity, but they have not been able to interest many students in applying to Swarthmore. The small number has led some Swarthmore students to accuse the Admissions Committee of being especially restrictive about Negroes. This is not true. The committee has been inclined to give the benefit of the doubt as much to Negro applicants as it always has to the children of Quakers and alumni. The number of American Negroes has been supplemented over several years by about a dozen students who have come from Nigeria or the Gold Coast. Most of these students were graduates of English schools and have passed matriculation examinations for the English universities. On the whole, they have been very successful both academically and socially. There has been no attempt to limit the social activities of the colored students, and colored and white students have mingled freely at dances; inevitably, students have been drawn together across race lines, perhaps in the beginning by their idealism and their desire to show a complete absence of racial prejudice. It does not seem to be true, as has been sometimes alleged, that the attraction of the races for each other is entirely on the lower social levels. The colored males seem to have a decided attraction for the white girls, and a few white boys have selected colored girls as their partners, temporarily or permanently. The Student Race Relations Committee has attempted to see to it that there were no forms of discrimination in the village that would make it uncomfortable for students of the college of any race.

The most notable area of conflict has been in the barber shops. Two of the three barber shops in the village have declined to cut the hair of Negroes. They have said that their reason was a fear of losing patronage in the village and of not being able to get enough help in their shops. The students have attempted to boycott the shops that have not given haircuts to Negroes, but this boycott has not been notably successful. When appeals have been made to administrative officers of the college, they have been quite willing to say that the college hoped that no form of discrimination in the sale of goods or in providing services would exist as far as college students were concerned. The issue has seemed to be slightly academic, since the one shop that proclaims its willingness to cut the hair of Negroes has had virtually no colored customers. The owner of this shop said that he felt he was making something of a moral hero of himself in announcing that he would cut the hair of people of all races, only to be disappointed to find that no colored people came to him. This has not been a real problem in the village, for the few colored people living within its limits seem to prefer to go to barber shops in near-by towns where the prices are lower and they can find more people of their own kind. Student committees have also circulated questionnaires in the village to attempt to find out public sentiment in the matter, but for the most part these questionnaires have been worded so as to increase irritation. The college naturally hopes that this situation may be remedied, but since the numbers involved are so small, it is difficult to maintain public interest over any length of time and it does not seem likely that the barbers will change their customs in the immediate future.

The small number of Negro and oriental applicants has prevented the discrimination issue from becoming serious in this area. But it has become acute in the question of the admission of Jews, and students have led a determined fight for participation in the admissions procedure.

In 1933 the Jewish students formed about 6 per cent of the Swarthmore student body. The vocal opposition to this state of affairs came from conservative alumni, who felt that the number of Jewish students in college should never exceed their proportion of the national population, which was then under 5 per cent. By 1949, the intellectual reputation of the college had raised the number of Jewish applicants to something over 50 per cent and the number of acceptances to a yearly average of around 20 per cent. This time the vocal opposition came from the students, who thought the Jews were unduly restricted. They asked the dean to address a student meeting called to consider the issue and, in speeches and letters to the *Phoenix,* vigorously attacked his defense of the situation. The Student Council sent a memorandum to the Board of Managers, saying that the current admission process did not carry out the democratic aims set forth in the catalogue and requesting a meeting with the Board to discuss the issues. The Board replied that "the application of the admissions policy is primarily for the administrative staff of the college, and the Board of Managers believes the current admissions procedures to be in accordance with the admissions policy of the college as stated in the catalogue."

This rebuff aroused the ire of the students to a fighting pitch, and they more vigorously repeated their demands for a hearing before the Board. When this was again refused, the Council turned its attention toward the student members of the Admissions Committee. Early in his administration President Nason included student members on most policy-making committees of the faculty and on the Admissions Committee. This had worked satisfactorily for a short period, although it was obvious, from strong suggestions that the Board of Managers be represented on the Admissions Committee to keep the Board informed and that alumni representatives should be present to be able to explain the refusal of the children of alumni to their outraged parents, that the committee was in danger of becoming too controversial to proceed effectively. As the students pressed the issue more strongly, Student Council appointments to the Admissions Committee became the most-sought-for offices; naturally enough, the appointments were most sought for by those most opposed to all forms of discrimination.

In this situation the meetings of the Admissions Committee were bogged down in endless controversy. In spite of preliminary attempts to agree on general policy, practically every applicant was the subject of endless debate. The college had previously removed questions of race and religion from application cards, but the students in particular were prone to argue for every applicant thought to be Jewish and to challenge every Gentile. This situation was reported to the president, who reported it to the Board in the light of the student demands for a hearing before the Board. The result was that the president and the Board agreed that it was impossible to continue the custom of having student representatives on the admissions committees. It was also agreed that there should be no Board or alumni representatives and that the matter of admissions should be left to the administrative officers and faculty representatives appointed on the grounds of competence, interest, and continuous service.

Rather than go through the long process of debating this with the Student Council and its representatives on the Admissions Committee, the president accepted the unanimous recommendation of the faculty and administrative members of the Admissions Committee that the students should be dropped from it. The students were informed of the action by President Nason, who suggested that, as an alternative, they might sit with the Admissions Committee on policy discussion, but should not sit in on the selection of individual applicants. This aroused student resentment that lasted a number of years and resulted in the publication of letters, resolutions, and editorials in the *Phoenix*. President Nason later admitted that the students were justified in protesting their removal without a hearing, but added that in his opinion the experiment of student participation had proved it to be practically impossible. He suggested that student representatives might help select the more important holders of scholarships, whose cases would not come up until their admission had been decided upon. This offer was accepted, but it did little to mollify student feelings.

Students carried the issue over into President Smith's administration. There has, however, been a steady refusal on the part of the administration and the Admissions Committee to include student representatives in the process of selection.

The removal of students from the committee did not, of course, stifle controversy. It is a matter of public interest now reflected in books, magazines, papers, and "scientific" studies of psychologists and sociologists and in national meetings of admissions officers, high school guidance counsellors, and the College Board. But we are here concerned to recount the feeling of the students that they should help to select their own community members and their confidence that they could resolve the deep-seated differences among themselves.

# 5

# Students speak for themselves

The accounts of the revolts of the intellectuals have thus far been concerned with public utterances and actions on the part of students to gain new freedoms. To what extent those public actions provide an emotional climate that affects their private lives is hard to say with anything like scientific certainty. The students constructively use these freedoms for an imposing array of achievements in curricular and extracurricular activities. The extracurricular activities gain from the intelligence required to make the highly-valued academic records. There are fewer pursuits of the kind described as "goat feathers" by students of the early twenties. There is real intellectual distinction in the student organizations devoted to public affairs, philanthropy, drama, music, and departmental clubs and to individual works in writing and in arts and crafts. The over-all picture is so good that some observers have said that nothing short of Utopia could be better. It would be quite plausible to say that anyone who doesn't develop properly and even happily in such a community should get out.

This has not been the attitude of the Swarthmore administration, but student difficulties, so far as they are due to the intellectual standards of the college, do not seem likely to grow less. They are the defects that go with the qualities, and apparently must be accepted as such. To quote from the 1959–60 report of Dean Susan P. Cobbs:

The virtues [of the college] can become abuses. The degree and nature of all these qualities can become too intense, can weigh too heavily on some individuals. Diversity and individualism may invite in some students eccentricity, or rebellion, or a foolish non-conformity, or they may become divisive rather than stimulating. The pursuit of academic excellence, where faculty are excellent and students able and serious, can become too fast-paced, can produce anxiety that threatens the joy of the undertaking. The "small and residential" can be "too much with us," can seem too pervasive. Surely, at times, for all students, the picture darkens in these and other ways. These are problems implicit in institutions like Swarthmore. They can be recognized, eased, partially resolved. They cannot be wholly eliminated. If they are, another institution emerges; another set of problems is substituted; another series of abuses presents its problems.

A national group of educators concerned with improving the quality of American colleges recently published a resolution declaring that an institution truly committed to intellectual excellence by its faculty and students would have few problems. This is to be blind to Dean Cobbs's statement that "there are problems implicit in institutions like Swarthmore." The increasing volume of published studies of student attitudes, achievements, and mental health in institutions of high academic standing will bear out Dean Cobbs's statements. This, in fact, is my principal reason for writing this study of adolescent intellectuals. A common, enthusiastic belief in the primacy of the intellect as a determinant of status cannot but have some implicit problems that need to be "recognized, eased, partially resolved."

In the attempt to discover what factors in the development of personality may have been influenced by the impact of the intellectual and emotional climate of the college, many students in an experimental course were asked over a period of years to write essays on what they liked most and least about student life at Swarthmore. They were also asked to invite their friends to volunteer statements; many of them did so. There is, of course, a wide range of moods, attitudes, and temperaments in such opinions; they may sometimes reveal more about the personality of the writer than they do about the college. But this study is primarily concerned with student moods, attitudes, and temperaments. A dozen statements by undergraduates have been selected as representative of student attitudes. They were all written by upperclassmen who have since graduated with above-average academic standing. Most had participated actively and responsibly in student affairs, some had held prominent offices, and none had suffered from any disciplinary penalties. The student opinions seem to be a representative cross section of what it felt like to be in the Swarthmore of their day, and the student comments illustrate some of the problems summarized so well by Dean Cobbs in her report.

## 1. *Swarthmore's ineffable something*

The more I think about it, the less able I am to dissect Swarthmore into its components and say "this I like" and "this I don't like." These elements are scattered about in other colleges. It is Swarthmore's particular combination which makes her unique. I can talk about these parts but I still won't have spoken of Swarthmore. What I love about Swarthmore is that ineffable something (I suppose I can call it "atmosphere") which infuses the components and binds them together into an entity.

I am very fond of Swarthmore. I feel comfortable and happy here. Part of this feeling is, no doubt, a result of mere familiarity with the place (though I suppose I wouldn't be fond of a familiar concentration camp) and of having a lovely group of friends here.

Much more important, though, is the exquisite delight I feel in having people my own age to whom I can *talk* and who have enthusiasm and ideals and—and *intelligence!* I lived in a farming community over half my life and went to a high school which I can only look upon with horror. Narrowness and mental stagnation are the best terms with which to describe the attributes of the students. Even the teachers were people of very limited abilities. The town itself—the whole area, even—was a cultural desert. So you can understand the heady experience which college is for me. This, of course, doesn't have any particular application to Swarthmore College. All I'm saying, I'm afraid, is that college is a good thing.

We all know about Swarthmore's academic standards and there's no point in running the thing into the ground. I'm glad about it. We're all glad about it. I should be very unhappy were it otherwise. Learning and knowledge are exciting things. The grades and diploma with which the student is rewarded are completely irrelevant to me.

A thing that especially endears Swarthmore to me is her informality and her strict lack of emphasis upon this thing called "Social Life." (The calendar is certainly overflowing with activities of all sorts, but by "Social Life" I mean something very different. I certainly hope you understand because I can't be very coherent about it.) I am an extremely frumpish, careless person and enjoy not having to wear white gloves on Sunday afternoons and being able to, quite casually, go about and do things without belonging to the club or organization involved.

Swarthmore's program of activities, lectures, and guest artists is simply marvelous. I've had opportunities to see and do things here that I will not likely have (without trouble and expense) in the "outside world."

I'm so glad to be studying with people of such diverse nationalities and races. They invariably express fresh viewpoints and ideas upon matters that I had considered "settled."

How lucky we are to have the woods and stream, and Philadelphia as well! It's an ideal location for a college.

I can only think of three things that I dislike, and these concern the attitudes of some of the students. Number one is the search for a controversial issue at all costs, be the problem ever so slight. I admit this is all a great deal of fun. But the situation is pretty ludicrous and regrettable when the students descend to the issue of food and "Should we show school spirit at the Haverford football game?" Number two: Why must there be this lurking suspicion that the diabolical administration is plotting against the student body? The very presence of a RULE turns them rabid with anger. Number three: I fear some of our much lauded intellectuality is simulated. A real scholar among the students is the exception not the rule.

Might a poor overburdened student complain that sometimes she really borders on nervous breakdown because of the amount of work? Five courses is a bit too much, if one really wants to do well in anything. It spreads you a bit thinly.

## 2. Self-centeredness and the feeling of inadequacy

To the incoming freshman, Swarthmore presents an exciting and imposing picture. Rather than the usual hazing that freshmen at most schools go through—the freshmen usually find that after the first week of orientation they are suddenly on their own, they are Swarthmore students—they are expected to put forth work of standard Swarthmore quality, are treated for the most part as adults, mature and independent. It's a little overwhelming—but also stimulating, not to say flattering. One soon finds that the principal, unspoken (usually) standard is that of the intellect. There are no campus leaders or Big Men on Campus in terms of athletics, personality, activities alone. Instead there is a sea of individuals— a few standing out because they are more individual than the rest —a fact usually coupled with the knowledge of their superior creativity. Artistic and intellectual creativity are, I think, valued above all else—this is true for play writing, acting, musical composition or performing, poetry and prose or even "he or she is terrific in seminar!" This whole general atmosphere breeds among freshmen and sophomores (after the initial thrill with everything has worn off)—more than any other single cause—a strong feeling of intellectual inferiority and loss of confidence. Very often those social characterisics stressed in high school—personality, sociability—seem not to count, and the intellectual (which was often previously underplayed or overcompensated for) is suddenly the all-important. This causes a shift in standards which in the process brings on loss of confidence. Various things can develop out of this stage— the person can gradually become adjusted to what he feels is the norm—perhaps intellectual and social individuality and gradually adapt to it—speaking out in class, find a "group," dress more casually or sloppily, etc., and gain a good deal of satisfaction. Another person might become increasingly disappointed and dissatisfied with what he feels to be a very reserved, cold atmosphere—no campus spirit, no unified effort or feeling about anything, no one willing to help another because each is too busy with his own affairs. Another might find a small group of compatible friends with whom he keeps very close—building a little framework within which he studies, plays, etc. with the security of sameness—feeling fairly content with this orbit—but perhaps wondering if there isn't more to college than this somewhere. I think all of these things happen to some degree with everyone—the new feeling of freedom, giving up of responsibility to discover the all-important self, the clinging to a few close friends, the feeling of aloneness in the midst of many people and activities, above all the feeling of inadequacy.

All this paints a rather gloomy, if incomplete picture. On the brighter side is the feeling that never in your life have you been in a situation in which there were so many people of such varied talents and interests—all are intelligent, all have something to offer, all are interesting. One of the first things one realizes, however, is that *time*, which is filled to capacity with work to be done, just doesn't leave enough room for really getting to know all the different people one is attracted to.

The basic problem at Swarthmore (or at least one of the biggest) seems to me to be centered around *identification*. To most incoming freshmen and sophomores, Swarthmore differs quite a bit from most colleges—or at least the high school idea of college—in that there seems to be a great indifference on the part of the students to everything—to school, activities, and often to each other. Loyalties, if they exist at all, seem to exist only among small groups of people—to each other or an organization, mostly, however, the stress seems to be on the *self*. The college doesn't at first seem to offer anything to take the place of the home and family which has now been partially left behind. A real struggle often sets in to try to arrive at a rational evaluation of the merits of the college, which usually turn out to be its high academic standards and the stress on individual expression and inquiry. I think these are often over glorified in an attempt to justify staying in an unhappy, insecure situation. Also, if the academic and the intellectual are the only factors stressed, the result can be a pretty self-centered group of people—each concerned with his own development and his rating in the eyes of his fellow students. Fortunately, I think other factors do develop which provide a somewhat firmer basis for identification—in the form of more general goals connected with factors outside of school, in the form of small organizations and activities, and gradually to a general, if rather nebulous "Swarthmore ideal."

If it is one of the basic aims of a college to provide an atmosphere for the maximum growth of the individual intellectually, morally and socially, then Swarthmore by its very nature fosters this growth. With its initial picture of intellectual prowess, non-unity of interest, and often indifference and self-contained attitudes, it causes a great deal of dissatisfaction, insecurity, and searching for purpose. The student is forced by his dissatisfaction and tension to try to evaluate what his former standards were, contrasting and comparing what he expected here and what he found—and in trying to reconcile his conflicts of feelings he may reach a more mature level of understanding of his basic goals and purpose in life.

### 3. The happy athlete

This evaluation was received from an "athlete," if there is such a separate student category. This athlete plays three sports and is captain of two. His indefinite plans for the future include, as one alternative, playing professional baseball. He seems happy and satisfied at Swarthmore but anxious for "after" college. He is not completely involved with the college as the limiting scope of his immediate experience, because he is "half in and half out"—looking, planning, making decisions in the outside world. He's beginning to feel, more than ever, the isolation and campus confinement and would strongly advocate cars for seniors although he feels they might be the source of too great distraction for underclassmen.

The extreme emphasis on intellectualism he sincerely approves as a good and necessary stimulus; "you come to school to learn." He realizes his capacities and limitations in the academic sphere and does not seem frustrated by constant striving to reach an unattainable goal. Rather than trying to "match" the more intellectual and intelligent students, he respects their ability and feels that he profits from contact with them.

He is irked by the seemingly "naive" idealism often exhibited at Swarthmore. Admitting his sometimes adamant prejudices, he agrees that he has learned to handle these in some measure, being influenced by the tolerant, accepting attitude prevalent here. He would advocate more administrative pressure on students for at least the minimum in social graces, since he feels a definite lack in any training or even much experience of this kind.

However, the most important point brought out was the importance of sports as a means of adjustment to the college (for this student). He felt that the sense of belonging, of group participation and acceptance was gained significantly more from playing on a team than as a member of a fraternity. In sports, the team must work together as one for best results. Individual excellence is admired and applauded (to a limited degree) and lends the factor of prestige. But more essential, there is built up a respect for the abilities of all the team members—for the bench warmers as well as the stars, because all are part of the same group striving for the same goal. It necessitates subordination of the self for the smooth running and success of the whole team. Here, cooperation and learning to get along with others is stressed. A sense of belonging, confidence and security is gained from such participation as well as a group of friends with whom you have much in common and have shared a number of the same experiences.

With a strong group loyalty, a prestige of a sort, a relatively homogeneous group of friends, the encouragement of leadership qualities, respect and tolerance—the academic pressure, social tension and "separateness" are substantially reduced. This does not mean that athletes are the happiest or best adjusted students at Swarthmore. I think it does show the need for group contacts, for a feeling of belonging to something and working together toward some end, whether it be a successful sports season, Little Theater Club production, or a moving musical concert.

### 4. Words, words, words

The Swarthmore student is excessively concerned with words and ideas. He shows little aptitude or interest in the application of them to his immediate environment, the college, or little potential for pressing home his opinions when he leaves college. He is not a popular persuader, he writes carefully, correctly, but limply. He is more concerned with dissecting his environment than moulding it. And he will, if he does have ideas, in all likelihood retreat to the safety of the academic atmosphere when he graduates. There he will continue to think, talk and write, but will never feel obligated to transmit his ideas into action. He forgets that first there is the idea, then the word, but the only compelling standard for evaluating an individual's productivity in the world is the material and ideological change which he stimulates.

I am unable to respect the college administration for its catering to public opinion outside the college.

There is unfortunately little communication between the different elements on the Swarthmore campus, although one of the primary purposes of diversity in the student body is to encourage the exchange of ideas and attitudes.

The emphasis on academic achievement at Swarthmore sometimes seriously distorts the perspective of students. They forget the importance, indeed the necessity, for corresponding emotional development.

Swarthmore students are the greatest rationalizers I know.

I am deeply aware of the effect Swarthmore has had in deepening and broadening my powers of perception and reasoning. I do not want to approach life from the academic point of view so I will be glad to leave Swarthmore and, at least temporarily, abandon my formal schooling. I appreciate my education, and feel obliged to utilize it in some way.

One of the most satisfying aspects of my life at Swarthmore has been sports. The school is small enough so that I have been able to participate frequently. The fellowship of athletic teams has been important to me. It is interesting, however, that many of my motives in sports have changed considerably over four years. As a freshman my primary concern as an athlete was the impression I made on other people. Now I find sports a much more personal thing to me, a way of testing my determination, confidence and courage. Incidentally, I find pride and hate the essential stances for the athlete; they can either alternate or complement one another.

## 5. The adventures of learning

The second semester of Senior year is a dangerous time for recording opinions about Swarthmore, at least for one like myself who must admit to a shudder of pride when the Star-Spangled Banner is played at ball games and who even enjoys Norman Rockwell. Another problem is that tomorrow is the first day of Spring and the campus is on the brink of—in Ginsberg's phrase—rehearsing Genesis. At any rate, I have already implied that (1) what follows will be influenced by a premature case of nostalgia, and (2) the Swarthmore campus is worth every ounce of sentiment it evokes.

Swarthmore without the magnolias and Clothier tower is far more difficult to assess but the attempt is interesting. Coming from a country day school, my sociological horizons were instantly expanded; e.g., in the first week I met my first professed anarchist, atheist, and even vegetarian. My initial reaction was confusion— "But they only wear beards in the Village!"—followed by snap judgments, usually narrow and unfair at that, and finally a present awareness that the Boy Scout Laws are not the only valid standard of conduct. Our college population is as heterogeneous as the IQ requirements will permit, and from this I think comes most of our collective energy. A catalyst to this seems to be the Quaker tradition, which has insured liberty without license and tolerance without indifference.

It seems almost an artificial distinction to start a new paragraph to consider the academic side of life here since the very air is heavy with young but often painfully sincere ideas. I was in a frisbee game after dinner in which we simultaneously discussed the nature —if any—of natural law; we were moving into determinism when it got too dark to play. Here, in all its glory, is the "casual intensity" that a Radcliffe visitor found so characteristic of Swarthmore. Any that I have myself I owe to the disconcerting but exciting challenge of the Honors program, in which for the past two years I have watched and even participated in the systematic demolition of cherished academic cliches; O.K., so maybe there was a Renaissance, but if so, Miss Albertson isn't telling. That's what I mean by disconcerting! I'm one of those people who love certainty, and the relativity of truth has been a traumatic discovery, but an invaluable one. Honors also exposes one to the infinity of knowledge, which might drive a hypersensitive mind to suicide, but in my experience has simply made learning more of an adventure. In this I owe more than I probably realize to the Swarthmore faculty, the first academic elite I have encountered and the most stimulating I ever hope to. My professors have been, along with the Arcadian campus and the apple pie, the most prominent constants in my opinions of the last four years—no matter how fed up I was with my roommate, upset by tragedy at home, or irritated by what I considered irresponsibility in certain campus elements, I have never overcome my amazement at the happy blend of brains and humanity that graces the Clothier stage on Thursday mornings. There's more camaraderie in seminars, of course, where professor and student storm the fortress of wisdom together over their teacups, but equally impressive to me is the spectacle of a Ph.D. reaching up to a beautiful obscurity with one hand and down to a scared Freshman in the back row with the other.

Mr. Hoffman once said that you don't learn about Europe when you travel abroad; you learn about the United States. I found the same perspective at two national conferences in the last year, the more significant revelations coming out of the Mortar Board Convention. Swarthmore was the wonder of the other hundred members because of the peculiar nature of our problems; while we're trying to liven our social activities, most other schools are trying to suppress them! In fact what to us are sources of tension—e.g., Mary Lyons vs. C Section—give us a diversity that Ohio State's 20,000 can only approximate on an unwieldy level. I was bombarded with questions that often seemed to boil down to "Gee, what's it like to be able to talk about deep things whenever you want to without being laughed off?" In my experiences as a freshman counselor for two years, I found more people considering transferring at one time or another than not. But whatever we lack —and it's usually social—is made up for by a combination of other elements that simply no other school has. I know this from personal investigation: I considered transferring myself!

A witty cynic once defined a classic as a book no one wants to read but everyone wants to have read. There are times when I have wished that I was not going to Swarthmore, but already I can see that I shall be very very glad to have gone there.

## 6. The exaltation of intellect; ethical relativity; inferiority feelings

Swarthmore's good points are also its bad points, depending on the extent they affect the individual and on the background of the individual before coming to college. Expectations of gains from college life also play a part in determining the effect of Swarthmore on students.

It is my belief that there is a great lack of any moral judgment on people's activities. The pressure to conform to any ethical standard is rarely applied even by close friends, and then only in extreme cases. There is no general moral code by which all the campus lives. This is a strong point for the college in that intolerant gossip which can be so harmful to a person is avoided. Also a person who has strong ideas and firm convictions does not find these challenged by the college community. This lack of moral judgment can be a bad point in that a person who has been conditioned to conflicting standards during childhood tends to be even more confused here when he sees one friend doing "this" in a certain situation and another friend doing "that," and all of his friends accepting both situations. It is this person who needs the most help in coming to accept certain moral standards in keeping with reality. The lack of judgment here I do not believe is found elsewhere (or at least not to this extent).

This lack of moral and ethical codes is carried over into other fields. There is a general attitude that intelligence is above all other factors in determining the worth of a person. This is a very important quality, but kindness and consideration and other such factors tend to be forgotten as being important aspects in the complete analysis of personality. This tendency is probably due to the fact that the most important personality aspect of most of the people at Swarthmore is their intellect, emphasized in childhood either as compensation for some inferior aspect (as poor motor control) or especially encouraged in home and at school. This emphasizing of intelligence found in assessing oneself tends to be emphasized when evaulating other people.

Another point about the Swarthmore campus is the unlimited amount of knowledge which is made available. When a student has been challenged all his life according to his capabilities, then this may not be as pronounced an effect as on a person whose environment has not been so stimulating previous to college. This new stimulation leads a student to take an active interest in all subjects because of exposure to them by interested people. A desire is created within the student to learn a subject not for the simple grade, but for the purpose of testing his own ability. A student meeting such an intellectual challenge for the first time rises to meet it. When the consciousness that there is far more material than one man is capable of learning begins to be apparent, then this very strong point for Swarthmore is tested. An individual who has depended on intellectual achievement for feelings of self worth may tend to feel inferior in this capacity because of not living up to his own standards within himself and failing to meet the challenge found there. This can lead to a terrible feeling of inferiority which could be compensated for in other ways. As intellectual compensation has been the pattern in childhood this is difficult to accomplish. Some students are able to meet the intellectual challenge successfully, and some are able to live up to the standards set for themselves although these are not the same as the college's. Some students do not accept their limitations but keep fighting by such measures as staying up all night studying and continually driving themselves. Some leave college. The students who accept their limitations turn to other fields in which they can excel.

It is my feeling that Swarthmore tends to emphasize the intellectual capacities so far above other personality factors that any sort of compensating activity is looked on as one that is not quite adequate as a substitute. Perhaps in order to keep up the high standard here this emphasis has to be prevalent and this realization of limitations is a good thing. This realization seems only good if a person can accept it and I do not think the atmosphere is especially conducive to this acceptance. Certainly the type of student selected to come here is of the type that finds this kind of failure even more crushing.

I think that some of the close intimacy found in Swarthmore couples may be due to the tension here which is so great. This tension causes people naturally to group together for support and this group breaks down into couples who find satisfaction in being together and actually need each other as a source of compensating for feelings of inferiority. People who have found satisfaction in dating before, date even more here. Those who have never found satisfaction in dating date even less here.

Perhaps this extension of old patterns is true in every new situation, but I wish there were some method here at college to bring out people who have anti-social ideas simply because they have been intellectually superior in other situations. Probably they found they excelled and were different; here at Swarthmore they are intellectually on a norm and can bring out the other aspects of their personality (such as consideration, responsibility, social consciousness).

I may be too critical of the intellectual atmosphere at Swarthmore, but I do feel it tends to hide other characteristics of people that I feel are important. I dislike intellectual considerations coloring all reactions to other people. If the intellectualism could be accepted and not emphasized as outstanding but as simply one important aspect of a person's whole personality, and if the college itself could help emphasize other aspects of the students' lives then I believe that many more students would be much happier at Swarthmore.

## 7. Humanizing the life of the mind

I have always liked the intellectual stimulation and companionship here. The stimulation found both in courses and seminars and among students and faculty is very exciting—the sudden insight you have into new ideas or connecting facts and ideas. On the other hand, I have just thought lately that we don't know how lucky we are and that we may be having it too good in the line of intellectual excitement. This feeling arises with the realization that I'll soon be away from Swarthmore and may be more dissatisfied living in an average middle-class suburb or town somewhere where the main concerns are gossip, flower clubs, PTA, than I would have been had I not known about Swarthmore. But again, even if this were the case, I'd still be glad for my participation in the Swarthmore life for a while at least. It is the Life of the Mind which is the particularly exciting thing.

I like the Honors program very much—that is, the whole setup. The two years in Course before going into Honors were necessary for me at least in training me to think and to study. In Honors I think at least a short period in which requirements are pretty specific—e.g., papers every other week and assigned reading—is necessary to get one oriented in the seminar system of studying things. Then I am in favor of more freedom in getting away from this rigid pattern than is usually the case—although real advances are being made this year it seems.

The relationship with the professor in Honors is very important— something which is never quite the same in Course. There is more feeling of communication as equals, that you are mutually concerned in *learning* about the subject and that each different individual may have an entirely new viewpoint to add. One gets to feel that some professors are really quite human in the seminars where there is enough mutual respect and freedom for the professor to talk about his own opinions, feelings, experiences, and sometimes even his homelife and family.

The relationship between students is equally important and very dynamic. Here there is a vital interaction of all sorts of different personalities, the opportunity to learn how to communicate as well as how to understand others and appreciate *their ideas* as well as their difficulties. I think that seminars can help in the growth of the individual toward psychological maturity: one learns something about responsibility which accompanies a certain amount of freedom, one must learn how to participate in an intelligible discussion, contributing to it and learning from it in a willing manner; especially difficult, one must learn to take the really critical (sometimes harsh) discussions of his work and papers, realizing that it is usually not of him as a person or his abilities—which would be damaging—but of that particular performance or of the ideas expressed which may not be his at all. The last problem involves an understanding that everyone there is mutually involved in the learning process, etc.

I would criticize the relationship between faculty and students. I think this is hard for the freshmen and Course students more than for the Honors student. When I was a freshman I definitely felt that professors weren't at all interested in me as an individual and were making unjust demands of conformity to an intellectual ideal pattern. This was in spite of the fact that I liked many of them. This is probably a relative problem.

A stock criticism of Swarthmore is the in-groupness of groups, or cliques. I resent this. I think the heterogeneity of the student body is very valuable. This heterogeneity means that there will necessarily be nonconformists and people with many differing interests. People with these very different interests given the freedom they have at Swarthmore not to conform (in relation to the conformity demanded at many other colleges) will naturally group with people of like interests. The grouping I do not think is a harmful or snobbish thing but is natural in our situation and adds many elements of richness and variety that would otherwise be missing. I am not dissatisfied with any particular rules at Swarthmore. I think we have lots of freedom and that there is a pretty intelligent attitude toward the rules, penalties for infractions, etc.

A last stock criticism that I don't go along with is that at Swarthmore the individual is not important as an individual and that he does not feel accepted. On a superficial level everyone is accepted and the individual is really valued as an individual because of the whole liberal philosophy, tolerant Quaker air, etc., etc. But deeper than this—I think it's pretty common for people to feel at particular times, as I have when I was depressed, that no one appreciates them, accepts them or loves them. But there has never been a time in my four years here, except in these temporary periods, that I did not feel that I was appreciated, accepted, loved by at least four or five of my closest friends, if not more. My experiences with other people and observing them in relation to others also supports the idea that they do have real concern for one another, and even for those who may not be directly aware of their concern. A problem is that this is often manifested in a rather sophisticated manner and that one does not have the innate assurance built up with his family over a period of years, that he can count on his friends no matter what. But on the whole I would say that most Swarthmore students do feel accepted and valued and most are concerned for others as well.

## 8. Finding one's self

Most students entering Swarthmore have not reached maturity, they are still wondering just who they are, where they stand in relation to others. Generally speaking they are anxious to establish themselves as individuals, to break the ties with their parents, to assert their independence. The curious thing is that most of them do not know where they are going; it is as if they were walking through the door into a different room, but the room is dark, they know not what they will find. This poses the difficult problem of seeking an environment where they will be both free to experiment with gentle gropings, their new found independence, yet protected from stumbling over unseen obstacles. Moreover this environment should stimulate continual seeking of knowledge and self-knowledge—both for those who lack any inner stimulation and those discouraged by the many blocks they encounter in trying to learn about life. In another sense this new environment should serve as a sort of hidden security to replace the security of the home. This "new" environment in this stage of an individual's development is, I feel, very important, for the individual will probably go through a great change in passing from childhood to maturity, a change that involves every aspect of his being, not just his intellectual life.

Swarthmore attempts to afford just such a new environment. The freshman at Swarthmore is soon aware that he is faced with a serious task. It becomes urgent that he apply himself totally and completely to the pursuit of knowledge. By establishing strict academic standards, the college hopes that learning will become necessarily so much a part of its students that a desire to learn will be inculcated in them, and they will go on learning the rest of their lives. It is hoped that by having to meet these standards, students will grow to love the process of meeting them. This implies a certain amount of self-knowledge, an awareness of one's abilities and limitations and emotional needs. This too is a difficult task and requires discipline of the individual. Likewise it requires a desire to know and be one's self.

The students at Swarthmore pride themselves on being more mature, more aware of life and themselves, more intellectual than students in other colleges. Actually we see them practicing the same fetishes, in different disguise, that we see at other colleges. All students seem to need some sort of "in-group" to which to cling for a while. One need only read an occasional "Grouse" to realize that the Swarthmore students cling just as desperately to their Bohemian, fraternity, and anti-fraternity cliques as other students do to their various eating clubs, etc. They are essentially the same thing—a vestige of the security of childhood, not quite yet totally discarded, a type of regression, although a necessary one, in disguise. It is interesting to me that the goal of intellectual rigor and love of knowledge established by Swarthmore to help students become mature people has been twisted into a game by so many at Swarthmore. I am talking about the student who calls himself an "intellectual," who deprecates the "unintellectual," the student who feels a compulsion to eat, sleep and drink his studies. Despite the stiff requirements at Swarthmore, it is not hard to find what I label the "sterile" student—that is, the student who makes it all the way through Swarthmore, perhaps with extremely good grades, and yet has no real interest, no real emotional grasp of what he has learned, in short no real self-awareness.

## 9. *Pains of overwork*

One thing that has impressed me greatly is the general friendliness of all members of the college community toward each other, regardless of huge differences in taste and group affiliation. There is respect for people who are different, and respect for that which makes them different. There is personal consideration, such as the effort generally made by students to refrain from disturbing the sleep and study of other students. In sum, people here are generally pleasant and nice.

Secondly, people here are quite open and communicative, which makes it easy to learn quite a bit about "human nature" and other ways of doing things. Such information I have found extremely helpful in the process of my own development, both intellectually and emotionally.

A third very appealing facet of Swarthmore is the critical intellectual orientation. While this at times goes too far toward cynicism and nihilism, it is a refreshing change from the everyday world of the "expert" opinion and the accepted norm.

Perhaps the biggest drawback to Swarthmore is the constant heavy study pressure, particularly in Honors. It is literally impossible to read *carefully* everything that is assigned, much less what is suggested. Perhaps part of the pressure is necessary to create motivation to study, but it seems to me the present amount is above what is essential for maintaining serious interest in learning. The present pressure might even tend to discourage such interest, especially in the long run (after graduation). Of course, maybe it is not educationally desirable to read everything as carefully as I sometimes feel it is, and then certainly the pressure would be less.

I do think, however, on balance, that there is something of a work overload, and that one result is a somewhat superficial understanding of the subject matter on the part of some students, due to necessary "skimming." This seems to me particularly true in the "intensive" Honors program, where 400 pages of common reading per seminar per week is the rule for many social science seminars.

A further criticism of the present Honors set-up (though I don't think this inherent in the system): some professors feel the Honors student is so much more motivated to learn, more likely to have his work done, and more intelligent, that they tend to slight the Course student. Unfortunate faculty attitudes toward the Course student such as antagonism, pushing, and lack of enthusiasm in teaching situations sometimes develop.

Another criticism, this one of student attitudes: grades in themselves, regardless of how achieved, are too highly valued. A person who spends most of his time on activities and still maintains a fairly high grade average, as I did my first three years, is quite highly thought of despite the fact that his knowledge may be quite superficial [N.B., above remarks on "superficial" Honors student knowledge may be largely projection!] and temporary.

Even the honest intellectual approach has its drawbacks. A tendency to cynicism and nihilism has already been mentioned. A remoter consequence is one stressed by Dr. Richard Hey in this year's Marriage Course—i.e., that Swarthmore is turning out graduates who are emotionally underdeveloped because intellectually overdeveloped (or at least overoriented).

Despite the criticisms covering more space than the bouquets, my overall impression of Swarthmore is quite favorable. It has done much for me, and provided me with many close and valuable friends. I leave with real regret.

## 10. *Realistic individualism*

It would seem that some of the outright objections and many of the vague, indeterminable anxieties of Swarthmore students stem from the oft discussed atmosphere of extreme *intellectualism* and *individualism* which prevails. This has its strengths and weaknesses; my objection to some of its varied aspects lies in degree rather than kind.

Intellectualism as used to denote the growth, expansion and maturation of the "intellect" by stimulation of rewarding contacts in many varied fields of knowledge and areas of experience is a valuable part of Swarthmore. We are offered speakers, drama, music, films, debates, discussions which often awaken new interests and desire for pursuit. Academically, an overwhelming amount of material is presented and a great deal is required. Professors, classes, seminars and fellow students can be exciting and fulfilling in their "intellectualism," their own store of information and their method of presentation.

However, there is a tendency for some (for me, anyway) to become supersaturated with, what often seems, an overdeveloped and undersensitized intellectual consciousness. This seems to be the ultimate standard by which to judge others. Such extreme emphasis is laid upon it that other aspects of life, equally important, such as social consciousness and "infantile" recreational enjoyment, are suppressed. Yes, probing the depths of philosophical ideas or arguing the admissibility of national and international policies can be vitalizing and satisfying. But not all the time. Discussing the relative merits or discredits of established ideals and institutions often helps to formulate more clearly your own opinions and beliefs. But these are the elements not the compounds of life. We are inclined to spend a great deal of time destroying previously and often precariously constructed foundations. This is not a bad thing since re-evaluation and reconstruction are valuable and desirable. But we do little rebuilding—many students whose "underpinnings" are weakened or shattered completely never regain a basic strength of conviction upon which to operate, which I consider essential. Are these people misfits or is Swarthmore unfit in some way to cope with the problem most effectively?

Much of Swarthmore living and learning is unrealistic. This objection is aimed not at idealism but rather at the lack of interrelation between college life and "outside" society. We have the cultural opportunities of Philly and the surrounding communities offered but academic pressure sorely limits our ability to take advantage of them. There is so much to see and do in this area, places to go which are culturally satisfying and aesthetically exciting (Valley Forge, Longwood Gardens, Bucks County and the Penna. Dutch region) but the beauty of the country and the points of historical and recreational interest are inaccessible without a car. There is a strong feeling of isolation and confinement here even with our freedom from actual rules and restrictions. Just to get off campus—to Marra's for pizza or Barson's for a double banana split—helps relieve the stifling frustration of academic and social pressures. I find it much easier to buckle down and work hard when I've had a chance to be completely free of the campus for even a few hours. Babysitting, tutoring and church activities help, too, in readjusting to the outside world; feeling the warmth of a home and family and making contact with outside people.

The extreme individualism which has become the accepted and

*expected* mode of the Swarthmore student has a dual edge. It enables many students to strike out against and relieve pent-up reactions to established convention through individualism in dress, action, and thought. This, for the most part, is acceptable here where tolerance and respect for individual rights are paramount. Perhaps for four years, it's good to "get it off your chest." But after college, returning to the less idealistic society can be a real jolt. Most people are not so tolerant—(indulgent)—are often hostile to the extreme "nonconformist." A mutual rejection, between him and society, may be acceptable since he professes complete indifference to society and the rules and conventions by which she is maintained. I'm not convinced. I don't think the question lies in a dispute of conformity or nonconformity. *Nonconformists conform to the intense desire to be different and are unified on that account. Conformists may pursue many and varied directions—without having to throw their energies into proving to themselves and to others their "separateness."* Individualism then is the key word—and rightly so since the merits and contributions and uniqueness of the individual are to be highly valued. But why not realistic individualism—society is here, we must eventually adjust to some degree to it if life is to be (to my way of thinking) not only meaningful but enjoyable.

We have decided that heterogeneity presupposes individualism which in turn promotes separateness and aloneness. Because of its size, Swarthmore in some ways compensates for this situation, while aggravating it in other respects. The student body is small enough so that most everyone is recognizable if not known. The small classes and seminars encourage individual participation, "active" learning, as well as enabling personal relationship between student and faculty. I have been impressed by the sincere interest of many of the professors in the student as a real and important personality, their generous offers of individual help and advice and genuine enthusiasm over achievement. I have been disappointed in the clear distinction made in many factions between Honors and Course students. Having experienced both methods, I think I can appreciate the inherent value of each system to some extent, but refuse to be convinced one way is best for most of the people, most of the time. Here, I'd have to fall back on my case for realistic individualism as a deciding factor—ability does not preclude interest and vice versa.

The Quaker "matchbox" may have a real germ of truth in relation to the loneliness of Swarthmore life. Couples are often drawn together and held together through the common ground of social tension, academic pressure and aloneness, yet they are unable to apply their relationship to the real world. *It's possible, I think, to go with one person for several years at Swarthmore, seeing them every day under almost every condition and in many situations and yet not truly know them.* This separateness fosters more intense emotional reactions to everyone—there is little neutrality of personal opinion here. Dormitory life helps in some respect to learn to live in close proximity with people who have different patterns of social and emotional response—to share and benefit from this contact is an individual matter. *However, the number of singles sought each year is indicative of our separateness—and intensifies it.* Dorms such as Woolman, Robinson and the Preps give a feeling of "going home," a relief from the frantic hubbub of Parrish—a return to the womb, if you like. There, the rooms are not monotonous; the parlors, fireplace and piano offer opportunities of "living room" congeniality.

We are stuffed with literature, science and philosophy but we know terribly little about getting along with others—nor do we often even make the attempt—and the so-called social graces are part of the tradition which no longer applies to our sophisticated society. At the risk of echoing verbatim the Fifth Century Greeks, I would venture to protest that Swarthmore educates only half a man—or at least only very selective parts. The whole man is important too, and we have difficulty putting the parts together.

## 11. *The lonely struggle to swim*

I came here for a rigorous liberal arts education and feel that I have gotten this, possibly sacrificing on the way many pleasant and valuable byways for the sake of study, but yet not losing on the larger scale, for the byways can come later and more profitably with the solid background.

Academic work I am on the whole very satisfied with. I have been able to get most of the courses I have wanted, and have found most of them high-quality and exacting. Some freshman courses, though, I think rather a waste of time especially for freshmen, since they are too general to be of any use. Relative freedom from required courses I think is on the whole good, and I am glad to have been able to take a wide variety of courses.

The less satisfactory side of this is that it produces a fragmentary education, or at least it has for me. Each course and particularly each department seeks its own compartment, making any useful correlation between areas of study very difficult. This also means that the non-major finds it difficult to get appreciable background in many subjects. I decry "cultural" courses in the sense of grade-school surveys, but on the other hand wish it were possible to get introductory work without an act of total commitment.

While I think it is possible to get a good education in either Course or Honors, on the whole I do not think the present arrangement a good one. I found the scope I wanted in Course; those who are ready to specialize before I was can find good training in Honors. But I think the generally-made dichotomy, assuming that naturally the "superior" student will select Honors and that therefore Course can be neglected, is a false one. But the program does mean that many of the better students are removed from the general community, thus depriving others both of their ideas and of a considerable amount of faculty time.

Swarthmore's general atmosphere I think a good one for study, perhaps excessively so. The amount of pressure in some quarters (chiefly but not exclusively among Honors students) can be very unhealthy, especially since it often seems directed to grades or to work done as such, rather than to learning. It also tends to be isolated and ivory-towered for the campus as a whole, although of course many students are extremely active and concerned outside the college. But on the whole I find this almost hothouse atmosphere good for the few years involved; if restrictive and neurotic while it lasts, I think the result at least can be worth it.

Again, in general, I think the faculty excellent and probably Swarthmore's chief resource. While I've had poor professors, I think these were more than balanced by the really outstanding ones. I'm disappointed not to have gotten to know more professors well outside the classroom (one of the chief assets, supposedly, of a small school), but grateful for those I do know. I would have appreciated more positive advising at various times—lack of this, coupled with the compartmental nature of departments, produces the lack of *universitas* which I feel is such an outstanding characteristic of our educational system.

This lack of *universitas,* this fragmentation and lack of purpose, is even more marked in the social "structure" (if there is such) of the campus. While individual freedom is a very great thing, and perhaps the greatest asset to one's education is being tossed into the sea to sink or swim alone, I do feel the lack of communal sense often reaches a point of selfishness and *mini solum* which is anything but good. This is not a plea for "togetherness" or school spirit, faceless phenomena which are even more deplorable than our 900 islands, but rather for a minimal sense of identity and common responsibility. As it is, the largest social unit is the clique, which often destroys the values both of individuality and of contact with many diverse people. This diversity is surely a positive good, and individual friendships are probably my most permanent single gain other than the purely academic from the college; but the cult of diversity as such sometimes seems to reach the point of secession from the human race.

In conclusion, and in a sense as a summary of what I've said, I think the college's, and the community's, attitude of *laissez faire* is probably more good than bad, at least for those who finish after surviving the lonely struggle to swim. Socially, intellectually, and religiously I feel I am the stronger for having had to battle a particularly rough current alone. Sometimes I wonder if it's worth it, if the same result couldn't be achieved at less cost and agony; surely for some people it can, and there are many casualties. But I'm grateful for it nevertheless.

## 12. *Swarthmore and the outside world*

One of the things I do not like about Swarthmore College is that I don't have the time that I would like to spend expressing my opinion of it.

Just one observation though: it has hit me hard in the last few weeks that Swarthmore is too unlike the "outside world." This I had forgotten until lately when I have been embarrassed by dressing too casually, trusting to the intelligence of university admissions offices, trusting to finding loop holes in masses of red-tape. I wouldn't really want to change Swarthmore but I wish I had remembered that Swarthmore ideas do not go far out of Swarthmore.

*(The entire speech was printed at the demand of the class and carried away
as a symbol of their new sentimentalism.)*

Those who are educated in the bad sense, then, talk a special language, which may be either pretentiously Latinate or may consist
simply of slogans, but which in both cases cloaks obscurity, and
they talk this language to one another in comfortable little groups.

For one of the curious attractions of being esoteric is that one can
be esoteric in comfortable little groups. In the little group of contemporary Swarthmore one escapes from the Lonely Crowd into a
*tribe* which discusses the deep truths of David Riesman; one en-
thuses over the rococo prose of Mr. Lawrence Durrell, a writer who
speaks to our condition with the most miraculous tongue by en-
veloping a mystery story in thickly Freudian purple sunsets; one
discusses the infinite superiority of musical compositions designed
for instruments with only one string; one virulently abjures the
bourgeois habit of wearing neckties. One rejoices in Swarthmore's
creativity and its lack of conformism. And the fact that these tendencies are discernible features of Swarthmore is a demonstration
of its tribalism. Swarthmoreans are tribal with a vengeance—I remember the baffled husband of a woman who was in college with
me observing, after several years of being married to Swarthmore
College: "It's not that I dislike Swarthmore people; it's simply that
I wish they didn't all behave as if they knew a beautiful secret
which no one else could ever share."

The tribal traits change over the years, but the essence of tribalism
does not. The symbols of our superiority change, but our conviction that we possess it does not. We are now, as a group, proud of
having emancipated ourselves so completely from the shibboleths
of the rah-rah era of higher education. We sneer at secret societies, football rallies, hazing and school spirit; we are unable to
repeat one line of Alma Mater. We are mature; we are rational;
we are intellectual; we are serious; we resist conformism; we belong, it is comfortingly certain, to the best college in the country.
But this is all poppycock. Fifty years ago the loyal alumnus also
believed he belonged to the best college in the country, on grounds
no more spurious. Our peculiar creativity, our intellectual distinction, are merely phrases cloaking tribalism as great as that which
characterized the class of 1901. It is for this generation as much an

expression of tribal loyalty to boast that you don't know a word of Alma Mater as it was for an earlier one to boast of knowing the third stanza. What we are doing is just what they were doing in 1901, solacing ourselves with mutual congratulation.

The selection of these comments upon life at Swarthmore recalls a student meeting scheduled by the Student Council at Swarthmore early in President Aydelotte's administration. The subject was announced as a student review of the Honors program. Quite by accident, several representatives of the General Education Board had arrived the day before on a tour of inspection to determine whether to terminate or increase their appropriations in support of the Honors program. Seeing the placards about the meeting scattered all over the place, they insisted upon attending it. For over two hours the discussion raged, intensely critical in tone, with hardly a good word for the Honors seminars. They were overorganized or underorganized, the teachers were too dominating or too passive, and so on and so on. Any observer could see that President Aydelotte was very uncomfortable. But the next morning he beamed in the halls as he told his friends that the inspectors from the Board were delighted and had said that any educational program that could produce such intelligent student criticisms deserved increased appropriations for its support.

# 6

# Some disturbed personalities

We have seen the vigor, determination, and intelligence with which our young intellectuals attacked those campus institutions, customs, and rules that seemed to them to repress their individuality. We have also looked at the feelings that many normally successful students have developed toward their new intellectual and emotional climate. But thus far we have considered students who have functioned effectively in spite of some antagonisms, frustrations, feelings of inferiority, and loneliness. Now we turn to a group who have not fared so well, who have needed supportive counsel or leaves of absence to enable them to carry on college work successfully. Such groups exist on all campuses, usually in unsuspected numbers. One advantage of the university is that it can have a more complete health center, where all combinations of physical and mental ailments can be studied and treated. From such centers have come various books[1] on student mental health, written by specialists and often for specialists, that can give these problems a more authoritative treatment than these desk-chair observations of an English professor turned dean.

In spite of all the attention given to adolescents in popular magazines, paper backs, current fiction, and the scientific books of specialists, most parents who came to the Dean's Office to discuss their offspring were under at least two illusions: (1) their son's situation was unprecedented (an illusion usually shared by the son); and (2) such things happened only at Swarthmore and were the result of the unique Swarthmore environment. A specialist might say that cases like these cited here do not need any more public attention than we give to the infirmary statistics on common colds and athletic injuries. But these cases have a much greater influence on the atmosphere of a community; they raise many questions relevant to admissions and other administrative policies, and they call for a sympathetic understanding that should be spread as widely as possible within the limits of discretion. "He jests at scars who never felt a wound"; these wounds ought to be protected from the jests of misunderstanding.

In the cases here presented some pains have been taken to conceal the identity of the persons involved, without making such changes as would destroy an understanding of the problems. The observations date back far enough so that there are now no campus memories of them.

We shall start with some manifestations of the widely felt feelings of inferiority, although it is impossible for a layman not to mix his lines of classification. When I sent for a boy to come to the office to receive news of a family disaster, he came in a little late and apologized by saying that he had swallowed a couple of bottles of poison to put himself out of the way. All day he had felt an acute sense of not being worth the space at college allotted to him. He thought that he was sure to be dropped from college before long and that he might as well beat us to it. Luckily, the college physician was close by, the stomach pump worked, and the student recovered. However, he had to be hospitalized for a period with hallucinations. Up to this time he had made no grade in his major subject below 90, and from the dean's naive point of view he had no reason whatever for such acute feelings of inferiority. After some months of psychiatric treatment in the hospital, he expressed a desire to attend an easier college. This he did; he relaxed and graduated. His background, of course, was much more complicated than was immediately apparent, and his reaction to the college environment was greatly influenced by his past.

Another case of acute inferiority feeling was that of the boy who required united action on the part of the dormitory proctors to quell his assaults on fellow students. During the first semester of his freshman year he was one of the most popular boys in his class. He was an intellectual who yet received bids from all the fraternities. But in his second semester he became moody, truculent, and aggressive. He was induced to explain that he had satisfied his longings for prestige in secondary school by excelling in the field of his special interest and by holding prominent student offices. But when he joined the campus bull sessions as a freshman, he was dismayed at his ignorance of literature and philosophy. He started a program of reading to establish his ascendancy in discussion groups. However, since upperclassmen were often quite at home in these fields, he could not establish a superior role. For a period he turned religious and violently anti-intellectual, and picked fights whenever he was irritated. This student required hospitalization and continued treatment before he was able to perform at anything like his intellectual capacity.

Less dramatic are a number of similar cases of boys distrustful of their own capacities and interests whose doubts are only increased by receiving large graduate fellowships for advanced work in the fields of their college majors. These awards are sometimes accompanied by letters telling them that they are already assured of being leaders in their fields and that their future is looked to with pride and confidence. Such boys have come to the office to say that they had not yet chosen their fields and did not want to be committed; that they had classmates who really should have received the award; and that they needed a leave of absence to be able to sleep again.

Changes of goals to assure status have often been recounted. By the end of their sophomore year at college, boys of intellectual capacity whose leadership in high school had been assured by participation in athletics and other activities have had a revulsion against all such pursuits as commonplace and ordinary, as opening no path to distinction. They talk contemptuously of gladhanders and Rotarian conformists, and amaze their friends by a sudden concentration on specialized scholarship that will lead to "real distinction." Others, sometimes of no less ability, are overcome with the loneliness of scholarship; they renounce it as cold and self-centered, turn for warmth and companionship to the activities of the campus, and begin to talk of the pleasure of "working with people." Some of these students have reversed themselves several times in college, saying that they struggle between the desire for the cold heights of a distant fame and the need for the warmth of immediate companionship.

In many cases there seems to be little relationship between a student's estimate of himself and the opinions of his teachers or his classmates. Parents have repeatedly come to say their son has warned them that he expects to be dropped at the end of the semester or that they should not come to commencement because he has no chance of graduation; then the grades turn out to be A's and B's. Students who are really in danger of being dropped often seem quite unworried about it. Those whose social success is particularly marked often confess to a continuous strain to overcome their feelings of inadequacy in all social situations.

Students often complain of the "exaggerated need to compete at Swarthmore." They say it is continuous and unremitting. Some, of course, are able to exult in this, and many are glad that status at Swarthmore is more dependent on achievement than on membership in any class or organization. But even exclusive and undemocratic organizations can afford occasional respite from continuous, self-centered competition. A student can occasionally relax in a feeling of companionship within his organization, and even take an easy pride in the reflected glory of his fellows. Apparently one of the penalties of extreme individualism is the necessity of perpetual self-assertion to silence the doubts arising from a sense of inferiority.

The roots of the rebelliousness so prevalent on the campus often go back to the earliest years, but occasionally it bursts out suddenly in the midst of the college career. One wise headmaster who followed his students' college days with interest and affection used to say, "John Smith shouldn't give you much trouble, he has largely run his course of rebellion in school"; or, "You should look out for Bill Jones, he hasn't begun to rebel yet, but he will." And he always insisted that this period of rebellion was a prime necessity for growth and that it should be met with understanding, even when it called for firmness.

World literature is so full of the rebelliousness of youth that our researchers often seem to be reminding us of ancient observations. A few typical college cases may, however, illustrate the current manifestations of this eternal characteristic in the contemporary college of intellect. One can with almost equal facility cite cases of young liberals rebelling against conservative families, or young conservatives rebelling against liberal backgrounds. The truth behind the Gilbertian observation

That every boy and every gal,
    That's born into the world alive,
Is either a little Liberal,
    Or else a little Conservative!

lies quite largely in the rebellion against the family background, whatever it happens to be. Many parents come to the Dean's Office to complain that they had always suspected the college of radicalism and that their worst suspicions have been confirmed by the careers of their sons at Swarthmore. One such boy, whose rebelliousness was so well controlled that he was not only a leader of every radical campus group but also a president of the Student Council and a scholar of distinction, was an especially effective denouncer of the college administration and an irrefutable Marxist in student discussions. In asking for a college room over vacation time he volunteered an apology for not accepting the cordial invitation of his parents to fly home. He felt considerable guilt about disappointing their affection for him, but he said that he could not enter his home without a loss of all personal significance. He seemed about to be absorbed in a social system that he lived to denounce. Social gatherings were unendurable, although when he presided over the Student Council, where his leadership was acknowledged, he was a model of courtesy, even to the "bourgeois" members. Not until he had been for some years a rebel against those of his own political and economic faith did he begin to doubt that he was destined to political power as one of the country's most conspicuous rebels. In the atmosphere of academic freedom to study all views of political and social issues his early rebelliousness was always the controlling factor in his discussions, although he was a master rationalizer. His parents could and did say, with some truth, that his college experience had greatly increased his faith in his ability to defy his own social group.

A contrasting case was that of a student who wrote themes attacking campus radical groups with a rage that became more and more incoherent and that seemed to lead to an obsession that made it impossible for him to study. His father was a liberal who had himself revolted against the conservative background of his inherited wealth. The father was also a successful athlete and a fan at football and baseball games, and had another son who followed his political and athletic interests. The student in question presented the somewhat unusual case of denouncing with equal vigor all liberals as communists and all athletes as childish. This rebellion developed such heat that he needed an extended leave of absence for psychiatric treatment before he could successfully resume academic work.

It is, of course, a widely held opinion that intellectuals are rebels; a professor is usually thought to be a man who "thinks otherwise." It seems to be difficult to decide whether they are rebels because they are intellectuals or intellectuals because they are rebels. But as the impulse to rebel comes much earlier than intellectual achievement, it is pretty certain that the instinctive attitude is the dominant one. Anyone who is sufficiently interested to read some of the literature [2] on intellectuals in America will wish the college of intellect success in helping rebellious intellectuals to develop from their adolescent turmoil some degree of constructive balance.

Early commitment to specialized interests often seems to quiet this turmoil (but some exponents of liberal education are always telling us that the major function of liberal education is to create turmoil, not to quiet it). An increasing number of students enter Swarthmore from academic families. Many of them on entrance know not only what graduate school they want to attend, but with what distinguished scholars they want to study. The path lies straight ahead, and there is no rebellion. Those students whose eyes are fixed on law and medical schools have standardized guidance, with increasing freedom. Most of them proceed happily ahead, but if something happens to change the pattern their confusion is increased. A boy reared in an eminent scientific family took it for granted that he would be a physicist. He had had A's in mathematics and physics in high school, but at the end of his freshman year at Swarthmore he had A's in philosophy and literature, a C in mathematics, and a D in physics. This continued throughout his sophomore year. He regarded philosophy and literature as playful relaxations; only science was serious work. In his junior year he made more friends among the humanists, but he continued to taunt them about their uncertainties and mere probabilities. In his senior year it became obvious that he could not gain admittance to any reputable graduate school in science, and he reluctantly changed his major. It was a great humiliation to him. His father professed perfect willingness to see the boy do as he pleased, but the humiliation, and even guilt, remained. When he graduated with a distinguished record in the humanities, he still suffered from the conviction that he had turned playboy.

Another boy from a distinguished academic family was brought up, he said, on the wrong side of the tracks. He desired to be a good fellow among the boys of his high school and did all he could to conceal his bookish interests, but he made A's in spite of himself. He looked forward, he said, to coming to an intellectual college, where he could talk freely of his own interests. To his surprise and disappointment he did not like the young intellectuals. He thought them cold, arrogant, self-centered, and became depressed with nostalgia for his old friends. Gradually he came to feel that he was achieving his niche in the college community by listening to the problems of unhappy classmates. He became a sympathetic listener, but he offered little advice. He found that he was most happy when he was most comforting to someone. He did not at this point have any theological interests, but he did go to a theological seminary, graduated, and now does mostly what might be called social work among the underprivileged. He calls it his return to the wrong side of the tracks. What he owes to Swarthmore, after a period of severe depression, he says, is a conviction of the emptiness of the merely intellectual life. He merely felt compassion, he adds, for the intellectuals who professed a great scorn for the "do-gooder."

This type of nurturant personality is often associated with religious interests, but is even more often identified, perhaps, with the maternal instinct. It was not my function to deal with the women students, but they came inevitably to my attention in connection with the men. Many disturbed male students owed their ability to keep going to the sympathetic care of their steady mates. Some of these girls persistently sought out such men as something of an antidote to intellectual interests or, at times, as a means of intellectual companionship. Girls such as these, with excellent academic records, have been turned down by schools for social work as "overmotivated."

Religious interests have been infinitely varied in their effects on the development of adolescent intellectuals. Some young professors of philosophy, with a morally earnest desire to rid the world of the incubus of God, have won enthusiastic disciples, but they have also encountered indifference and opposition and have created surprisingly little disturbance. The Christian Association has occasionally dropped the word Christian from its title, and has become the Society for Religious Understanding. This in turn has divided into different groupings. Many members of the Presbyterian, Methodist, Episcopal, and Quaker groups have continued actively and contentedly with their earlier affiliations, but many members of the Society have asserted that they had no concern with such nonintellectual organizations as churches. The less self-conscious intellectuals have often and in large numbers given their attention to social work in various forms—reading for the blind, neighborhood houses, week-end and work camps—and have gained great satisfaction from helpful cooperation.

The relations among religious, philosophical, and philanthropic groupings sometimes reveal strange associations. At a widely publicized meeting a prominent Zionist student who was presiding announced that the services would begin with a Quaker silence, followed by prayer, the singing of a Whittier hymn, and the reading of scripture. Then he said, "Our speaker today is an eminent psychiatrist who will speak to us on sex, and next week we shall have an informal bull session on Christ." Some time later, groups met to hear records of liturgical services accompanied by jazz.

Surprised denial usually results from attempts to generalize about the religious life of the students, especially when free-thinking is asserted to be completely dominant. One day a student objected that a lecturer on Milton had dwelt on Milton's use of Genesis and of classical mythology and had assigned the reading of Fraser's FOLK LORE OF THE OLD TESTAMENT. "This," he said, "threatens my salvation, and I have lain awake for three nights trying to decide whether to read it. I have finally decided that I will not." When asked about his major subject he said it was biology, with a minor in psychology. When asked if anything in these fields had ever threatened his salvation he said that he had never heard anything mentioned that had any bearing on religion. Some time after dropping the Milton course he came back to explain that he was sleeping well and that his other symptoms of anxiety had disappeared.

That same semester a freshman came in to say that he was leaving college because he had come to Swarthmore to form a comprehensive philosophy of life, and nothing he had heard in his classes seemed relevant to it. He left Swarthmore, journeyed to China and India to continue his search, and found some peace in the teachings of Ghandi. Later he returned to college and graduated with distinction; now, as a university professor, he lectures on oriental solutions to problems that had troubled him.

For a number of years a group of fundamentalists flourished. They came from widely separated areas and objected to the liberalism of the pastors of the local churches of their earlier loyalty. They invited fundamentalist evangelists to the campus, and compelled the dean to fight the battle of free speech against the student members of the Forum for Free Speech, who thought it a disgrace to the intellectual standing of Swarthmore to have an old-fashioned revival meeting, even if it was attended by very few students. The academic records of these students were somewhat better than those of the Forum, and many of them were science majors. They were dedicated to a cause as earnestly as were the advocates of free speech who invited Alger Hiss and Minister Oumansky to speak on the campus.

The fundamentalists were a close group, eating and praying together in noon and evening meetings. They disturbed some boys seriously enough to send them to a mental hospital. When some of these zealots were asked to read such books as RELIGIOUS FACTORS IN MENTAL ILLNESS,[3] a few did so, but most said that their religion had nothing to do with psychology. A number of these later went to theological seminaries and, for the most part, greatly changed their views. It was surprising to learn that many of them had come from families of liberal views in their Unitarian, Presbyterian, Episcopal, and Methodist churches, and that part of the adolescent rebellion was to attack vigorously what they called the emptiness of the pseudo-religious attitudes of their parents. Where no convictions were imposed upon these boys to rebel against, they sought a cause that would give them the mental satisfaction of "commitment."

The more traditional type of reaction to "free thought" came, as might be expected, from foreign students from "undeveloped" areas, many of whom had prepared for college in fundamentalist mission schools. Some of them made excellent records in scientific subjects and showed little interest in religion. Others anxiously tried to pursue courses in religion and philosophy along with those in science. One who felt with many others that the course in "Neo-orthodoxy" offered most promise came jubilantly to say that the study of Harry Emerson Fosdick had answered most of his questions. But a month later he was sitting on his dormitory stairway saying resolutely to all questioners, "Go away, I'm dead." When carried to the infirmary and questioned, he said, after some hours of silence, that he had felt his spirit come from his stomach and that nothing around him now had any reality. After a couple of days he began to talk coherently and said that he had lost his sense of reality in trying to understand John Dewey. After a period of outside employment at manual labor, he returned, graduated, and went on to graduate study before returning to his native country.

An intellectually sophisticated student with strong religious interests took a deep satisfaction in quoting from favorite authors, especially poets. He took a violent dislike to the intellectualism of much literary criticism and would denounce it explosively, saying that literature was to be lived and felt and not reasoned about. He would ask to open seminars with quotations, and did so with such feeling and reverence that it seemed like opening the session with prayer. Even the most irreverent students treated him with profound respect. His visiting Honors examiners reported that his final written examinations omitted all philosophical and critical aspects of the questions, but quoted relevant passages with such facility and extensiveness that he must have somehow concealed a large group of books and copied from them. It was suggested that he be tried on quotations in the final oral examination. He outquoted all five examiners so amazingly that after much debate they gave him highest honors. The boy went on to theological seminary. There he developed the same aversion to theology that he had for literary criticism, and he left to enter a mental institution. Some years later, when visiting the college, he recounted his success as a sales and business manager and said he felt that he had been out of touch with reality all during his college years.

A very considerable number of disturbed students whose difficulties manifest themselves in social behavior find solitary intellectual work a relief from the strain of personal relations. Their parents frequently come to request that the college do something to make them "well rounded." The parents of a startlingly successful physicist came repeatedly to urge that their son be induced to take part in dramatic productions. With exceptional docility he made unfortunate attempts in the try-outs. His suffering was so acute that his parents finally decided to allow him to be content with the self-esteem that came from his superiority in science. He graduated with distinction and won a coveted graduate fellowship, which added to the prestige of the college and caused his classmates to quip about Swarthmore being a school for Einsteins.

An increasing number of such students proceed to graduate school as the place that allows most freedom to concentrate on their own interests. The prestige of winning awards in graduate school is perhaps the most unquestioned symbol of individual and college success when friends and parents come to extend congratulations at commencement time. For admission to the professional schools of law, medicine, and the ministry, personal qualifications play an increasingly important part, and new methods of testing personal qualities are constantly being developed. But a career in research is not expected to lead to public life or to involve the graduate in personal relations. Personality may seem irrelevant. This may be a new area of freedom that will yield great returns in the productivity of research. The trivialities of social custom may be ignored, and intellectual distinction may gain increased prestige. The undergraduate who is sometimes warned by his parents that he will eventually have to conform to the ways of the world may reply that he is preparing for a career in which he can realize himself in complete independence of its ways.

In a public lecture at Swarthmore, Professor Gordon Allport of Harvard commented enthusiastically upon the number of "odd balls" who came from the individualistic freedom of Swarthmore to do distinguished research at Harvard. He hoped that Swarthmore would continue to attract such researchers and would continue to direct them to Harvard. But apparently some of the difficulties of late adolescence continue into the graduate years; students in graduate school have more difficulties and less stability than those in professional schools, and stand in some need of humanizing.[4]

One of the commonest phrases used to describe the adolescent turmoil is "He hasn't found himself." This applies to the period when a youngster is aware of a great discontinuity between his past and his present. He may be quite unsure what his past leads to; he may be all too sure and dislike it; he may know what he would like to be, but is not sure that he can thereby win recognition; he may feel quite superior to all the routines he knows about; he may feel that only in a new world can he find scope and therefore rush off to fight Franco or join Castro or found a new society such as William Penn attempted.

In the past, various cultures have had traditional rituals to offer support and guidance for these years. To be told firmly by tradition just who one is can be experienced as freedom, whereas permission to make original choices can feel like enslavement to the unknown. The older college traditions were the equivalent of many primitive rituals and supplied an element of participation, of loyalty, of common aims. But the newer college is the greatest artificial postponement of adulthood, emotionally speaking, that could be imagined. Older cultures would lead at a reasonably early date to the individual's entering the life of his people as a worker, earner, and homemaker, with a new independence of his parents' home. But college provides one of the longest apprenticeships of our time. There is a radical postponement of some satisfactions and a replacement of them by others. It fosters some forms of childishness and stimulates certain types of precocity.

Professor Erik Erikson of Harvard, who has long worked as a specialist in late adolescence, has listed some of the main symptoms that he has observed as characteristic of this period, which he calls one of "identity diffusion." First, there is a great disturbance in the sense of time. Some young persons feel everything to be mortally urgent—career, immortality, love:

. . . at my back I always hear
Time's wingèd chariot hurrying near. . . .

Or, on the other hand, nothing matters enough to be in a hurry about it—as exemplified by the engineering student who stayed away from classes until he had read all of Aldous Huxley. Secondly, there is a great increase in self-consciousness— a constant preoccupation with one's type, physical appearance, sexual character, anticipated occupational role—and a bisexual confusion, a doubt as to whether one really is a man or woman. The symptoms resulting from this are often an inability to concentrate on a required task, a preoccupation with excessive reading, or listening to music, or watching sports. The final common characteristic Erikson calls negative identity: a scornful and snobbish hostility toward all the roles offered as proper and desirable in one's family or community.

In his Introduction to EMOTIONAL PROBLEMS OF THE COLLEGE STUDENT, Erikson declares:

Such a *moratorium* is often characterized by a combination of prolonged immaturity and provoked precocity, which makes colleges not only good study grounds, but—as surrounding communities have been most eager to note—breeding grounds for deviant behavior of all kinds, whether such behavior is attributed to the influence of scholastics or humanistics, radicalism, existentialism, or psychoanalysis. . . .

[The book's authors, "Harvard men dealing with Harvard problems," Erikson goes on to say,] display a pragmatic and democratic orientation toward emotional problems universal to students. . . . If Harvard cannot deny its ten per cent quota of [student] emotional problems, neither can other colleges get away with the assumption that what is described here is essentially (and predictably) typical for Harvard. . . . There are always some, in any setting, who must be steered in their erratic growth or kept from being crushed by a transitory condition. The relevant questions are only what kind of problems receive public recognition and attention; who is appointed to deal with them; and what these caretakers will make of these problems—medically, conceptually, and ideologically.[5]

# 7

# The intellectual community

## Students

The development at Swarthmore that I have attempted to describe has much in common with the traditional American college in its religious origin, its gradual conformity to worldly ways, its acceptance of conventional standards of success as the basis of campus customs, traditions, and morale, followed by the intellectual revolution, with its student attacks upon the institutions that seemed to require conformity, both on and off campus. Along with all this has come for most students a new source of morale in their pride in the growing prestige of Swarthmore due to the intellectual distinction of graduates as shown in their professional achievements. But too many others have found themselves lonely, unhappy, and frustrated, and altogether too many drop out of college.* This is true both of the small colleges that have attained intellectual distinction and of the large universities where community life is hardly expected.

The Jencks-Riesman study of the Harvard House Plan, which President Lowell hoped would create more community life where it was painfully lacking, suggests some of the difficulties in creating a community among intellectuals:

* A different view now gaining acceptance is that dropping out is often a healthy part of the adolescent's attempt to find himself and should be sympathetically encouraged. For an understanding account of the dropouts at Harvard, and the attitude of student advisers toward them, see William Wertenbaker: "A Problem of Identity," *The New Yorker,* Vol. 38, No. 41, December 1, 1962, pp. 68–117.

In all that we have said . . . there has been a tension between the ideal of solidarity, friendship, security, and the ideal of diversity, conflict, and adventure. Neither of these ideals can endure alone. Students must be stretched, but not to the breaking point. They must become involved in conflicts, but they must have enough security to believe that they may emerge victorious, for otherwise they become rigid with fright and learn nothing, or only by rote. . . . In small provincial colleges the houses and the utopias they suggest . . . are likely to be so supportive and homogenized that there is neither incentive nor room for original or imaginative thought. . . .

. . . in a world where togetherness based on superficial similarities makes rugged individualism nostalgically attractive, an appeal for solidarity on any basis seems untimely. . . . Nevertheless we are convinced that closing the gap between the academic and the intellectual will become an increasing problem for higher education as the academic values spread throughout the university world.[1]

There was an earlier hope, still cherished by a few, that restricting admission to the top-ranking students might produce an intellectual community. This standard of admission has been retained in some places because of its simplicity of administration. It has often been difficult to make the more complex "nonintellective" factors seem comprehensible and consistent to school advisers and parents. When a national magazine attacks a college for rejecting a student with high scores, it is difficult and embarrassing to make a public explanation of all the factors that make an applicant a desirable member of a small academic community, especially when that community is known for its intellectualism. But experience is repeatedly confirming many well-worn observations that too many intellectuals will not make an intellectual community. One of the final comments made by President Taylor before he left Sarah Lawrence was:

. . . in the selection of a student body to function in a free community it was of first importance to consider the personal attributes of the applicants every bit as seriously as their academic qualifications. . . . Intellectually ambitious students with a drive toward personal gratification could, if present in sufficient numbers in a given residence, produce sufficient tension and difficulty within their own environment to prevent the healthy development of the students around them and block their own growth. To choose a student body with regard mainly to academic competence and achievement is unwise not only in the decision it implies to give the privilege of private education only to a particular kind of student, but unwise in the effect it has on the conditions for the development even of those most intellectually gifted.[2]

During many years of my own chairmanship of the Men's Admissions Committee at Swarthmore we were entirely delighted at the great increase of applications from young intellectuals. We did not wish to keep any promising student out merely because he was a nonconformist. We often felt that the prospects for creative talent and rigorous scholarship were greater among the "odd balls." But the result of some years of this was to give more attention to personality factors. This is evidenced in the analysis of each freshman class that Swarthmore now publishes and distributes to secondary-school guidance officers in asking their assistance in recommending a wide variety of applicants who may successfully meet Swarthmore standards for graduation. Some individualists among the students have complained that the campus is now less picturesque than it was when they were freshmen, but at this writing the Admissions Committee is now ready to read with sympathy Dean Bender's final report on his retirement from the Admissions Committee at Harvard, in which he contributed his views to the heated controversy over admissions:

The make-up of the Harvard student body was determined by natural forces, not by conscious planning, for over three hundred years, and the College has had a significant degree of selectivity for only about ten years.

Does Harvard want only the top one per cent of American college students? I do not believe this would bring to Harvard the highest proportion of genuinely powerful, creative, and useful minds.

The student who ranks first in his class may be genuinely brilliant. Or he may be a compulsive worker, or the instrument of dominating parents' ambition, or a conformist, or a self-centered careerist who has shrewdly calculated his teachers' prejudices, or he may have focussed narrowly on grade-getting as a compensation in other areas because he lacks other interests or talents or lacks passion and warmth or normal healthy interests or is afraid of life. The top high school student is often, frankly, a pretty dull and bloodless and peculiar fellow. . . .

My prejudice is for a Harvard College with a certain range and mixture and diversity in its student body—a college with some snobs and some Scandinavian farm boys who skate beautifully, and some bright Bronx pre-meds, with some students who care passionately if unwisely (but who knows) about editing the *Crimson* or beating Yale, or who have an ambition to run a business and make a million, or to get elected to public office, a college in which not all students have looked on school as a preparation for college, college as a preparation for graduate school, and graduate school as a preparation for they know not what. Won't even our top one per cent be better men and better scholars for being part of such a college? [3]

If Harvard really had had such a diversity in its student body, it does not seem likely that the Harvard chairman of the Center of Research on Personality would so readily accept the stereotype of Harvard men as "indifferent, superior, and slightly disillusioned, with very few committed romantics among them."

There are those who are troubled by the power that research on college applicants may give to admissions committees and who ask if there are to be no natural forces left in the formation of college communities. One natural force that the most-expert committee cannot entirely control is the effect of the college reputation on those who will not apply because of it. How many "Scandinavian farm boys who skate beautifully" think they would care to associate for four years with "indifferent, superior, and slightly disillusioned" boys? To be sure, there have been in the Harvard of the past many different types, and they have distributed themselves in the different houses whose local designations have showed the delight of adolescents (and others) in expressing their easy contempt for those of a different type. There were, for example, the House for nonconformists and Bohemians, the House for aristocratic intellectuals and unfriendly socialites, the House for Midwestern hustlers and organizers, the House for varsity athletes, known as "jocks," and the House for academic high-brows and "grinds." These stereotypes of houses grew so influential in controlling membership that the masters established a system of academic and social quotas designed to make each house representative of the college as a whole. This made it difficult for the sophomore to find himself or change himself.[4] Yale has tried I.B.M. machines for this selective process, and there are those who strongly urge the replacing of expensive personal interviews with machines for college admissions. All this makes the replacement of natural forces a little frightening.

Statistical studies now indicate that at some colleges the aesthetic and artistic type is dominant, that in others the political type holds sway, and that in still others religious and social values are most esteemed. According to several reports, in large universities the economic type prevails. Robert Hutchins laments that the success of courses in the production and sale of mobile homes portends the end of civilization. For a time the greatest proportion of distinguished scientists came from small grass-roots colleges, and a theory was promptly developed that since the colleges were not good enough to have caused this, it must be that science attracted poor boys who did not expect large incomes. But all this has changed, and the increase of scientific rewards and the burgeoning of large laboratories in the universities have taken the lead away from the small colleges. All these differences in institutions and groupings seem to show that planned selection has not entirely overcome natural forces.

Some of the forces operating on adolescents before they come to college seem to make the college situation easier for them to cope with, and some make it harder to maintain the intellectual community. In the earlier stages of the intellectual revolution students who had the courage to be "brains" in high schools often entered college with strong tendencies toward nonconformity and an arrogance that in earlier years would have invited hazing. Or they were meekly submissive and entirely conformist. But the high schools are now changing rapidly; many young intellectuals now enjoy enough prestige and leadership to be humanized by these characteristics. This has allowed a greater tolerance of different interests and personalities, particularly among the smaller colleges. Studies of personality in different fields of study show that the influence of the smaller communities moderates the diversities of temperament in the different fields. Statistics show that in large groups in large universities the students with the most fears, worries, and conflicts are usually found in the fields of literature or fine arts. Apparently the more neurotic, complex, or troubled persons are drawn to intangibles, or, conversely, they are repelled by the mundane. Other studies show that students in psychology and sociology are more rebellious in their attitudes toward authority and convention. By contrast, the most conservative and conformist people are the engineers and the students of the applied sciences.[5] These differences are tempered (not always easily) by the understanding that comes from life in an intellectual community, where the influence of the college as a whole is greater than the influence of specialized colleagues.

An outside social influence that seems to make it more difficult to maintain the intellectual community has been commented on by Harold Taylor, former president of Sarah Lawrence. The progressive program that allowed most unlimited social and intellectual freedom to Sarah Lawrence girls, and that expected in return both responsibility and initiative, was highly successful in the 1930's and 1940's. But in the 1950's liberation into freedom seemed no longer to exhilarate the students; they lost interest in their self-government and wanted more definite study outlines and requirements. As a result, there had to be a general return to a more authoritarian approach. President Taylor explains this by saying that the greatly increased freedom in the home and school made freedom in college no longer interesting and that it ceased to be a source of morale. What the students wanted was an escape from freedom.[6] Whatever the causes, such changes call for study and concern by the colleges.

Student apathy at Harvard has become sufficiently notable so that a study of alienation among adolescent intellectuals has been undertaken by specialists in the Department of Social Relations.[7] The notable lack of commitment to adult values and rules is not only characteristic of the beatniks, but common to many teen-agers. The term adolescent has formerly seemed to imply a goal of adulthood, but the society of the modern teen-ager is so complete that he often prefers not to grow up. He has come to see adult life and work as dull, repetitive, purposeless. Society offers few objects of loyalty and parents are poor models of the good life. The past is irrelevant, the future uncertain, and the present best occupied with private and personal experiences. The various beliefs that lead an alienated youth to fear "growing up absurd" have been set forth by various critics, playwrights, and fiction writers, and naturally are found reflected in many *avant-garde* intellectuals on the campus.

Kenneth Keniston, who has been studying such youth at Harvard and later at Yale, believes that giving moralistic lectures about the need for social responsibility and the perversity of withdrawing into private life is not likely to be of help. Students should somehow be encouraged to understand the significance of their own stage of life and the problems that are likely to affect their generation. What is needed is an understanding both of the personal relations that have molded the adolescent before he came to college and the psychosocial forces that will affect him all his life. Academic instruction is often so concerned with being objective and scientific that it does not allow for the personal involvement without which there is little insight. But undergraduates since World War II (as contrasted with those in the period after World War I) have turned, perhaps from a sense of helplessness, from economics and politics to the arts as an expression of their emotions and to the study of personal relations in psychology, anthropology, and sociology. The Department of Social Relations at Harvard, established in 1946, was almost immediately near the top in enrollment, in spite of the skepticism and opposition of older departments. The course in "Culture and Personality" at Chicago immediately attracted a large following of really concerned students. Similar courses at Stanford, California, and Michigan are meeting with the same kind of response. This interest, too, may pass with the social changes of the future or may wear out as novelty wears off. Or it may become so scientific and impersonal that it becomes strictly a professional field. But this interest should not now be ignored.

At present several courses in the Social Relations Division at Harvard seem particularly worthy of attention for their help in developing the human understanding that is so necessary for an intellectual community. Professor Erikson's course, "The Human Life Cycle," studies "those lawful stages of life which every human being is born to live through, and which every functioning society must be set to support." His books, CHILDHOOD AND SOCIETY,[8] IDENTITY AND THE LIFE CYCLE,[9] THE YOUNG MAN LUTHER,[10] and YOUTH AND SOCIAL CHANGE,[11] have had a great influence in directing attention to late adolescence. "Psychological Study of Life Histories," given by Professor R. W. White, uses case histories pursued over a number of years to introduce and illustrate the general ideas that go to make up a scientific account of personality. His coordination and illustrations of the biological view of man, of man as seen by dynamic psychology, and of the social view of man are set forth with admirable clarity for the undergraduate in his volume LIVES IN PROGRESS.[12] "The Interpretation of Interpersonal Behavior" is an interdisciplinary course that aims to "develop the student's understanding of his values, attitudes and perceptions as they affect human relations." Professor Bales also uses the case method here; as the director of the Department and Laboratory of Social Relations he also directs research and publishes continually.

Such courses as these are not usually given in small colleges because there are few qualified teachers who have a broad interdisciplinary background, because of the lack of financial resources, and because of the skepticism of well-established academic departments.[13] One explanation of such skepticism, with possible reasons for its disappearance, is given by William G. Perry, Jr., director of the Bureau of Study Counsel at Harvard, in an article entitled "The 'Human Relations' Course in the Curriculum of Liberal Arts":

The study of the concrete events of daily human life has had an odd history in the liberal arts curriculum. Before the development of productive analytical tools, the commonplace incidents of which life is made seemed unworthy of intellectual care. As a result this complicated and vital subject appeared traditionally in the curriculum only after being dignified by art, as in literature; by morals, as in ethics; or by destiny, as in history. At the turn of the century such new subjects as social anthropology, sociology and psychology attained their first probationary acceptance by maintaining a high level of generality. These concepts now enable us to develop college courses in the disciplined observation of individual events. . . . There is now a place for the observation of human situations in a liberal arts curriculum just as much as for training in observing a frog or a poem.[14]

Although small colleges like Swarthmore have had neither the resources nor the interdisciplinary staff members to support courses like those being developed at Harvard, some experiments have been made. Professor Peter Madison of the Psychology Department was interested in conducting extensive and concrete studies of student personalities as seen in their Swarthmore setting. There was some faculty skepticism about what was considered an invasion of privacy, but the students were eager to offer themselves as subjects for prolonged study. They were often gratified to find that experiences that they had regarded as unique could be so much better understood in the light of concepts that might become scientific. Professor Madison was chiefly interested in the study of the normal personality as a means of correcting and supplementing some generalizations drawn from psychoanalysis. Finding it very difficult to define "normal," he asked faculty members to nominate small groups of students whom they regarded as most effective. He wished to generalize from their growth and development rather than from the study of students who had been driven by suffering to the psychoanalyst. But in defining the personality concept as "the individual's characteristic reaction to events of emotional significance in living," he was, of course, no nearer to a line between the normal and the abnormal. Some of his results are incorporated in the book TO-WARD UNDERSTANDING HUMAN PERSONALITIES.[15] Many students stated emphatically that this was the most interesting and helpful course they had taken in college, and they expressed keen regret when Professor Madison left Swarthmore.

Another attempt to study the normal resulted in the same ambiguities. Dr. Earl Bond entitled his research paper "The Student Council Study, An Approach to the Normal."[16] He took as his subjects sixty-four students who had been elected to the student councils of Swarthmore, Haverford, and Bryn Mawr. He was assured by a college president that if there were any normal people, they would be these students who had passed their admission requirements and then won the approval of their student bodies for their interest in student affairs. He was therefore surprised to have to report that although half of them were efficient, easy, and happy, the other half stood in need of help to assure mental stability, and that about one-fourth were on the lower edge of the range that could be called normal. Of the substantial group who "carried the burdens of retreat into fantasy, marked insecurities, obsessions, snobbishness, intolerance, fears, hostilities," Dr. Bond remarks that their chances for success seem much greater than their chances for happiness. He does not consider colleges responsible for these characteristics, but he thinks that to publish the fact that so many gifted students have neurotic handicaps makes it easier for such persons to ask for help. It also helps the college to be more tolerant of the unusual personality.

Another study of the development of personality at Swarthmore was made possible by the financial aid of the Grant Foundation and the experimental cooperation of the Department of Psychology. The basis of this study was the direct observations of a dynamic psychiatrist in clinical practice, Dr.

Leon J. Saul, who is consultant in psychiatry at Swarthmore and a member of the faculty of the University of Pennsylvania. Dr. Saul is the author of BASES OF HUMAN BEHAVIOR,[17] EMOTIONAL MATURITY,[18] TECHNIC AND PRACTICE OF PSYCHIATRY,[19] and other well-known books. In an unpublished account of this experimental course he has written:

The need for the course has been expressed by the students as wanting something "closer to home," a course which deals with what is most real, pressing, and poignant to them in their lives at the time—loves and hates and rivalries, shyness and loneliness and sexual drives, senses of inferiority, of being different, undefined confusions and anxieties, wishes to come to grips with the emotional life and relations between people and what these are all about and what can be clarified and systematized. The basic human emotional problem is regularly intelligible in the same terms—as a problem in feelings and motivations which have a particular source and origin.

The psychiatrist sees these human problems not only in his practice, but in his consultations with students. As the years pass he sees how each student with his own individuality and specific problems represents only a different continuation of the same few motivations and feelings, of what might be termed, for convenience, "emotional forces." Like a kaleidoscope of a few varicolored pieces, these dozen or so major motivations and reactions and the thirty or so defense mechanisms, combine into distinctive patterns. But although no two patterns are alike, many of them are of similar nature. And the emotional problems occasioned by disturbed patterns trace back with monotonous regularity to troubled relations with parents or others responsible for or close to the student. . . .

Psychodynamics, and not psychoanalysis, is what this course is about. Psychodynamics is the new embryonic science of the development and interplay of the emotional and motivational processes. The impetus to its genesis came chiefly from psychoanalysis, but by no means limits itself to these. It draws freely on all the related behavioral sciences—anthropology, animal etiology, sociology, experimental psychology, and other disciplines. . . . Psychodynamics may illumine all we experience, in work, in living, in recreation.

To achieve a proper balance between concrete experiences and interpretive concepts is not an easy pedagogic problem, and success or failure in doing so is partially measured by the autobiographies students wrote toward the end of the course. They show how little the teachers know of their pupils, and often clearly indicate progress in self-understanding. Coming of age in college is rather more difficult than coming of age in Samoa. There is being developed a cultural anthropology of college students that is at least as scientific as the literature on the Samoans or the Navajos; it may help us to see how tribally ritualistic even the Bohemians and the rugged individualists really are. Such studies give us an increased sympathy for adolescence, and for late adolescence in particular, as a necessary, significant, and inevitable period that is one of the major justifications of college as providing a "psycho-social moratorium" before the great decisions have to be made.[20] We are only now realizing that the more intellectual students often require a more prolonged adolescence.

## Faculty

What does the study of adolescent intellectuals imply about the place of the faculty in the intellectual community? A recently published volume of more than 1,000 pages, entitled THE AMERICAN COLLEGE: A PSYCHOLOGICAL AND SOCIAL INTERPRETATION OF THE HIGHER LEARNING,[21] edited by Nevitt Sanford of Stanford, presents a very full summary of the research of thirty psychologists and sociologists on what happens to students in American colleges; it is very frankly critical of colleges for knowing so little about students. Its fundamental assumption might be said to be that the prime purpose of a liberal education is the development of the student's personality. If this is accepted (and this cannot be assumed), it follows that educators should design curricula to this end and should support research to see what effect their teaching, along with the total life of the college, is having. At a national conference called to discuss this volume a number of college professors reacted typically. Some thought that the personal and social development of students was the responsibility of family, church, and state and that faculty members should restrain their missionary impulses and get on with their research. Others thought it eminently desirable that a student should be stimulated to develop himself, but that his development was obviously his own responsibility. Still others feared that the suggestions of the authors of the volume might degrade the college into a super secondary school. Professors also expressed their fear that turning the attention of an adolescent toward himself would almost inevitably do more harm than good. They felt that the college should lead the student to forget himself in his work. The conference was like many faculty meetings: there was little agreement on the questions discussed.

It is not likely that a faculty will ever agree about its functions, and this kind of diversity is probably stimulating. Some whose talk is most hard-boiled are sometime more successful with students than those whose "missionary impulses" are strongest. And the small college often humanizes teachers in spite of themselves. If the college had no power to do this it might as well be absorbed by the university, where, Beardsley Ruml has charged, faculty members have become such technicians that they should not be allowed a voice in university policy.[22] President Killian of M.I.T. has admitted that expansion of research has greatly diminished the university's effectiveness in undergraduate education.

One reason for the disagreement among professors on their function, aside from the normal differences in temperament, is that they are influenced in different degrees by their changing roles in education. Older professors in colleges that were once church-related still feel the effects of the tradition that they should be concerned with the inculcation of moral principles (now usually referred to as "values") and the development of character. Teaching was allied with the ministry. But the preaching function, as we might, with evident condescension, call it today, is fading rapidly. If we were to read to undergraduates of today some of the eulogies of outstanding teachers and personalities of the earlier Swarthmore (or Harvard or Yale or Oberlin or Amherst or "Mark Hopkins on a log"), they would be received with incredulous remarks about the sentimentality of the times.

The aim that succeeded the pastoral one was the informational function, the transmission of the cultural heritage of man. In this there was usually some remnant of a belief that such knowledge was an aid to the development of wisdom. Teaching was also sustained by an abiding loyalty to the college and its campus life, by an interest in students, and by a pleasure in watching them develop. As the rate of change in universities increased, this group of teachers more and more became the old guard, which seemed hopelessly conservative and an obstacle to progress. If they had been progressive they would have moved up the academic ladder as a result of their publications. And yet David Riesman admits:

Strength of ties to a particular college is not always, of course, a sign of stagnation or lack of intellectual discipline. A number of colleges—Antioch, Reed, Amherst, Swarthmore, for example—that set themselves as models for the nation, yet develop an intense devotion to the local institution and its total program.[23]

His examples could surely be multiplied.

The third and newest function of the teacher, which emphasizes research, is rapidly replacing the others. It has been described in its praiseworthy aspects by Professor R. H. Knapp of Wesleyan, as

the very general function of extending and coordinating human knowledge. . . . [The professor] must move intellectually into unexpected domains, obtain new information, and then return and report it with his interpretations to the main host of society. In this function boldness, improvisation, astuteness, and even courage are all at a premium. . . . This includes not merely scientific research in the narrow sense, but also humanistic scholarship and the reinterpretation of all kinds of accumulated learning.[24]

This function will seem to many temperaments to offer a much more exciting career than staying within the realm of the known and accepted, to say nothing of the greater rewards in status, mobility, and salary. And it has its appeals to the intellectual adolescent, too. Various studies of student reactions to teachers have reported that students have rated warmth, friendliness, fairness, and humor above scholarship and intellect. But the adolescent intellectuals of today are likely to be quite unsatisfied with the accepted. They prefer the newly discovered learning of their own generation. Technical terminology is accepted and repeated enthusiastically as a sign of superior intelligence. In some quarters Mr. Chips may still be the ideal professor, but today the status of the professor's intellectual achievement is more impressive to his intellectually minded students. A student saying reported from the University of California is typical: "It is better to be fifty feet from a great man in a lecture hall than five feet from a small man in a conference."

And yet even today the persistent efforts of student committees to examine student-faculty relationships show that even the young intellectual craves a nonauthoritative relationship with the faculty. The small college is the place where this can best be achieved, and where the capacity for this relationship can best be recognized and even rewarded. Those psychologists and social scientists who are doing the most intensive research on late adolescence in college do not believe that a specialized knowledge of psychology and psychiatry is as important for a teacher as a warm humanity that makes him an effective counselor as well as teacher. And they recognize that faculties do not crave the advice of alleged experts in human nature on their relations with students.

But the classroom is not much longer to be the professor's private domain. Many colleges are being subjected to consumer's research investigations. Swarthmore, as other colleges, is proud of the number of Merit Scholars who choose to enroll. The college careers of these scholars are followed with interest and pride, and when occasional failures and disappointments occur, caustic comments are made about the processes of selection by which the students were admitted. But the Merit Scholarship Corporation has a much greater interest in all this, to say nothing of its greater funds. It is now publishing research studies on the home influence that helped to mold the students, the relation of their high school records to their creativity, their vocational choices, their selection of colleges, their college careers, the intellectual and social quality of the colleges that received them, their personality development and its effect on their later careers. Nothing remains hidden, and every college teacher may be involved in the public judgment of the influence of the college on the kinds of students it attracts. The professor cannot readily separate himself from the life of his intellectual community; in sheer self-defense he will have to support efforts of the college to conduct more of its own consumer's research on the intellectual community.

## Alumni

What should be said about alumni and their influence on the intellectual community? The most uniform characteristics of all alumni are their loyalty to their own generation and their habit of viewing with alarm the beliefs and actions of their successors. Most undergraduates shudder with horror at the thought of becoming alumni and joining the "old guard." The alumni of the era of guarded education were intensely loyal to it; they expressed their disapproval of conformity to worldly ways in many letters to the *Friends Intelligencer* and to the president of Swarthmore. We have already discussed the concern that the successful in worldly ways have displayed about the intellectual nonconformists. Many of these nonconformists have returned to the campus to express their fear that conformity is creeping back to a greater degree. But others have returned to laugh at themselves as they once were and to tell of their complete recovery from their adolescent turmoil, now only an affectionate memory. Many Princeton alumni were greatly shocked at the student philosophies recently published in THE UNSILENT GENERATION,[25] but most Harvard alumni felt a renewed pride and affection in reading in their alumni publication the scathing remarks of Thoreau, Henry

Adams, and Francis Parkman as powerful dissenters from the Harvard life of their day. If the rebels are distinguished enough, and from far enough back in the past, their criticisms only enrich the traditions on which alumni are nourished. Even the most critical alumni come to unite in affection for the scenes of the campus and hope that it may remain unchanged. An undergraduate of not more than ten years ago, while drinking tea with his classmates at a seminar, led them in singing a parody on Alma Mater that he called "How I hate this rustic place." Not more than five years later, on returning for a visit with his professor, he said, with a depth of sentiment that he had never displayed in the seminar teas, "I wonder if you realize how fortunate you are to have lived so many years between the library and Crum Creek."

There have, of course, always been gaps between the generations, but as social change is increasingly accelerated by technological advances, the adolescents too will change more and more rapidly. It has been seriously proposed that colleges should reduce the retiring age of professors to fifty, so that the faculty should not get so far out of touch with the youthful experiences of their students. A hopeful bridge over the gap between the generations is being built by the new methods of communication that make the alumni active participants in the intellectual community. The *Swarthmore Alumni Bulletin,* under the imaginative editorship of Maralyn Orbison Gillespie, '49, has developed prize-winning journalistic skills for including in the college news the most significant events on the intellectual and artistic life of the campus and for reporting the achievements of the alumni that increasingly show the development of intellectual interests of college days. There is increased understanding of what classmates have done and what their achievements have demanded of them. News of their successes leads some to say, "I knew it all the time," and others to exclaim, "Who would have thought it? How he must have developed since college!" Both will feel something of warmth for an earlier common experience and will hope that their children may fare as fortunately.

Alumni magazines are arriving at a stage of national organization and are helping to build a national intellectual community, influencing alumni to weld in their consciousness their own personal experiences in college, a warm regard for their fellows, a knowledge of college problems, a critical interest in educational theory and practice, and a pride in their education leading to increasingly widespread support. Naturally, personal news in these magazines will concentrate on the conspicuously successful. But the thoughtful articles in the realm of ideas that they are now preparing to syndicate and publish will exert a humanizing influence on intellectuals throughout the country.

To revert to the quotation from David Riesman at the beginning of this chapter, those aspects of the intellectual community that stimulate discovery, creativity, independence, conflict, and adventure have been greatly strengthened by the intellectual revolution wherever it has struck the colleges. Almost all the forces bearing on college development today make the continued power of these forces desirable and inevitable. Perhaps many of the students by temperament will be most effective as happy warriors. Some may even denounce appeals for elements of solidarity, friendship, and security as conformist influences that impede progress. But for all of our students except the most self-sufficient of adolescent intellectuals, there is an increasing need for cooperation and understanding in an environment that can inspire trust and sympathy.

# Notes

## Preface

1. Clements C. Fry: MENTAL HEALTH IN COLLEGE, The Commonwealth Fund, New York, 1942.

2. Nevitt Sanford, ed.: PERSONALITY DEVELOPMENT DURING THE COLLEGE YEARS, *Journal of Social Issues*, Vol. 12, No. 4, 1956. The entire number is devoted to this account.

3. Dana L. Farnsworth: MENTAL HEALTH IN COLLEGE AND UNIVERSITY, Harvard University Press, Cambridge, Mass., 1957, p. 13.

4. Bryant M. Wedge, ed.: PSYCHOSOCIAL PROBLEMS OF COLLEGE MEN, by the Staff of the Division of Student Mental Hygiene, Department of University Health, Yale University. Yale University Press, New Haven, Conn., 1958, p. viii.

5. Graham B. Blaine, Jr., Charles C. McArthur, and others: EMOTIONAL PROBLEMS OF THE STUDENT, Appleton-Century-Crofts, Inc., New York, 1961, pp. vii–viii.

## Introduction

1. Frank Aydelotte: THE OXFORD STAMP AND OTHER ESSAYS, Oxford University Press, New York, 1917.

2. Bernard Berelson: GRADUATE EDUCATION IN THE UNITED STATES, McGraw-Hill Book Co., New York, 1960.

## 1. Awakened colleges

1. Clarence Cook Little: THE AWAKENING COLLEGE, W. W. Norton & Co., Inc., New York, 1930.

2. I. M. Rubinow: "Revolt of a Middle-Aged Father," *The Atlantic Monthly*, Vol. 139, No. 5, May, 1927, pp. 502–604.

3. Robert H. Knapp and H. B. Goodrich: THE COLLEGIATE ORIGINS OF AMERICAN SCIENTISTS, The University of Chicago Press, Chicago, Chap. 9. Copyright 1952 by The University of Chicago.

4. Robert H. Knapp and Joseph J. Greenbaum: THE YOUNGER AMERICAN SCHOLAR: HIS COLLEGIATE ORIGINS, The University of Chicago Press, Chicago. Copyright 1953 by The University of Chicago.

5. Philip E. Jacob: CHANGING VALUES IN COLLEGE, The Edward W. Hazen Foundation, New Haven, Conn., 1957.

6. Thomas Harold André Le Duc: PIETY AND INTELLECT AT AMHERST COLLEGE, Columbia University Press, New York, 1946.

## 2. William Penn and guarded education

1. Frederick B. Tolles and E. Gordon Alderfer, eds.: THE WITNESS OF WILLIAM PENN, The Macmillan Co., New York, 1957, p. 113.

2. Isaac Sharpless: THE STORY OF A SMALL COLLEGE, The John C. Winston Co., Philadelphia, 1918, pp. 71–72.

3. Edward Parrish: EDUCATION IN THE SOCIETY OF FRIENDS, J. B. Lippincott Co., Philadelphia, 1865, p. 38.

4. Homer Babbidge: SWARTHMORE COLLEGE IN THE NINETEENTH CENTURY, unpublished Ph.D. thesis, Yale University, 1953, p. 46. A copy of this thesis, valuable for many interpretations, is in the Friends Historical Library, Swarthmore College.

5. Edward Hicks Magill: SIXTY-FIVE YEARS IN THE LIFE OF A TEACHER, Houghton Mifflin Co., New York, 1907.

6. Emily Cooper Johnson: DEAN BOND, J. B. Lippincott Co., Philadelphia, 1927.

7. *Ibid.*, p. 128.

8. Babbidge, *op. cit.*, p. 135.

9. Elizabeth Powell Bond: WORDS BY THE WAY, Vols. I and II, Philadelphia Friends Book Association, Philadelphia, 1895.

## 3. Conformity to the ways of the world

1. All the inaugural addresses are contained in the *Swarthmore College Bulletin*, Vol. 1, No. 2, March, 1903.

2. This volume of letters is now in the Swarthmore College Library.

3. For a fuller discussion of this subject, see Richard Weaver: THE ETHICS OF RHETORIC, Henry Regnery Co., Chicago, 1953.

4. The three quotations given above are from the *Phoenix* of October 28, 1913.

5. For Ivy orations up to the time of World War II, see the commencement issues of the *Phoenix*.

6. Ralph Lee Smith: "Why I Resigned from Annapolis," *The Atlantic Monthly*, Vol. 180, No. 4, October, 1947.

7. For a sense of the public excitement over this issue, see the news articles and hotly controversial letters in numerous editions of *The Philadelphia Ledger* during October, 1907.

8. Alan C. Valentine: TRIAL BALANCE, Pantheon Books, New York, 1956.


## 4. Revolt of the intellectuals

1. Frank Aydelotte: ELIZABETHAN ROGUES AND VAGABONDS, Clarendon Press, Oxford, 1913.

2. For a full account of President Aydelotte's athletic program, see AN ADVENTURE IN EDUCATION, by the Swarthmore College Faculty, The Macmillan Co., New York, 1941, Chap. 10. See also Frank Aydelotte: "I Believe in Athletics," PROCEEDINGS OF THE THIRTY-SECOND ANNUAL CONVENTION OF THE NATIONAL COLLEGIATE ATHLETIC ASSOCIATION, New Orleans, La., December 28–30, 1937.

3. The *Phoenix*, November 24, 1931.

4. This statement and the one that follows were printed in the *Phoenix* for February 28, 1933.

5. G. W. Pierson: YALE: THE UNIVERSITY COLLEGE, 1921–1937, Vol. II, YALE: COLLEGE AND UNIVERSITY, 1871–1937, Yale University Press, New Haven, Conn., 1955, Chap. 14.

6. *Ibid.*, p. 286.

7. Pierson: "The Yale Approach," in SEVENTY-FIVE: A STUDY OF A GENERATION IN TRANSITION, Yale Daily News, New Haven, Conn., 1953, p. 19.

8. Adam Yarmolinsky and others: RECOGNITION OF EXCELLENCE, Working Papers of a Project of the Edgar Stern Family Fund, The Free Press of Glencoe, Ill., 1960.

9. Carl A. L. Binger: "Emotional Disturbances Among College Women," in Graham B. Blaine, Jr., Charles C. McArthur, and others: EMOTIONAL PROBLEMS OF THE STUDENT, Appleton-Century-Crofts, Inc., New York, 1961, Chap. 10, p. 181.

## 6. Some disturbed personalities

1. Graham B. Blaine, Jr., Charles C. McArthur, and others: EMOTIONAL PROBLEMS OF THE STUDENT, Appleton-Century-Crofts, Inc., New York, 1961.

Erik H. Erikson: IDENTITY AND THE LIFE CYCLE, *Psychological Issues*, International Universities Press, New York, 1959, Vol. 1, No. 1, Monograph 1.

Dana L. Farnsworth: MENTAL HEALTH IN COLLEGE AND UNIVERSITY, Harvard University Press, Cambridge, Mass., 1957.

Clements C. Fry: MENTAL HEALTH IN COLLEGE, The Commonwealth Fund, New York, 1942.

Group for the Advancement of Psychiatry: THE COLLEGE EXPERIENCE: A FOCUS FOR PSYCHIATRIC RESEARCH, GAP Report No. 52, formulated by the Committee on the College Student, New York, May, 1962.

Bryant M. Wedge, ed.: PSYCHOSOCIAL PROBLEMS OF COLLEGE MEN, by the Staff of the Division of Student Mental Hygiene, Department of University Health, Yale University. Yale University Press, New Haven, Conn., 1958.

Robert W. White: LIVES IN PROGRESS, A Study of the Natural Growth of Personality, Dryden Press, New York, 1952.

2. See, for instance, Merle Curti: "Intellectuals and Other People," *American Historical Review*, Vol. 60, January, 1955, pp. 259–282. Also note the reservations about the intellect alone in Jacques Barzun: HOUSE OF INTELLECT, Harper and Brothers, New York, 1959.

3. Wayne E. Oates: RELIGIOUS FACTORS IN MENTAL ILLNESS, Association Press, New York, 1955.

4. Blaine and McArthur, *op. cit.*, Chaps. 11–13.

5. *Ibid.*, pp. xiv–xv.

# 7. The intellectual community

1. Christopher S. Jencks and David Riesman: "Patterns of Residential Education: A Case Study of Harvard," in Nevitt Sanford, ed., THE AMERICAN COLLEGE: A PSYCHOLOGICAL AND SOCIAL INTERPRETATION OF THE HIGHER LEARNING, John Wiley & Sons, Inc., Chap. 22, pp. 763 and 772.

2. Harold Taylor: "Freedom and Authority on the Campus," in Sanford, ed., *op. cit.*, Chap. 23, p. 791.

3. Wilbur J. Bender: "A Blunt Warning," *College Board Review*, Fall, 1961, p. 28.

4. *Cf.* Jencks and Riesman, *loc. cit.*

5. *Cf.* Carl Bereiter and Mervin B. Friedman: "Fields of Study and the People in Them," in Sanford, ed., *op. cit.*, Chap. 17, pp. 563–596.

6. Taylor, *loc. cit.*

7. Kenneth Keniston: "Alienation and the Decline of Utopia," *The American Scholar*, Spring, 1960.

8. Erik H. Erikson: CHILDHOOD AND SOCIETY, W. W. Norton & Co., New York, 1950.

9. Erikson: IDENTITY AND THE LIFE CYCLE, *Psychological Issues*, International Universities Press, New York, 1959, Vol. 1, No. 1, Monograph 1.

10. Erikson: THE YOUNG MAN LUTHER, W. W. Norton & Co., Inc., New York, 1958.

11. Erikson: YOUTH AND SOCIAL CHANGE, Basic Books, Inc., New York, 1963.

12. R. W. White: LIVES IN PROGRESS, Dryden Press, New York, 1952.

13. For a brief statement in support of this widely prevalent attitude, see Arthur Schlesinger, Jr.: "The Humanist Looks at Empirical Social Research," *American Sociological Review*, Vol. 27, No. 6, December, 1962, pp. 768–771. See also the replies from readers of the article that were published in the following issue of the *Review:* Vol. 28, No. 1, February, 1963, pp. 97–100.

14. William G. Perry, Jr.: "The 'Human Relations' Course in the Curriculum of Liberal Arts," *Journal of General Education*, Vol. 9, No. 1, October, 1955.

15. P. W. Leeper and Peter Madison: TOWARD UNDERSTANDING HUMAN PERSONALITIES, Appleton-Century-Crofts, Inc., New York, 1959.

16. Earl Bond: "The Student Council Study, An Approach to the Normal," *American Journal of Psychiatry*, July, 1952, Vol. 1, No. 1, pp. 11–16.

17. Leon J. Saul: BASES OF HUMAN BEHAVIOR, J. B. Lippincott Co., Philadelphia, 1951.

18. Saul: EMOTIONAL MATURITY, J. B. Lippincott Co., Philadelphia, 1947.

19. Saul: TECHNIC AND PRACTICE OF PSYCHIATRY, J. B. Lippincott Co., Philadelphia, 1958.

20. See Erikson: IDENTITY AND THE LIFE CYCLE.

21. Sanford, ed., *op. cit.*

22. Beardsley Ruml and Donald H. Morrison: MEMO TO A COLLEGE TRUSTEE: A REPORT ON FINANCIAL AND STRUCTURAL PROBLEMS OF THE LIBERAL COLLEGE, prepared for and transmitted by the Fund for the Advancement of Education, McGraw-Hill Book Co., New York, 1959.

23. David Riesman: CONSTRAINT AND VARIETY IN AMERICAN EDUCATION, University of Nebraska Press, Lincoln, Neb., 1956, p. 86.

24. Robert H. Knapp: "Changing Functions of the College Professor," in Sanford, ed., *op. cit.*, Chap. 7.

25. Otto Butz, ed.: THE UNSILENT GENERATION, An Anonymous Symposium in Which Eleven College Seniors Look at Themselves and Their World, Rinehart & Co., Inc., New York, 1958.